THE ROAD FROM DAMASCUS

Rob‎ lish
mo‎ nsively,
working as a journalist in Pakistan and teaching En‎ four Arab
countries. He now lives in Scotland.

The Road From Damascus

ROBIN YASSIN-KASSAB

PENGUIN BOOKS

PENGUIN BOOKS

Published by the Penguin Group
Penguin Books Ltd, 80 Strand, London WC2R ORL, England
Penguin Group (USA) Inc., 375 Hudson Street, New York, New York 10014, USA
Penguin Group (Canada), 90 Eglinton Avenue East, Suite 700, Toronto, Ontario, Canada M4P 2Y3
(a division of Pearson Penguin Canada Inc.)
Penguin Ireland, 25 St Stephen's Green, Dublin 2, Ireland
(a division of Penguin Books Ltd)
Penguin Group (Australia), 250 Camberwell Road, Camberwell, Victoria 3124, Australia
(a division of Pearson Australia Group Pty Ltd)
Penguin Books India Pvt Ltd, 11 Community Centre, Panchsheel Park, New Delhi – 110 017, India
Penguin Group (NZ), 67 Apollo Drive, Rosedale, North Shore 0632, New Zealand
(a division of Pearson New Zealand Ltd)
Penguin Books (South Africa) (Pty) Ltd, 24 Sturdee Avenue, Rosebank, Johannesburg 2196, South Africa

Penguin Books Ltd, Registered Offices: 80 Strand, London WC2R ORL, England

www.penguin.com

First published by Hamish Hamilton 2008
Published in Penguin Books 2009
1

Copyright © Robin Yassin-Kassab, 2008
All rights reserved

The permissions on p. 350 constitute an extension of this copyright page

The moral right of the author has been asserted

Typeset by Rowland Phototypesetting Ltd, Bury St Edmunds, Suffolk
Printed in England by Clays Ltd, St Ives plc

ISBN: 978-0-141-03564-2

www.greenpenguin.co.uk

For Rana Zaitoon

It is only when you know the Higher Factor that you will know the true situation of the present religions and of unbelief itself. And unbelief itself is a religion with its own form of belief.

Ahmad Yasavi

Atheism indicates strength of mind, but only up to a certain point.

Pensée 157, Pascal

Contents

Contents

I

The Other Path

Uncle Mazen drove Sami into the city as far as the parliament building, then shrugged and peered out through the windscreen. 'The car wouldn't make it up there,' he said, pointing an ear at the mountainside. 'There aren't any roads anyway. Just steps. Perhaps you can walk.'

Sami disembarked and straightened on the pavement. A man of average height, somewhat hunched, with a pale complexion, a sensitive, moving face, black eyes flashing with an intensity called beautiful by those that love him, and thick and curling hair, also black, grown longer than in his youth to distract from climbing baldness. Still handsome. But a body ageing quickly, increasingly swell-bellied. Thirty-one years old.

And feeling foreign now, unsteady in the heat, among balloon salesmen, bootblacks, cassette stalls, exhaust fumes. Sami searching for breath in the smothered heart of Damascus, home of his ancestors, the former city of streams and orchards the Prophet had refused to enter, not wishing to commit the sin of believing himself in Paradise. But Sami, unconcerned with Paradise, for better or worse, had entered. Damascus was supposed to offer him answers.

He'd been here for a month, in order to (he listed): reconnect with his roots; remember who he was; find an idea. And the tourist stuff too: to bathe in the wellsprings of the original city, the oldest continuously inhabited city on earth. A city that had briefly ruled the world. Where jasmine and honeyed tobacco scented the evening air. Where Ibn Arabi wrote his last mystical poetry, where Nizar Qabbani wrote 'Bread, Hashish and Moon'.

Years ago Sami thought he would write a doctoral thesis on

Qabbani. Not thought; assumed. It had seemed inevitable, and it had never happened. Nothing remained of whatever that idea had been. So he was here to find a new idea, gather material – and then return home, write the thesis, become Dr Sami Traifi. As a proper academic, like his father before him, he'd be able to get it all back on course, his place in the world, his marriage, his mother. So he believed. A new idea, a turned leaf. It was time, it was perhaps his last chance, to leave childish things behind.

In front of him the mountain was sandy red and imposing, shiny with whitewashed shacks and satellite dishes. One of those buildings, his maternal aunt Fadya's house, was his destination. To his right as he walked there was the rubble of destroyed four-storey Ottoman homes: tangled wood and plaster and a back wall still intact with a mosaic of dead rooms printed on its surface. You could make out the hitherto private squares of paint, entire inescapable universes for their inhabitants, now brought border-less into promiscuous intimacy. On one patch there was some religious calligraphy. On another, what looked like family photographs. Though the demolition was some days old, white dust motes swirled thickly. History refusing gravity.

Just about all the women Sami could see were wearing the hijab, many more than on his last visit. He didn't like it. He didn't like supernaturalism, nor backwardness in general. And in this country a return to religion meant a return to sect. It was just under the surface, just under the smiling face of this hospitable people, the secret loathing of the other path. They don't respect each other, Sami thought. They fear the strong and despise the weak. This cacophonous country: each individual playing from his own score, ignoring the others. But it was his country too. His father's country.

Struggling upwards against the descending swell of well-wrapped ladies, across Corncob Square with its melancholic bronze president, Sami imagined roadblocks, men with armbands and guns and armed identities. That's what it could be like, very easily. The wrong identity would end you at the intersection. Dead for wearing a cross. Dead for wearing a hijab. Dead for Ali's sword swinging from your car mirror. It had nearly happened in the eighties when the Muslim Brothers took over the city of Hama, and the government had stopped it, rightly. In the face of the Brothers' fanaticism the government stood unwaveringly firm. Sami's father, Mustafa, safe in London, had explained it to him. Beards disappeared. Surely a good thing. The headscarf tide was reversed. Hair breathed freely. What rational person would disagree with that?

And as he bobbed past coffee merchants, past careening taxis and minibuses, past a line of shawarma furnaces flaring the afternoon into more surreal heat, he asked himself what his father would think if he could see this determinedly Muslim population, hairy and hijabbed not twenty years after the Hama events. What would his father say? It would represent the very end of the world he'd hoped for.

Back in London, Sami's own wife was threatening to wear the hijab, which somehow seemed to represent the end of everything Sami had hoped for too.

The road stopped as Uncle Mazen had said it would. Up here mucky children replaced traffic, children loud as traffic, smudge-eyed, tangle-haired, brandishing bleeping plastic weaponry. There was the occasional fruitless mulberry tree. The ground was dust, mud where something had spilt. In the winter it would all be mud. Mud and dust alternating, flesh and bone, life and death.

He breathed outside Fadya's wooden door, then swung the knocker. Fadya opened up with a show of surprise and welcomed him, thanked God for his safety, told him he had illumined her house. Her family crowded around him, everybody kissing solemnly and shaking hands. Fadya welcomed him again. Her hair was collected under a white scarf which she didn't remove, despite her blood relationship to Sami, even after the door was shut. His two cousins asked him dutifully for his news, and asked him to make himself at home, following the formulas. Then they sat on the floor in front of the TV, their large backs to him, their lined and stubbled faces immobile.

When Fadya brought Turkish coffee with sweets and joined him on the sofa, Sami's eyes hadn't yet adjusted from the glare out-side, so he saw in black and white, with patches of blindness, as through a photographic negative. The room was windowless and dark, lit dimly by the Intifada on the TV screen. Boys throwing rocks and flaming bottles at armoured cars, the cars shrugging it off, dispensing the occasional efficient bullet.

Through the door to the darker interior of the house Sami sensed something shuffling.

He unslung his shoulder bag and brought out a notebook. He had a page of questions already prepared for this interview. Fadya and sons would provide the responses of ordinary people, ordinary Syrian Arabs, to Sami's poetic enquiries. Doctoral material.

'Aunt,' he began. 'Let me ask you a question. What kind of poetry do you like?'

Fadya aimed at him the eyes of someone used to staring through storms. She staged a smile. They watched each other, stalled. And then a cousin stood up and faced Sami, with blue chin raised, slight moustache quivering.

'I'll tell you, cousin, which poetry is important to us. Probably not to you, but to us.'

'Tell me,' said Sami. But why the defiance? Sami hadn't had anything to do with these boys since playtime in the distant past.

'The Qur'an,' said the cousin. 'The Noble Qur'an. The Perspic-acious Book. That's what.'

'Aha,' said Sami, creasing a new page, and writing: *The Qur'an as poetic text*. 'Please go on.' But his cousin sat down again sideways on, face back to the Intifada, making tutting and clucking noises. Why the anger?

From the gloom of the house Sami heard a cough. Something was stirring also in the inner chambers of his memory.

'Who's there, aunt? I should greet them.'

'Never mind, nephew. Leave him alone. Will you drink more coffee?'

'Please, don't treat me as a guest.'

And suddenly inexplicably dizzy, and with an English petulance,

4

he stood up, Fadya rising with him, the cousins too, all watching him narrow-eyed, heads inclined. He watched them back. And stepped towards the inner door.

Sami saw Fadya nod at her sons with weighty significance. Then she looked at him, her too, with malice. And a palms-up shrug.

'Go on,' she said. 'Go ahead. My house is yours.'

On the other side of the door: a square airless room, no TV, no shelves, no pictures, and another door, into further gloom. In the middle of the room, on a chair, doing nothing, facing nowhere, a man. There was a secret here which Sami alone had not penetrated.

Sami advanced. 'Hello, uncle,' he said, stretching out a hand. In Arabic every older man is called uncle. Uncle looked up. His white-flecked mouth, salt-and-pepper beard, wispy salt-and-pepper hair, salt-and-pepper skin gleaming a little in the TV light from behind Sami. Not returning Sami's greeting. Not bothering to wipe away the sweat which dripped from his head into blinking fish eyes. Just worrying prayer beads – click, click – in a relentless chain of cause and effect.

This was the skeleton in the backroom, then: a loonish relative. This was what they were ashamed of. With an inward smile, and a wrinkling of the nose against the hot mustiness, Sami returned to the others.

'So tell me, aunt. Who is this?'

'You want to know who this is?'

'Yes. Tell me his story.'

Fadya's eyebrows were raised high. 'You've come here to learn. So I'll teach you something. Just listen. Don't write in your notebook. I'll tell you the story of a man in this country. Let's call him Faris Kallas.'

Kallas is Sami's mother's name, his aunt's name. But he'd never heard of a relative called Faris.

'Faris is a student, twenty years old, hasn't even begun his life yet. He studies at the university. What else? He wants to be an engineer. He wants to get married, have children. He wants to build a house. Don't we all want the same things?'

This assumption of Fadya's, that everybody knows what they want, marked her foreignness to Sami.

'It happened in the eighties, when you were happy with your father in London. It was chaos then. But Faris went to his university lectures, always interrupted by mukhabarat coming in and reading out the names of people whose names were never spoken again. When people disappeared their families didn't dare enquire about them, didn't mention them. The mukhabarat could do magic, you see. When they read names the owners of the names ceased to exist. God only says "Be!" and it is. With the mukhabarat it's the other way round. They cancel by speaking.

'So when any sensible man would keep a sweet smile on his face and his mouth shut, this Faris decided to join the Brothers. He didn't do anything, mind you. No plots or bombs. Just said yes when another student asked him if he wanted to join the organization. They said they'd fight corruption and the Communists who'd surrendered our land to Israel, and this donkey Faris agrees with them and lets them write down his name.

'After three months of earnestly doing nothing but go to engineering lectures, Faris is informed on. Someone tells someone that he's a Brother. Then they came to his home. They walked in and got him, beat him in the kitchen in front of his parents and sisters until they couldn't see his face for blood, and then put him in their car.

'They drove him somewhere in the city. He doesn't know where because there was a hood over his head. His blood stuck the hood to his skin as it dried, but loosened again with slaps and kicks when he arrived. In a cell smaller than this room, and forty others in there with him. No food, no water.

'Then they took him to Tadmor, in the desert. You'll have visited the ruins, the tourist sites, not the prison with the words over the entrance arch: "Who enters here is lost; Who leaves is born again." First they made him write his name, his family's names, and his address. Then they burnt the paper and stamped on his hand. Because he had no name or family or address any more, nothing to write down. They slapped him and spoke to him politely. "Please step this way, Mr Nobody."

'He was kept alone in a cell too small to stand up in. They gave him rice with stones in it and dirty water. After sleeping he could think properly, which meant he wasn't able to sleep again. The fear was worse than the pain. He thought he was going to die.

'They tortured him for a time and left him for a time. Then tortured him again. It became a normal routine, so he no longer feared death. He feared life instead. A routine, except a routine requires ordered time. In there, there's no time. They live in darkness. No suns or moons. And what was left of him outside was darkness too. His family stepped around his shadow in the house. They couldn't forget him and neither could they assume he would come back.

'Later, after years perhaps, time returned to Faris. Ways of telling the time. He had yoghurt for breakfast, rice for lunch, a potato for dinner. Once a month he was shaved. But when they shaved him they slashed his ears and nose and lips with the razor. Why do that? What's the point of it? Why?'

Sami spread his arms in innocent incomprehension. 'I don't know. Why are you asking me?'

'Why do you think I ask you, nephew? Why do you think?'

Sami was open-mouthed, almost tearful, too warm.

'Never mind,' she went on. 'What you don't know you're innocent of. And if you don't know the answer to the question, then neither do we. What was the point of any of it? What was the point of ripping women's hijabs off in the street? What was the point of murdering tens of thousands in Hama?'

In other circumstances Sami would attempt a partial answer, about Hama at least. His father had explained it to him. The Brothers murdered plenty of Alawis and Party members in Hama before the government responded. The response had been harsh, certainly, but the alternative was also harsh. The Brothers in control of the cities and the Party in control of the army. It would never have ended. But this was no time for historical debate.

'If there were men they left alive,' continued Fadya, 'that's because they'd killed the man inside them. Before they released Faris they asked him about his politics. Politics is men's business, so he had nothing to say. He had no opinions, no desires. That's why his family didn't recognize him when he walked in. Twenty-two years had passed. His father was dead. His mother ill. His sisters married. Your mother had left the country before they took him. There was almost nobody there to recognize him. Only his little brother. And he didn't recognize him. He remembered a man, not a ghost.

'That's what we call lucky here. We thank God, anyway. Many men never came out. Some came out but found everyone dead. Some found their homes but the key wouldn't fit the door. There were strangers inside.'

It reminded Sami of Palestinian families in the refugee camps, and their useless keys sometimes brought out of a cabinet to show to a guest, sometimes hooked on a nail in the reception room, thicker and heavier than keys of today. The image extended. Entire countries, and pasts: houses without keys. Houses no longer homes.

'And what should he do?' Fadya continuing. 'He couldn't marry. He couldn't work. He cries and has bad dreams. Look at him.'

But the door had closed, and Sami had seen enough.

'You mean to say, aunt, that the man in the next room is my mother's brother? Faris?'

Fadya nodded twice.

'I didn't know about this. I've never heard of an uncle called Faris. My mother didn't tell me. I wish she'd told me. She should have.'

Sami didn't talk to his mother, not any more, because she hadn't talked to his father, even when he was dying, and because she'd betrayed his father's secularism by wearing a hijab. She'd stayed in London after her husband died. Lived alone, and worked in the man's world of a halal butcher's shop. And now she'd humiliated her son. She must have known he'd visit her family in Syria one day – and she'd let him grow up without telling him this essential piece of family information, about her brother.

The cousin who'd mentioned the Qur'an spoke again, this time very quietly and without defiance, as if only to himself.

'I wonder,' he said, 'I wonder who informed on Uncle Faris? I wonder who told the mukhabarat?'

And the other cousin asked, almost wistfully, 'Who betrayed him?'

'Well, there's a question indeed,' responded Fadya. 'Faris told only close family members he'd joined the Brothers. Not including his little brother, who was too young. Of course we didn't speak in front of children. There was the danger they might repeat what they heard. So it was only us who knew.'

Everyone's eyes rested expectantly on Sami.

'So?' he asked.

Aunt and cousins waited, eyes unmoving.

Sami stood, shouldered his bag, took two steps towards the inner door. Manners as well as curiosity suggested he should make his new uncle's better acquaintance. But something stopped him. And then a flush of anger followed that impulse as if to clothe its too obvious nakedness. What did he want with broken Islamists? And Sami was too old to be discovering new relatives.

That's the way he left. Seeing himself out, without any eastern courtesy. It was too much information of the wrong sort, this Faris story. Nothing that would help his thesis or his fraying life in London. Sami endeavoured not to let it set him off course. And in the wind and the muffled city sound and the blanket of warmth it was easy not to think, easy to forget.

But before awakening with a bolt into the next day's voice-cluttered dawn – his last dawn in Syria – Sami dreamt an uncomfortable dream. Of a galloping and a heartshaking. An acceleration of hooves. Sami beginning to run, slapping into boughs, becoming entangled in newly sprouted undergrowth, his feet disobedient. Unable to push the panic from his brain into his body, into action.

Horse saliva showered his neck. He could feel its breath. He opened his mouth to scream.

Yet in place of the scream he heard a mighty crash, and its aftermath, a backdraught of air. He wheeled around to see the dead horse, which was not at all cartoonish. An ordinary, dead, brown-flanked, sweating horse, with only one difference from the normal model: this horse wore the face of Sami's dead father. Mustafa Traifi's face, elongated to fit the equine muzzle. Hence the bolt of awakening.

Sami had never before been visited by his father in nightmare form. All his dreams of him had been burnished memories, night nostalgia of the kind that occasionally provoked wholesome tears. There was nothing wrong in the father–son relationship, nothing except the fact that the father was dead, had been dead for sixteen years, was dead, embalmed and mummified. Mustafa Traifi, porcelain sepulchre. Mustafa Traifi, enshrined in Sami's head. The only member of Sami's family who Sami had no problems with. None at all. Mustafa Traifi who'd shown his son the stars, taught him his history, protected him from womanly superstition, planned for him a career – all this before the boy's sixteenth birthday, before turning still and cold in snowy North London, leaving Sami alone on this dried ember of a world.

So nothing wrong in the father–son relationship. Not until now. Bubbles were rising – marsh gas, deadly methane – from the trowelled-up earth of Sami's brain. What could it mean?

It took him all the hot morning, until Uncle Mazen dropped him at the airport, to regain his frozen-hearted cool. Sitting in a grey area of the departure lounge, against the evidence, wishfully thinking, he pieced together his thesis theory. And beyond that, the pride and peace of mind his achievement would provide him, the improvement in his marriage, the future of professional success, respect, wealth.

And then in this transition between worlds the hashish of his thoughts momentarily released him, and he lucidly conceded that things were complex, that nothing was simple. There were paths other than the one his father had trodden. Other, but not necessarily mistaken. Paths taken, for instance, by his wife, or by his mother. Other, valid paths. He conceded it just for a few moments. It would take a summertime for the realization to sink into his core, corrosively, like salt into snow.

2

A Mirror for Sami

To avoid hostile airspace the plane looped east and north over sudden desert before turning west, above dry brown hills and valleys like scar tissue, and green mountains, and then to where the shining sea and the sky spat photons at each other. The gnaw of the engines, and the carbon spreading behind them into the fizzing, popping sky. Sami watched until the dazzle hurt his head, too narrow to contain it, and called for wine and paracetamol, slammed shut the plastic blind, and set to thinking. Arrowing westwards like his father before him, faster than the sun to where the day was younger, he thought of the past. Of the wife he was returning to.

What had he first noticed about her? That her laughter was like the scattering of birds? That her eyes burnt their target in soft fire? Or was it just that she seemed preordained, that she measured up to something he was waiting for?

Summer 1991. The British Museum. Life stretching before him like a creature to be conquered.

He'd had previous girlfriends, if girlfriend is the word. Perhaps 'willing victim' is more suitable. Not that he was fierce. It was a mutual victimizing, and as innocent as looking in a mirror: he was prey too of the grainy sensation-hungry English girls he found clustered in dance halls or in the student-union bar, drawn so easily, by their own momentum, into his careful net of difference.

And what was *he* hungry for? Sensations, certainly. He was twenty-one years old then. But also, more importantly, he hungered for confirmation of the difference he flaunted. Like a tiger that killed in order to be assured of the sharpness of its teeth, he sought the sensation of his own reality. He observed his image in the (frequently dilated) eyes of women. The girls too saw in reflection what they wanted to see of themselves.

The image he saw in his conquests' eyes was a definite, deliberated image, constructed of solid elements. These included, firstly, Arabism. He had come to terms with what he now described as his heritage by means of a transplanted nationalism in which the significance of signs had swivelled away from their original focus. He often sported a kuffiyeh, either the black and white check of the (first) Intifada or the red and white worn by Syrian labourers and farmers. A member of his class in Syria would never wear one. Wouldn't be seen dead in one. But this wasn't Syria. To distinguish himself from the students who wrapped kuffiyehs around their necks like braces against the whiplash of adulthood he wound his tightly around his head, actually in a Kurdish style. He wandered about the campus with it, above a firm expressionless face, as if wearing it were a question of asserting rights. He also wore it in the bar, and during lectures. He had a T-shirt of the Palestinian flag, and another which read Darkness Never Lasts in both languages. On top of these he wore a crinkly black plastic jacket with ACID written on the back. It communicated, he felt, a fine mix of hedonism and anti-imperialism.

Recycling third-world meanings: again, there was nothing special about him here. From body tattoos to nose rings, his contemporaries were all at it. Striking poses, claiming allegiances. Sami's allegiance, in memory of his father, in homage to himself, was to a sexy version of the Arab world.

And Muntaha was an Arab. A proper Arab. Baghdad-born, she had an accent. The way she dressed, tidy and formal, declared her. So did the careful way she walked. Her movements and her speech were upright and courteous. She was every bit as Arab as the kuffiyeh he checked in the mirror before leaving his flat.

How he'd loved mirrors in those days. A couple of years before then he'd accepted his face only reluctantly, and only after hours of precise mirror-bound analysis. If he compared his face with the

English people's, there was something overdramatic about it. A face that was trying too hard. There was too much crammed in, too much life. The features were too big, too expressive for his English-style emotions. They suited someone else. Someone foreign. That's what schoolboy Sami felt. But with his maturity, in his university years, he came to amicable terms with his appearance. He was an Arab, was all. He contrasted well with the blandness of Englishmen. The English girls believed so, and he could see the evidence himself. His full, tasting, mobile lips. His passion-heavy eyebrows. His pale unblemished skin. His curls. He felt love for the face he'd been ashamed of before, and compensated with pouts and meditations which pulled him in to the centre of the reflection, into the dark dreamy eyes. They made him dream of his destiny. Of poetry.

Poetry: the second element of Sami's identity. He'd done his first degree in Arabic, and he'd known for years that, as his father had before him, he would write books about Arabic poetry. Modern stuff, not old. He kept sleek volumes visible on tables in his flat. He carried them with him to meetings in bars, the better to explain their importance. Poetry still mattered in Arab societies, he expounded. It was appropriated by pop singers. It had political relevance. And Sami had grown up on the simple, revolutionary language of Nizar Qabbani, language which smashed both literary and social conventions. This was particularly important. Its eroticism, secularism and defiance all contributed to the sexiness of Sami's Arabism. And Mahmoud Darwish, national poet of Palestine, was a further source. Sami would gloweringly recite Darwish in Arabic to the bar girls:

> Record! I am an Arab
> And my identity card is number fifty thousand . . .
> I have a name without a title
> Patient in a country
> Where people are enraged . . .
> Beware . . .
> Of my hunger
> And my anger!

Poetry wove a web of wonderful origins: jasmine-scented, fruit-laden, tasting of dusk. Even the despair in it seemed romantic. Despair which expressed a nobility of perspective.

Add to these jazz or hip hop for embellishment and you had the theme tune to Sami Traifi. Black music, Arabism and poetry: these were what he considered himself to be made of.

And Muntaha was a girl it was easy to read in poetic terms. To visualize her skin colour Sami had only to think of the crops of the earth. The colour of mature wheat on a Levantine afternoon. The darkest olive oil. Her skin which looked smooth as butter and felt smooth as milk. He had to speak like Qabbani to describe to himself what he meant. The feminine flow of her compact body, thickening like a trapped river towards her hips. And her voice, the dis-embodied projection of the body, the intermediate station between body and soul, soft, various and intelligent in its gentle penetration of his ear. There was also harshness in its depths. It spoke with incense breath. It sounded like the voice of home. All this was poetry. And that her name, Muntaha, meant The End. That it sounded like Moon.

Poetry too in their meeting. Summer 1991. They were in one of the Mesopotamian rooms at the British Museum. Sami turned from an ancient diadem and glimpsed her, the kind of woman who would have worn such jewellery. Muntaha was caught in sunlight (was there a window in the room, was there a clear sky that day? He remembers the atoms dancing around her, the light and shade). Gazing at the Sumerian ram and tree, a gold and lapis offering stand to Dumuzi the shepherd god, she didn't notice him. She was entirely still, like an exhibit herself. A Mesopotamian woman in communion with Mesopotamian art, about to launch herself from its past into Sami's life.

This was the sort of meaningful coincidence that the inexperi-enced believe is only found in fiction. People like Sami believe this. It seemed to him that there had once been meaning in the real world, when he was a child, before his father died. But to his adult brain meaning had become diffuse, scuttling out of sight behind curtains, draining through floorboards and through the cracks beneath doors. Meaning had left the earth with his childhood reflection and taken up residence in a realm of artificial images, where it was caught, concentrated so it could be tasted. As he read the final page of a novel and then sat still until the traffic outside or rain against the windowpane retrieved him. In poems, of course. In the fullness of his heart at the climax of a film. In the music which released a hormone flood into his bloodstream. Even an advert could make him alert and tearful. These triggers detonated his soul (though he would dispute this word) like a baton swung against a gong. Not God's real world that made music of him but the worlds made by men. But here, in her Sumerian shapelessness, in her awe-struck eyes trembling before the ram, and in what followed when she looked at him and began to speak, was the shiver and the stern inner silence, the moment of clear vision prompted only by art.

'Does this have a special meaning for you?' she addressed him in Arabic, as if continuing a conversation.

'It does. How do you know that?'

'You were looking at it with such passion.' Her accent confirmed she was Sumerian, Iraqi.

'And so were you.'

She smiled. 'Tell me why it's important.'

'My father used to bring me here. This was his favourite exhibit. I suppose it makes me feel nostalgic. And why is it important to you?'

'I don't know if it's important or not. It depends on what you're looking for. It's beautiful, and very old.'

'It comes from your land. You must be proud of it.'

She laughed. Birds scattering from the tree. 'I'm from Iraq, not Sumeria. We have different gods today. Gods with moustaches.'

Sami laughed too.

She had met his eye and begun walking with him as if introductions were unnecessary. He liked that, particularly from someone not born here. Tradition over there demanded introductions, and false modesty, and all kinds of pointless etiquette. Sami considered tradition a concrete and formidable enemy, and saw her immediately as Qabbani's new woman, self-created from conflict with the East.

He listened as they stepped from Sumeria to Babylon, from Babylon to Assyria. She spoke through pomegranate lips. He was already captivated, already entranced.

'I learnt about all this at school in Iraq,' she said, 'but it was taught only to make a point. It doesn't mean anything until you see it yourself. Of course I saw the museum there. They took us three or four times and marched us round. The teacher read nationalist poetry and made speeches about the people and the leader. I had to get away from her to feel what it meant.'

He allowed her to talk.

'It didn't make me more proud to be Iraqi. It made me think how strange it is to be human. Believing in your gods, thinking you understand things, making beautiful statues, and then dying and waiting for people to guess who you were. The teacher said it showed the eternal nobility of the Arab nation. Maybe that's right too. It can mean different things to different people. But you have to get away from other people's ideas to know what it means to you.'

For him, the real world held no surprises; it had to be turned into poetry first. She was saying the opposite. That it's necessary to escape from poetry to see the world in front of your nose.

The world in front of her nose made Muntaha overbrim with excitement; that was clear from her breathing, from her expressions, her tone of voice. He presumed she was excited by him.

They walked around the British Museum from Egypt to India to Mexico. They observed each other sideways. He noticed the luxury of her hair, and her beauty belatedly made him nervous. He moved heavy eyes, an anaesthetized tongue.

Fighting the paralysis of this awe, Sami started to take the lead, showing her round, explaining things. This was a pattern that would continue through the coming decade. Here in the museum, spending too long on the wall plaques, he asked himself what he could teach her. Not much about the Arabs, he expected. But jazz and hip hop. Probably sex. He knew more about those than she did.

He did most of the talking. She seemed to be encouraging him.

'You know so much. Did your father teach you all this?'

'I learnt a lot from him, and a lot after him.'

She noted the implication of his father's death, this most important fact about Sami.

'I like knowledge,' he said. 'It puts you in charge of the world.'

They'd stopped speaking Arabic once they left the Iraqi rooms. She'd been in London for all her teenage years, and was used to meeting people in English. To him, English felt more natural. And her voice was still more authentic in her second tongue, tripping a little, rolling too much. He decided never to correct her pronunciation.

'How does it put you in charge?' she asked, with more range of tone than a native woman. 'I thought money did that.'

'The world respects money, yeah. But knowledge lets you see straight. That's the advantage.'

'Knowledge illumines the mind,' she said, 'while wealth darkens it.'

'Exactly. That's a good way of putting it.'

'When knowledge is distributed it increases. When wealth is distributed it decreases.'

'Excellent! Who said that?' And it was excellent. She could speak in quotes. Arab, and educated, and eloquent. She reflected him.

'Imam Ali.'

Sami frowned. 'Are you Shii?' Here was the drawback of an Arab woman, the shackle-weight of history.

Muntaha halted. 'Don't you like the Shia?'

'I'm not sectarian. I don't think much of the whole religion thing.'

'Neither do I. I'm not Shii, anyway. My mother was.'

Sami noted the death of her mother. He stopped frowning. So

religion was dealt with, out of the way. He noted too, once again, her beautiful free-flowing hair: black as . . . moonless darkness . . . black as emotional disarray.

They arrived at the exit. Huge grey columns reached above them with all the mocking solidity of London. Fat grey pigeons stumbled in the low grey sky. It smelled of rain, beer and petrol fumes.

Now they shook hands. Both had large, strong hands with long fingers. Muntaha's hands were large, out of proportion to her body.

'Fursa saeeda. Happy chance,' she said, translating the Arabic literally, comically.

'Pleased to meet you too. I really am.'

He really was. But Sami also felt disabled by happiness, as if it was a trap, a drunkenness necessary to make him fall. Muntaha's happiness, on the other hand, was unalloyed.

'I am Sami Traifi.'

'And I am Muntaha al-Haj.'

'Do you study, Muntaha?'

'I'm going to study history. And then be a teacher. What about you?'

'I study too. Arabic literature. I'm starting my doctorate.'

Then they exchanged phone numbers. She nodded goodbye and moved off with Iraqi intentness until she merged with the crowd and the cars beyond the railings, leaving a tingling in Sami's groin and a more impactful churning in his intestine, rising to his chest and throat. The beginning of addiction. The memory of her warmed him like the memory of fire.

This was who she would end up with. Sami chose Muntaha. And she chose him. He was good with her family. Polite. He was also clever and funny, which seemed to please her father as well as her friends, although her father's target virtues in a son-in-law were steady religion and morality, not cleverness and wit. And Sami befriended her brother, Ammar, who needed befriending.

So he was a decent man. A good choice. They had a civil marriage and a honeymoon in Scotland, wilder, quieter, more hidden than she'd ever been. Clouds of midges danced in the thick wet air.

Trees creaked on heavy hillsides. Fertile darknesses, greens, blues and browns in the ponderous northern dusk, drained into one. A lightening moon in the sky full enough to be a lamp. The land feeling old to her, and them too, as if they'd been together for years. And after that she loved their long conversations, their gentleness to each other, their sex. Sami looking after her, bringing her breakfast in bed, preparing coffee for her when she came home from work. She loved that he was an educated man, and that he talked to her about his ideas. All his enthusiasm, all his passion. His hopes for the future, for them together.

3
Sami Hurries Home

Ten years later Sami still had good intentions – new ones from Syria concerning Muntaha and complexity – but these became complicated even before the plane touched the ground. High up and unattached he'd been calm, light and balanced, but as the descent began he panicked. He felt fate. He felt the force of gravity. A headache curled its claw around his skull.

He sped up: his breathing and heartbeat and the flickering of his eyes. He popped two more painkillers from their wrapping into his mouth. He jigged his legs and clicked his tongue. He snorted and swallowed against the cabin pressure. And with the first flashing of wheels on English earth he was already on his feet, reaching for the luggage locker, scowling back at the frowns of the nearby stewardess. He wobbled and tutted and bounced and said 'fuck'. Portly, circle-bald Syrian men and their hijabbed wives tutted in response, covering their children's ears.

The plane decelerated to a point of silent decision. Everybody stood up and shuffled in the aisle, closer and closer in the unexpanding space. Sami, ignoring the laws of physics, tried dodging and weaving in the crush. Faster and faster. He felt speed give him buoyancy. Speed battling gravity.

He spilled with ejaculatory force from plane to walkway, from tube to tube, increasing his velocity as human density thinned. Trampolining the conveyor belts, rushing past the multilingual warnings to refugees, striding through the appropriate channels, still faster. In such aimless, frenetic speed, in the daydreaming allowed by fuzzy lack of focus, he discovered the illusion of potency, of freedom.

He spied a toilet. Banging through a cubicle door he unshouldered his bag, unzipped, and released a flow of analgesic-laden urine. Before he'd properly finished he gave himself a superficial body search, hands fluttering over chest and hips and arse, the pocket areas, and swiped from somewhere a packet of Lucky Strikes, and a lighter. He shook, zipped, lit, inhaled. A sour cumulus of smoke bloomed and glowered about him. His nostrils clogged. He felt the London wheeze catch in his lungs, the wrong chemicals tickle his stomach. And a yellowish smile spread over his face. Home again.

He submitted to the gaze of passport control, feeling as unaccountably guilty as any normal citizen does in the presence of the law.

'Where are you coming from today?'

Sami breathed deeply, slowly.

'Syria.'

A moment of full eye contact.

'Nice trip?'

'I'm glad to be back,' said Sami.

And he surged onward. The process was efficient, but he was maddened by impatience nevertheless. He saw himself progressing through the airport like a worm through waterlogged soil, eating it steadily and steadily pushing it out. His aim was to arrive in his own life as quickly as possible, his normal London life, to escape from that other life claiming him.

He fed a card into a cash machine. Muntaha had put five hundred into his account. He withdrew half, then headed for the express train, calculating how long it would take to reach home. In the train, on the tube, walking. Time lost on platforms. An hour and a half, two hours. And then ... And then he'd stop. He'd come to rest. Have time to think and remember. The other, foreign life waiting for him at home, travelling faster than he could. He had to slow down.

Also, he told himself, being home was excuse for celebration.

At the Arrivals bar he treated himself to a triple whiskey.

Jameson's. Mustafa's drink. He held the glass up to his dead father. 'Cheers,' he said aloud, and felt tough and nihilistic. It was nothing sentimental, drinking with the dead, but a gesture consigning this world and its living inhabitants to hell.

Two minutes later he was engaged in debate with himself. He wanted another. Should he give in? Desire nearly mistook itself for need, for more whiskey and more smoke to chase it. But Sami was a man of half principles, and these won out.

He dialled Muntaha.

She answered after one ring.

'Habibi!'

'How did you know it was me?'

'I always know. Where are you?'

'I'm in Heathrow.' He glanced uncertainly at his bag. Brown leather, compact, with a long shoulder sling. 'I'm still waiting in the baggage hall. They say there'll be a delay.'

'You checked your bag in? I thought you were going to travel light.'

'I was, but it got heavier. You know, presents.'

'All right, then. I'm waiting for you.'

Her voice trilled. She was genuinely happy about his return.

'I'll be there soon, Moony. I'll see you soon.'

At this stage, despite his lie, he still believed he would head straight to her. To her breasts and arms and thighs and hair. But first, to protect his lie, he needed to bulk out his luggage. In the morning he'd deliberately forgotten the jumpers, pyjamas and boxes of sweets intended by various relatives as presents for Muntaha. He'd left them under the bed in Uncle Mazen's spare room on the grounds that they were too burdensome. If he'd known then what his lie would be he'd have brought them. Bad planning. In the concourse commercial area he touched and rejected distinctively English chocolate bars, toys and bathroom products. About twenty books in the Middle East section with titles suggesting kidnap and domestic violence, fully veiled women on the covers. Men's magazines. London A to Z. None of it looked like presents from Syria. But there was a fluffy white toy dog. In Muslim countries dogs aren't considered cute or fluffy. But it looked like a present, and it made his bag bulge. He bought an Arabic newspaper too. He'd already paid and walked away when he remembered that this paper, independent and London-based, was banned in Syria. Muntaha wouldn't know that.

Down some steps. Through one tube, and into another. It would be a while yet before he breathed open air. Not fresh air, not clean, just open. Down in the distribution system air rushed and stopped through channels and valves. Stop and go. Travellers marched or slouched to platforms, waited for the roar and the shunting of doors, and entered the train as obedient as haemoglobin. Sami sat down, bag bulging on a leg which he began to jig, fast and faster. The train shot smoothly into London's heart.

A screen unfolded from the ceiling. A voice, more avuncular than chirpy, welcomed the passenger to an exclusive in-journey news bulletin. The busy, important passenger. And the helping hand of the voice. 'Keeping you in the picture,' it said. 'Making sense of it all.'

Sami pushed the bag off his leg and took out the newspaper. He surveyed the front page. More teenage deaths in Nablus and Jenin. Houses demolished in Gaza. Families made refugees for the third or fourth time. More useless keys. A photograph of a peasant woman carrying rocks in her gathered skirts to resupply the frontline youths.

He repacked the paper into his bag. The ache in his head had slipped to his shoulders and the hollow between his shoulders. Hunched, shrunken, he resolved vainly to straighten himself.

Through the window grey bubble structures flashed by. Fenced and rounded things which were perhaps gas works, Sami didn't know. Art deco buildings stranded by sixties development. Brownish low-rise blocks of flats and empty expanses of park. Box-shaped shopping centres. Vast concrete storage spaces for cars waiting to be used up. Everything passing quickly under a flat grey light. A succession of film stills.

Nearing Paddington, however, as the train slowed down, he saw the city unclothed, its private parts. He saw the backs of houses, and railings, and grime-coloured brick. Slipped roof tiles and barbed wire. The loneliness of potted plants.

He stood, and hastened down the corridor, and back again. Passengers flinched as he approached and subsided into their worries as he retreated. Moving along the carriage in this way he created a ripple. Fear, relief, fear – like a strobe. Scrambling, rushing, thudding against seats. Hurtling from Syria towards more Syria, from cell to inescapable cell. The distance from the airport to his front door was all the freedom he had. He used the space, the speed. Stopping was like bars slamming down.

The train itself stopped, not with a shudder but a hi-tech hiss. People slipped diagonally and unmeeting from the doors, and rapidly vanished.

On the tube, the real tube hurtling into tunnels, he worried the passengers as he'd done before. They watched their knees or read the adverts. Anything but contact.

Spat out on to the final, most familiar platform of his journey home, Sami paused by a no-smoking sign to light a cigarette. Not much further to dash, not much more time until his life-redeeming trip would have to be described and accounted for. The gains and the losses. The new academic idea. His dribbling Uncle Faris, if he would tell her about that. He stood and smoked where modernity receded and dusk encroached, in the eye of a transport police camera, under an archaic station clock. Roofed-in and tower-shadowed but open to the air at last, to the smell of London. What did it smell of? Of his childhood, and the ineluctable present.

He knew he was in a state. Hardly surprising, he told himself, what with the change of air, being cooped up in a plane, the rest of it. Hardly surprising. But he was surprised to find tears springing from his eyes. Even a great hiccup of grief rushing from chest to throat. His father. His Uncle Faris. He stood for a minute startled in the headlights of his emotion.

He transmuted grief to anger – ah! that's better! – and rubbed his face. Then strode, furiously, from the tube station, hand luggage swinging from his shoulder, and turned in the opposite direction to home. Hurrying down the Harrow Road, fast and faster.

He arrived at a barber's shop. With a thrill of clandestinity, and the cheering sense of getting things done, he surveyed this way and that. Cloak-and-dagger stuff. Satisfied that nobody authoritative was in sight, he pressed an unlabelled intercom button.

A full minute passed. The defunct launderette at his side was plastered with words. Icons, flyers, alerts, calls to arms. There was the difference between Damascus and London: all the extra information. But was any of it wanted?

Crackling and breathing emerged from the intercom, and a slow voice: 'Ye-es? Hello?'

Sami gave the code. 'Beam me down, Scotty.'

'What? What you say?'

He flushed cold red. Had the code changed in the month he'd been away? It made him ridiculous if it had, there in the gathering dark inaccurately whispering a *Star Trek* line to the middle-aged and elderly Trinidadians below.

He repeated himself. And this time it worked.

'Yes, man. Come down.'

He leaned through the buzzed door and into a cramped stairwell, a few brown carpet fibres remaining on each splintered, rotten step, the walls green-dull and the ceiling stained with coughing. A comforting environment.

At the bottom he rounded a corner to find Harry the Barber – short, white-whiskered, spry – rising from a blue trade chair to greet him.

'Sami! Where you been? Got a tan!'

Sami grinned, and raised a finger to acknowledge his audience of men, some paying close attention, some already reabsorbed in dominoes or newspapers.

'What, just from the airport?' Harry pointing his head at Sami's bag.

'Straight from the airport.'

Harry chuckled. 'Getting your priorities right, I see. Now what is the priority, herb or a trim?'

'Herb, please, Harry. And if you have any Rizla I'll build one right now.'

'Aha. The herb holds precedence. The trim later.' He rummaged in a drawer before handing over a packet and some loose papers. 'You'll have a drink too.' Splashing silky liquid into a tumbler. 'Sit down, boy, sit down. Make yourself comfortable.'

So Sami sat and raised the glass. Harry and a few others returned his salute. Sami drank, and the sweetness and the heat melted one more piece of ice in his heart. There was warm liquid oozing there now, liquid at the centre of him. The muscles in his shoulders and neck eased as he sniffed and crumbled the fresh weed, and he became mesmerized by the building of the spliff, this fetish transcending the real, offering light, colour, depth, resonance.

He always felt comforted by the company of older men. Men drinking rum or ginger beer receding down a long table into blue smoke, pipes or cigars between their teeth, clothed in the remnants of the day's formal dress: waistcoats and rolled-up shirtsleeves, old-style hats, loosened cravats. Respectable old blokes. No skull-caps or African robes here, not for this generation. They had cricket and church and English names long before they reached England. It was only when they arrived in the Mother Country they learnt how alien they really were, how black their faces, how strange their speech.

'It was back home, then? The old country?'

'To Syria, yeah.'

He sparked up. The deep green crackle brought memories of parkland, cut grass, sunbeams.

'Must've been good, then. Better than over here?'

'That's right,' he lied. 'Much, much better. Plenty of sunshine.'

He breathed slow and soft through pursed lips as if blowing feathers away or keeping a balloon buoyant. Spliff spread from his throat to his lungs and up through the nerve cable into his brain.

'Yeah,' he continued, pursuing common ground in the longing

for light. 'Plenty of sunshine over there. And the fruit tastes better where the sun shines.'

'Ah, yes indeed. You don't need to tell me. Nothing like a Trinidad mango.'

And this brought forth a chorus of nostalgia from the men nearest.

'Guava!'

'Pineapple!'

'Papaya!'

'Plantain!'

What was Sami going to contribute? Lemon? Olive? Fig? He remembered the Damascene wind that whipped up every sunset, warping the sound of the prayer, making him sneeze. How he burst into paradoxical sweat as darkness fell and the temperature dropped.

But he'd come home. He strained to perceive present information. He thought there should be calypso playing, but what bled from a small speaker behind the chatter sounded like Capital Radio, showy unaccented talk cutting into commercial music.

He could feel thought bubbles rising and bursting and dispersing in frenzied series. 'Must pay,' he thought. 'Must remember to pay.' He unpocketed a note and offered it to Harry.

'I'm going. I haven't been home yet.'

Harry winked. 'Minister of the Interior won't be happy if you're late. I'll see you, man. Come back for the trim.'

Back outside, with heartblood still thawing, Sami calculated lost time. Forty minutes in Heathrow after the phone call. Forty-five on train and tube. Thirty more on the street and underneath it. Makes about two hours.

He was suddenly hungry.

Along the Harrow Road – tensed up again, hurrying after burst-bubble thoughts – and through the open entrance of the Tennessee Bird Bar. (Or the Louisiana Chicken Shack, or the Mississippi Fry House, perhaps the Memphis Wing Palace. They're all there.) Behind the counter a nocturnal, paper-faced creature blinked into perpetual neon day. Sami placed and at once received his order:

battery chicken in batter, a potato and grease ensemble, a syrup and caffeine mix.

He ate leaning against a low wall. A piss-fed hedge twisted up from behind it. Cars whizzed by trailing carbons and distorted sound. As he chomped he was conscious of his butter-churn stomach, the enzymes working.

He rolled another spliff, licking the paper with stunned tongue. Green in the dark, the smoke plunged and divided in his lungs, coating the walls, dribbling through to pollute the blood. He could see all this. The smoke used merely to disappear within and become abstract. Not now. He was losing his ability to not notice.

There was the danger of tears. Dear me, he felt tired. Dear me. So he strode homewards, finally homewards, the bag swinging against his back.

Then his stride froze, as if he'd walked into a rope pulled taut.

He was at the door of a pub called The Scud. Twinkling coloured light hinted from beyond the door, the chink of glass, a rumble of amplified music. Beeriness and mould. The Scud's windows were covered by blackwashed chipboard. And chalked on the chipboard: Exotic Dancing 7–11.

Sami, in need of distraction, seeking to extend the length of his leash. Sami, requiring just one last drink, shoved through the doorway and entered the pub.

An expressionless black man just inside. Security, measuring him. After that, the clientele was blanket white. There were probably Poles and Albanians, certainly Irish. But it was undifferentiated to Sami. Low-slung jeans, football shirts, tattoos. The multicoloured neighbourhood hadn't made it across the threshold of The Scud.

He padded over sawdust to the bar. Men drooped all around it, using it to stay upright. Disconcertingly, there was a woman pouring the drinks, frail but brisk. Not much talking going on. The occasional forced laugh. Otherwise each man trapped inside himself. One more woman visible – very visible indeed through her lingerie – who dodged and wormed between the drinkers' slablike hands, collecting coins in a pint glass. She winked and grinned and inclined her head, thighs trembling, straw hair limp on yellow shoulderblades.

Sami ordered a pint of lager and carried it to a table snug between a stained wooden stage and a wall. He lit a Syrian Lucky Strike and smoked like the others, watching his cigarette closely. Pulled at the warm lager, like the others, watching the plastic glass. Puffed and swilled and puffed.

This is where you'd expect commercial pop music, but it was in fact a calypso that banged from tinny speakers when the coin collector mounted the stage. Looking into the mid-distance, into the smoke, she began her routine. The enfeebled audience feigned indifference. As she shook and wobbled they surveyed the gloom behind her, open-mouthed in vague enquiry, searching for dart-boards, calendars, directions to the Gents. And so two minutes passed until the performance reached its resolution, the dancer discarding a final flimsy garment before lying on the stage and splaying her legs in joke abandon. This was irony: the veil between her body and the real.

Among the men there was a listless straining for a better view, as if absent-mindedly, and a display of boredom, glassiness of the eyes and puffed-up lips. From his knobbly chair Sami had a perfect perspective on the intricately folded vaginal package. The flesh flower. The possibility of its yielding, being reshaped by him. He concentrated. No signs of arousal from his body whatsoever. Bodies are better clothed. The occult best left unknown.

He scanned the pub's brutal good cheer. A man in a suit, who'd just happened to stop by on his way home from the office, was stroking a cigarette machine. Others coughing into the sawdust. Others limply slapping each other's shoulders and backs, straight-faced, cold. And nearest of all and therefore unseen until now, right across the table from Sami, a round, red, roaring man. Sweating through his burst-button shirt. Damp hair crawling over the collar. Far enough gone to be openly rapt by the performance. There was a wall of empty glasses in front of him, and a perspex box full of change, for more drinks, more bodies. But sensing Sami's horrified gaze he turned his hot eyes and spongiform nose on him, and barked through salivating lips.

'You're me brother, you are!'

Sami ignored him.

'Not my brother. You're a youngster, son, isn't it? You're my son, my long-lost, my real and genuine boy.'

He started pawing at Sami's arm across the table. Sami pressed against the back of his chair, the dirty wall.

'I'm not your son.'

'Not exactly, I'll grant you that. Not precisely. You're ... you're ...'

Did Sami believe in coincidence yet? The music of events?

'... my nephew. My sister's son. My sister's little boy.'

Sami found his feet, heaving the bag to his shoulder, and pushed to the door. His new uncle roaring above the stereo.

'Oi! Come back, boy! That's my nephew! Bring him back!'

Sami scurried muttering along the canal. Clumsy now, he'd lost the excitement of the spliff. He knew the rushing was an attempt not to see what was in front of his nose. But what did he have to aim for except illusion? There were tears on his face again, and no poetry for miles. Unusually, most unlike him, he felt hot through and through.

Three minutes later, panting, head spinning, he raised a hand to strike his front door.

4
Sami's Thesis

On the Saturday afternoons of Sami's dead childhood his father would take him to the cinema. It was a ritual as educative, as acculturing, as a Friday mosque visit. It anticipated the shape of life to come.

Each film followed a similar pattern. We find our hero in a mysterious, problematic world. Conscious of his weakness, he grows in strength and knowledge, winning love and admiration along the way, until he forces an explosive climax. Victory is his (and therefore ours). The death star is destroyed. The world set to rights. If it's a good enough film all the kids in the audience applaud. Then there's ice cream before the bus home.

Little Sami waited for life to happen as a boy in a cinema awaits the start of a much-hyped film. The kind of film talked about in the playground. The kind whose spin-off picture cards you collect from packets of chewing gum, and whose action figures you ask for on your birthday. A really exciting, really important film.

He looked forward to life enthusiastically. He'd go to university, probably the same university his father worked at. In the first year after graduating he'd travel around the world, learn to speak the major languages, have all manner of tropical adventures. Then he'd write some volumes of globe-shaking poetry. In awe of his soul, universities would offer him chairs. He'd choose one, and write about Arabic literature, and become famous for that too, like his father. But better than his father. Leaping forth from the giant's shoulders, he'd go further. After that the future became fuzzy. Surely there'd be more good things, more achievement, stretching into the interminable distance. The thought of it made his small heart beat fast.

This little Sami felt to the adult Sami like his dead, innocent child, buried in the blind years. Everything since that particular funeral, since adulthood, had been enveloped in an anticlimactic fog of mourning. Except for meeting Muntaha. Except for beginning his PhD. There had been hope until then. It was the start of the PhD that marked the transition.

His doctorate made him as emotionally overworked as the worried and fretted spines of his academic books. A high frequency of Re and Post among the titles: Re-presenting, Re-interpreting, Re-thinking, and Post-colonialism, Post-modernism, Post-structuralism. Never noticing the present moment, but doing the event again, after the event. A sigh for theory, his sometime love. The attraction of the Posts was their decentring not only of religion but also of the imperial West. Everything decentred and flattened into meaninglessness. Sami liked it, but kept a contradictory corner of his consciousness – a small centre – for the Great Arab Nation narrative. A story told in Mustafa's voice, with Qabbani's words.

His first PhD plan had been to show how poetry improved language and therefore the world. He set out to prove that Qabbani-isms had infiltrated and revolutionized everyday Arab speech. But it hadn't quite worked out. However much he trawled through newspapers and transcripts of TV shows, and advertisements, speeches and pop songs, reality wouldn't quite submit to his vision. He'd even sat in on exile conversations on the Edgware Road with a surreptitious dictaphone. A particularly bad tactic. The discussion became bland and coded as soon as he switched it on. On the third occasion, somebody smashed the dictaphone. 'Do you think I'm scared of you here?' rattled this paranoid Egyptian, thick arms suggesting violence. 'What more can you do to me? You want to hear what I think of them? Just ask me. Just ask.'

His first supervisor sat him down and told him to pay attention to the texts themselves. Fate opened the page at the poem called

'Declaration', where Qabbani, in imitation of the declaration of faith, had written: *I declare / There is no other woman*. So Sami made notes on the sexualization of religious language. Piles of earnest notes. The supervisor pointed out a comparison with English Renaissance poets, who'd also described physical desire in terms of divine love. Sami read the poetry, and the prose, and the (post-psychoanalytical, post-feminist, new historicist) criticism. Using up a lot of paper, and more time.

The supervisor went to work in America. He was replaced by a German expert on Sufism who drew Sami's attention to Arabic poets who'd sexualized spirituality in previous centuries. Anti-Qabbanis, drooling for divinity, but in their own way subversive (more subversive, Dr Schimmer held). Certainly there appeared to be very many parallels between their God and Qabbani's man-burning, man-drowning woman 'wordlessly sensed by the mind'. The rapture of union. The lover-moth longing for the beloved flame.

Sami listed Sufi symbols: wine, eyes, breasts, skin. A long time in libraries. Reams and trees of notes.

Then Dr Schimmer instructed him to learn Farsi.

The first fingers of panic were poking in Sami's insides. Withstanding lectures on the Farsi programme, perusing medieval grammars, filling more files with notes.

Another year before he made a stand. From high up, unstable atop stacked notes, he called down his complaint. He hadn't intended his thesis to become bogged down in the stagnant waters of mysticism. All that soupy soul stuff, that Iranian heavy breathing, that he'd been brought up to despise.

'No, No, Mr Traifi,' intoned Schimmer (but Sami, merging Anglo-Arab prejudices, heard 'Nein, Nein'). 'When you study poetry you must be interested in the soul. And the Arabs, you know, didn't make the spirit–reason duality until the, aa, incurable stage of their decadence. They had their greatest material success in their most religious period.'

Outraged, disdainful, even briefly considering lodging a complaint against Schimmer's racism, Sami strode out of the office.

Slamming the door as if firing the first symbolic shot of a liberation war. He strode all the way to the library, where he barricaded himself behind impenetrable books. More notes produced, paperthin, insubstantial. As firm a defence against Schimmer's ideas as the Arab states' armies had been against Zionist expansion.

With tail between legs, and lowered gaze (his back and shoulders had begun their trouble), he crawled back to Schimmer. Back to mysticism after his Setback. From here on, he drifted. Then Qabbani died, after writing his last great, angry work, 'When Will They Declare the Death of the Arabs?'

Years by now had passed, and the world had changed since Sami made his academic plans. The blocks with which he'd built his personality – Arabism and poetry – had begun to rot. Which wasn't only Sami's fault. The whole world rotted. It heated up, grew smokier, more fetid. The Arab part in particular rotted faster than the rest. Arab culture and ambition shrivelled. Poets died and were not replaced. Religion grew in response.

In truth, Sami was an academic only because his father had been. Professor Mustafa Traifi, renowned (to an unheard-of coterie) author of *The Secular Arab Consciousness*, the great formulator and compartmentalist of Sami's youth. Sami following a map that had been drawn for him years before, but not arriving anywhere, floundering in libraries and lecture halls, failing to produce a doctoral thesis. Making him, in his own eyes, not much of a man – unsettled, out of place, unexplained. And he had the feeling that there was a core of truth and direction nearly visible yet decisively hidden, frustratingly, something only noticed in its absence, a purpose for him, somewhere out of reach. And he thought it was his failing, his lack of clear sight, that stopped him from grasping it. He began to despise himself, and his behaviour degenerated.

He became argumentative. He whinged and whined. Muntaha dealt with it. She knew he was having trouble and supposed it was temporary. She wished she knew enough to help, but never did, despite her best efforts. This because Sami grew defensive whenever she spoke about his life and work.

She persisted on memories of what she thought of as his true self: Sami preparing meals and conversations, or running his fingers through her hair on the tube, showing her off a little, the great value he had seemed to place on her. She persisted on the thought that his true self might yet re-emerge. But for that to happen, it was clear he needed more than just an idea for his thesis. He needed a spiritual change. But this was another area Sami wouldn't discuss. However vaguely and carefully she addressed the issue, talking about perspective and attitude instead of prayer and fasting, he cut her off. He accused her of sounding like his mother, the mother he didn't talk to. Muntaha knew better than to advise him to pray – Islam had been taboo since she'd begun to express sympathy with it. Another to add to the list of forced silences they now had: his work, her ideas. Her feelings. Important subjects.

So when Sami declared a year off for the world travel and the poems, Muntaha, having observed things slide the hill from bad to worse, and hoping he would find direction on the way, was supportive. Plus, it was no loss to her to have the house free of smoke and noise. She was engaged now in the practical business of an East End school, teaching history and geography to children replete with these same qualities, marking homework when it came, managing decidedly unspoilt students and, in equal need of guidance, their world-spoilt parents. So off Sami set, chewing his lips, to south and east. One of the reverse refugees, fleeing the leisure to discover himself.

Apart from Morocco (plenty of spliff), he avoided the Arabs. There were vodka and Gypsy festivals in Bulgaria. Efes beer and raki in Turkey. He inched through Anatolia from bar to harsher bar. In the contested borderlands he ascended a mountain whose summit was a burial mound littered with vast stone heads, sculptures of god-kings, and on the way down had his foot run over by a car swerving to give him a lift. It did him no harm, except to add to the accumulation of harm in his spirit.

Back in London, he smoked, he drank, he avoided things. He gazed moon-faced at Muntaha. He received her comforting embraces, but was not comforted. In an iconoclastic fit he hurled Qabbani books at his study wall. He never looked up at the stars. He limped around the university campus like a wounded animal, his back hunched up and his neck tied in memory knots of pain. He flicked through old notes as you might flick at a mouth ulcer with your tongue. He smoked some more.

By now his early sets of notes couldn't be found. Someone may have carried them out with the rubbish. They may have been burnt to join the other carbonates in the sky. It made little difference. And by now too, Sami's money had run out. Half of his inheritance from Mustafa sunk into the mortgage, the rest into the vortex of his daily needs. He lived off his wife's labour.

Of his doctorate, he'd produced nothing. Dr Schimmer should have given up on him, but instead agreed to start him again, registering him as new, for his father's sake.

'Perhaps you will settle down to the work now? Perhaps, like your father, you will produce, aa, greatness? Perhaps it's in the blood, yes?'

To prompt the sensation of turning over a new leaf, Sami took a long trip to Paris. A sabbatical, he said. He planned to study second-generation North African rap in French. It seemed complex enough, important enough, to necessitate nine months in a flat in the 18th arrondissement learning street French and smoking Algerian hash. Every few weeks he ate a lump for the ten-hour bus and ferry ride to his benefactress in London. Happy times, unfamiliarity breeding respect. Then back to Parisian Babylon to congregate with clandestine Maghrebis, those homeless and paperless, fallen between borders. By this stage, Sami felt he belonged with victims.

In April 2000, however, Hizbullah drove the Israeli occupation out of Lebanon. It was the first Arab victory in living memory. Could the age of defeat have an end? There was a hint of that possibility in the air.

In September confrontations with the occupation spread across Palestine. Teenagers challenged tanks – new-born children of the stones absorbing live ammunition in their bodies. After three or four days of escalating demonstrations it was obvious they weren't going to stop. The second Intifada had erupted like a poisonous boil, and so, for Sami, had an unexpected moment of bliss. He was still young enough for wasted years not to matter much, and to be young in that morning of the rejuvenated Arabs was very heaven. On wings, he alighted again in London, and with passionate but chilly fury began a new book of notes, on Mahmoud Darwish and the poetry of immediate engagement, on Qabbani's Jerusalem poems, on the Palestinian revolution. He loved his wife. Saw no need to smoke. For Muntaha, the real Sami had come home.

Alas, the uprising provided a false dawn. Sami produced political enthusiasm rather than scholarship, transcribing each morning the emotions provoked in him by the previous day's body count. Merely that. When he recognized it, there were no longer any delusions to accommodate him. It was a decade since he'd graduated, and what had he actually said in that time? What wisdom would he bequeath to the coming generation? Sami had meant to add his distinctive stone to a particular cairn on the mountain of knowledge, but he held no stone, could find none to fit his palm. The father whose inheritance he'd squandered towered above. Our Father Who Art. In the high places, at the sacrificial sites. On Sinai. In Muhammad's mountain cave of meditation.

The mountains crowded and loomed and threatened to shake with the shaking earth and crush him. He was blinded, unable to distinguish between the Straight Path and all the intercrossing goat trails. Or between fathers and gods. Between reason and religion.

There was still Syria. It's a misfortune of our age that we have returned to roots to find solutions. The roots are shallow, and mythical; we all come from everywhere at once, and we are floating creatures. Sami as much as anyone was inheritor of the great postmodern diversion. So it was with the sense of a last chance that he planned a summer month in Syria. His reasons for going: to reconnect with his roots, remember who he was, find an idea. In that causal order.

When he got there he realized there were roots he didn't want to dig up.

As children we sense mystery but expect all to be explained. As adolescents we sense mystery but understand it as an extension to the glories of the self. There's time later for universal questions, we think, but right now I'm busy preening. As adults we sense mystery but have become by then accustomed to it. It's the solid ground beneath us, easy not to notice. And there's no longer any time. We're busy, so we put it from our minds.

That's how it's meant to be in the society we've built. Busyness keeps our noses out of mystery. But Sami, being a failed academic and international layabout, living on his wife's honest earnings, wasn't busy. Whatever he was accustomed to was falling away beneath his feet.

5
Reunion

The door opened almost immediately. Muntaha's head appeared round its side, the heartshape of her face and her long eyes. Her pupils expanding with human warmth, despite justified disappointment, into the nearly black of her irises. Her dark skin shadowed in the streetlight. Her hair like a curtain, like a veil, promising revelation.

'You're back, then. Why did it take you so long?'

'Oh you know how the tube is, I don't need to tell you. And I don't know how long I had to wait for my luggage. Much more than an hour.'

She nodded sadly and stepped back to let him in. The hall was clean after his absence. It smelled of flowers, coffee and perfume. Sami unshouldered the bag and put it on the floor. They both examined it. It looked like hand luggage.

'Come on, then,' said Muntaha, drawing a line.

He walked into her extended arms and lowered his nose into her hair. She pressed against him. She and Sami in each other's arms. She was wearing a man's blue gellabiya, loose for the London heat. Sami clutched at it in handfuls. They held each other tight, fitting together well.

Muntaha disengaged.

'You've had a drink on the way home.'

Sami, in hot turmoil, didn't know what to say. All the melted ice was splashing about inside him. Still melting. He concentrated on not crying. But should he cry to win her sympathy? It was an opportunity, after all. He hadn't been able to cry since they met. Since before that, since his father's death. And now he had these

burning tears to struggle with. In the end, like a man, but not much
of one, he again transformed his confusion to anger.

'I'm not a child,' he said. 'I'll do what I like.'

'I know that,' she said quietly. 'But I thought you might have
wanted to say hello first. To leave your bag. Then you could have
gone for a drink if you'd wanted.'

'But I didn't want to say hello first.'

'Apparently not.'

'I mean I did . . . but it happened differently.'

There was a long silence during which Muntaha studied the wall
behind Sami's head, contemplating anticlimax. She'd been hopeful
for his Syria trip. She'd even – whisper it – prayed for his success
there. And here he was returned, also considering anticlimax. Sami
saw his brain exhale a little puff of illusion and then deflate into
itself, sunken, crinkly, grey. The same swirl of light and dark greys
that made up London. If illusion was sustainable anywhere, it
wasn't in this city. Meanwhile he felt her eyes on his face, peering
through and underneath him to something that didn't exist.

His bladder, it struck him now, was much fuller than his
brain. 'Anyway,' he said, dragging sawdust-stained shoes over the
floorboards. He locked the toilet door behind him. The house was
divided into spheres of influence, and the toilet was in his. Large
enough to rotate in if you kept your arms to your sides. Dark red,
and decorated with political cartoons from the same Arabic paper
he'd bought in the airport. There was a small deep handbasin, a
mirror he flinched from, a low toilet bowl. He pissed long and
thickstream, dizzy in the enclosed space. Knowing he was in the
wrong, he tried to feel more drunk. Why was it him always in
the wrong? It wasn't fair.

When he emerged Muntaha was in the kitchen. The kitchen
and bedroom and upstairs bathroom belonged to her. And since
he'd been away she'd reclaimed the hall and stairway. The kitchen
had a wooden surface and washed-out blues and greens for
walls, furniture and plates. There were salty, bitter odours, like on
a beach.

'Look, I'm sorry. I had a bad time in Syria.'

She softened immediately. 'What happened, habibi? Tell me.'

'I wish I hadn't gone.'

'Tell me what happened.'

'No,' he frowned. 'Nothing.'

'What do you mean nothing? Tell me.'

'We'll talk about it later.'

That was Sami, opening doors only to slam them shut again. Muntaha shrugged and moved to the open window. Darkness hid the neighbours' patch of garden.

'I love London in the summer,' she said. 'It smells so warm. So full of colour. Everybody relaxes. Everybody smiles.'

Struck dumb by her optimism, Sami rubbed an aching shoulder. And in a sudden white flash there were tears in his eyes. Muntaha was still sniffing at the window, and he turned from her, breathing the tears away as you would control nausea, getting on top of it, calming down.

Then he asked, 'Do you want to see your presents?'

Crouching in the hall he unzipped his bag and brought out the newspaper. He held it, wondering what to do.

'That's not a present, Sami.' Muntaha was amused.

'No.' He tossed it to the floor, and then the fluffy white dog burst out of the bag. He threw this to his wife.

'A present from the family.'

She threw it back, laughing. 'It has a Heathrow price tag on it.'

'All right. Fair enough.' He smiled. Her laughter made everything good. 'They did get you presents. You know, Arab stuff. Clothes and sweets and stuff. But I'd have needed another bag to bring it all.'

'And you only brought hand luggage.'

'Exactly.'

She looked at him. He looked at the floorboards.

'You're silly, Sami. If you didn't want to come back straight away you could have just said so.'

'Silly.' Now she knew the word. Previously they argued whenever he'd used it against her. She used to translate it into Arabic, where it had more offensive significance.

He groped to the bottom of the bag, and handed over a thin brown paper package.

'The postcards! Thank you.'

She'd requested these to use in the classroom, for projects on foreign countries. There were pictures of mosques, castles, water-wheels, mountains, women in embroidered dresses, old city doors, water sellers and other self-consciously traditional street life. Tourist Syria.

Sami stood up, unfurling a heavy necklace. This was the best moment of his day. It may have been the best moment of the whole summer. He stepped to his wife, swept her hair up, and arranged the cord around her neck, fastening the clasp on the nape, touching the downy skin with his long fingers, shaking lapis and silver pieces into place over the top slope of her breasts. Her slender neck and her swelling breasts.

'That's what I wanted,' she said, turning her warm face to his. 'Something chosen and given with love.'

She kissed him. Her lips on his.

Sami felt sexual desire. More precisely, he felt a will to live – a power that was entirely other than him – pulling strings through his body towards her. He also felt anger, moving in another direction, moving upwards with the rush of melting ice. And he felt failure, a sense of smallness, crashing downwards, from his skull deep down into a plunge pool of despair. He was a battleground of forces.

Disordered, he retreated from her through a brown door. Instead of a sitting room they had a study, and that was his. His smell was preserved in there among crowded bookshelves, generalized English mustiness, humid curtains, the fibres and spices of rugs and favoured clothes, and other ancient ritual objects, his relics. Furniture inherited from his father, memories his mother hadn't wanted. A low desk and a dwarf-sized upholstered Moroccan chair to go with it. A wood and leather camel stool. And a red felt burst-spring sofa, into which Sami sank.

The room stank of nostalgia.

Muntaha walked in with a mug of tea. She set it carefully on the floor next to his booted feet. Early in the marriage she'd tried to make him leave his shoes at the door, to recognize a distinction between outer and inner, as the Arabs do. In vain. After some months of low-volume dispute she'd stopped trying.

'Baba's ill again,' she said, seating herself on the camel stool.

The room darkened.

'I'm sorry,' Sami said. 'Is he in hospital?'

'Not this time. Hasna's looking after him. And they send a nurse to visit him every day. I've been going there after school. You should come tomorrow.'

'Yeah. Tomorrow. Good idea.'

'He had another heart attack. A small one, but he looks so old. He can hardly breathe. Just moving around the house is a big deal for him.'

Sami grunted.

'I don't know if he's going to survive this one. Allahu 'alim. God knows.'

'Yeah,' said Sami.

She looked at him. He shook himself.

'I've brought him new prayer beads from Damascus.'

'Thank you, Sami. He'll like that.'

'Wooden beads.'

'That's nice.'

A man in a gloomy room worrying prayer beads. Click, click. Cause and effect.

Sami ran out of things to say. He picked up the mug and breathed into it. Steam breathed back.

'So tell me,' said Muntaha. 'Did you find an idea?'

She was referring to his doctorate. Sami had told her what he'd convinced himself, that his visit to Syria would crystallize his academic thoughts, that it was his talismanic last-chance cure, that the visit would produce what study and thought and time had failed to.

'Sort of, yeah.'

'Excellent! What is it?'

'Something about the city's defeat of the countryside versus the countryside's defeat of the city.'

'Meaning?'

'You know. Rural–urban tensions. Social change. That kind of thing.'

'Go on.'

'What do you mean, go on?'

'I mean explain it to me.'

He stretched. The muscles in his neck were curled and tight. His headache was returning. What he really needed was another spliff.

'All right,' he said. 'All right. This is what I mean. It always used to be that political power was centred in the big cities, in Damascus or Baghdad or Cairo or whatever. The sultan was in the city, the local governor at least. The army was in the city. But poetry came from the countryside. Linguistic standards set by the Beduin, by the desert. The urban rich sending their sons to live with the tribes, to learn proper Arabic.'

'Yes.'

'But now, after independence, since the revolutions, it's the other way round. Political power is held by rural people, villagers who came from the mountains and plains. They staff the army. They're the ruling class. And, paradoxically, for the first time, the city sets the standard for language. Radio and TV stations broadcast city language everywhere. Poetry deals with urban problems and uses urban imagery. That's it.'

'It's a good idea.'

'Thank you.' Sami had cooled down during this exchange. He had his old frozen control back. And Muntaha liked him less.

'But can I ask a question?'

'Of course.'

'Abu Nuwas and people like that. They lived in cities, didn't they?'

'Yes, but that's only one kind of poetry.'

'I see.'

'Anyway, it's more than that. I'll show how rural people get changed. They arrive in the city and hear the revolutionary poets, the new music, and forget their old references. The Qur'an becomes irrelevant to them.'

'Are you sure?'

'Yes, I'm sure. There's been some development. Reason has superseded religion. It's defeatist to think otherwise.'

'But that's not what's happened, is it? The Qur'an hasn't become irrelevant. And is the Qur'an really rural? It was the product of two cities, wasn't it? Mecca and Medina. And the countryside was never as religious as the cities.'

Sami's shoulder twinged. Muntaha continued, innocently.

'And isn't modern poetry full of rural imagery? Olives, wheatfields, the moon, and so on.'

He radiated anguish.

'Maybe. But the images are used differently now.'

'I'm not trying to annoy you, habibi. I'm helping you to think it through.'

'And since fucking when . . .' – he couldn't help himself – '. . . is the moon rural?'

Muntaha walked with compressed lips to the kitchen. He could hear her closing and locking the window. When she returned she was wearing her tolerant look, an expression which unfailingly maddened Sami because it reminded him he needed to be tolerated.

'I don't know why you're getting yourself so wound up about it,' she said. 'Just do the work. You'll write something good. Insha'allah. And if you don't, it's not the end of the world.'

He stared at her. 'The end of the world. Maybe it is.'

'Of course it isn't. You could get a job. It might make you happier.'

'What job?'

'You could be a teacher. You could translate. You could work in a business. We know people who'd give you a job.'

'West London Cabs,' said Sami, full of sarcasm. When he wasn't in his underground mosque, Muntaha's little brother, Ammar, drove a cab.

'Why not? It's a job.'

'There's ambition for you.'

'It's a job. You could do something else if you don't want to do that.'

'And one day, if I played my cards right, if I reached the heights, I could branch out on my own. My own cab empire. Traifi Transport. From North Kensington to South Kensal Rise. The world at my feet.'

'Don't be so cynical. Or arrogant. It really doesn't suit you. There are people who'd kill to have a decent job.'

'I wasn't born to work in a cab office.'

'What were you born for, then?'

'Not cabs.'

'It was your example. And you weren't born for any job. Nobody is. You do your best. That's all.'

'Very wise.' Anger prickled his scalp. 'Words of wisdom. Very fucking wise.' He knew he was in the wrong.

'Control yourself. Remember jihad against the nafs, struggle against the self. Cool down. Imam Ali said the strongest man is he who fights against himself.'

'Jihad? You sound like Ammar.'

'No, I don't. His jihad means something different, as you know, Sami.' Muntaha stood above him and sighed. She briefly tousled his hair. 'I suppose you're tired. That's half an excuse. Be better in the morning.'

He heard her switch off the lights in the hallway and kitchen. He heard her on the stairs. She was undressing. She was washing. She was arranging herself on the bed. In the summer she slept naked.

He knelt to roll a spliff on the desk's low surface. Before he lit it he sat back into the sofa and surveyed his room. His past. His childhood. All the local history implied by objects and odours. He'd have liked to burn it all. He'd have liked to say, like a savage finding enlightenment, the gods of this place are not my gods. To burn it all, and move on. But he wasn't ready.

He heard a creaking from a bedroom floorboard. So she wasn't on the bed yet. She was praying.

6
Relics

Sami had one collection of Mustafa relics in his head and another in his desk drawer. The desk-drawer collection was more satisfying. He could handle it when he liked, each item fully present to his touch, unlike his vapourish memories which burst on him at odd moments and disappeared again into the insect whirring of his thoughts. Anyway, as time progressed the internal pieces came more and more to resemble the external, so that he considered the external, the empirically verifiable, the trustworthy, to be the originals.

He opened the drawer and withdrew them one by one. The constellation map on card thinned to paper by age, Mustafa's thick bold biro ticks across the patterns Sami had learnt to recognize. The Gilgamesh epic in Arabic, on the flyleaf of which Mustafa had written: *To my own little Enkidu, my wild man*. A signed first edition (there had been two: not bad for an academic work) of *The Secular Arab Consciousness*, losing weight as Sami rocked it in his hand. The miniature whiskey bottle, the one they'd shared in the hospital room, glinting with a little not-yet-extinct mystery. Then a wad of photographs – of him and Mustafa only, no mother, no uncles – curling at the edges, glossing into sepia forgetfulness. Sami held one away from himself to see it more clearly, and lowering it back to the drawer caught his own reflection in the window, as old as his father had been then. His mind filled with this image, and he lost Mustafa's.

Before he died Mustafa had told his son to look for him in the sky. 'I'll be up there,' he said, pointing weakly at the hospital window. 'Among the stars.' At night the window was not transparent. It reflected back the light of the ward. And in any case it was London winter. When Sami and his mother walked from hospital to tube there was unbroken red cloud above them – coloured from this side, not from that. To look upwards would expose his throat to the air, and it was too cold. Sami dug his hands into his pockets, hunched his shoulders inside his jacket. Wrapped inside the city wrapped inside the sky.

Mustafa hadn't intended it seriously. He was an atheist. For all of Sami's life he'd told him the courageous thing was to look death in the face honestly, without inventing stories to console yourself. Men are atoms of nations. They are replaced, and the nation continues. Even the nation is replaced eventually, but humanity continues. Then humanity dies, but the universe continues. Perhaps the universe will die too, but we won't know about it. We'll have rotted long before. Don't shirk reality.

When Mustafa talked about the sky he was evoking their shared past, not the future. And he was doing what Qabbani did: it was the self-ironizing consolation of poetry. It meant nothing concrete. Words are terrible liars.

So Sami never looked at the sky. He could do without the sentiment.

He had a composite memory of numberless instances of star-gazing, from infancy to his teenage years, from the perspective of their London home and from British fields and mountainsides. Also from dry nights on trips to Syria. All these scenes collapsed into one, in which Sami stood enclosed by one of Mustafa's arms, the other pointing conically upwards into darkness. Mustafa's dark manly odour, cigar smoke, aftershave, and the greenish cold air. Little Sami surrounded by rough warmth and the giant shape of his father. Mustafa pointing at brief atoms of light.

The best nights were moonless. Otherwise they had to wait for the moon to fall. Then the sky would clarify and harden, losing some cheap romance but gaining detail and (so Sami imagined) intellectual force. Mustafa, joining the dots, found lines and arcs in the chaos.

Their favourite constellation was Orion, bright enough to distinguish from their urban doorstep. Sami followed Mustafa's finger as it traced the warrior's belt, bow, scabbard and upraised arm. He repeated the Arabic names of the stars. Al-Nitak. Al-Nilam. Mintaka. Shapes with meanings, histories.

'This is a warrior you know already. His real name isn't Orion, but Gilgamesh. Gilgamesh our great ancestor. It was us who named him first, in Sumer. You know the story.

'And over here' – swinging his arm rightwards and Sami's small weight with it – 'is the red eye of Taurus, the Bull of Heaven. You see Gilgamesh's arm raised to strike him?'

Ishtar the love goddess convinced her father Anu, god of the sky, to send the bull to earth. The bull destroyed crops and slaughtered men. It unleashed havoc where there had been order. But Gilgamesh fought it, and restored peace.

'There, Sami. Watch Gilgamesh's arm. This is the moment he strikes. Gilgamesh and his friend Enkidu, the wild man. They slew the bull on Cedar Mountain. It's called Mount Lebanon today.'

Sami said his part. 'Then Enkidu fell ill and died.'

'Yes. Enkidu fell ill. That was his punishment for killing the bull. Ishtar's revenge.'

Mustafa could map genetics and geography on to the sky. Sami half expected to find the map of Syria up there. He expected to find himself.

Mustafa used to say any Arab could feel pride simply by observing the stars. It was Arabs before Greeks who had navigated by their light. Arabs who had narrated the first sky stories. He said the Arab nation had brought writing and irrigation and myths and cities to the world. By the Arab nation he didn't refer merely to its latest embodiment, the Muslim Arabs who had ridden out from the Hijaz. He meant all the Semitic peoples in their eternal consecutive march. Sumerians, Akkadians, Assyrians, Canaanites, Phoenicians, Hebrews, Nabataeans. These were his Arabs.

He used to say the Arabs had no need of religion to make them great. He saw the Islamic period as a falling off from previous glory.

'We'd always had gods,' he would say, 'but we didn't surrender to them. We always knew they were our creations. We invented them and destroyed them at our pleasure. We used to make gods from date stones when we were bored.'

And then he told the story of the Arab whose camels strayed while he was praying to a stone idol. The Arab ran to gather his camels and then returned to address the idol in verse. What use are you to me? he asked. Keep in your place. I am flesh, and you are only rock.

'What,' asked Mustafa rhetorically, 'has kept us backward for a thousand years? What makes us think we're starting the fifteenth century, according to the moon, and not ending the sunny twentieth? What has subjected us, the fathers of civilization, to thick-headed Turks and Albanian slaves and bloody Frenchmen?' The answer followed with an exasperated waving of hands. 'All this false consciousness. All this focus on the unseen. All this superstition and bloody otherworldly stuff. It's out of character for us. We should be a people of worldly power. We should be contributing to material culture, as we did before.'

His academic work focused on the ancient and the contemporary Arabs, cutting out the fourteen hundred years in between. He wrote about the pre-Islamic Age of Ignorance (which he campaigned to rename), about the priests of the old religions and the desert poet-prophets, and then left them stumbling and sinking into a morass of Islam, averting his gaze in distaste until he caught sight of them climbing out from under it in the late colonial period.

'It's a crumbling edifice. It's already nine-tenths gone. It only kept going so long because of our energy accumulated beforehand. Now it's all over and we're unmoored from tradition. Well, it's a bloody good thing. We can wake up, take a step back, see who we really are. We can get back to the essentials of being Arabs.'

According to Mustafa, voices like Qabbani's were leading the Arabs to a better future. If the Arabs felt a lack where there had been religion, then poetry, and freedom, could compensate. He used to talk about a 'god-shaped hole' (Salman Rushdie's phrase).

A wound remaining after the extraction. The chief concern of the responsible intellectual, he argued, was to heal this wound. 'Man doesn't live on bread alone,' he said. 'You need some hashish, some moon, to fill in the gap.'

Sami heard different mythology from his mother. When Mustafa was out of the house they curled up together and she told him the adventures of God's messengers. Of Khidr the Green Man. The tales of the Rightly Guided Caliphs. And as well as the history of the past she told him the history of the not-yet-happened. The signs of the end of the world, the Day of Standing, the final judgment.

Sami learnt early on to separate these two narratives. If, for example, his father was talking about Egyptian gods and Sami brought up the story of Pharaoh and Moses, Mustafa would turn to his wife with darkened face.

'What's this you're telling the boy? I want an educated son. Leave him alone with your superstition.'

And he would calm himself, pacing between chairs and coffee tables, by reciting Qabbani. Usually 'Bread, Hashish and Moon', which railed against Arab backwardness.

> What does that luminous disc
> Do to my homeland?
> The land of the prophets,
> The land of the simple,
> The chewers of tobacco,
> The dealers in drugs?

Sami's mother's name is Nur Kallas. She sells halal meat on the Harrow Road, wears patterned hijabs, prays five times a day. She dared do none of these things when her husband was alive. In those days all she had was a copy of the Qur'an, which she hid on the top bookshelf behind other volumes. She would kiss it and press it to her forehead before reading. Holding Sami to her breast at bedtime she would quickly mutter its protective verses. If Mustafa caught her reciting, he declaimed more Qabbani, stamping and tutting with the rhythm:

> The millions who go barefoot,
> Who believe in four wives
> And the day of judgment;
> The millions who encounter bread
> Only in their dreams;
> Who spend the night in houses
> Built of coughs . . .

Worse still, Nur told stories about the jinn. First- and second-hand anecdotes of how they inhabited Damascene houses, and their good or evil interactions with the human occupants. She strayed into supernatural territory absent-mindedly, forgetting her husband's sensitivities. Mustafa tolerated ghouls (an Arabic word), plus sprites, leprechauns, dryads and goblins. Also dwarves, elves and hobbits. He read Tolkien to Sami. But he drew the line at jinn, because these were mentioned in the Qur'an.

'But everybody believes in the jinn. Even party members. Even Christians.'

'Show me a jinn. Measure me a jinn. Weigh one. Can you? We want logic in this house. Two plus two equals four. It can never equal five. That's how we talk here.'

Then he would quote Qabbani's 'Stupid Woman':

> Shallow . . . stupid . . . crazy . . . simple-minded . . .
> It doesn't concern me any more.

The poem's intention was to protect women from the mockery of men, but Mustafa felt his use of these lines against Nur was somehow appropriate. Wasn't belief in the jinn part of the whole repressive package? Didn't his raillery therefore contribute to liberation?

Even as a young child Sami wondered what had brought his parents together. He knew they'd met at university. Nur had also studied literature, and had planned to be a teacher, but she'd accompanied her more successful husband to London instead. Photographs of the early years showed her as an impressive extension to Mustafa's cosmopolitan intellectual, with her bouncing brown hair cut short, her eyes shining with energy, her body bursting from low-cut dresses. Strange, unreal depictions. In his memory Sami saw her wearing her hair long and lank in protest against the lack of hijab. Her face closed. Her eyes directing their light inward.

At some point she'd become more religious. At first she'd innocently mixed Islamic language with that of nationalism and modernity, not understanding how they could exclude each other. When she did belatedly understand, she chose Islam. In silence. With immovable determination.

By the time Sami entered high school Mustafa had grudgingly accepted that the boy needed to know something of the patriarchs. For the sake of Sami's secular education he gulped back his discomfort. These Semitic myths, after all, were essential to the literary traditions Sami would study. So Mustafa delivered his interpretation of religious pre-history. He explained that, as with Oedipus or Achilles, there was psychopathic drama in the lives of the heroes, a drama in its essence no different from that of today's Speakers' Corner soapbox types, or of the schizophrenics following mysterious itineraries through the city's streets. The scriptural heroes heard the same internal mumblings and insinuations, but as they belonged to an epic age, with epic genres, these were granted mythic status. It was pre-psychological, pre-ironic. There was high seriousness everywhere, blowing out of the desert and rolling up from the sea. There was prophetic articulation of destiny. There was the terror of God's voice.

This raged, for instance, in the ears of Ibrahim. Where monotheism started: in the ears of Ibrahim and at the neck of Ismail. Mustafa told the story as he thought it deserved to be told, at hysterical speed. Ibrahim and Ismail. Another father and son duo. The old man despite his barren dotage begging God for a child, and the Voice after the passage of tears and time saying Yes, and the man bringing the boy up as the apple of his glinting eye, his only heir, only to hear the same Voice ringing in his raddled brain, telling him the unsayable, the obscene. Commanding him to cross dust fields and lakes of rock to a certain craggy mountain top, there to bind the perfect child, to sharpen the stone, to cut the slim throat. To wet the rock with his son's lifeblood.

The Voice relented, but the man had been ready to do its murderous bidding, that was the point. The boy too. The boy who, against both instinct and logic, helped prepare the place of slaughter.

The foundational event of three religions. Attempted murder. A proud-humble refusal of logic. It filled Mustafa with righteous anger.

'The voice in my head is God, especially when it urges me to perversity. Especially when it asks me to kill what I love. From now on I will ignore human law. From here henceforward I will fuck up the world for the sake of the unseen.'

He raised his voice when Nur was near. Let her hear! Let her learn!

Sami heard of the prophets from this voice that vanquished them. He learnt religion through the prism of civil war. Qabbani versus Qur'an. Mustafa's bookish noise, and the unspoken but resistant verses of the Book. These were the opposing camps of Sami's childhood.

It didn't take long for him to choose his side. He couldn't accept a supernatural truth. If he had chosen one, his mother's for example, he'd have had to deny all the others. And there were so many others. Just on his bus route to school there were as many one-and-only truths jostling for attention as there were fast food outlets. Jehovah's Witnesses and Seventh Day Adventists. The Nation of Islam in natty suits and carved hair. Rastafarians, both black and (absurdly) white. Anglicans, sagely complacent despite the coloniz-ation of their churches. Hare Krishnas singing while lapsed Catholics wolfed their free curry. Sikhs with daggers and briefcases. Freemasons with briefcases only. A Hindu incarnated as the bus conductor bowing inwardly to the elephant god. Scientologists offering personality tests. Grinning Discordians. A Sufi roadworker at his drill, pruning the rose garden within. Rebirthers. Crystal healers. Buddhists of the latest version. To name but some. All of whom had found the exclusive answer.

Sami smiled from the rocking top-deck seat. All these people had to do was to stop and talk to each other and listen carefully and reflect for a moment. It wouldn't be difficult for them to realize that they couldn't all be right. In fact, that none of them could be.

Belief X cancels belief Y. Leaving zero belief. Religion can't last much longer. It had developed in deserts and villages. Here it's an immigrant thing. It can't survive the cosmopolitan city.

Things looked like that then.

Of course there were times when, because of his name, because of the expectations of neighbours and acquaintances, it became necessary to visit mosques. London mosques. This usually meant the suffocating lethargy of suburban living rooms, or maybe the neon vacancy of a disused warehouse. There were calligraphic plates on the walls instead of triple ducks in flying formation, but behind them there was mildewed wallpaper or damp pocked plaster. Instead of dry air swirled by ceiling fans, the stagnant soupy stuff of central heating. The odour of besocked feet instead of frankincense. It didn't work. It didn't fit.

The mosques smelled of feet and mist and moss and wood. Wheezes and groans invited the faithful and atheists alike to prayer. Sami yawned back tears, shivering from his teeth to his anus, and settled and rocked on thin folded legs. An old man croaked the Qur'an in an Arabic deprived of a third of its consonants. Someone half coughed, like an engine failing on a frosty morning. And among the nostril noises, palate clicks and throat-clearings of older, heavier bodies, Sami in his isolation did in fact pray, blowing the time faster through a tiny hole in his puckered lips, but only for the prayer to end.

How long it took. And Islam taking its time to die, oozing

like blood in a geriatric's hardened veins, sluggishly, soporifically, dripping and dropping away from an unseen wound.

Accompanied by Mustafa, however, these mosque visits were also a kind of tourism, a glimpse into other people's slightly sad, slightly exotic lives, a glimpse which reinforced the stable comforts of his own. Crouching at the back of a wintry English mosque, touching his forehead to the musty colour-bled thread of carpet, was for Sami what a stroll through dusty farmland might have been for a gentleman of the Raj, what a visit to a refugee camp would be for a portly American journalist. He was slumming it, in among cringing Old World reptiles, and Mustafa snorting quietly at his side, making him snigger, a wink and a ludic nudge after the prayers as they sat down to eat. The irony was delicious. The storing up of joke details for later in the car. The unsuspecting earnestness of the godbothered. They were – Traifi senior and junior – disguised by curling hair and thick eyebrows, by black eyes, wrapped in the mufti of their own faces. They had superior knowledge, so it seemed.

It was an entirely different matter when the mosque invaded his home. When his mother had visitors and dared to roll out her prayer mat with them. Mustafa slammed doors and played Egyptian dance music as loud as the stereo would allow, screamed 'For God's Sake!' – in English, so that it wasn't an invocation of the supernatural but an entirely realist expression of bad humour. Sami, swirling in a vertigo of shame and self-loathing, observed his mother from the height of his disdain. The worst of it was, he felt an urge to jump.

There was certainly something attractive about the ritual movements Nur made, standing, bowing, crouching and kneeling according to an invisible logic. Despite Mustafa, and in contrast to her usual flustered manner, she performed each section of the prayer at a leisurely pace. Bangs and crashes failed to make her flinch. It was as if she was deaf. To Sami's eyes – sickened, fascinated – a halo of peace and slowness surrounded her. It was with incomprehension he turned from her to the window, and saw rain, cars, people scowling under umbrellas. His father's noise, the TV, and then back to his mother looking intently in front of her, moving her lips, her back straight, her fingers outstretched. There were conflicting worlds in this scene, worlds which could never be reconciled.

Even as he frowned he felt a breath of wonder. Nur repeated holy words whispered or sung by hundreds of millions, their prayers rippling over the earth at times determined by the sun, as shadows progressed and dawn advanced behind. It was, despite the coughs and splutters that defined it locally, a chorus he would have liked to join. Part of him. In a way. Beyond the chorus there was a – he thought the word quietly – a civilization. A civilization made of sound instead of pictures. The names of its centres – Lahore, Samara, Isfahan, Timbuktu – resonating like the ancient desert poetry his father recited and which he couldn't understand.

Were the world's objects and his inner feelings signs of something greater? Was another reality glimmering through the surfaces of things? Should living be a struggle to read the universe like a book? If he fell into his mother's way of seeing, this is what he would believe. He had the sensation of knowing something but not remembering it. And the visible became transfigured. Almost.

His mother had taught him this:

> sa-noor-ihim ayaat-ina
> fi-l-afaaq wa fi-unfuss-ihim
> hatta yatabayan-lihum
> innahu al-haqq . . .

Which meant: *We shall show them Our signs on the horizons and in themselves until it becomes clear to them that It is Reality.*

He would catch himself humming it in incantation. Even that. In dark moments, the darkest, he asked himself why Mustafa was so determined not to appreciate the poetry. Everyone recognized the Qur'an as the peak and glory of Arabic poetry, even if it wasn't the word of God. Everyone except Mustafa Traifi, Professor of Arabic Literature. What was he so scared of?

Here Sami stopped himself. Stepped back from the abyss. Was he not a proper man? Was he not prepared for the twentieth century? Some adolescent males worry about homosexuality. Sami worried about religion, about being religious. No, he needed another identity.

He sided with Mustafa. Religion was the long childhood of a people. If an ancient people still had the habit, it was no longer childishness but senility. When that people lived in London, among the healthy, among the sane, religion was humiliation.

It made him bow his head, not before God but before man.

'Syria's a Muslim country, isn't it?' asked his teachers, or his friends' parents.

And he would answer, 'It's a Mediterranean country. Would you call the Mediterranean Muslim?' or 'It's a mixture of everything, really,' or better still, 'I don't know. I don't have a clue.'

His origin was nothing to be proud of, at least not before his student days, when he refigured Mustafa's Arabism as his own. From a schoolyard perspective all origins except his had something going for them. Some credibility. White English through strength of numbers, and because it was the normal standard. Black was stronger still. It even made converts: many whites adopted black speech, tastes and hairstyles, as far as was possible for them, at least while in school. There was a mutual fascination between the whites and the blacks, watching and imitating each other, fighting and fucking each other, while the Muslims tiptoed in the gloomy spaces around the beds and dance floors where the drama was played out. The Muslims got in the way. They ruined the whiteness of the city, and the blackness too.

The blacks who subverted and enriched England with reggae and hip hop, the Carnival, spliff smoke. It looked impressive in the playground.

The Sikhs. The Sikhs had bhangra and, more recently, gangs. Nobody bothered messing about with the Sikhs any more.

The Irish. They were funny and tough and pissed. They lived in pubs on the Kilburn Road. They had tattoos, and – what was it called? The gift of the gab.

The Jews were not so enviable. His schoolmates didn't emulate a Yiddish-coloured English to toughen themselves in the playground. Nor was the two-dreadlock haircut ever in vogue. There weren't any Jews in Sami's school, not that he was aware of. They lived further north. But the idea of the Jews was attractive. They had almost single-handedly invented everything that made the West the West and not the Middle East. Modernism, Psychology, Marxism, atomic bombs. They owned the culture as much as the English did. They were neither insiders nor outsiders. Unless they dressed the part you could scarcely tell them apart from the natives. Sami had heard people say this is what made them dangerous. It certainly made them sharp. They understood London, and Europe, from within, looking out with conquering European eyes. But they'd never feel comfortable. They'd never nod off. Never grow fat and aristocratic.

But Muslims. In Britain Muslims meant Pakis, which meant crumbling mills and corner shops. Which meant anoraks and miserable accents and curry houses. Dismal northern towns where day never truly dawned. They had a proletarian role in the economy, and a bourgeois conservatism. Neither sexy nor strong. Badly dressed and poorly educated. Islam's cobwebs in their eyelashes, and its mould on their tongues.

'So you're from a Muslim family?'

'Perhaps originally. A long time ago. Not any more.'

Sami wasn't a Paki. But there were so few of what he was that it barely qualified as a community. This was before the Iraqis arrived. The visible Arabs were Gulf Arabs, tourists and princelings, obese, wealthy, stupid.

'So you're an Arab, then?'

'I'm a kind of Arab, yeah. But not like the Arabs you see on TV.'

The Arabs of his acquaintance were one or two of Mustafa's friends from the university, ideological secular-nationalists like him, and their children. Nur's friends, who smoked a lot, drank a lot of Turkish coffee, talked a lot, and prayed. Uncle Mazen from Damascus who visited in the summers 'to taste the civilization'. Those of Nur's family she was able to arrange visas for, who stayed for extended periods to make the price of the ticket worthwhile. Old Grampa Kallas, Haj Ahmad, who sat with long serious face topped by a red tarboosh, what the English called a fez, gazing through the living-room window at the English street. Once he was accompanied by Fadya, who didn't wear a hijab then, and once by Nur's much younger brother, Shihab. They huddled, the Kallas family, to complain about the coldness of the London people. Shihab clicked his prayer beads and studied school textbooks. Mustafa sighed too obviously in their presence, shrouded his face in a mask of wooden tolerance.

There came a point when Nur's family stopped visiting. Around the same time the relationship between Nur and Mustafa ended. They didn't divorce or live in different houses, but the marriage was as dead as if it had never been. Mustafa no longer talked Islam down when she was nearby. She no longer spoke to him at all. She moved into the guest room. When Uncle Mazen visited he had to stay in a hotel. Nur cooked meals, washed clothes, she helped Sami with his homework when Mustafa wasn't there. Silence spread between them, as grey and thick as Mustafa's cigar smoke.

Sami started seeing his mother wearing a hijab in the street. If Mustafa approached she would sullenly remove it, her hands working heavily, with the blank expression on her face of a teenager obeying absurd commands. Having her hair uncovered when Mustafa was there was one of the minimal duties, like cooking, like sleeping under the same roof, whose performance was required to keep them officially married.

Nur offered little comfort when Mustafa was diagnosed with cancer. There were no smiles, no tears, no soft words. As soon as he was hospitalized she boxed up his books and music collection, threw away the bottles, distributed his clothes around charity shops and mosques. She visited the hospital daily, going through the motions, changing the flowers at his bedside, bringing newspapers he was too weak to read. But she still didn't speak. Fifteen-year-old Sami couldn't forgive her for this.

Then Mustafa was gone. An atom dismantled. As dead as if he had never been.

Sami cried only momentarily before he found his cold strength. Nur didn't cry even that much. No, she seemed relieved. Their family, his childhood, was dissolved, and Nur, his ex-mother, was pleased about it. Sami couldn't understand from what distances the hatred had surged up within her and broken through her surface. What Old World, Middle Eastern curse had possessed her at the same time as her hijab? What evil, unregarded star was responsible?

7
Marwan al-Haj

Marwan al-Haj, Muntaha's father, left his country for ever in June 1982. This was four years after the cultural blacklist, two years after the outbreak of war, and three months after his release from prison. Looking back, leaving home was for him a release from the absurdities and irrelevance of his early life.

He had spent sixteen months in prison. Not a long sentence according to the standards of his homeland, but still long enough to repent being an Iraqi, or an Arab. And long enough also for his slight, well-proportioned body to stop being a source of pleasure and pride and become instead his enemy. Through his body they had broken him. By splitting his lips and ears, smashing his nose, crushing his spine, and tugging out handfuls of his full hair, from scalp and pubis, they had taught him at once how physical he in fact was, despite his earlier disbelief, and also, or therefore, how expendable.

Part of the lesson was cleanliness. Being next to godliness, this was a supreme virtue, essential for his development. They washed away all the illusions concerning an expansive soul that had hitherto rolled about within him like lemonade in the belly of an overstuffed spoilt child. Which made things simpler. They washed too the uneven concrete floor of both his cell and the pain room with his blood and urine, bucketloads, really sluiced the place shiny so that he thought of himself in the end as a large blood blister, a viscous membrane containing too much red, sweet, sickening liquid. A surface. Something savagely, uselessly, physical, better burnt and buried and unseen.

They used his body as a door to his soul. They climbed in

through it, keeping their boots on, found the soul and kicked it down to size. In quieter moments they reasoned with it gently, convincing it that if it did exist, it certainly had no right to. Then they hoovered it up, all except a grain, a peppercorn of hope. I will live, it said. I will see Mouna. She will make me better. We will start again.

When they beat him he would gasp or belch God's name. It meant nothing to him. It didn't help him. He had been too long out of the habit of seeking help in religious quarters. He didn't even intend to say it, but heard the sound on his animal breath: *ullahullahullahullahu*. 'Maku Allah,' the beaters said. 'There is no God.' They wrote it on the wall with his blood, using the wall as a blackboard and the blood as chalk.

After the first timeless beatings time settled into order. They beat him one day a week, except for the week before they let him out. Sixty-eight Tuesdays (he thought they were Tuesdays). He had no secrets to spill. They never even asked him questions, except rhetorical ones. There was no point to it beyond his metaphysical education, to satisfy the demands of routine, and his beaters' zeal.

This zeal he had to admire. They set about their work with unflagging dedication. Sometimes he detected exhaustion in their eyes, but they kept on at it. They did it as effectively as possible, so he supposed, although he was no expert. And a lot of thought had gone into his torture. The chair in which his back was shortened, for instance, was a quite ingenious device. Made in Iraq by Iraqis too, not imported technology.

Now he thought about it he realized how many people his being here depended on, what careful planning the whole complex system required. A network of informers, party men, officials, wardens, revolutionary guardsmen, police and soldiers. Taxi drivers were famous for listening, and the shopkeepers who opened early and closed late, and watchful tenants in every building. How many people? He estimated, from the suspects in his own neighbourhood, and the population of the country, he estimated hundreds of thousands. All of them with families. All of them with some poetry in the soul. But he'd learnt about the soul now. He knew what human beings really were.

Out of prison, he found the city stunned by heat and war. He returned to his flat and sat on the sofa in a layer of dust, wondering vaguely what would happen next. Mouna and the children were not there. He waited for them, looking out of the window. The sky and the street were bleached by the sun. He heard amplified counting songs and patriotic anthems from the primary school at the corner. He heard the chattering of women in the stairwell and children's laughter among cars. He heard policemen's whistles and the crowing of cocks. He heard the prayer called five times a day.

Old men from the nearby flats came one by one to greet him. The young men were away at war. The fathers and grandfathers spoke softly, closed the door behind them before they embraced him. He held them without warmth and thanked them for their presents of food and tobacco. Many of the neighbours didn't come at all. He would have come, in their position, in his stupid days. But he wasn't stupid any more, and so he understood. He had some bites of the food, rice and beans prepared in pity, and smoked the cigarettes, for something to do.

On the third day his brother-in-law, Nidal, knocked on the door. Seeing him through the spy hole, his hollow cheeks and sharp jaw, Marwan's hope exploded in him. 'God is great!' he cried, tugging him into the flat. Resurrected thought ran about inside him. Mouna would come back with the children. He'd keep himself out of trouble. Life would start again. He wept with huge movements of his chest, like an old, rusty engine heaving into motion, the tears dragged from him in bursts and blusters.

Nidal stood back and watched with a helpless expression. He shook his head slowly from side to side. He raised and lowered his hands, and finally clasped them across his waist.

'She is dead,' he said. 'God have mercy on her. They beat her on the night of your arrest. We took her to the hospital but it was no use. They beat her on the head and she bled inside. God have mercy on her. There is no might and no strength save in God.'

Marwan stopped crying. It was hope not sorrow that made him weep. He blew his nose and washed his face while Nidal made tea. They drank the tea, and Nidal continued talking.

'Muntaha and Ammar are with us. They're fine. Of course they're upset, but they're fine. Muntaha's still going to school. Ammar has become a bit nervous. He cries a lot. That's understood. He doesn't really know what has happened. He'll be all right. Both of them will. You all will. We'll bring them to you whenever you're ready. Or they can stay with us. It's up to you.'

At the beginning of June a mukhabarat man rapped at the door. Marwan looked through the spy hole and the mukhabarat man looked defiantly back. Looking was his profession. His shoes shone in the absence of light. His trousers were so black they shone too. His polished leather jacket reflected the yellow ooze from the landing bulb. Marwan opened the door and stood with head bowed.

'You are Marwan al-Haj.'

'Yes.'

'Do you want to leave Iraq?'

'No.'

The mukhabarat man cleared his throat. He tried again.

'Do you want to go away?'

Marwan, unsure, whispered, 'No.'

'Nevertheless, it would be better if you went away.'

'Perhaps.'

'Certainly it would. Here is your exit visa.' He removed an envelope from a shimmering inner pocket and thrust it towards Marwan. 'This is valid for one month only. Do not make trouble where you go. Wherever you go, we are there too. Go with peace.' He spun with a squeak of the shoes and strutted to the stairs.

Unheard, Marwan thanked the retreating back, and slid the door closed again, frowning, pensive. The future had been decided. He had no feelings about it either way.

The next day, returning on foot from the Jordanian embassy, Marwan saw one of his former torturers at an intersection sandwich stand: a large man crammed into a small plastic chair on the pavement, legs in a diamond shape bowed outwards at the knees and converging at boyishly side-rolled feet, chest and shoulders bulging over a white plastic table, a water-coloured face, unlined and uncomplicated, sunk into the shoulders. He was looking into the traffic blankly, perhaps sadly. An ordinary man. Marwan stepped behind a tree and watched until a boy brought the torturer's order. A tightly wrapped sandwich and a tall glass of red juice. Fruit cocktail. Customer acknowledged service with a weak smile and a slightly timid nod, but the boy was already at another table. Marwan, out of sight, watched the torturer eating – he ate slowly, with both hands – and asked himself what kind of revenge he'd like, if it was possible. His response was, none at all. He wasn't even angry. He said a silent goodbye across the exhaust fumes and moving crowds, and went home.

He sold the flat to Nidal for as much as could be mustered in a week. He took Muntaha and Ammar and two suitcases packed with their clothes and toys. Also some photographs, for the children's sakes, not his, and the album of their drawings Mouna had collected. He didn't take his books.

The children eyed him cautiously, circled him whispering in-cantations against doppelgängers and possessing jinn. Muntaha was excessively correct with him, behaving with a politeness he hadn't seen from her before, although at times she would forget and leap into his surprised, unready arms to nuzzle her face in his beard, or sidle up to him and slip her brittle hand in his. Ammar, much smaller, was governed by his sister. When she came close so did he, and then Marwan nodded to himself, ah yes, the children loved him. He felt the warmth of the memory of paternal love. He remembered how it had once brought tears to his gazing eyes, given him a sense of meaningless things like meaning and achieve-ment. But he couldn't feel these things again. Sometimes, when his children touched him, he flinched. That enveloped him in nebulous guilt, but he fought it off, knowing it to be illogical. Greater than love or other abstractions he had duty, and because of duty – to his children, his dead wife, to himself – he would do his best.

On the day of departure, Nidal made himself busy with the suitcases, and keys and addresses on scraps of paper. A hot wind blew up the stairwell against them as they descended. Dust was yellowish and thick on the roofs of their mouths. In the tiled entranceway Nidal turned around, panting.

'You should be happier than this,' he said. 'Good things will happen now. You'll see. And think of us.' A portrait of the president was pasted to the wall behind his head. 'We're staying here with this bastard.'

Nidal shut them into the taxi and leaned in through the window, dispensing sweets, blowing kisses, fixing his brother-in-law with a significant stare.

'Go with peace, Marwan. It will be a new start. God be with you.'

'I've already made a new start,' said Marwan, his eyes on the windscreen.

The car pulled out into the noise of the street – children wailing, mothers screaming at children, a cart man crying his wares, television sets, pop music on tinny radios, patriotic songs, the clank-clank of the gas-bottle man. Tattered flags flapped in the breeze. An old man stood in the road rubbing his back and groaning. A harsh indifferent sun glared, fixing details in memory, embellishing them with meanings to be retrieved later, meanings which they perhaps did not deserve.

8

The Immigrant

Marwan had been a minor poet. Very minor. And very poet – in attitude, lifestyle and aspiration. There were lots of poets in those days – lots of young people, lots of words, and plenty of cash.

Iraq was the only Arab country with both oil wealth and a large urban population, the only Arab country where something constructive could be done with the wealth. Money flowed into the sandbanks of the two rivers and the future sprouted. You could see through Baghdad's crumbling shrines and markets and under the surface of recent slums to a coming metropolis as greenly luxuriant as Haroon ar-Rasheed's. The hospitals and universities were already as good as those in Europe, and cleaner, newer, more gleaming. Parties characterized the city as mosques had done in the past. A cigarette-smoke and perfume miasma spawned vegetal words, verdant ropes and webs of words, of ... renaissance, progress, unity. Everything seemed to matter, every word.

Verses were currency as much as commodity. A well-aimed panegyric would buy you a job, a villa, a car. Verses came easily to Marwan, but he was an ethical investor who avoided direct toadying. He was able in good conscience to praise more generally, and the bulk of his poetry consisted of such innocuous fare: short laudatory hymns to the city, the nation, to brotherhood and other abstractions. He lovingly ornamented the present and future, and also conjured the dusty provincial town he'd grown out of, representative of the primitive past.

He sat on the editorial committee of *Revolution in Words*, a state-sponsored literary review for a coterie readership. The editors played their roles as seriously as method actors through flashing afternoons of theory and whiskey which ended in table-thumping to punctuate socio-poetic points, and then laughter. They belonged to a class which had liberated itself from rural inhibitions. They were open about their girlfriends and boyfriends, their atheism, their experiments with hasheesh and opium. Wild love and intoxication, they said, defined Baghdad in its Golden Age, and would again in the age of black gold.

Mouna was one of this group, Marwan's girlfriend before she became his wife, his wild lover, his accomplice in experiment. The object of erotic verses.

Marwan, secular and romantic, believed he was a model citizen of the new Iraq. He made no mistakes in his writing or living, not that he was aware of, not until he made the mistake he must have made in order to be arrested. He thought on this when he had time between Tuesdays in prison, and afterwards, and decided his blunder had most probably been to copy and circulate the wrong poetry. Of course nothing directly political, nothing he expected would cause offence, but he'd copied poems by disappeared Communists, translated Iranians, sectarians. He'd used the *Revolution in Words* photocopier and distributed the poems to friends and visitors who accepted them out of politeness and who in most cases never read them; Marwan standing up when they were sitting, waving his hands the while, becoming overexcited, babbling too loudly about modernism and radical diction and liberating the unconscious and God knows what else. For such noble activity he'd murdered his wife and lost his country. If he could feel anything he'd feel shame. For his absurdity. But then, the copied poems may not have been the mistake. Someone may have made a false report about him and, in that case, his arrest had been a mistake. And he asked himself, could Mouna's death have been caused by a mistake? Could the death of his own soul and the orphaning of his children and the end of consequence and depth in the world which left only silhouettes where there had been well-dimensioned people and houses, could all this be mistaken, or was there a reason for it he couldn't perceive? A logic which determined events? A set of rules?

In Amman, from a rented house on a rocky hill, Marwan wrote to Jim Clark for help. As poet and editor he'd had such international acquaintances. Jim Clark: former cultural attaché at the British embassy in Baghdad, Arabist and Arabophile, who'd arranged bilingual poetry evenings in the British Council garden and translated Marwan's poems for London magazines. Marwan posted the letter and waited for a reply.

He sat on a mattress in his bare accommodation. Without the furniture of books and words his life was as empty as the house. *Better like that*, he thought. *Free of illusions. Simpler. Uncluttered*. On Friday he walked to the nearest mosque and half listened to the sermon like the other men, cross-legged and nodding on the tired carpet. He prayed the congregational prayer for the first time in twenty years. Stood and bowed and prostrated and knelt in conformity with the crowd. He bought fruit in the street outside and carried it back. During the week he stayed in the house. He didn't read. He didn't pray.

The following Friday, and the next, he returned to the same mosque. He took pleasure in the uniform movement of the praying men, and hurried away from their extended hands and questioning glances as the mass splintered afterwards. He didn't wish to know them as individuals. As individuals they would be sharp as shrapnel.

In three weeks Jim Clark arrived, sweeping sweat out of grizzled eyebrows with the back of a heavy hand. He attended to Marwan's every gesture with the grim sympathy he judged due. Marwan – exile, torture victim, persecuted artist – was unable to play his roles properly, or to reciprocate Jim's friendship. But he did what needed to be done; was taken to doctors who noted and recorded his limp, his twisted spine, his sudden bald patches, and to British officials who regarded him with the same focused attention as Jim, dispensing with paperwork, patting him cautiously on the shoulder, afraid he would break.

Jim, tree-tall next to Marwan's withered shrub, explained that political asylum had already been applied for. A formality. In the meantime, here were three visas, and plane tickets. Marwan could pay him back later. It was the least he could do.

'Call yourself lucky,' said Jim, flinching from the inappropriate adjective. 'I expect half the country would like to get out.'

'They would,' said Marwan, 'and they wouldn't.'

'Yes, I know, I know.' Jim puzzled over it. 'It's our fault of course. It usually is. Us and our American friends. He's our man, you see. Keeping the Communists down yesterday, knocking the Iranians about today. He can do no wrong. It's a sorry state of affairs.'

Ammar wheeled around the adults on the mattress with a peal of high laughter. A screech of brightness. Muntaha followed with a water pistol. Jim was talking about the poetry Marwan would write in London. Marwan gazed at Jim, and at the abstractions like steam clouding his face. And he thought: *If I'd died at thirty I might have died happy. My eyes might have entered paradise open, still searching for something. I might have had the smell of paradise in my nostrils as I died.*

The next day they arrived in London.

It astounded Marwan. Stately-solid, autonomous, indifferent, history bowed before it. He tried to compare. More prosperous than Baghdad but harsher, tidier but more desolate, it revealed Baghdad as a ramshackle shapeshifter, built in haste for a shuddering moment, all its wiring and dirt showing. London, in contrast, was sculpted and seamed like a fortress, for permanence, with its rolling acres of pavement and wall and its tunnels underground channelling sewage, rats and trains, everything functional enclosed coffin-tight and buried again in stone. With its big stone houses, its blocks and rows and crescents, its entire streets carved from the same rock, its red zones and its white zones, its brickwork, the tremendous trunks of its trees, the city could withstand anything. Even its dwarfed and cowed inhabitants, who seemed to be there by accident. Was that it? Baghdad was an accident that happened to its people, but the people here were an accident happening to London. Crawling over its face like unwelcome insects. Getting in the way. Including him now, Marwan and his children accidents too.

Could people be merely accidents? Was it humility or arrogance to think so?

Everything was tied down in its proper place. The streets had names. No discrepancy between the written and spoken names. Even the dogs, labelled around the neck, had names and addresses. Squirrels, less timid in their residence than Iraqi human beings, lived unharassed in the trees which burst from the pavement at regular intervals.

He didn't sneer, not even at the combed and collared dogs. There was nothing wrong with order. Order meant safety. Order kept people within limits.

And there were people, he gradually understood, who belonged in the city more than accidentally but as part of its fabric, people made of stone flesh and cold stone blood. Of every colour and class, arriving from everywhere, for every reason and none, and staying when they came in the shadows until they moved invisibly into death, and even the shadows were fixed, and the air hanging between the buildings, the exhalation of lungs and engines, the cloud and the metal sky in permanent residence, fixed in situ for ever and ever and ever.

Unrelenting, eternal London. A piece of the earth's crust reared up and separated from the rest of the planet. A stone mountain.

Wonder soon hardened into resentment. He cast bitter glances at the imperial centre, at Buckingham Palace and Whitehall, the great museums and opera houses, at banks, theatres, department stores. *Why don't we live like this?* he asked the emptiness. *Do we not qualify? Are we a different species? Are we not human beings? Or are we human beings and these the gods?*

But he was giving up metaphysics. He developed a sense of perspective. Weaned himself away from symbols and observed the world by its letter and surface. He attended to his hours as assistant librarian in the Arabic department of the School of Oriental and African Studies (Jim had guided him into the job). He paid the rent for the small house Jim had found in West London. He attended the local mosque. He bowed like the others – the Turks, Indians,

Nigerians – prayed as he'd been taught as a boy, before abstraction set in. His prayer was not meditation but a habit establishing itself, a practice and a rhythm, the string attaching him to his place in the city.

There were other sides to London Marwan discovered only as time passed. After a leaden wintertime he found less reason to be jealous of it. He noticed shabbiness, hollowness, randomness. How the lives hurtled into collision, unplanned, each scouring the other's surface. A sandpaper world. People tied individually to the city but not to each other. He wasn't the only one to avoid meeting eyes in the street; the natives too were foreign to each other. He watched the aggressive youths, beer cans in knuckly hands, navels exposed, sometimes pierced, and remembered with shame his own extended youth in Iraq. And for that association among others he didn't miss it. Any happiness there had been illusory, mistaking hell for heaven. For the world is made of the same material, London or Baghdad, it makes no difference.

One humid evening walking from the tube station Marwan passed a blood-sticky body hugging the kerb. Matted filthy beard and tangled long hair. Passed it and half turned his head, his peeled eyes. Nobody else was stopping. So with the now characteristic hard-set, turned-down expression about his mouth he went back and crouched, holding his breath to keep his lungs unsoiled, and slowly rolled the corpse face-up. And the corpse came to life, spitting froth from its lips. Marwan sprang back upright. 'Fuck you,' groaned the corpse. Marwan walked on quickly.

He stayed inside when he could. But inside was no relief. The little rooms were dark and damp. Varieties of mould tattooed the walls. He had that mushroomy sour smell always in his nostrils. The windows didn't open unless you unscrewed anti-burglar locks, and the air outside was anyway gusty and cold, and tasted of beer and traffic. Gusts like the squalling tears of a derelict. When the wind rushed along the street the windows rattled. In the winter, ice formed on the inside of the panes.

Marwan's room, downstairs, guarding the entrance hall, also

served as dining room and living room. In the daytime his bed became a couch. No pictures or books. He had the TV which revealed further little rooms and compartmentalized English people gossiping and whingeing within them. Through the window he heard the immanence and distance of the world outside.

The children were upstairs out of harm's way. A room for the girl and a room for the boy. They cut pictures from magazines and stuck them to the walls to reflect what they imagined inside themselves. They were allowed to jump around and make noise. Marwan was not an unkind father. He questioned them about their schoolwork and the friends he never saw. He worried about them and warned them away from danger, but never beat them or raised his voice. He did his best. He played his part.

He would pray at home and at work as well as in the mosque, measuring out the day by the allotted times. He performed fifty press-ups and fifty sit-ups in the gloom of each morning. He memorized sections of the Qur'an as an exercise to maintain his mental health. With a sort of quiet pleasure he felt age descending upon him.

Once on the tube he intervened in an argument between a man and a woman. They cursed in one of the stranger accents. Irish? Scottish? Subdued swearing burst into shouts, and then shoving and flailing hands. As slaps became punches Marwan found himself standing, stretching an arm between them. 'Madam, how may I help you?' He heard his croaky foreign voice and his diction suited to the British Council garden or to Shakespeare seminars thirty stale years old. Bleating ridiculously, 'Madam, madam . . .' until the couple interrupted themselves and looked at him with shocked disgust.

'Piss off, you old Paki fucker,' the woman said, and pushed against his face with a wet hand, a fingernail scratching blood from the corner of his eye.

Marwan leaked tears back to the house, locked the door, and shielded himself from Muntaha's concern.

Thereafter, in the English phrase, *he kept himself to himself*. Didn't presume to interfere in anything beyond himself. He began reading again, but not poetry. He read the pamphlets he picked up at the mosque or in Islamic bookshops concerning the laws of God established and fixed by the Righteous Predecessors. The laws by which God made Himself known in the lives of His servants. These were straightforward, plain texts. Facts you could be sure of. No mistakes or accidents. Nothing elitist or vague.

The pamphlets provided another reason not to miss Iraq, which they said was the realm of unbelief as much as London. No country could call itself Muslim if it refused to submit to God's laws. And no individual. Marwan remembered his soul-bloated former self mocking the laws, how in his foolishness and arrogance he'd assumed men to be angels. Worse, he'd attributed to men qualities owned only by God, such as interpretive control over life, such as absolute independence. *I seek forgiveness from God*, he repeated. *Forgive me my faults. Forgive me my faults.*

It was clear to him that the laws offered a solution to the agonies of the grimy city and its brawling populace. That the laws could tie the people together with the twine of common humanity and shared purpose, could tame them with humility and restrain them within proper limits. Strict punishments and the prohibition of drugs and alcohol could establish peace and safety. Modesty and honour in sexual matters could allow men to regard their fellows as brothers rather than competitors. Then the city could be clean. Not sandpaper, but harmony and balance. Five times a day it would pause its commerce and bow as one body to its Creator.

But that wasn't his business.

He ordered his own life and left the people to their fate. If it was God's will to guide them, they would be guided. But he still felt a kind of pity as he walked at a distance behind them, striving for invisibility. He raised his eyes under lowered lids as the Londoners flitted or staggered from pub to betting shop, those most commonly in the poor areas, or wandered blankfaced and numb in shopping centres, or stood nervous at cashpoints, guarded, locked into themselves. Marwan followed them breathing quick and shallow, worrying his prayer beads, either seeking forgiveness on their behalf or protecting himself from repeating their sin. *Istughfurullah*, he muttered. *Istughfurullah, I seek forgiveness from God, I seek forgiveness*.

Computerization and cutbacks, meanwhile, made Marwan redundant. He wasn't sorry to lose his job, for two reasons. First, he found himself incompatible with the bookish, youthful environment of the university. The undergraduates – noisy, brash children – he could bear. But the ever drawn-out youth of the graduate students and unkempt professors he could not. Their academic froth of visions and revisions, their satisfaction with unreality, they mirrored too much his younger self. Not a mirror he wished to look into any longer. And secondly, this: in his former academic life, back there, he'd been a student and, more or less, a teacher. Student and teacher of nothing much, but at least those, an agent with knowledge as his supposed object. He'd been made a fool of only by himself and God. Until his imprisonment. Whereas here, he himself was an object of study. In this respect undergraduates were worse. They peered thoughtfully over the tops of books into the middle distance, not into space but at him, the Arab. Sometimes they would ask for his point of view on a particular issue, not because they respected his opinion but from a desire to hear an Arab voice, any Arab voice. It spiced up their day. Saved them a trip to the Edgware Road. Just standing nearby could authenticate things for them. Breathing the air he'd breathed was like treading the Mesopotamian soil, like waking in a goat-hair tent. An undergraduate once asked him, with admirable honesty, 'Mr al-Haj, what's it like, being an Arab?' He didn't say: *It's not like anything. I know nothing.* He was never more than formal with them, although they were often too friendly with him, these sons and daughters of a cold uncourteous people, introducing their sexual partners as if he was interested, or badgering him into group photographs with their large arms around his shoulder. In some way he couldn't define and therefore couldn't repulse they recorded him, fixed him, pinned him down. He expected at any moment to be dissected.

So it was a relief to be freed from this. His health was degenerating too. As loyal as a sheepdog – a dog in English is a fine and trusty animal – Jim Clark arrived to organize another transition. Shaggy, stumble-footed, he led Marwan between hospitals and government bureaus to confirm again the official existence of his bad back and persistent limp, plus now the laboured beating of his heart. Jim did the talking, ponderously, with significant nods and movements of the eyes.

Marwan's retirement present was a cup overflowing with empty time. What would he do with the yards and folds of it? He interested himself in the children's homework and exam revision. He expanded his daily routines, walking to the mosque for every prayer and spending twenty minutes after each glorifying God on his prayer beads. He did press-ups in the afternoons as well as the mornings. He reread his collection of pamphlets, finding comfort in the repetition. He memorized more of the Qur'an. Still there was time.

He explored further afield, on wide-ranging circuits of Arab London. To the Syrian grocer's on the Uxbridge Road where he bought olives and salted balls of cheese. To Moroccan stalls on the Golborne Road where he drank steaming bowls of harira against the weather and listened to the gruff, almost incomprehensible Franco-Arabic of the market men. To cafés on the Edgware Road or upstairs rooms in Kilburn where he smoked a narghile – his one occasional vice – between voluble Egyptians and Lebanese. He stepped around plotters, journalists and other exiles, and closed his eyes to the vulgar young Gulf tourists.

He walked alone, uncherished, but the city softened to him by degrees. He expanded his acquaintance. Before long he had hand-shaking knowledge of more than two dozen men. Shopkeepers, security guards, eternal students and tourists who'd lost their way home, a poet, businessmen, embassy staff, waiters and managers of restaurants. He knew their names and origins, the storied versions at least. He presented himself as a mild critic of his country's regime, but a patriot, who'd settled in London for the sake of a good job (perhaps he exaggerated its importance), and who was now waiting for his children to finish their education before returning home. Most of them talked of going home, even the Palestinians from disappeared villages.

They bought each other lunches or glasses of tea or pipes to smoke through bawdy or fantastical narrations of Haifa or Beirut, Cairo or Riyadh, or of London itself, what scandals they had heard or seen or imagined. They talked a lot of politics, but seldom involved themselves in the opinions they gave, cloaking every thought in so many layers of irony or parody that even the speaker of a statement rarely felt sure of its intention. They preserved the survivalist suspicion they had brought with them. There was a lot of laughter in these meetings, and the steam of vain words again, but Marwan allowed himself the indulgence. He wasn't engaged to words this time. That was the difference. He didn't have faith in them any more.

On warmer days he would walk on to Hyde Park or Regent's Park or Queen's Park, worrying his beads to excuse himself from the café's frivolity or from the corruption of the streets. On these days women were more than usually naked and lovers more than ever intent on flaunting the drunkenness of the body. He would choose an unoccupied bench and flick non-committally, inviolate, through a pan-Arab newspaper until he fell into a doze punctuated by cloud-interrupted sun. Then he would awake from kinder parallel worlds into a brief bitterness, sour and cramped, before he remembered himself, stood up, and limped towards the nearest mosque.

It was in the Regent's Park mosque, after Friday prayers, that marriage was proposed to him. He was kneeling far beneath the dome as the congregation picked its way past those still stationary in prayer or meditation when the face of Abu Hassan, a huge and craggy Baghdadi, loomed close. Eyes burnt from deep sockets in Abu Hassan's bone-white cheeks. Tufts of brownish hair sprouted from his ears and nostrils. He wore a grey suit and an open-collar pinstriped shirt for the mosque, but Marwan saw him always as he usually encountered him, with a triple-extra-large Union Jack T-shirt pulled shiny tight across his barrel chest. Such was the uniform Abu Hassan had selected for the staff of his Queensway shop, which sold royal regalia, novelties and tourist goods. In among the plastic patriotism that made his living, the policeman's hats and postcards of mohicaned punks, Princess Di dolls and rubber caricatures of the prime minister, he looked like a toy himself, with his simple movements and uneven proportions, like a bear-sized, vastly over-grown child. Like many people that big he was an unexpectedly gentle man, happiest at home with his little wife and his shipwrecked sister, Hasna. It was for Hasna that he clutched Marwan's arm in the mosque and announced, 'My brother, marriage is half of religion.'

Hasna's first husband had been an officer and party member who at the close of an illustrious career of casual barbarity had committed the folly of idealism. He had intervened to avert an entirely irrel-evant act of murder or torture. As a result, he was exiled from home, property and reputation. In sullen recognition of her duty Hasna had obliged herself to go with him, to London because her brother was there, leaving her adult children behind. It was hard for her to forgive her husband, so she didn't. She put her energy into building a shrine to Iraq in the tiny flat they bought, representing her sacrifice in an iconography of lost bliss, in photographs of family and in traditional craftwork items she'd never been interested in before. She bemoaned her reduced circumstances and ignored her husband until, with admirable promptness, he was thrown down dead on the linoleum kitchen floor by a tremendous shaking of the heart. Then she kept the shrine for religious purposes only, and moved into her brother's house.

Marwan seemed to her a steady, uncontroversial man who would spring her no surprises, and she was largely right. He made few claims on her. She found him regular in his habits and respectful, if also uncommunicative and on occasion suddenly harsh. His chil-dren were polite although secretive and wayward, and at least half English, particularly the snake-eyed boy who refused to speak his own language. She moved Ammar into the living room and took for her and her husband, purged of its supernatural posters, the bedroom he'd occupied. She did her best with the dank little house which was not much more than stairs, corridors and cupboards. She double-glazed the rattling windows. She painted the living walls, but the paint never really dried. She overstocked the kitchen with food, and invited guests at least once a week.

Marwan remembered to thank God for his blessings. Hasna was a handsome woman, large and white, round-eyed, round-faced, round-bellied. Her breasts were rich and heavy circles. She contained as much femininity as he could bear. He felt properly human when he was imam for the prayer at home, with his wife praying behind him, as if his body carried weight and consequence.

Sometimes at night or in the deserted hours of the morning when the children were at school and habit made him think himself alone she found him weeping without noise or reason. It was only because she saw him that he realized he did it. In such ways she made him more lucid. He was thankful for the light, this shrivelled man who did his duty and tried to do his best. Ammar barely noticed him. And in his daughter he provoked only a dull ember of love, half extinguished but burning still. Light in the warmth of a glowing heart.

9
Muntaha

Muntaha loved her father, but she was embarrassed by him.

Like all teenagers, she wanted to fit in. The usual desire to belong increases in proportion to the feeling that you don't, and she, with her stumbling sing-song accent and instinctive politeness to teachers, knew she didn't. But it was more than that. Beyond adolescent narcissism, teenagers want the world to fit together better than it does. Their childhood assumptions of jigsaw accuracy in the world's interconnections have given way to anxiety. They realize there are pieces missing, that the edges are jagged. Muntaha considered her world especially awkward, and for this she had a good excuse. She'd arrived when she was twelve, straight into school at an age when coolness and conformity are the big issues. She had to work it all out very quickly.

Her father didn't fit her memory of him, so changed he was since his imprisonment and her mother's death. And he certainly didn't fit London. People looked at him in the street. It had nothing to do with his race. Muntaha is darker, like her mother was, and anyway there are enough dark people about for people not to notice. So that wasn't the reason. It was the way he looked at others, and the way he moved, as if he was guilty of something. His limp more like a shuffle, he walked sideways, like a crab, and then twisted himself straight before stepping forward again. Muntaha knew how shameful it was to hold that against him. It wasn't his fault. But it wasn't a question of fault. It was a question of fitting, beyond morality.

The way he dressed annoyed her. She tried to make him buy smart clothes, at least new clothes. He got his jumpers and jackets and trousers from Oxfam and Age Concern. Said it was vanity to spend money on clothes. She half agrees with him now, but then she was a teenage girl who understood clothes to signal qualities beneath the surface.

He wasn't part of the image she wanted for herself. Girls at school called him shifty. 'There's your shifty dad!' they said, when he came to pick her up at the end of the day. She told him not to come; she'd walk back with her friends. For the same reason she never wanted to go shopping with him. On Saturdays when they went to the market in Kilburn she tried to walk three or four people behind him in the crowd, and frowned to show she was there under protest, just in case any of her friends saw her.

At school she'd found a clique to fit into. Six or seven or eight of them at a time, very conscious of their exotic charms. Muntaha plus Nita, Lakshmi, Asma, Jenny, Randa, and then temporary members, Pakistanis, Indians, Jamaicans, Arabs – depending on who was beautiful that month. Beauty was the criterion, and being brown. Jenny was Irish, but very brunette. Blondes didn't qualify.

The other thing was, they didn't have sex. They practised eyelash flutterings, bestowed smiles, stopped conversations almost as soon as they'd started them. Kept boys enthralled. But no sex. That way they attracted more interest than the girls who did it, than the 'slags'. Boys competed to see who could make them give in first. In Muntaha's case, nobody won. When it happened, with her husband, with Sami, she didn't give in. She gave herself, very consciously.

It wasn't religion that made her guard her chastity. She wasn't interested in religion then. She was conscious of what her father would feel like if he discovered she'd been sleeping with boys. It would have made him feel even smaller, even more of a failure. But that's not what stopped her either. Her clique stopped her. Like most teenage decisions it was a group decision. They were chaste for the same reason other girls were trying to have sex and to let everyone know. Just to be cool. To fit together by being a bit different.

She had to have extra English lessons for the first year. After that she was one of the best students in her class. She had the advantage of spending her free time reading. The TV was downstairs, in her father's room, so she never watched it. She only went down to make cups of tea or for meals. She made the meals. Otherwise she sat on her bed for hours in the evenings reading Victorian novels. Dickens and Hardy. *Wuthering Heights. Middlemarch.* It meant she couldn't join in conversations about *Eastenders*, but she soon had a bigger vocabulary than your average West London girl. There was a teacher who made a big deal of it. She put Muntaha in front of the class with her hands on her shoulders. 'This Arabian girl speaks better English than the lot of you, so-called British children included.' Called her Arabian, like a flying carpet. Even that didn't dent her reasonable popularity.

Her favourite teacher was the history teacher, Mr Sorrel. He was a self-declared member of what the tabloids were calling 'the loony left', and an overt social engineer. 'My job as a teacher,' he announced, 'is to create a classless, multicultural society.' And, more pertinently to history lessons: 'If we stick to the curriculum you aren't going to learn anything that'll help you understand the news. Nothing that'll help you understand how this country has shaped today's world, for better and worse, mainly for worse. The curriculum won't teach you about the Falklands, or the Middle East, or Ireland.' Except he called the Falklands 'Las Malvinas'. So they did Cyprus and Portugal and the Miners' Strike, each student choosing a project. Muntaha did the 1920 Iraqi Revolution against the British. But after a term Mr Sorrel was told to stop. It was causing fights. Cyprus caused a fight. So did the assassination of Indira Gandhi. Knowing the world didn't make it easier to live in.

Those classes were what made her decide to study history as a subject at university. She was interested anyway, because she came from somewhere else, because she couldn't take her present position for granted. She knew she came from ancient depths, like a fish emerging from dark water, knew it was her turn in the historical process to emerge now for an instant into distinction. The generations a stream rushing uphill, and then a waterfall crashing in silence, into caves. Everybody coming up looking around themselves at the world, and waiting for the hidden descent.

The descent her mother had already made. The fact that Mouna had died in Iraq by thuggish mistake, that she'd never seen the streets Muntaha was living in, wouldn't have been able to imagine them, added to the mystery. Muntaha was aglow with the strangeness of it. There was no dividing line between her personal circumstances and what was discussed in Mr Sorrel's class. Beyond the beauty clique, she fitted, jaggedly, into historical narrative. She even dreamt about it. Nearing the top of the Up escalator, her brother, Ammar, pressing close a step behind, her weathered father with his head lowered in front. Everybody going up and falling down in fated order, but the view on the ascent looking different to each. And here she was with familiar foreign London as her view, free to examine any corner she chose.

She met Sami for the first time in the British Museum. It's a good memory. They spent an afternoon walking around the rooms together, and it was all very natural and informal. Accompanying a stranger, leapfrogging over conventional greetings to intimacy, in Iraq it would seem very untraditional, very 'modern'. But the distinction is a false one. Nobody anywhere lives in smooth connection to the past. Only the shape of tradition remains, only folkloric stuff for tourists. Only oppression justifying itself as tradition. Muntaha has nothing against tradition – she even wishes it existed – but she understands its absence. Whereas Sami was impressed by her supposed victory over it, astounded that she'd become his girlfriend, as if she was doing something revolutionary. As if Iraqis don't have relationships. Sami in his dreamworld.

She didn't need dreams or miracles. London was more than enough. And then him in it, walking close enough to produce electricity. He was very handsome, with the bluish pale skin some Syrians have when they keep out of the sun, and deep black eyes, and blue-black, curly hair. A face you could see his feelings roaming about in, it made no difference that he tried to hide them. His body well enough put together. And she could tell he liked her – he got nervous around her – which is always exciting. Muntaha infected by him.

In the museum she allowed herself to be led. They didn't touch, but later she remembered being taken by the hand. She trusted him as if by intuitive recognition of her fate. She let him do most of the talking, about the Egyptians and Assyrians and the various exhibits. It was clear he wanted to show off his knowledge, and she appreciated that. If a man wants to show off, that's a good way to do it. And she probably liked him being so talkative because her idea of a man then was someone as depressingly silent as her father, who you could barely squeeze a word from. So when she already knew what he was telling her she kept quiet. She even pretended surprise, rounding her eyes and raising her eyebrows, to encourage him.

He was thoughtful, obviously intelligent. They had a lot in common, a lot of shared references. But not so much as to be predictable. He was more English than her, without trying. He seemed to fit. He took the place for granted.

He took himself for granted. He was brought up that way, which was not necessarily a bad thing. It was fine until he stopped believing his own myth. His arrogance was tempered by a vulnerability linked to his father's death. It was his father who'd filled him up with self-belief, so his dying when Sami was young undermined him and made him bearable. All kinds of trauma nestled in that event, all kinds of scar tissue. Sami didn't talk to his mother. He still doesn't. He blames her for not loving his father enough. A coldness descended when Muntaha tried to talk seriously about it. Sami became wintry, and she had to change the subject.

After the museum she met him a couple of times with Ammar in tow. Ammar entering his hip hop stage, and Sami very proud that he could hold his own there and be an intellectual talking about that too. On the second occasion he gave her a lapis and silver necklace, lapis lazuli being the trademark of Sami's gifts to her for reasons related to the Sumerians and their first meeting. But much more touching was the poem he'd copied in both shaky Arabic script and surer English translation, on a folded sheet of paper crammed into the lid of the jewellery box. Not his own poem, but one by Nizar Qabbani.

> Do not say my love was
> A ring or a bracelet.
> My love is a siege,
> Is the daring and headstrong
> Who, searching, sail out to their death.
>
> Do not say my love was
> A moon.
> My love is a burst of sparks.

Who would be able to resist it? Not her.

These symbols had great importance for him. There was one night early on when she, whispering with that sound-modesty imposed by the dark, called him 'amri', my moon, and he started quoting Qabbani's 'Bread, Hashish and Moon' about the moon being a narcotic for the Arabs:

> What does that luminous disc
> Do to my homeland? . . .
> On those eastern nights when
> The moon waxes full,
> The east divests itself of all honour . . .

And so on, lifting his hand like he had an orchestra to tame.

She fed him more rope, enjoying his rages and sudden frowns.

She'd say, 'But this isn't the East, and you're not my homeland, not quite.'

'Exactly! Exactly!' he shouted, enthusiastic. 'It's a new land, a new start. We'll leave the moping moon behind us.'

And that was attractive too, all that passion about a metaphor. The politics of metaphors. She told him she'd let him have his dream if she could keep the moon, and he accepted that at the time. Later he developed the attitude that if his dream failed everyone else's had to fail as well.

Of course, Sami with his spliff habit wasn't the best person to complain about narcotics. Not even sky narcotics. On those evenings by the canal or in the park he'd tell her about constellations, about Orion and Gilgamesh, repeating mythology he'd learnt from his father, teaching her the lesson in turn, waving his arm at heaven without actually looking himself.

She'd tease him. 'What do you think you're on about? Who's the romantic now? That's not your friend Gilgamesh up there.'

'Who is it, then?'

'It's just rocks and ice and explosions. It's metal and minerals. The stars aren't even where they seem to be. What you're talking about is only a story for people to share when the moon has set.'

Back to the moon. You could see his anger. She thought it very beautiful.

'You're denying the Sumerians,' he said. 'You're denying our Arab ancestors the Sumerians, and those who came after them.'

The Sumerians weren't Arabs. They didn't speak a Semitic language. She pointed this out, and he was very disconcerted. Silent. More wounded than angry. Like her father would behave if someone doubted the credibility of the Righteous Predecessors.

She knew she was a challenge for him. Just by being herself, a bit Iraqi, she unclothed him of his symbols, stripped the power from the idols which were visible in his flat – the signs of his Arabness, the kuffiyehs and the gellabiyas which he used to impress English people. Seeing him floundering a little, wondering how to talk to her, how to behave, was very flattering. He tried hard.

They had a long courtship, long for England, stretching into the cold months. So many afternoons spent walking and talking, crossing wet roads or coming up from under canal bridges for coffee and cakes in dim cafés. Making a lot of the cold, stamping their feet and puffing out steam with their frosted words. Well wrapped up but still finding excuses to slap and pat each other's arms and shoulders, helping with collars and hats and scarves.

Circling each other. Behaviour that Muntaha has since realized is inherently religious: heightening pleasure by putting it off. It's the opposite of hedonism. Paradise tomorrow instead of today.

They talked about her school and his college, why she was going to study history and why he liked his Arab poets. He wanted her to remember Baghdad for him, which she did as far as she was able, in disconnected, non-narrative memories. Pictures seen through cloud, in bursts of noise. She speculated on what had now been obliterated. Their courtship happened in the autumn of 1991, after the Kuwait war.

Sami tended to support Saddam, but quietly out of deference to her. He was disturbed by it all. She could see him turning away from his Arab rhetoric, feeling unstable on his symbols, as if they were unreined and getting away from him. Everybody was disturbed, all the Arabs. In the war there had only been evil options. No heroes to support except your enemy's enemy. Whichever enemy you hated less. Perhaps there was the invisible heroism of people dying staunchly, conscripts under carpet bombing and families in their shelters. But heroism didn't really come into it. The dying was done pointlessly, in blind screaming and choking blood.

Iraq had been the most developed Arab country. After the war it was in the Stone Age again, worse than the Stone Age, the Depleted Uranium Age, children born deformed or dying of cancer, people wading through sewage to go to the market. Muntaha loses her sense of wonder when she thinks about Iraq in the decade since, or she experiences the wonder as horror. For Iraqis, for all Arabs, history started to run backwards in 1991. Contrary to the stuff about progress that we learn, explicitly or not, in British as well as Iraqi schools.

Maybe, then, it was the news as much as meeting her that challenged Sami. Both happened to him at once. Her, and the realization that the condition of being an Arab was impotence, which is certainly not the idea he'd inherited.

The war had its effect on Ammar too. He went from a lisping

Anglo-boy into dungeons and dragons and maths to some kind of counterfeit gangster. Started saying 'yo' instead of hello and 'negative, motherfucker' instead of no. His age and where they lived had something to do with it, but it was mainly the war. And his father's lack of response to the war. Marwan would shrug, say whatever happened was what God willed, that it was nothing to do with us.

The war disillusioned them, which gave them another reason to hold on to each other. It's only by being disillusioned that you know you had illusions in the first place. In Muntaha's case, she'd believed, she discovered then, that this was a free country they'd come to, that the newspapers told the truth, that the people made the decisions and only after careful thought. She didn't know the people could be manipulated. But look what happened. Half of them didn't know where Iraq was, and none of them understood the Iraq–Kuwait issue, but still they were ready to send their brothers to kill and die. They really seemed to think a lot of them would die. They thought it was 1939, not 1991. There were people on her street who put the *Sun*'s Support Our Boys poster in their windows. And half of her beautiful friends getting excited about tanks and planes and soldiers and what they could see on TV. How much like a game the world was for them.

Marwan said the Arabs are freer inside their heads than the English because the Arabs never believe what they're told. That's why Arab governments need police and guns and torture chambers. For the English, who are trusting and sheeplike, those things aren't necessary.

Maybe that's too harsh. The English don't complain because they have less trouble, less reason to complain. Anyway, they dose themselves to get by with their lives, with TV and football and pubs and drugs. The desire for numbness suggests they know something's wrong.

It was a dose of English numbness that Muntaha decided to take, numbness administered by Sami's hands. To make herself properly English. Not so much doing the drugs as watching him do them, although she smoked spliffs once or twice to see what they were like – and they were all right, a bit fuzzy, a bit tickly, no more than that. He smoked and drank and took Ecstasy, and thought he was very cool indeed. She pretty much agreed with him. She was boundlessly tolerant, anyway. He took her into underground ware-houses where the music was so loud she felt it squashing her ribs instead of hearing it with her ears, and where the people who'd been so uncommunicative in the queue outside stroked each other's floppy hair, where no one danced in couples but there was plenty of groping in the strobe-light. It was in those places he took his little ochre pills, and then danced very well, and when they emerged in the daylight into birdsong and car-noise she used to feel, although she'd taken nothing, that the world was transfigured and strangely fresh. Not actually numb at all.

It was one of those mornings they first had sex, before they married, and she's not in the least ashamed of it. She chose it. She chose him. She knew what she was doing.

It says in the Qur'an husbands and wives are like clothing for each other. A husband is an adornment and a protection and a comfort. And it often felt like that. But less and less lately, as his self-hatred came to a head. As he sank into unhappy lethargy her tolerance became less unbounded, more staged. Inevitably so: he wanted to punish himself for his failures so he made himself impossible to live with. Being too lazy to punish himself he hoped she would do it for him. At the same time, he wanted to be pampered, caressed and forgiven. Wanted to be treated like the children they hadn't had, the children he clearly wasn't ready for. He felt children would distract from his search for direction.

Given that his directions turned out to be dead ends he resented Muntaha finding her own. Her hijab upset him most of all. Who'd have thought a headscarf would cause so much fuss? It was the catalyst. She couldn't understand what it represented for him.

Like the world, she had become more religious. She realized she fitted into a community, that she wanted to belong to this Muslim community. That there are things you shouldn't be embarrassed by, things you should be proud of.

But more than that, it was the settling of her sense of wonder. She'd absorbed plenty of alienation, plenty of atheist ideas, breathed all the agnostic air around, but her default mode was still belief in God. That's what she returns to. The Qur'an, and prayer, and the sense that God is next to her, closer than her jugular vein. She knows her sense may be wrong, but it feels right to her. Why should she struggle against herself to deny what she feels? If someone brings her proof that God is a fiction, then she'll have to disabuse herself of the notion. But she doesn't believe anyone can prove there's no God, any more than she can prove there is.

She remembers the prayer of Rabia of Basra, an Iraqi woman, a Sufi, who prayed:

If I worship You for the sake of heaven, deny me heaven. If I worship You for fear of hell, cast me into hell. But if I worship You out of love for You alone, accept my worship.

Muntaha worships like that. Maybe there are Muslims who believe because they're afraid, or because they want what they don't have, but not her. For her, belief is only the expression of wonder.

One way of asking the belief question is this: Are you going to respond warmly to the universe, or not? It's a choice you make. Sami's trying very hard to answer no, and she can understand that. It isn't stupid to decide the universe is cold. The interstellar spaces, the emptiness of inner space, the animals eating each other. Cold is true. But you could equally be warm. Everybody's warm towards something, their team or teddy bear or pint glass. Their authentic Iraqi lover. But you could feel warmly towards not just one piece, not only sentimentally and a little sarcastically, but towards all of it, towards all reality.

Muntaha read someone saying it would be impiety to believe in a God who created a world as bad as this one. But she thinks the writer is cheating. To be certain that the world is so bad he has to be already certain that there's no God. He's using retrospective logic, propaganda logic. He won't say that the things which worry us so much, death and war and betrayal, that those things might make sense from a higher perspective. He denies the validity of that perspective because he can't see it or measure it. Like an empirical scientist. But religion isn't science.

It's a choice, and not one you make consciously. You need to be attentive to know what you believe. Muntaha experiences God's comings and goings. Because it goes too; it isn't always there. Inside her, hot and cold alternate like the seasons. And she knows which she prefers. She aims for summer. She aims for light.

10
Hijab

Sami was woken by Muntaha shaking a foot, making him rock from side to side in his sweat. A bad start. If he'd looked at the expression on her face, if he'd noticed that her grip on his heel was also tender, he might have responded differently. But he didn't notice, and he hated to be woken by anybody. It made him feel vulnerable.

Predictably, he had a headache. From the spliff, the alcohol, the dehydrating aeroplane. The bad temper. His brain like an anemone in search of moisture was swelling against his skull. Photophobic, he clutched his brow. He moaned. He said 'fuck'. This his version of *good morning, darling*. Muntaha shrugged shoulders and went down to the kitchen.

When the gurgle of coffee arrived upstairs he stirred again, with groans and curses. Hauled himself up and rattled around the morning-broken room. He went through the routine to make himself better. Poor suffering Sami. He pissed. He attempted weakly, vainly, to shit. He stood in the over-oxygenated shower jet. He underwent a self-administered head massage.

Downstairs his wife was preparing for a day of work. She'd already eaten, to musical accompaniment, an omelette and a piece of buttered toast. Brushed her teeth. Packed her bag: keys, tissues, water bottle, notebook, pocket Qur'an, purse. A photograph of Sami inside her purse. She'd drunk her first measure of coffee, and that was enough for her. It was kindness and a will for all to be well that made her wait to drink a second cup with her husband. She looked at the clock. Five more minutes and she'd be late. She checked her trousers, shirt and jacket. Everything in order. Her shoes were ready to be slipped on at the door. Only one more piece of clothing to put on, and she thought she'd better wait for Sami before she did so, to make him ready.

The clock again. She turned up the CD a notch, her Rachmaninov. She liked the broad otherworldly sweeps of it, the surges and swells. Perhaps it would hurry Sami up a bit.

A minute more, and into the kitchen he fell, full of drama. His first act was to fumble through the medicine box on top of the fridge. He could have found paracetamol in the bathroom upstairs if he'd wanted, but he preferred to find it here, in view. Deathly pale, breathing shallowly, eyes squeezed to bird-feet wrinkles. He swallowed the pills dry.

'Headache? Poor thing.'

She put a long hand on his shoulder but he turned to the sink and hunched down to dip his head under the tap. Muntaha gave up waiting and moved to the window. As she closed and locked it (not trusting him for security) she looked at the neighbours' garden. A patch of muddy grass. A black wall held together with ivy. Then she turned to the clock again.

'So are you coming to see Baba tonight?'

'Yeah.' Sami standing, tap water drizzling from his hair on to his T-shirt.

'I'll be back by six. I'll meet you here then. All right?'

'All right.'

She cocked the cafetière.

'Cup of coffee?'

'Yeah. I will.'

Deep Italian coffee, not Turkish. Its thick smell and its heaviness anchored him to the floor. Necessary stability. He hooked his nose inside the mug, inhaling. Beyond the mug's semicircle he saw the wooden kitchen surfaces and the blues and greens of walls, cupboards, the fridge. He could be on a ship's deck. Rachmaninov came like waves. He felt seasick, but the coffee kept it under control.

'Any more?'

'There is.' Muntaha poured. 'Are you getting better?'

'A bit better, thank you, yes.'

He tried a smile. The sides of his mouth moved. He told himself to be on his best behaviour. He too, in his own way, had a will for all to be well.

She switched off the music.

'I have a surprise for you, Sami.'

'Oh yes?'

'Now you might not like it.'

His eyebrows made a half-shrug.

'So I want you to keep cool about it, all right? If you're not happy we can talk.'

'All right.' Curiosity as much as the coffee was diminishing his headache.

The capillaries in Muntaha's face and neck flared. With both hands she reached and picked something up from the surface behind her, and clumsily raised it towards her head. A patterned cloth.

Above newly narrowed eyes, a furrow appeared on Sami's brow.

The mainly cream cloth swirled like Rachmaninov. She unfolded it over her hair, wrapping her chiselled ears. Crossed her throat with it, and brought it up on the other side, securing it with a pin.

'I've decided,' she said, quiet and firm, 'to wear the hijab.'

Sami's fingers unfurled from the coffee mug. His lips were loosely parted.

'Don't be angry. It's something I want to do. You'll get used to it.'

Now what was it he had decided? Things are complex. Nothing is simple. Be calm, therefore.

Muntaha glanced at the clock. 'You know I've been praying, for a while now. And I fasted last Ramadan. These are things I used to think were silly, or I didn't pay any attention to them, but once I try them I find they help me. I mean, I really enjoy them. I even wish I'd started before and not wasted so much time because, you know, the more you pray the better you are at it, the better able you are to concentrate. The more peaceful you feel and the greater the reward.'

She regarded him coaxingly. His face twitched with internal dispute.

'So if praying and fasting work for me, perhaps this will too. It doesn't mean I'm becoming conservative or something. We've talked about it before.'

Indeed they had, on several occasions. On each, as Muntaha had warmed to the idea of covering her hair, Sami had become increasingly desperate, the ground shifting beneath his feet so that before long he wasn't dismissing the backwardness of religion in general but actually engaging in theological dispute. On the Qur'an's terms. Where had his earth gone? He was all at sea.

He argued that the injunction to believing women 'not to display their charms in public beyond what may decently be apparent thereof' could be understood in relative terms. The text was deliberately vague, to fit a variety of social situations. The principle of modesty was more important than any specific garment. He argued that 'let them draw their head-coverings over their bosoms' stressed the necessity of covering bosoms, not heads. That the head-covering was an accidental specificity. That it just happened that the Arab women of the Hijaz had worn head-coverings, like the men, because of the sun.

He argued all this, and she agreed with him. But it didn't stop her wanting to wear the hijab. The more he won the argument the more he lost.

'Just what is your issue with this?' he wanted to know. 'Why this hijab obsession all of a sudden?'

'Yes, I do have an issue,' she said. 'I'm not afraid to admit it. I want to belong to my nation. That's my issue. If you want to make a psychological thing of it, go ahead. I want to show myself that I'm not ashamed of who I am.'

'What are you on about? What nation? You belong to the Arab nation. If you want me to explain it I will.'

'Sami,' she said, 'I don't need your lessons.' And then she attacked. 'It's nothing to do with the Arabs. I'm British anyway. I'm a British Muslim. Please tell me what *your* issue is, that you can't see what's happening in front of you. Nobody talks about the Arabs any more. Don't you realize that the Intifada you're obsessed by is called the Aqsa Intifada? The catalyst was Sharon visiting a mosque. The Aqsa mosque, not a flag or a border.'

'But it's using the mosque as a flag. They mean a flag.'

'If they mean a flag why don't they use a flag? What mobilizes the people but Islam?'

And on it went, round and round, a spinning wheel of incomprehension. A wheel whose spokes, by centrifugal force, span out as far as childhood, as far as foreign lands. The entire spinning universe.

'Sami, it's a headscarf. It's material to cover my hair. That's all.'

'It's not the thing itself. It's the principle.'

'Exactly. All it is is principle.'

'But what about *our* principles? What about loyalty to me? Can't you support me? Can't you stand by me? Can't you back me up?'

'Those are my words. That's what I should say. I want you to be supportive.'

'A bit of loyalty. That's all I ask.'

For Sami now in the kitchen, considering the history of this marital dispute, still not speaking, watching her wrapped in the swirling cream hijab, watching her watching him, the hijab issue felt like a wheel spinning in the silence after a crash. The crash had already happened. Irreversible. To cover this silence he began to make snorts of disdain, pacing, grabbing chunks out of the suddenly thick kitchen air. He shook his head with great vigour and pushed out his chin Mussolini-style.

'What the fuck?' he demanded. 'What the fuck is this?'

'Habibi, please. I don't have time for an argument.'

'What the fuck? Not this. What have I married? What have I done?'

'I don't know what the problem is. Why should you be upset if I want to feel and look more like a Muslim woman?'

'Why should I be upset? Because you look like your stepmother. You look like Aunt Hasna.'

Muntaha managed to smile. 'No I don't look like Hasna. I look like me.'

'You look like my mother, for God's sake.'

Muntaha breathed. 'That's a weird thing to say, Sami. And I don't look like Nur. As if you know what she looks like these days. Go and talk to her if you want to know what your mother looks like. But I don't look anything like her, and that's a silly idea. I've told you already. I just want to look and feel more like a Muslim woman.'

Sami stopped pacing, as if he'd found what he'd been looking for. 'That,' he said, 'is shit.'

'What's shit?' She stopped herself. The Prophet said if you're angry you should sit down. If you're still angry you should lie down. The Prophet said in the case of anger you should wash your face. Muntaha looked at the clock. Then she tried again, in a concessionary, almost conspiratorial tone. 'I'm not completely convinced of it either. Not one hundred per cent. Just let me try. We'll talk about it this evening.'

'Women shouldn't have their dress code dictated to them.'

'Well, exactly, habibi. Please listen to yourself.'

'What will people think of me? They'll think I make you wear it.'

'What do I care about people?'

They confronted each other from opposite ends of the kitchen. Muntaha heated, Sami icy. Light spilled orange and yellow from the window to her hijab, illuminating blues and greens on its passage. Too much light in there for Sami's taste. Their breath came in bursts. Sea blusters.

He said, 'I didn't think you were actually going to.'

'Well, I am.'

'All I'm saying,' he said, at lower volume, 'is that this is a step backwards. You don't need to look like a Muslim woman. You don't need any symbol like that. We've progressed beyond the hijab. Women should wear what they like.'

'I'd like to wear the hijab.'

'No. I mean, you shouldn't feel you have to.'

'I don't feel I have to. I want to.'

'But.' And Sami felt great weariness, like a mariner fighting a week-long storm, and then a brisk overwash of indifference concerning the hijab, this symbol the Muslims and the anti-Muslims use to whip each other with. Nevertheless, he had a position to hold, a reputation, loyalty to a certain image. Otherwise, what did he have? 'But,' he said, 'it's shit. It's just backward, and shit.'

'So you want me to take it off?'

'Yes,' he said. 'I do.'

'Sami Traifi,' she said, 'you aren't a man. You're a contradiction.'

And she turned on her heel, slipped on her shoes, and left the house before he thought of a response. He watched the closed front door. Then he returned to bed.

II

Tom Field

After lunching on breakfast cereal, Pot Noodle and spliff, Sami set out across the city.

It was a tough, harsh day, full of shards of light and broken noise, the air soupish and sweat-inducing. Sami noticed sweat wherever he looked, and he looked mostly at uncovered women. At the bulge of their breasts, the tracework of their nipples, at stubbly or willow-haired armpits, at moist midriffs. Glistening skin. Clean lines of sweat patterning it like wind-driven rain across a dusty windscreen. At clothes stuck puckered to backs and bellies, and caught in crevices. He nodded in approval.

But scattered in among these women, like shadows across the sun, were dark, occult, hidden females. From the top deck of the bus he saw Saudi wives and daughters rushing from taxis to continue their summers of shoplifting. Draped and masked like demons. Like antimatter. There were also women springing athletically along the pavement in sock-shaped hijabs which pulled their hair up and around into the form of a question mark, leaving the neck visible. Actually quite fashionable. Actually alluding to Rasta bonnets or hip hop bandanas. Then where Sami changed buses there were gum-chewing British Bengali girls in heavy brown or green jilbabs, projecting defiance and bursts of cockney. He noticed too earnest Levantine housewives or office workers, family women and providers, in neat pastel or flowery hijabs, and raincoats or business suits. Pallid white from fear of the sun, they flitted seriously about their affairs.

What were they symbols of? What did it all mean? Where would he fit Muntaha into this? And what did it mean for him, being the husband of such a sign? What was he now? What was he a symbol of?

These were the questions he took to Tom Field. Sami in search of wisdom.

Tom Field: an academic of a different stripe. A success, for a start. Several books published, one of which – on the militia move-ment – has popular appeal. You can find it in bookshops, this attempt to rescue the militias from their fanatic reputation. For not all, Tom argues, are right-wing lunatics, racists, religious nuts. Some are brother-loving associations of free men and women bright enough to sniff the inevitable on its way. They organize in logical response to the gargantuan organizations ranged against them. And beyond these, but tarred with the same brush, are unpinned-down individuals, self-defined and invisible, those who have had them-selves wiped from the official records, freed of contracts, who have withdrawn within, into secret circles, away from the empire.

Tom sympathizes. No disjunction for him between real life and his research. This is why he has turned down TV appearances. He understands the usefulness of an unrecognizable face. Not only face. His name sounds suspiciously like a pseudonym. Ask him for an address or a driving licence and you're liable to be disappointed: he's not one to be plotted on charts or filed in databases. His ideal is anonymity. For Sami, who would love more than anything to be recognized, this is admirable, infatuatingly so.

Tom Field is a man of movement, evoking a density not seen since the early moments of the universe, energy bound in, straitened and tied down, but heavy with explosive potential. A furiously labouring physique of vigorous lines, tight, sparse, taut, with a dent graven deep in his small chin. Pulsing eyebrows, raggish hair which is purely functional, peppery beard sheathing wind-raw skin and erupting jowls, and grinding stubs of teeth, a muscular tongue.

In his book bunker, sipping at something free of genetic modifi-cation, far more natural than supermarket organic, perhaps culti-vated by his own hand in a guarded pocket of air, in the last clean soil, he addresses Sami's problem as a grandmaster addresses his board. With intensity. With yogic focus.

'Let's look at it two ways,' he says, and as he speaks his Adam's apple jumps and falls like Newton's apple hitting a trampoline. 'Way one: She wears this hijab. She changes her appearance. She confuses those who saw her before. She becomes representative of something else, something new for her but well established in the crowd outside. She buys into a new group. The Islamic group. She deepens her ties of belonging to it. She identifies with it. It defines her. So, in a definite way, she becomes more than herself. We are all more than ourselves, but few of us consciously so. And what does she achieve by this? She blends in. And this is a wise move. The blended individual ceases to be a definite target. There is spiritual continuity, and thus an increased chance of survival, in a group. And there is also the firm root of belief. Of religious belief, in the meaning-giving sense. This is of benefit too.

'Think of this. In a hundred years' time the population is going to be significantly less than it is now. Dramatically less. We could say decimated. Decimated may be an understatement. There's going to be a cull, most likely the most thorough cull the human race has ever experienced. Big like the comet and the dinosaurs. Like the mass extinction at the close of the Permian period. Almost that big. For us at least, for what we consider the higher life forms – probably not for the cockroaches and the rats – but for us, we're reaching the end. Now the question is' – Tom stands up to jab a clawed hand at his little window, the only porthole in his Noah's ark – 'the question is, who's going to still be here? Who, if any of us, is going to survive?'

Sami looks out and frowns obediently. Sees figures moving darkly on the concrete garden. Under the glassiness or haze of his recurrent headache, or of the hot and bothered ageing afternoon, students are clustering and separating like bacteria busy under a microscope, like particles in Brownian motion. Each one calibrated for just the right concentration of oxygen in the air, for a particular gravitational force, a narrow temperature range, each sixty-five per cent water and evaporating steadily. Invisible steam rising above synapse-crammed heads. White shells colonized by flesh. Palpitating organs. Heart and brain. All fragile. In the main, oblivious. Each with a fixed number of years programmed on its body clock, which could nevertheless be interrupted – and at any moment – by superior technology or other blind intervention of the environment.

Tom is fanning his fingers back and forth as if inviting the bodies in from outside, offering them a place in the ark but knowing all the while, sadly, knowing human nature, that his invitation will go unheeded. His expression of inevitability shows this, the stoic pursing of the lips.

'Not many of these will survive. The bright young things. The stagy revolutionaries. The followers of fashion. The ideology tourists. The postmodernists. The mass culturalists. It's goodbye to all of them. They're going down with the sinking ship. But, on the other hand, people with firm belief, with independent – or group-dependent – insight, with the ability to retreat: such people may have a chance.'

Sami, breathing through his mouth, nods. He follows ponderously. Muntaha's hijab will save her from the apocalypse. He tries the thought out. But Tom has wound up again and started off.

'That's one perspective,' he says, thyroid cartilage still bobbing in unrestrained rebellion. 'But the other way of looking at it is this: your wife won't blend in, not into the dominant strain, and so she won't survive. The social body will reject her. The culture will spit her out. This multicultural culture, let me tell you, is apt to eat itself when the crisis grows. And it is growing. The signs are all around us. The return to religion, your wife's issue, is itself a sign. And the new forms of religion, the fundamentalisms, the blood and soil movements, the BNP, Le Front National, the megachurches, Louis Farrakhan's people. What else? The drugs culture. The subcultures. People feel it, even if they don't understand what they feel. They're looking for ways to keep themselves safe. You know, the hip hop people stick with hip hop people. The grunge people, the crusties, they stick with their own kind, their own values.

Society is splitting up into sects, into fraternities, usually mutually hostile. So who trusts his own judgment now? All we can do, most of us, most of them, is choose which set of experts to submit to. And where is real power? I ask you that. It's invisible for the most part, guarding itself. Transnational, above and behind the theatre of governments, living in gated communities, well tooled up. Preparing itself.'

Sami, at the foot of his shaikh, has crouched on the dead wood floor. He listens. The torrent moves through him.

'All this is happening while things are still easy, here at least, though not so easy in other parts. In your lands, Sami, in the Middle East. In Africa. South America. But the trouble will reach us soon. You can take my word for it. You can mark my words.

'Think about it. Logically. Economics. Capitalism has to grow, it can't stop. Standing still is for it a disaster. It has to use more, manufacture more, sell more. And what happens then? Reality will set a limit. Resources are finite. The oil, my friend, think of the oil. You've heard that one day it'll start to run out, one day, in the unthinkable future?'

Lightning flashes from his brow. His eyes are cups of blood.

'Think again. We've already reached that point. Demand is outstripping supply. Wells run dry. So you'll have to contemplate the coming world without oil. Meaning a world without cars or planes, without plastic. Think what is made of or wrapped in plastic. Think! Think of no electricity. Think what one night without electricity would be in this city. Consider the murders, the raping, the terror.'

Needle points of sweat have appeared amid his stubble, on his trained arms. The day is hot, and it is a delicate task in the most temperate times to keep a body's temperature stable. To still his heart's drumming Tom meditates upon his sandalled feet. He breathes slowly, audibly, a sweet warm stream. When he speaks next he is collected, his words weighted. He won't look at Sami, who looks, awestruck, at him.

'Which element of the oil collapse will hit us first? The shortage, or the global warming? I would say both at once, striking from either side. Lights dimming and nations submerged. And don't imagine that our hidden rulers are waiting passively for the hour to come. That's not how they work. Something is planned. Something decisive. That oil war in '91, that was just the beginning. So when the next stage starts, when the pieces fall into place, there'll be no quarter for misfits, no quarter at all. This is my warning, Sami. This is what I can say.'

And there wasn't much that Sami could say in reply. The hijab would be Muntaha's salvation or her undoing. One of the two. He thanked Tom for this paradox and took his leave, the guide watching after him as he went, his hunched posture and uneasy gait. When he left the building Tom saw him below through his porthole, a body among bodies.

Sami walked towards the SOAS building, swinging his arms monkeywise to loosen the spasm in his shoulders, knots there like rocks, like gnarled roots. He was headed for his supervisor's office, thinking what he would tell him about Syria and wondering how convincing it would sound. He remembered the sound of the previous night's excuses to Muntaha. How his hand luggage had looked like hand luggage. Then he thought better of the meeting, and turned for home.

There was time for a spliff before Muntaha returned. Musing on the two distinct bands of coiled smoke – a thin blue and a more substantial grey (one was transformed tobacco and the other the weed; he'd never been able to ascertain which was which) – he saw them as the human beings and the earth incinerated together in the pyre of Armageddon. The elect – but he wasn't sure how this worked out, how much his imaginings owed to Islam or Christianity, or to popular culture – the elect would be hovering cool and unruffled somewhere in this scene, above the flames or within them, incombustible. And would the elect be bearded, or wearing hijabs as fire screens? Or not? Would the beards be the first material to ignite, crackling like the seed and stick of his spliff? In any case, he felt more relaxed about the hijab now he understood it as a response to contemporary events. Perhaps he'd been wrong in the morning. He *knew*, in fact, that he'd been wrong. Perhaps it was him who lagged behind the times, lagged behind Muntaha, who he saw since his visit to Tom as a creature of struggle and identity, making a choice at least.

This was what he tried to express to her half an hour later over chilled orange juice (she'd come from the tube via Freezerland: fish fingers, bagged peas, frosted broccoli stalks spilled over the kitchen table towards him, and also, he noted, mince from the halal butcher). The citrus freshening him up, he felt not dazed but enlightened by his smoke. He bubbled with affection. He found himself capable, even, of an apology, which she received with grace.

'I knew it would be a shock for you,' she said, 'but you'll get used to it. And you're not the only one. It feels strange to me too, I don't recognize myself in mirrors, I almost forget to put it on before I go out. But I'm happy with it. I'm happy with myself in it.'

'Well, good. That's the main thing.'

'Thank you, Sami. Thank you, habibi.'

She skipped around the table to bestow a string of kisses. He inclined to her neck and nuzzled there in the slender softness, as slender and as soft as a decade previously. Her sigh, her trembling, permitted him, so he directed her to the stairs, helping her with a hand between her legs, pushing her up.

Afterwards she showered while he lay, dead to thought, on the bed. She came back dripping reflected light, towelled herself unselfconsciously before him. She revolved as she worked, turning from the orange window through degrees of her own shade. Turning on the axis of her mystery. Sami, wordless, closed his eyes. When he looked again she beamed at him, her glowing planet of a face ringed in the sea-blue garment she had pulled over her head. He grinned without mirth.

'You're not going out like that.'

'No.'

She faced into shadow to start her prayer. Standing with head bowed, eclipsed, hands crossed over hidden breasts, silent, still, intense. Sami could hear a car stereo, waves of traffic, birdsong. The innocence of the world. She leaned forward, fingers he imagined webbed on her knees, raised herself erect again so far her back arched inward, and sank slowly to the floor, prostrated.

Mental activity crept back like a sullen rat. What he would tell his supervisor would be the failure of the city to end superstition, the failure of modernity. He remembered how many more Damascene women wore hijabs than on his last visit, the gathered brown pollution cloud over the city, the rattling plane as it attained height, the closeness of the entubed air. And here, how carbon in the atmosphere made dusky London softer. It was jungle music out in the street, children fighting in a muddy garden. A ball banged off brick. Signs on the tube walls. He wondered where his tube pass was.

Muntaha stood, pulled off her prayer cloak, naked, everything springing into place.

'What's that?' he asked.

'It's the Asr prayer. Just in time.'

He couldn't prevent himself. 'Is all this necessary?'

She wore her tolerant expression. He saw her ribs move as she sighed.

'Not strictly, no. What's necessary is modesty. Everything in its time and place, including the body. I know the arguments.' She sat on her side of the bed, putting on underwear. 'The Qur'anic ambiguity. That the Arabs always covered their heads but the women before Islam kept their breasts uncovered. I know the best veil is in the eyes of men. I know what Fatema Mernissi says.'

'Qabbani says . . .'

'I know what Qabbani says too. But the hijab is what Muslim women wear. And I want to wear it as well. It's as simple as that.'

At risk of losing his composure, Sami restrained his voice.

'I thought, Moony, I thought that we stood for something else.'

She said, 'We don't stand for anything, Sami. Don't be silly.'

12

A Family Visit

Rebuked, quietened, Sami sat beside her on the train. This the first journey he'd made with Muntaha and the hijab. He supposed she must look prim in it, prudent and stern with the motherly calm she'd assumed since he'd voiced, once again, his agitation. He shouldn't have done that, not before a journey on the tube, not before a public showing.

There were four viewers to see them in the carriage. Firstly an old Jew in toned-down Polish clothing, black hat and coat but no ringlets, no fur, reading the *Jewish Chronicle*. A well-established – if still religious – suburban sort of Jew. Next a long, thinly featured black woman, with fingernails occupied in wave-frizzed hair, also at home, also at ease. And then a fatigued pair of suited natives shooting out unembarrassed glances, mumbling to each other news of the fat, round world, him and Muntaha now part of it. Sami supposed they must look like a proper Muslim couple, what with the hijab, Muslims out on dark business, their trauma children and a string of austere relatives left behind in an unfurnished overcrowded room. Four or five children already, that's what it probably looked like. These two Muslims at large.

Sami was thirty-one years old. He reflected on this. In his mind's eager eye he looked twenty, at a stretch twenty-two. Twenty-two next to Muntaha – Muntaha aged, in reality, twenty-eight, and in a hijab. Did he look younger than her, then? Unlikely. Her skin was unravaged, her eyes fresh, while his bore the marks of nicotine, alcohol, insomnia, oversleep. Un-Islamic capillary damage. He hoped that was apparent, the un-Islamic part.

It was less difficult in the street, because darkness hid them.

They avoided conversation; this, her carefulness, a reminder of his instability, his unsuitability. A fragile fellow, Sami, swiftly provoked, a little unhinged.

There was more rebuke waiting. Aunt Hasna, Muntaha's step-mother, stoutly imposing as she opened the door, uttered the correct welcome for a returning itinerant: 'Thank God for your safety.' She stood aside for Muntaha to slip into the corridor, but blocked the way for Sami, glaring at his boots until, cold-faced, he removed them. Muntaha looked back to observe: Hasna in charge of her house, like a real Arab woman. Unsmiling beneath a spreading nose Hasna made a quick nod, to register victory, and allowed him to pass.

For all its lamp-lit islands the al-Haj sitting room remained sombre. A bulky flatscreen TV glowing in one corner. There in front of it, reduced into an armchair, teary and dribbled-mouthed, was Marwan. His wasted limbs sticking out of him like drought-struck branches. Cropped grey hair like the doomed stubble of last winter's sparse rains waiting to be uprooted by the wind. Lips and skin the same colour. His body packed, inexpertly, into grey gellabiya and dressing gown, the shape filled by his chest seeming disproportionately large. Sami, in a rush of dizziness, was reminded of a hotter, dryer, but equally gloomy room, in Damascus.

Taking the air in sips as if it were unpleasant medicine, Marwan wheezed in Sami's direction, 'Welcome, welcome,' and frowned at the effort this cost him.

'How are you, uncle?' Sami advanced to lift and squeeze a brittle hand. 'Well, insha'allah?'

Marwan made a sluggish blink, cast brief warmth on his daughter, and settled back to the TV. It looked like the news. Sami released his hand.

Muntaha removed the hijab and shook out her hair. Aunt Hasna kept her hijab on, for she wasn't Muntaha's mother and so theoretically, very theoretically, Sami could marry her. She could be halal for him, according to sharia, and so he was haram for her. Strands of dyed hair escaped at her sturdy neck.

'Your father's no better,' she said. 'His strength isn't returning yet.'

The room smelled like burst tomatoes and simmered minced meat. Hasna sat on stocky, boneless ankles and spooned the food into her husband. She'd grown in these last years with the padding and thickening of extended domesticity.

She had grown in power too. Her importance had ballooned with the size of the exile community. No shame now in a London life: all the best people were here. ('Hasna, it's unlivable at home,' her ladies told her. 'The situation, it can't be expressed.') In addition, she'd had immediate cause for pride when her doctor son, her youngest, arrived from Iraq. A practical help, her bright son Salim, coming to check on Marwan every other day. Speaking with real Iraqi courtesy and a real Iraqi accent. Not like these British children. Doctor Salim. She'd be able to marry him to the finest class, to some 'daughter of a family' as they said at home. Several of her old acquaintance – well-bred Baghdadi ladies – had recently made the migration, and several had daughters or nieces of the highest quality.

These ladies bore witness to the old days, the old glitzy social life. Hasna took the wives of generals, professors, surgeons to Bayswater restaurants, and as an act of charity she always paid. This is how she profited from sanctions.

She'd entrenched herself in the al-Haj home, her family photos mounted on the walls. As the space became hers, as the bus ride to her old flat became tiresome, her Iraqi memorabilia had moved in too. Karbala tiles propped against window sills. In the hallway, a wooden chest inlaid with mirrors, bearing a Kirkuk ceramic urn. A copper brazier on a copper table at the bottom of the stairs.

Down these stairs and into the sitting room sloped Ammar. As he entered, Hasna left, carrying spoon and bowl. Ammar skinny, vulpine or weaselish according to the light, shaven-headed in a skullcap, with drooping, wispy beard and a hard-set expression. Obedient to one interpretation of the Prophet's sunnah, his upper lip was plucked bare. He wore a baggy, long-sleeved shirt. Printed in green letters on black background: **Islam: The Only True Religion**. He surveyed the room darkly.

'As-salaamu alaikum,' he intoned.

'Wa-alaikum as-salaam,' his sister responded, with raised eyebrows and smiling eyes.

'Yeah, cheers,' said Sami. 'How are you doing, Ammar?'

'How was the homeland?' asked Ammar, with only a touch of irony.

'The homeland?' Sami in satirical mood. 'The homeland? I wasn't visiting a bantustan.'

'Whatever, brother. We'll talk later.' They embraced, then Ammar arranged himself cross-legged, straight-backed, in the line of the television. An Intifada documentary. Muntaha spoke softly to her father from a stool at his side. Sami lounged on the sofa. Ammar increased the volume.

The documentary focused on the bombing of the Dolphinarium nightclub in Tel Aviv at the start of the previous month. Twenty-one Israelis killed. Tony Blair expressed personal sorrow at the deaths of people who looked and behaved like his own sons. Not so much sorrow over more numerous Palestinian deaths. Palestinians were people who didn't go to nightclubs. People who threw stones at jeeps in the open spaces of their refugee camps. People who didn't look like little Blairs.

Sami couldn't feel very sorry about the Israelis, but he wondered about the bombers.

'How can they do it?' he said. 'How can they go like that to their deaths?'

Ammar's head swivelled around.

'You're thinking like an Englishman. Better to die on your feet than live on your knees. These brothers will be granted jannah. They're the most honoured of our community.'

Muntaha frowned at the screen. She asked it, 'How would you react if your country was stolen?'

'I mean,' Sami continued, 'how can they be calm enough to choose their moment? How can they be fired up and cool at once? It's not like dying in battle.'

Muntaha said, 'I suppose believing makes you strong enough to do anything. And they're used to self-control. At roadblocks, checkpoints, crossings.'

Ammar, a finger raised, feigned a quietness wholly alien to him: 'The Last Day will not occur until you fight the Jews and defeat them. Then the trees will call out, "O slave of Allah, a Jew is behind me." All except the ghardaq tree.' Addressing the reported words of the Prophet to nobody in particular, his gaze filmed over. 'You know what the ghardaq tree is? The Jews do. They're planting it all over Palestine.'

Sami was a little amused – and slightly comforted – to hear Muntaha speak in the tone she used in the mornings, or in his agitated evenings.

'Don't you think, habibi Ammar, that the hadeeth may have a symbolic meaning?'

Ammar vexed. 'Symbol of what?'

'Well, I don't know.'

'Sister, be very careful. You're about to say the hadeeth isn't true.'

'I'm saying it may be true, but not literally.'

'True is true. I thought your Islam was growing.'

She answered slowly, calling him Amoora and habibi. But just as Sami felt himself satisfied with his subtle wife in conflict with the simpleton, felt himself on the same side as her, she left with Ammar for Ammar's room, to pray.

Sami said 'fuck' inside his head.

Marwan lifted a stick arm towards the TV. 'What will be their response to this, the dogs, the pimps?'

Sami shuffled over, taking the vacated stool. 'They're killing us anyway, uncle.'

Marwan turned to Sami, and seemed to resent the exertion. He resented Sami disturbing his private ruminations. In truth, there was a great deal he resented in this boy. His snivelling self-worth, for instance. His uncalled-for vanity. His vision of himself as above God's law. I seek refuge in God from Satan, Marwan thought. From the whisperer of trivialities. From the boy's refusal to submit himself to system. And what was this boy who refused to work? Who'd pranced around the university for over a decade, and probably would for ever after, until death seized him by the forelock and shook the stupidity out of him. Who was always too young to have children, to take responsibility. There was no wisdom in him, no sobriety. He was a boy, a mere boy.

'Why,' Marwan coughed, 'do you not join your wife in prayer?'

'Not my thing, you know, uncle.'

Marwan thought: Belief is a duty. It isn't a choice. It isn't something you pick up in the market because you like the colour or you have enough coins in your pocket.

He'd expected more from a son-in-law, but he supposed he had no right to. He should have done more for the girl, guided her better. She'd married in a registry office, not a word of religion mentioned. Marwan hadn't presumed to interfere. And what an apt punishment this Sami Traifi was, this failed Syrian, this fake Englishman, neither fish nor fowl, its head full of froth – what a terrifying reminder of Marwan's early self, floundering in the hollow words of men. He was conscious of the shame of it still, as keenly as if he'd repented of it only that minute. It prompted further leaking of the eyes. My God, he thought, supplicating, let this just punishment expiate my sins and save me from the fire on the Day of Standing. Have mercy on me, unworthy slave that I am.

Now he looked at Sami with the expression of someone emerging from the sea. Labouring at the task of injecting oxygen into sluggish, pulpy blood, blue-faced, he opened his mouth, waited for the impulse of language.

'I will die,' he said. 'I want to see my grandchildren first.'

Sami squirmed on the stool, then contrived to chuckle.

'Don't say it, uncle. You'll be with us a long time yet.'

Even now, could the boy not talk like a man?

'We all will die. You will die too. And what will be left of you?'

Marwan trembling, betrayed once again by his body. This short lifelong struggle to balance an oily bubble of selfhood atop this body, a bubble of consciousness, of pure idea. To balance it steadily so it wouldn't pop. Inevitably a losing battle. Who can hold the sea back? Who can still the wind?

And Sami, horrified, seeing blood on his betraying hands, not answering, or perhaps making sounds – 'O no, uncle, but hmm, but yes' – didn't know what he could do to satisfy them, these people, this old Arab. To bring children into this ending world? And what else? To fall into the role of patriarch? To grow a beard? (Always, with Sami, issues returned to hijabs and beards.)

At that moment Muntaha returned, and gloomy Ammar behind her, like night chasing her daytime, and she saw her father's flared nostrils and fury.

'Baba, what is it?' she cried.

'Uncle is a little upset,' said Sami, surging to his feet.

'Pimps,' spluttered Marwan. 'Sons of pimps and dogs and whores.'

As Sami left the room he heard Ammar's attempt to soothe: 'The Jews, Baba, I know. Don't worry. Justice is coming. Don't worry yourself. God is greater than them.'

At the stairwell Sami passed Hasna's solid, flat-mouthed face, inexpressive but ever judgmental.

'Bathroom,' he mumbled, banging up the stairs.

Spreading Rizlas and grass on the cistern, he skinned up. His hands worked against his spreading bulge of belly. Already he was assuming the shape of his uncles – squat, solid, barrellish. Thick-blooded Levantine market men. Cancer had rescued his father from that, just in time. The shirt adhered to his sweaty back. He spat into the toilet bowl. This wasn't going well at all. He'd been behaving, for fuck's sake. He'd been doing his bit, for Moony, and nothing worked out, and everything went wrong.

There was no toilet roll in which to fold the signs of his spliff, only a bottle of water set on the linoleum floor, so he hoovered up the stray tobacco and seeds with his mouth, and swallowed.

He stood on the front step to smoke, watching the fierce, foolish street, empty of sense and divinity. A dog barking. A distant siren. Boozed-up men loping from the pubs. It was chucking-out time. Cars trailing exhaust. Carbonates accumulating, spiralling upwards to the point of critical mass when the catastrophe would begin. More traffic, and raucous voices left hanging on the air, and more pollution, ticking, ticking, grains of sand through the waist of an hourglass. So there was, perhaps, divinity somewhere, at least in the shape of judgment, waiting to fall. Sami heard his heart beating deeper and deeper till it shook all his body and drowned the traffic noise.

He hadn't heard the door swing but here was Ammar at his side, taller than him, gathering himself for a declaration.

'Still smoking the herb, I see.'

Sami looked at the spliff and didn't bother replying. It was clear enough.

'That's bad shit, man. It'll do you no good.'

'Bad shit, is it?' Sami cocked an eyebrow, lifted the side of his mouth.

'Yeah, I know what you want to say. But those days are well over for me. I've repented of it. I've sorted myself out. Allah is forgiving.'

'Anyway,' said Sami, and took a long drag.

'Yeah, anyway. I knew you'd be smoking. But I didn't come out about that. I came to congratulate you.'

'Congratulate me?'

'Yeah. Congratulations, brother. Mabrook.'

'Congratulations?'

'That's what I'm telling you.' Ammar extended a steady hand. Sami observed it, bewildered.

'Congratulations for what?'

'For Moony, brother. For her becoming muhajjiba. It's been a long time for her to do it. You must be proud.'

'I must be proud?'

'Fuck, man. Why do you keep repeating everything?'

But Ammar realized he'd come out of character, and mumbled 'istughfurullah' under his breath.

'Excuse me. Yeah, you should be proud. It's a rare thing in this country, a modest woman. A woman with religion. A very rare thing. These Englishmen don't care if their women walk around topless. These women, anyone can have them. Even our women in this country, they got the sickness too. That's the tragedy.'

'Our women?'

'Look at them, just look at them. This is Babylon, man. No, I mean this is Jahiliya. The days of ignorance.'

Fortuitously, a couple of pub women were staggering on the other side of the road, supporting each other, laughing. Mini-skirted on the hot pavement.

'Well, I hadn't thought of it like that.'

'You should, Sami. You should. You're a very lucky man. You're blessed. You've got a diamond as a wife instead of a dog. A real lady. A diamond wrapped in silk.'

'Yes,' conceded Sami. 'You're probably right.'

He was talking to her brother after all. And she was a diamond, true. He remembered their lovemaking before the tube journey, her skin rosy in the evening light, the slack buoyancy of her breasts, and her tenderness. He breathed gently, forgetting the incident with Uncle Marwan. A meaningless incident, the product of an invalid's irritability, a passing shadow. Marwan would have forgotten it too.

Sami's brain was floating easier in its fluid at this close of day, and he listened to his brother-in-law with something approaching equanimity. Ammar was just a bit of an enthusiast, was all. Hip hop last year and radical Islam this. Sami felt fondly towards him.

'I know you, Sami,' he was saying. 'You're a Muslim underneath it all. You'll find yourself. You'll sort yourself out. It's just – and don't get vex now – it's just it's better if you sort it out soon. These days, you see . . .'

And he paused here, with significant eye contact.

'These days are important days. You know what I'm saying, not any old days. The other side knows it, so we should know it too. Look who they've got for a president now: Born-Again Bush. You know who he represents. The Christian Zionists. The Crusaders. History speeding up, man. Tings coming to the end. That's how to understand Palestine. They want the Jews back in Palestine so the Last Hour will come, which they think will be a benefit to them. Oh ho . . .' – Ammar, greatly amused – '. . . oh yes. That's what they think. But the point is, everything's speeding up. When the major signs of the Hour come, they'll follow one another fast. And the signs are coming, falling into place.'

Sami, suddenly disorientated, wants to go home. It's been a long day.

'All I'm saying, Sami, brother, is it's time to wake up. Know what time it is. You're an intelligent man. You can see it. In these times now, we need every Muslim awake.'

Sami stepped on his butt and went inside. Feeling suddenly very spliffed in the furiously sober house, guarding eyes which he felt to be bloodshot, he said goodbye to Uncle Marwan and Aunt Hasna as politely as he could manage. They watched him as if they knew something he didn't, something out of deep history. Muntaha wrapped her head for outside. Then Marwan gave him a parting line.

'I want to see them,' he said, 'before the end.'

Walking in the street, Muntaha asked: 'What did Baba mean?'

'I don't know,' he said. 'Nothing. Palestine.' He saw her from the corner of his eye, her hijab. 'Has your brother not heard of the feminist movement?'

'What do you mean?'

'The emancipation of women. The suffragettes. The modern world.'

'What's he been saying?'

'He's been congratulating me on your hijab.'

With a burning smile: 'He's excitable, Ammar. He's young.'

'He's very fucking excitable. "Allahu Akbar, brother. Mabrook for the hijab. Allahu Akbar, brother. Mabrook for the jihad. Yeah man, a thousand mabrook. Big up the Muslim posse! Booyakka for the Islam crew!"'

In his imagination mimicking his brother-in-law very accurately, Sami danced along hip hop-style, cutting the night with jerking hands. Muntaha failed to laugh.

'He's probably a bit confused as well. He came here at the wrong age. He isn't comfortable with himself.'

'Oh everyone came at the wrong age. No one is comfortable with themselves.'

Now it was Hasna's turn.

'"Oh these children. They don't know what hot flushes were like back home. They'd have grown up better if they'd seen hot flushes in Baghdad."'

She snorted a little. Nearly a laugh.

'The miserable menopausal bitch,' said Sami.

'Sami, calm down. What are you angry for?'

'And then my uncle, my father-in-law.'

He affected an exaggerated Iraqi accent: '"The pimps, the dogs, the sons of pimps and dogs, God destroy them, the donkeys, God destroy their houses."'

Silence from Muntaha, her eyes forward, her skin taut.

'What's wrong?'

Further silence. A lake of silence.

'What's the matter?'

'Nothing.'

'Yes there is. What's the matter?'

'I said nothing.'

'You're not talking to me.'

'Yes I am.'

'No you're fucking not. What have I done wrong?'

The silence. The hijab.

'What the fucking hell have I done to you? Don't be so fucking temperamental. Talk to me.'

'Be quiet, Sami.'

'Well fuck you.'

On the tube there was only the rattle of carriages, the flash of advertisements, the rustle of someone's newspaper opposite. The lifestyle section. Muntaha glowing blackly in her heart. Two places away, Sami coldly fixed, infuriated to be wrong. Here was their lifestyle. The train shot into the dark.

And at home he built another spliff, superstrength to be dramatic. Interspersed tokes of brackish smoke with slugs of whiskey from the bottle. The yellow tang dulled by the smoke. When he came into the bedroom she was praying the Aisha prayer. He went to the bathroom and fumbled the shelves like a burglar, searching for pills, for toothpaste. He clattered and banged. Things fell to the floor. 'Fuck,' he said. 'Fuck. Fuck. Fuck.'

13
Death Number Two

Muntaha could look forbidding when she wanted to. At school. The skills of a prizefighter first entering the ring, before the uncloaking, these were the skills required of a lady teacher. Sucking at her lower lip. Arms folded and legs apart. Eyes and skin and mouth tight. Communicating: Don't Mess. Or trotting the tarmac yard, bobbing her head like the fighter, or like a fly girl, and also grinning. Too self-aware to take the pose seriously, although she could do it on the street without the grin. It was part of the theatre of everyday living, and it could make the difference between being attacked or not, whether in the playground or coming back from the shops.

There were other means of protection, such as the children growing their first beards who called her 'sister' since she'd started wearing the hijab. Boys that age should call her 'aunty' if they knew anything about Islamic manners. But this was respect of the street variety, pronounced without a t, with a sweeping movement of the hand, and she wasn't about to surrender any ammunition. Wryly she called them 'brother' in return, signalled irony with her eyebrows, smiled a downward smile. So it seemed that her mockery of their respect concealed deep wells of true respect, which was exactly what they wanted: her theatre to reflect theirs, and both hinting at a purer realm beneath.

As a result of these strategies, she had no fear of playground knives. The Muslim posse would look out for her. Furthermore, she knew like any sensible policeman when not to get involved. The boys and girls so publicly smoking spliffs, for example, dangling loose-trousered legs over the school wall, giving each other blowbacks or pulling smoke expertly through cupped fingers –

these wanted only to be confronted. Confrontation would make their day.

Her final source of strength, of this world, was Gabor Vronk, the man she patrolled the playground with. Gabor, her age but exuding the confidence of maturity, with his solid gaze, his firm face, his height, his muscles, his glowering brow, Gabor who considered himself Muntaha's protector. He had presence, a forcefield of it, which intimidated and deterred. Around him, like electrons around a nucleus, children danced in perfect order. They were sucked into orbit as he strolled the yard, and then, at increased distance, they fell back into chaos.

As well as protector he was her devotee. They paced beside the mural which walled the premises – religious and ethnic community symbols overwebbed with gang motifs – through the brands and bling which assimilated the tribes, through evidence of the drugs culture, the common denominator. They patrolled and talked, swapping ancestor stories. Gabor told her of his Russian, Jewish and Hungarian roots. She told him, in heroic version, of Marwan's flight from Baghdad, of Mouna's murder, and about Ammar and their stepmother Hasna. Gabor listened more than he usually did. The dark depth of her voice impressed him. And during their patrols he developed a lively and passionate interest in tawheed, the Islamic doctrine of unity, the oneness of God and the fundamental oneness of the creation emanating from Him, the One Origin of all. Gabor was taken by the idea, which fitted his own interests, both scientific and artistic (he taught physics and art). He was taken by her, his black-eyed guide. The curve-voiced Iraqi who'd given him a Qur'an to quote, a big, beautiful, expensive copy, with copious footnotes.

Gabor was also an artist. He recognized beauty wherever he looked: in the molecular structure of grey concrete, in a woman's wheatish complexion, in an exotic idea.

His art was often based on scientific concepts. Science and art. The material and the spiritual. He'd concluded that the borders between the two perspectives are entirely artificial.

Take the Big Bang. Here is what contemporary cosmologists say:

Once upon a time there was nothing, no time, no space, nothing but an infinitely tiny, infinitely dense dot of everything. And then one day (but not actually *one day* because this was before days, and not *then* because this was before chronology, and not even *before*, because this was before *before*) the dot exploded. The explosion still continues. You and I are part of it. We look out at the stars moving further apart. We reflect upon ourselves, our beginnings and our ends.

And version two.

God was a Hidden Treasure who wanted to be known, so He created the creation (Hadeeth Qudsi).

He says to it Be, and it is (Qur'an 19:35).

Are, then, they who are bent on denying the truth not aware that the heavens and the earth were once one single entity, which We then parted asunder – and We made out of water every living thing (Qur'an 21:30).

And it is We who have built the universe with power; and, verily, it is We who are steadily expanding it (Qur'an 51:47).

Gabor saw no contradiction. He told her so.

What Muntaha called tawheed sounded to him like basic relativity: properties are not only themselves, they are other things too. Time and space, for instance, are not the separate qualities they appear to be. Matter and energy are different manifestations of the same underlying substance. And, by extension of the principle, so too lightness and heaviness, light and dark, life and death. What manifests itself to our weighty, failing brains as diverse and multiple is, from an ultimate perspective, unified, singular, one. The great sameness from which all difference is born.

To apply one aspect of Einstein's theory: bodies are slowed-down energy. Weight is slowness, tardiness. Lightness is speed, and ultimate lightness is the speed of light. A body that we call dead is only slowed down a little more than usual – sluggish blood congealed,

ticking heart halted. And what of the soul, the Godstuff? The
Qur'an tells us the soul is from God, or of God, and also that God
is Light. What travels at lightspeed is not limited in time. There is
no beginning or end for it, no before or after.

Ten days had passed since Sami's visit to his father-in-law. Marwan
had been sleepless for those ten days.

Apart from the years of poetry when wine and love had kept
him awake he'd always managed to sleep, in brisk, dreamless
six-hour spurts, from ten or eleven until he rose for the Fajr prayer.
So insomnia distressed him. He experienced his wakefulness almost
as a dereliction of duty. There were unpleasant associations with
his unsystemized early life, which like now in a different climate
had been filled with empty time.

He didn't know what to do with time. He'd have read the
Qur'an, but it tired him, his eyes would not see. He could never be
sure if he was in a state of purity, so difficult it had become to keep
track of his dribblings and evacuations, and he coughed and spat
involuntarily on the sacred verses. He'd have read his pamphlets
on sharia but the very thing that had reassured him before – that
he knew them word for word – made them tedious to him now.
The dull rhythm of the sentences played like a repeated sequence
on a hollow instrument, again and again, hectic and fast until it
hurt. He began to suspect that these sentences too, as much as his
versifying, had been a vanity, a waste of time. His life had passed
quickly, and he still wasn't old, not in years, yet these strings and
loops of time, all this time, weighed upon him. It was an intolerable
burden, and so much heavier now when he didn't have the strength
for it, when he couldn't manage to break it up with sleep.

Worse, he knew the insomnia was a precursor of something.
Not only death, which he hoped would bring reward, but some
great labour looming. Whatever the thing was, he wasn't sure he'd
manage to do it. He had butterflies locked up in his disordered
intestines, flushes of adrenalin, a weakness unrelated to his physical
problems that reminded him of exam days at school and university,

of waiting for the critics' reception of his first published poems, of the first night he slept with Mouna. Memories he didn't want but couldn't help. Mouna laughing. Mouna painting the flat. Driving with Mouna on mountain roads, buying fruit from villagers who barely spoke Arabic. Mouna's breathing and his as they made love. Waiting on the stairs, chain-smoking, outside the hospital room where Muntaha was born. His daughter dancing on the kitchen table on her birthday. Toasting Ammar's birth with whiskey. How aged but small the baby had looked, never crying, too small for his big name. Fighting with Mouna at a party. Echoes and ripples. The untarmacked town of his childhood – palm trees, canals, flat-roofed brown houses – a beautiful place. His mother. The thoughts flitted past him like pictures, like bursts of light, more real than him. He would ask God's forgiveness for them if this too did not seem to be a vanity.

He was always breathless, coughing up a lot of bitter liquid, his lungs sinking and his ribs straining. He'd lost bodily comfort and couldn't find it again. Each position he shifted to was stiffer and more sore than the last.

Muntaha came every day. Ammar hung about him, ascending and descending the stairs in threes, praying in front of his chair so he could follow the recitation. Hasna tried to make him eat, and walked him to the toilet. His feet on the floor were just for show; really she carried him. They all saw the want in his eyes, seeking and uncomprehending, like a wounded animal.

But on his final night he slept. With much gesture and eye contact Ammar and Hasna transferred him to the sofa. He slept for ten hours and when he woke he seemed better, some force in him at last, the signs of blood working in his face. They were all smiles, Ammar, Hasna, even Marwan himself, ready for anything. Ammar helped him to his chair. When Hasna encouraged him to try some breakfast he straight away conceded. He'd have bread and cheese, an egg, some tea. She skipped on heavy feet to the kitchen and Ammar, believing the crisis to have passed, began putting his trainers on to walk to the mosque. Then they heard a noise like a high-pitched hiccup, a youthful, joking noise, and in the sitting room Marwan's head was hanging, and his time had come to a stop.

Muntaha and Gabor, at this particular moment, were tramping over the stumps of the history and geography building (burnt down in the Easter break). The children were on their long summer break, chilling on the nearby estate, some doing gangland apprenticeships, or learning better discipline in the lands of their parents. The teachers still came in for meetings, and preparation, and more meetings.

'If I were more conventionally religious,' Gabor was saying, 'I'd most likely become a Muslim too. This tawheed, this basic theme, it fits perfectly with modern science. No contradiction at all. The unity principle underlies all that we know about the evolution of life on the planet, all we know about the universe. In fact, it expresses my own thoughts, the conclusions I've arrived at. But I do my spiritual thinking differently.'

Muntaha, admiring his voice, became aware of her mobile phone trilling and vibrating. She unshouldered her bag to fish it out. The display read 'Baba', and she almost knew then, before she was told. So it was half redundantly that she answered. Ammar speaking. He told her in a sentence.

How did she take it? With a characteristic flush of warmth. The body felt it. Certainly that. She noticed the organism growing excited, weakening, trembling. She must have blinked a film of water, because Gabor and the background shimmered. And then something blew a breath of unreality over the day. The schoolyard, suddenly two-dimensional, quietened and shrank. The city beyond, the world itself, shrugged off both light and shade, became trivial, hollow, not entirely credible.

Gabor Vronk was watching her from whirlpool eyes.

'You've had some bad news, Muntaha.'

'Yes. My father has died.'

It was significant for Gabor that he was there with her. It was a moment they shared.

He accompanied her gravely to the staff room, along school corridors like hospital corridors to the nostrils, then to the arched exit, to the main gate. Not knowing what to do with his hands (he'd have hugged her if she hadn't been in the hijab), he patted her mannishly on the back.

'Whatever I can do,' he said. A lazy African lake of meaning in his eyes.

It took her a long time to cross the city, by bus, by tube, on foot. The world solidified by degrees, and as it did so her calm eroded, giving way not to grief but anxiety. She'd awarded herself points for her reaction thus far. She worried now that sorrow would strike her when she saw the body. Surely this calmness had been only a defence mechanism. And facing the house they'd lived in, the house they'd come to as refugees, the house which entombed his corpse, she was afraid. Fears like dark fish broke suddenly on the surface. She didn't know if she'd be able to enter.

But when she did enter and, ignoring Hasna's lamentation and Ammar's wounded glare, ran to the sitting room, to the centre of the horror, she found him strong and still and given weight by death. The same thing that had blown unreality over the day now held its breath, and she and Marwan were held motionless inside.

He was already washed, dressed in his death shroud and laid in the box that English law insisted on. In death he was a younger and more handsome man. He seemed what he should have been, given different conditions. This man of the open-cast slight smile and upward-tilted head had been absent at least since they'd come to London. 'O Baba,' she murmured, nodding. Her loss was an old loss. That's how she judged, watching, remembering.

She touched his hand, flinching at first, summoning herself to touch again. How strange to touch flesh which is not flesh, skin become leather, unyielding and soapish. Cold. She absorbed this.

Meekly, as if exploring something carnal, and in fact delving into the ultimate carnality, with all the wonder of girlhood, she let herself touch his short beard. She brushed his forehead with her lips. Stillness held in the room, which was cool and bright as it had never been before. So it seemed to her.

'As-salaamu alaikum,' she whispered. She was awestruck, contained by a lovely inertia, actually thrilled to be here observing this in the transfigured room. Slowly she recited the fatiha, then wiped her face with her hands as if with perfume. She grinned, unable to do otherwise. The inhuman human object, his corpse, man and earth at once (is this, she wondered, where the Christians found the God-man idea, in corpses?), the absurdity of it, the incomprehensibility, the unexpected reassurance it provided; all of this made her grin. Inside herself she recited:

Out of this have We created you, and into it shall We return you, and out of it shall We bring you forth once again.

And she thanked God without forcing herself to, not missing her father at all but loving him, and forgiving him for any fault, and filled unaccountably with happiness.

Ammar had also shed years, in form at least. He hadn't leapt forward to claim his best potential, not like his father's corpse, but had gone back, grown down. He'd lost the Islamist's poise and fervour and was again in his rangy adolescence, hungry, wired-up, hood-eyed. He blundered about the house in sullen anger, shoving furniture against walls, falling over his feet, carrying deckchairs upstairs for the women's ta'ziya.

Hasna, meanwhile, scuttled from the kitchen, where she made useless cups of tea, to the living room, shifting her view from the corpse to the wall clock. She stared at it with black reproach. Time was against her. In Iraq he'd be in the ground by now, in accordance with tradition. It was already half dark, already too late to do it today. In Iraq he'd have been trotted via the mosque to the cemetery hours ago. He'd have been prayed over and buried; the first visitors would have arrived. To be going through this in a foreign country was a cruelty and a wickedness she didn't deserve.

Thank God for her dutiful son. Salim came to stand by her. He occupied the phone, talking to doctors, the council cemetery department, taking notes. Hasna hovered busily nearby. But nothing could be done until the doctor brought a form. Something had to be signed. You had to seek permission from the English to be put in the ground. Not even from the English, not even that, but from the Hindu doctor. Dr Krishna. A worshipper of cattle. What did a Hindu know about dying? Hindus who burnt bodies like people in the slums burnt rubbish. This Hindu who still didn't come, too busy administering sedative potions to hypochondriacs, shaking hands with carriers of syphilis and AIDS, dispensing drugs to street criminals (she knew the bones of this from Salim and fleshed them out with details), this Hindu taking his overpaid time even as the long northern dusk settled heavier about the roof, as tradition was ignored. This Hindu, this reincarnation man expecting to find her husband's soul in a cockroach under the sink, or in a rat or a pigeon, or in the tree near the bus stop. It was all too much. It was a trial and a tribulation.

Ammar and Hasna bumped against one another at the foot of the stairs, mumbling, watching the floor. Salim and Muntaha in collusion suggested jobs to keep them busy. There was hoovering and dusting to be done, meat and coffee to be bought. Salim explained that at home grief was treated by activity. That was why everything was done in a rush, and by crowds of people. Here, though, in the absence of relatives, there was an excess of melancholy time to fill.

Dr Krishna eventually arrived, harassed and apologetic, to fill in the form. After conferring with Salim he prescribed a sedative for Hasna. Grudgingly she climbed the stairs for bed, and Ammar left for his mosque. Salim went to his flat, promising to return in the morning. Muntaha called her mother's brother in Baghdad, and her father's people, villagers she couldn't remember. And then, after the Aisha prayer, she lay down on the couch parallel to her father. She'd tried calling Sami too, but at home the answerphone was connected, and his mobile was switched off.

14
Vronsky

When Gabor thinks of who he is he skips his personal history. Avoids his parents too. Avoids as much of muddy contemporary England as he can and focuses instead on his Russian grandfather, Vronsky, and Saint Petersburg the city of his origin, city of orchestras and novelists, and the woman Gabor imagines Vronsky must have lost there. There must have been a woman – his grandfather was such a handsome man. Vronsky's Anna, or Ivanka or Sofia. Yes, Sofia – the name incarnating the eternal feminine, Greek for 'divine wisdom', Sofia which sounds like Sufi. A black-haired, high-cheeked, very Asian Russian. Perhaps a Georgian or an Armenian. Looking almost as eastern as Muntaha. So Gabor supposes. And Vronsky losing her as Marwan lost his Mouna.

But Vronsky never told his grandson much, and empirically speaking, there isn't a lot to work on. One lesson of quantum physics is this: it isn't so easy to separate the observed from the observer. What you're looking for, how you look, determines what you see.

What is certain is that Vronsky left Russia as the First World War morphed into revolution. While the soldiers who had dissolved his unit debated the extermination of the officer class, Vronsky, an officer, ran away in the dark. Dressed in a peasant's smock, eyes open and ears pinned back on his leonine skull, he waited and moved. Procrastination by means of movement. Village to village. In the end hunger pushed him westwards, little by little, until he had gone too far.

Gabor sees his ancestor trekking through interminable blue-black forests, through one-cart villages. Stealing from rabbit traps. Digging up fields in return for soup and a place in the barn. Sleeping well under dripping hedges, on pillows of moss and rock. Walled by the shadows of mountains at night, or on open terrain from horizon to horizon, brain and heart in his crumbling boots. Coming east to west, like the parents of the children in Gabor's class. Like Muntaha.

Vronsky ended up in London, in a sludge-streeted East End quarter where the Jews could remember Russia (Talmudic schools and pogroms rather than country estates and the opera), where he could read Russian newspapers and slip with maimed ex-servicemen into soup kitchens set up by the evangelical missions. His neighbours included offloaded Lascars – Yemenis, Somalis, Malays, Bengalis – and Irish and Chinese, and fallen Russians like himself.

He learnt English from the newspapers and from a leather-bound volume of Shakespeare. Most pertinently to his new environment, he noticed the newspapers worrying about the arrested development of the Jews. These, opined the *Daily Mail*, were more tribe than nation, an archaism in the machine world, suffering a morbid and occult religiosity. The way they treated their women, subservient inarticulate wigged shapes that they were, was abominable. The Jews had untrackable organizations, unknown numbers, a lust for subversion. The way they dressed was a clear rejection of the host civilization. They spurned British law and established their own religious courts. A colony within the capital of the mother country: they turned things upside down. That the Jews were disloyal was obvious; the greater danger was their international dimension. The colony – the hive, the nest – sent and received insect signals far overseas. Untraceable, cabbalistic signals.

To the same theme, remnants of the British Brothers' League marched past the Brick Lane synagogue. Set up a soapbox in the marketplace, their leader speechmaking amid a ring of supporters, their 'England for the English!' signs blotting out the un-English horde.

'Has the Aliens Act,' he asked, 'with the passage of fourteen years, made these squalid streets more British? Indeed it has not!

The establishment is in denial. We do not reject genuine refugees, no, but alien Bolshevik and Anarchist values! We reject the Shylocks and Fagins who abuse our hospitality, our sometimes naïve generosity. The destitute foreigners who plague us. The motley multitude. Our stand is a question of principle, of civilization entrenching itself in the face of barbarism. Let them go to their national home in the biblical land of Palestine. Let them return to the desert from whence they issue. Mr Balfour has proposed this. Mr Balfour who alerted us to these people, a people apart, who only intermarry among themselves, these who, in Mr Balfour's sensible expression, are not to the advantage of the civilization of this country. Yes, shout, Bolsheviks! And attend the reckoning! We know these hecklers are financed by the Jewish money kings. Decent men of England, stand your ground!'

Black-coated, with his natural religion and his Tolstoyan beard, too heavy and meaningful for the climate, Vronsky fitted into the clatter and conflict of this brick-walled democracy as badly and as happily as everyone else. The photograph on Gabor's desk, Vronsky's 1920s photograph, beams happiness. A framed portrait in black and white of the man in his virile prime. The high, lumped forehead, the hunter's slanted eyes, the smile. Something in his surroundings pleased him as much as the orchestral city he'd fled. Did he hear an East End harmony behind the noise? Did he notice unity, tawheed, beneath diversity?

He certainly noticed Lily. A Jewess, orphaned by dysentery. Orphaned, like Muntaha now. Too disconnected and defiant to stay inside her community, and Vronsky wooed and won her. The *Daily Mail* said one thing, but Shakespeare said another. There is nothing either good or bad but thinking makes it so. Vronsky thought she was good, very good. He came home early for dumplings, smothered Thames fish, lessons in her soon-to-be-dying language, sing-songs and sex. In form, in moving, thought Vronsky, how express and admirable! In action how like an angel!

Gabor's grandmother was a Semite, like Muntaha. And his grandfather, Gabor notes, was her saviour.

After the next war Lily bore a son called Richard, a name Vronsky considered Englishness itself. On the boy's birth certificate he wrote Vronk as a surname. Lily complained, tugging at his sleeve as he calligraphed, *Vronk sounds so silly, old man*. Vronsky nodded and ignored her. Remove the sky and you remove Russia, he thought. Richard Vronk. A real Englishman.

Richard was a timid, blank-faced thing. The compromise of Lily's swelling roundness and Vronsky's rugged lines was an uncontoured rectangle, a bland, in-between, utilitarian face. He had a mouth fit for eating with, a nose fit for smelling, eyes enough to see what needed to be seen. He fulfilled his functions and left passion to his foreign parents. He studied quietly, school, university, finally a PhD in nuclear engineering. He aimed for a well-ordered suburb, but overshot and landed in Bradwell-on-Sea, because the nuclear plant was there. After a couple of years of work he married Angyalka, another engineer, the daughter of Hungarian refugees. Stubbornly unexceptional children of exceptional parents, they lived together smoothly without churning up the depths.

Their son was given a Hungarian name, after his maternal grandfather. This was Gabor. Gabor Vronk.

His Bradwell-on-Sea childhood is not worth remembering. Only snatches of it seem to have something to do with him. He remembers instead walks in the East End with his ancient and indecipherable grandfather. Vronsky cheering on the underdog, whoever it was, and remembering Russian women. Remembering Sofia. Probably. It was a toothless mix of Russian, Yiddish and English that he spoke, plus a dash of senility. Gabor had to imagine it into shape. And what you're looking for, and how you look, determines what you see.

Grandfather Vronsky, ghostly deceased, but still in some way with him today. Certainly in his blood. Same genes: the height, the bulky head, the darkening brow. He is accompanied by him, or perhaps inhabited by him. Vronsky chuckling over his shoulder as he paints or shaves, or breathing somewhere in the room in the slow minutes before sleep. Old Vronsky's characteristic cough when nobody else is about, a cough full of laughter, right inside his ear. Vronsky's rich, clean, experienced smell. There when Gabor looks for him, and sometimes when he doesn't.

Most of us have seen our dead at night. We even fear them observing our shameful moments. And then we smile at our folly, the tricks we play on ourselves. But Gabor is sure his case is different. He's sure there's no psychology behind his visions, no regurgitated memories, no frustrated guilt or longing. No reason at all, other than that the presence is real and true, and that a profound identity exists between it and him, to meet it now in wisps of smoke.

15
Gabor at the Ta'ziya

Gabor crouched cross-legged on the floor of Marwan al-Haj's former residence, his head lowered respectfully, chewing on meat. He'd come, for Muntaha's sake, to join the mourning.

He sat in the furthest corner of the room, with Ammar diagonally opposite. It was Ammar who'd let him in from the street, clasping his offered hand in bonier, darker hands, and pressing a little more earnestly than Gabor was used to – but Gabor liked that warmth. He liked too the forceful 'as-salaamu alaikum', to which he responded with a well-pronounced 'wa-alaikum as-salaam'. He'd been practising the phrase.

He removed his shoes and joined them to the crush of male and female footwear in the hallway, and straightened himself. Ammar was watching.

'What mosque you from, brother?'

'Oh, from no mosque. I'm not actually a Muslim. Just a friend.'

Ammar's head clicked backwards to an English distance. 'One of Sami's friends?'

'No. A friend of Muntaha's. I'm Gabor Vronk. I teach at the same school.'

'Yeah, well. Peace, then. I'm the brother.'

Gabor sought to regain ground. 'You must be Ammar.'

'That's right.'

'Muntaha's told me a lot about you.'

Ammar, brushing the words off with quick nods, had turned towards the stairwell. 'Yeah. Follow me.'

Through a door rightwards into a hushed atmosphere. Men sitting on the floor like students in the night-time when they should

137

be writing their essays, but these men were straight-backed, not lounging. Ammar announced him – *Gaaboor Vrronk* – buzzing it on his lower lip, wrinkling his nose and rolling his head as if chasing a pesky insect. The men stood up all at once and waited to be introduced.

'This . . .' – a short bestubbled man in suit trousers and white, buttoned-up, tieless shirt – '. . . is Mr Veysel, one of my father's friends.'

Mr Veysel saluted, touched Gabor's hand, touched his own chest.

'And this is Mr Nader.'

Mr Nader shook Gabor's hand energetically, and smiled.

'Mr Nader is a Palestinian brother.' Ammar frowned significantly, so that Gabor searched in his own demeanour for a fault. He wished to explain his sympathy. That he was Russian. Eastern.

'I see,' he said instead. 'I see.'

Nader grinned apologetically.

'This . . .' – Ammar moving to a man of more than Gabor's height – '. . . is Abu Hassan, our uncle. I mean our stepmother's brother.'

Abu Hassan, strength rising up his back into a slight hunch, and sideways, to domed shoulders of terrible solidity, made a slow, deep nod.

'This is Mr Jim Clark. He helped us when we came to London.'

Jim Clark, bushy eyebrows under a shock of woolly white hair, shook an English shake. Then, clockwise, a young Pakistani Briton (so Gabor guessed from the sculpted haircut and cream shalwar kameez), introduced as Brother Sajjad from Ammar's mosque. And another young brother, a white one, shaven-headed, redly bearded, also in shalwar kameez.

'I'm Mujahid, brother,' he said, in an eager Ulster accent, making the 'j' of his adopted name a 'ch'. At higher volume: '*As-salaamu alaikum!*'

'No,' said Ammar. 'Not a brother. Not a Muslim.'

Mujahid's hand dropped. Ammar stood behind, preoccupied. Abu Hassan sent him a pale glance of warning.

The mourners sank to the floor, Gabor in the space made between Abu Hassan and Jim Clark.

'My condolences.' He addressed the room. 'I understand Mr al-Haj was a very good man.'

There was a murmur of approval. Abu Hassan said, 'Thank you. Thank you.'

The formal unity of the gathering relaxed and men fell back into groups. The Pakistani and the convert huddled close, whispering. Abu Hassan and Nader exchanged brief comments in Arabic and in accented English for the benefit of Mr Veysel, who Gabor supposed was Turkish, or Iranian. Ammar poured coffee into tiny cups and distributed them with his long, moist fingers. Not Turkish coffee but something stronger, something sharp and spicy. In the centre between them was a wide metal tray piled with rice and meat, which Abu Hassan shovelled now on to a plate for Gabor.

Jim Clark turned to Gabor with an old-fashioned smile.

'Gabor, I believe, is a Hungarian name.'

'That's right. From my mother's side. My father is Russian and . . . British-born.' He glanced at Mr Nader. 'British of Russian origin.'

'O what a lovely complex background!' Jim shifting his chair-accustomed legs across the thin carpet. 'What complex backgrounds we all seem to have these days. Such strange beasts history has made of us.' He chuckled at this cosmic witticism. 'And what brings you to Marwan's ta'ziya?'

Gabor received and swallowed the strangled word, assuming – correctly – that it meant the condolence ritual.

'I work with Mr al-Haj's daughter. I'm a teacher at the same school. I was with her when she heard the news.' Gabor remembered it, their shared moment.

'Ah yes. Muntaha. Wonderful girl. Very bright.'

'She certainly is.'

'I'm sure she's a successful teacher.'

Gabor burst into smiles. 'She must be. And not just for our

pupils. I've learnt a lot from her too. She's got me interested in Islamic philosophy.'

'Has she really? What do you teach, Gabor?'

'Art and science. Physics. Which ties in with my own stuff. I'm an artist, you see, as well as a teacher.'

'How interesting.'

'I do paintings and computer-generated art, a lot of it based on cosmology and quantum physics. The physical fundamentals of being. And Islamic philosophy.'

'Indeed. The doctrine of tawheed. Unity underlying variety.'

'Exactly.' Gabor warmed to both theme and Jim. 'Exactly that. It's a beautiful principle, and appropriate to modern discoveries. Time and space are one. Particles and waves are one.'

'The Qur'an certainly inspired some great scientists in its day.'

'I can see why. Muntaha gave me a copy. The scientific tone is the amazing thing. I mean, if I were inventing a religion today I'd put a lot of science in. Most people do their spiritual thinking when they think about science. But fourteen hundred years ago? You know . . .' Gabor pinching thumb and fingers urgently. 'It doesn't just say believe. It says, study the mountains and the stars if you don't believe. Look at biology and cloud currents if you want to find signs of God. That's why the Muslims were scientists. This oneness behind the signs, you know, beckoning its lovers, waiting to be discovered. There's something very seductive in that. I think it inspires my art now as much as anything else.'

'And Muntaha is also your muse?'

Gabor took this playfully, in the way it was intended. 'Yes, I suppose she is. She's got me reading all about it. Al-Ghazali. Suhrawardi's *Shape of Light*. Lots of classical writers. It's a fascinating field.'

Jim lidded bulbous eyes and shook his head in satisfaction. But Gabor noticed Ammar studying him over the rice, bending a frown towards him, and the convert and the Pakistani, no longer in conference, following Ammar's gaze. Gabor stopped talking.

'Ghazali, you say?' continued Jim. 'Yes, I recommend the Sufis. Lovely poetry.'

'You must suggest some reading for me,' said Gabor, his eyes on Ammar's.

A spasm passed through Ammar's kneeling body.

'Poetry? Philosophy?' he spat. 'Inspiration for your art?' Another long shiver grappled him. 'I don't think so. Islam is faith and action. Don't fuck with it.'

The young brothers grunted and pouted. Abu Hassan glared at Ammar, who inhaled sharply.

'He thinks it's an invented religion. What's this, on the day of my father's funeral?'

'Please eat more meat, Mr Gabor,' said Abu Hassan, carefully ignoring Ammar's appeal. 'Uncle Jim, please have more meat.'

Ammar half stood, thought better of something, and dropped his stare to his knees.

The silence softened. A spread of blood in Gabor's face and head tingled and receded, and he made a show of returning to Jim.

'So tell me, Mr Clark. How did you know Mr al-Haj?'

'We met years ago, in Baghdad. Dear me, thirty years ago! I ran the British Council there, and Marwan was a regular visitor. He came to read his poetry. Wonderful stuff it was. Wonderful.'

Jim talked until he held the room's attention, covering Marwan's commentaries on Shakespeare and Marx, the literary periodical and the volumes of poetry – and anti-communist terror, the police state, the purges, the Iran–Iraq war (digressing into chemical bombardments, ravaged Edenic marshes, population transfers). Then Jim's retirement and the rumours that reached him of Marwan's trouble. Marwan's understated letter from Jordan. How they'd met again, and the signs of Marwan's torture. How Marwan's first wife was murdered. How Marwan came into exile a limping broken man.

The three elder men sighed and hissed at intervals. They were like Shia listening to the martyrdom epics, glistening with tears, gripping and massaging their heads. Jim too, who had invested his best years in the bad returns of foreign lands, was wavering, restraining tears.

'He had such a bright future ahead of him. That whole generation promised so much.'

Across the room Ammar was staring either in fury or blind confusion not at Gabor or Jim but at the empty air between. Chin uptilted, his nose like a weasel's scenting danger. Fumbling, amid a whirl of feeling, towards confrontation. He wanted to say, 'What does this Englishman know about my father? What's this Crusader fantasy about my father and Karl fucking Marx?'

There were no copies of Marwan's poems in the London house. There never had been. They existed now only in Jim's library, and in the minds of the dead. Ammar, therefore, had no access to the largest section of Marwan's life, before the fall. None beyond an eroded Englishman's nostalgia.

He puckered his lips into a tiny hooligan 'o'. What violent thing was about to burst forth? His maladroit conspirators observed, imitating him with banal lip thrusts of their own. The convert's beard splayed out bloodish like a renaissance ruff, damp shaded skin quivering underneath. Mujahid wasn't sure what was wrong, but he was willing and poised for brotherly defence.

Truly, Ammar wasn't sure what was wrong either. Except that he had no country. Except that he was orphaned. Except that there was nothing for him to love. Except the endless gaping depths of space separating him from his father. Except that his father, even dead, was still an embarrassment. Except for powerlessness. Except for the earth and the heavens and everything in between.

Gabor, assuming control, pushed the rice bowl in the boy's direction.

'He was a good man,' he said. 'A good man and a fine father. He brought up two fine children. This is the proof of his success.'

Abu Hassan clasped Gabor's shoulder, and the grip remained, clutching Gabor to the family's bosom. No light thing, is what the grip conveyed. Nothing temporary. Nothing to trifle with. To join a family like this was to be pinioned to it, skewered to it by a javelin through the heart.

Ammar's hostility seemed to have drained away, and the brothers eyed the walls in disappointment.

Afterwards the Pakistani took his shuffling leave. Then the doorbell, to which Ammar replied. A woman clucking Arabic was ushered up the stairs which, creaking, stoppered further conversation. Ammar returned and kneeled closer in. Abu Hassan, Nader and Veysel took turns extolling Marwan's character, his mosque attendance, his steady morals. Mujahid fidgeted with his fingernails. And when speech lapsed Gabor, in his innocence, posed a dangerous question.

'Where's Sami? I'd love to meet him.'

There was a broad expanse of non-response. Abu Hassan tutted explosively, and clenched a fist to strike at the anvil of the other hand. Nader smiling at the rice. Veysel studying the carpet. Mujahid exhibiting outrage but, unsure of the etiquette, not doing anything with it.

'Sami is away,' said Ammar, coolest of all now. 'Unfortunately he couldn't come.'

After a few more minutes Gabor rose to leave. All rose with him, and the older men wanted to shake hands again. They went so far as to embrace him. Virile, crushing hugs and kisses on both cheeks. He liked these old Arabs. He liked their exaggerated features and overdone gestures, their delicacy, their complicated heavy heads. They reminded him of his grandfather.

When he had his shoes on he asked for his regards to be passed to Muntaha. Ammar in a light, high voice said to wait, he'd get her. While he waited Gabor resolved to buy a shoe rack for his own doorway. Civilized behaviour, the removal of shoes. Then he heard the stairs. She came down beaming, full-lipped. She looked up at him, slipped on her own shoes, and pulled the door open.

'I'll come with you. I need a break.'

It was a maturing afternoon, clouds clearing away a little abashed, yielding precedence to a self-assured but lowering sun.

'Are you going by tube or taking a bus?'

'I haven't decided,' he said. 'Let's walk for a bit.' And then: 'So how do you feel?'

'I think I feel fine . . .' – speaking to the rhythm of her footsteps – '. . . maybe I'll be upset later but I don't think so. I feel that everything's all right. And that he's all right. Does that sound silly to you?'

'Not at all. In some situations, feeling is the best judge.'

'In mysteries. When we don't have anything else to guide us.'

Under the surface of death, behind the pixilated screen, what was there? Human beings gone like rabbits bolted into holes, into what unseen unimagined warrens? He had a picture of an anthropomorphized warren in his head, with fluffy armchairs and bunny beds. From one of his children's books. Which was as close as his childhood home had come to a Bible.

He held a wrist in a hand at the base of his back and stepped on slowly enough for her to walk comfortably.

'I admit I find heaven difficult to visualize. But I'm sure he deserves to be there, the way you've talked about him.'

'Not heaven yet, although I hope somewhere like it.'

'Not yet?'

'Muslims believe no one goes to heaven or hell until the Day of Resurrection and Judgment. They're still here until then.'

'That could be a long time.'

'But time for them isn't like for us.'

Buoyed by the coffee, Gabor had to restrain a bounce. He kept at her pace.

'So they're here, seeing us and hearing us?'

'In some way, yes. It's mysterious. It's recommended to pray for them, to make them happy. You know, there's a hadeeth of the Prophet that he went to talk at the graves of people killed in battle. He said, "Look, do you see now?"'

They passed a scrubland park. From the bleached street birds darted wingless into shadow.

'In our prayer we greet Muhammad and call for God's mercy

and blessing on him, and we greet and bless God's righteous servants. What would be the point of that if they don't hear?'

In the petrol cough of a car in a side street Gabor heard Vronsky's chuckle.

'You know the Ghazali book I gave you?' Muntaha went on. 'There's another section of that which says the dead are fully aware for just a couple of days. They know what's going on for that long. That's why you shouldn't moan and shout at funerals. You see Muslims doing it on TV, but they shouldn't. The Prophet said crying disturbs the dead. Then after a couple of days they slip into a kind of dream called the barzakh, which is a barrier, an in-between state. The souls sleep and dream of the state they'll be in after the Last Day.'

Her face, which had been fluid with hope and eagerness, hardened.

'I feel silly thinking about it in too much detail, like I'm making things up to please myself. I'm talking about things I know nothing about. It's a mystery. Death and life are mysteries. It's arrogance to pretend they're not.'

'Although your religion has doctrines which I suppose you must subscribe to.'

'Not really. I mean yes, but doctrine is secondary to faith. And doctrine is open to interpretation. Near the beginning of the Qur'an, near the beginning of the second sura, after the first descriptions of heaven and hell, there's a verse which says, "God does not disdain to propound a parable of a gnat or even less than that."'

Not following, Gabor allowed three slow paces.

'Which means?'

'That God uses any image or symbol He likes to get His point across. He tells you that the fire and the gardens and the fruit in the gardens are not really fire or fruit like we have here, but imagery to describe what we can't understand.'

'I see.' Gabor nodded, eyebrows raised. 'That opens it up to interpretation. A different book to what the media presents.'

'Not just the media. The Muslims too. The first word

Muhammad heard was "read". The Muslims should read better. They should be less literal about everything. It was that verse that made me read the Qur'an again. It warns us not to take ourselves too seriously when we interpret. We only have images for what's incomprehensible.'

'Imagery. I see.'

'So I don't know what happens after we die. I don't know if dreaming of heaven is the same as being in heaven. Only God knows.'

They'd come to the burnt mouth of the tube station and moved beyond it to council blocks curtained by trees, half a mile further. Then there was a circle of shops – a pub, a newsagent's, a halal butcher – around a rearing white war memorial chiselled with the names of local boys fallen in the Great War, boys whose families had by now moved further out into the suburbs. The memorial ringed by low fence railings, which were violated by mountain bikes and chains, sheets of newspaper, cans. Gabor and Muntaha turned here, Gabor again slowing himself, and started back.

'And what of judgment?' Gabor asked.

'I believe in it, in the principle of it. Islam says we have an angel on each shoulder, one to record good deeds and one to record the bad. Everything we do is written down, and at the end we see it all, good or bad. I don't know how it happens. Are those real angels with wings, or metaphors for our conscience? I don't know, but I believe in them.'

Gabor's head was all ear. He absorbed her words, her clear ringing voice, stored her for remembering. His powerful heart was blotting paper. Soaked her all up, her skipping flowery smell, the thick tock of her shoes on the pavement, the bobbing of her face parallel to his chin.

'The idea of the record,' he said, 'corresponds to a lot of NDE accounts. Near-Death Experiences. A lot of people who die and come back say they've seen their lives played out in front of them. But that could be endorphins in the stressed brain. It's not hard science.'

'Whatever happens,' said Muntaha, 'something happens. I'm sure of it. I don't need the Qur'an to tell me. Something must happen afterwards, otherwise . . . otherwise it would just be absurd. And in some way there's justice in what happens.'

'I hope so.'

'Hoping so, believing so, that's all Islam is. To have faith in the unseen. In mysteries known only to God. God not as a person as He is in Christianity, but as the Absolute. If we believe there's justice from an absolute perspective, and believe this perspective really exists, even if we can't see it or understand it, then we can surrender to it, and we'll be at peace.'

The sun was sinking leisurely into a smooth deep sea of crimson. It was excess of pollutants that made the anticipation of dusk so beautiful, but it was beautiful nevertheless. Gabor's head floated in the sky.

'This is a true story,' he said. 'My mother told me, and she isn't a mystical type at all. Quite the opposite. Much too down to earth for her own good. Anyway. She had a friend whose husband was dying, and she was sitting with her in the hospital. In a waiting room. There was a vase of flowers on the table in front of them. They were sitting there talking when suddenly the flowers spun round the table. I mean the whole vase moved around in a circle. By itself. It can't have been a hallucination because they both saw it. And like I said, you'd have to pump my mother up with a load of drugs before she'd have a hallucination. They looked at each other, and a moment later a nurse came in to say the man, the husband, had died. It sounds ridiculous, but it's what my mother saw. My mother who's a staunch atheist. Who doesn't believe in anything she can't see. You can't imagine a more empirical person.'

Muntaha smiled up at him. 'It doesn't sound ridiculous at all.'

He smiled back. He saw the flowers whirling on the hospital table, the colours merging into one. She breathed. He breathed.

They arrived again at the tube station entrance. Winds and odours gurgled up from its throat.

'Do you want to go home?' she asked.

'What do you want to do?'

'I should go back.'

'Then I should go home. This has been an inspiring conversation.'

'It has. I needed it. It's good to talk about these things.'

Gabor looked into her dark eyes. 'If I can do anything. If you want to come round, or I'll come to you. Somebody to talk to. Anything at all.'

'Thank you,' she said.

They shook hands. Her large hand inside his.

'Well, then.'

'Thanks for coming, Gabor. It's nice of you.'

She walked back to her father's house noticing flying insects and leaves and the red light reflected in people's faces. All these were signs, meaningful and important. Signs of what exactly she couldn't tell. But she didn't need to tell. Signs speak for themselves.

Back she marched to the plodding niceties of the mourning ritual. Back to an outraged Hasna who had lost now two husbands to weakness of the heart, whose eyes (already making plans for redecoration) would escape around the room to her friends wobbling on white plastic chairs – repeating 'God be merciful' and 'may the years be added to yours' – and to the fierce young wives of Ammar's friends, who didn't know the traditions and so didn't know what to say.

Muntaha, filled up with oxygen, briskly galloped the stairs. Another twenty minutes is all it took, expressing gratitude, saying goodbye. It was easy to get away. She had the sorry excuse of a husband to go to.

Then she was on her way, by tube, on automatic pilot. Street, train, street, with weariness at last, the tug of her breasts and the pull of her back, sucked through a darkening tunnel to the pinprick of darkness that was home. No husband in it. She closed the front door, reducing the city's volume, then shut it out further, closing also her bedroom door. She let skirt and shirt fall to the floor, and then unhooked her bra. Stepped out of her knickers. Stood motionless under the shower. Afterwards she buried herself in her prayer robe and prayed the Maghreb prayer, too tired to follow the words but also too tired to wander into other thoughts, so her prayer was warm and wholehearted. With little of Muntaha present there was more space for God. God's presence closer than the veins in her neck. She felt surrounded and absorbed by God; although it can't be said that 'she felt', because she was asleep to herself and didn't feel anything.

She rocked back on her heels and found the sensation of herself again, somewhere between the hips and under the heart and fizzing up her spine to spill from her eyes and ears.

She considered herself: a bereaved daughter. Who wouldn't see her father again. She summoned pictures, first of him dead and then of him living. As she moved backwards into shadowy girlhood he became a memory of an odour, clean and rich underneath all the other smells, omnipresent. Or a physical memory like being enclosed in huge rough arms big enough to encompass school and streets and the river and even the wind. These were the constants in her life, in Baghdad or in London: streets harsh and various, an elderly grey river, an aggressive wind. And her father who'd brought her. Her Baba. How small he'd been in the coffin, the strength of all her origins compacted into that short folded-up package of corpse. It didn't fit together, his size and his mortality, his eternity and his shrivelled stopping. It couldn't be properly reconciled.

She listened to catch his presence still, nose pointed, ears pricked, but couldn't tell if he was there, or if only she was there, or only God, or if she and her father were only speckles of God anyway, and she soon found tears dripping from her mouth into the prayer robe, and her nose sludged solid, and she covered her face with her fingers. She wept. She heaved and sniffed and moaned. But after five minutes, looking through her fingers' grid, she said out loud, 'This isn't real,' and with that, dried up, took off the prayer robe, switched off the light, lay naked on the bed. She wiped her face on a pillow and stretched out until she touched the wall. She was perfectly happy.

Then she remembered Sami. 'The wanker,' she told herself in

proper solid English. 'The fucking worm. The stupid fucking piece of shit.' She swung her feet to the hairy rug and stood up. Switched on the light. Stepped to the phone on the chest of drawers.

She remembered Gabor. The other time today she'd been perfectly happy was when she'd been walking with him. How long since she'd last had a conversation like that? When she spoke he listened. Then he said something interesting. And she would reply. It wasn't much to ask for.

There were two messages on the answerphone. One from the headmaster, supportive and serious. The other from Sami. 'Yeah, Moony,' it said. 'I'm busy, so I won't be back. I need to be alone.'

Greta fucking Garbo. Where the fuck was he?

16
Sami Overheats

As Marwan sank from view Sami had been waging his own battle with time. Trying to make it stop, he avoided thought and activity. He avoided change. He tried to stabilize his temperature, and watched the weather, which was stuck in a loop. Not like London weather, it was neither hot nor cold.

He packed the hours up into bland portions: TV programmes and newspaper articles, internet chat sessions concerning nothing at all, walks towards the tube station and back again, passages spent loitering in supermarkets and video rental outlets. Told himself in justification that he was getting back in touch with the culture. He also shaved as often as thrice daily, removing skin only, plucked at his eyebrows with Muntaha's tweezers, smoked spliffs, took over-the-counter pills.

He rented disaster movies and lounged stiff-necked on the marital bed to watch them. The two classics of the genre, *The Poseidon Adventure* (1972) and *The Towering Inferno* (1974). Plus *The Swarm* (1978), in which foreign killer bees threaten Houston, Texas. Against his carefully maintained boredom, against the undramatic but naggingly tragic undertow of reality, he deployed the kick of the fake-real. Flames, blood and redeeming heroism in ninety-minute packets, triggering adrenalin emission – not enough to move him off the bed – and pulses of novelty, just enough, keeping him active but stable, ticking over like the economy.

He watched his anti-Arab favourites. They lived in his collection for their incorrectness, both for academic and visceral reasons. They gave him an apocalyptic buzz of victimized self-righteousness. *Raiders of the Lost Ark* (1981), in which a scimitar-wielding, Nazicollaborating savage emerges from a snake-charming, veils-and-dust backdrop to challenge Indiana Jones. The hero waits, allows the wild man to perform. Then – bang! – dispatches him with a casual pistol shot. Humiliation hits Sami in the gut. Wonderful. Builds another spliff. *True Lies* (1994), casting Schwarzenegger versus the psychotic Abu Aziz of the Crimson Jihad organization. Real-life Arabs acting in this one. Then coming up to date, *The Siege* (1998), in which shots of a mosque and men at prayer are juxtaposed with explosions.

Good viewing for the end of work hours. He tried taunting Muntaha when she came back from school ('Here comes the Mullah! Respect to the hijab posse! Make way for the believers!' and suchlike), but she wouldn't be provoked. Wore the tolerant expression as she brushed his crumbs and ash from the sheets. So nothing happened. Nothing moved on.

It was all procrastination and he knew it. The meeting with his supervisor was the logjam ahead against which events congested and refused to flow. The more obvious logjam. So in the end, after ten days of this, having picked at his books like scabs, having scribbled his Great Idea in spiderish and unconnected half-lines, he'd arranged and then attended the meeting. And now in its aftermath, in that same moment when Muntaha was unfurling on her father's couch in the proximity of death, Sami was ensconced in a central pub, at a corner of the bar, slurping lager and cigarettes in unsteady bursts. Descending into an underworld of drunkenness and self-pity.

Angular Dr Schimmer, in his plastic office, nodding his head with a chicken's abrupt inflexibility, had listened to his mumblings. It hadn't taken long for Sami to finish, so he recapped, paraphrased, spoke more slowly. But Schimmer arrested him with an upheld palm: 'To the point, Mr Traifi. For this is, aa, repetition.'

'Yes,' said Sami. 'Well, that's the bones of it.'

'The bones. Indeed the bones. Now let us, aa, deconstruct.'

So the idea was dissected, unemotionally, with Schimmer's world-class scalpel.

'There are, Mr Traifi, the following, aa, incongruities. To be rationalized. To be, aa, reconciled. Or else the dialectic you propose is, aa, problematized. For instance, the court poetry and the patronage. For instance, poetic contests in urban centres. And the, aa, standardization of Quraishi dialect as the pure language, aa, achieved by the grammarians in urban seminaries.'

Sami would have been well advised to take notes, no doubt, except his fingers were slippery, his concentration gone.

'Furthermore, Mr Traifi, poetry in the, aa, nationalist phase. It centres on imagery of land, I think. And there is a certain nostalgia for pre-urban life, is there not?'

Schimmer seemed not to understand that this was Sami's self-imposed last chance. If it had to be denied, it should be done more respectfully. There should be more weight, more ritual.

'Can you, aa, defend your thesis?'

Sami could not. He knew he could not. What was the point in dishonesty?

'Now this perhaps is the problem with grand schemes. With the, aa, big ideas. Better to be modest.'

Sami was on the threshold of clear sight, but a hot film clouded his vision. He took refuge in stereotype. Schimmer became a jackbooted Kraut. Jerry. The Hun. German academic justice goose-stepped into action, and with that Teutonic rhythm Sami's indulged indoor thoughts were shunted off to the death camps. The powers failed to come to his aid. His father was dead.

'As it stands, Mr Traifi, we have only the, aa, the germ of an idea. We need a body, a body of thought for this germ to inhabit. The germ will not stand alone.'

There it was. The concept dismantled so as to be better reconstructed, except there was nothing left to reconstruct. Deconstruction was the end point.

'Small is beautiful, Mr Traifi, as Schumacher declares. Now your father, for instance, in the, aa, *The Secular Arab Consciousness*, his mastery of the, aa, minutiae . . .'

And there was Mustafa Traifi, the flaking standard, the sepulchre.

You couldn't find *The Secular Arab Consciousness* in bookshops. It was known only to Schimmer's coterie. And if that was the case, what was the point of it? And if it had no point, neither did anything else, not as far as Sami was concerned. It was around *The Secular Arab Consciousness* that he had tried and failed to build his adult life.

'I've tried the minutiae, Dr Schimmer, as you know. I've tried analysing details, words in isolation.'

'Ya, but always the big idea looming behind. Always you have wanted to map the details on the big idea.'

'I've looked at details in Qabbani and the Sufi poets and Darweesh and Arab rap. It's just that there doesn't seem to be much to say when you concentrate on details. Not enough for a book.'

Schimmer's head jerked in mock hilarity. 'Not much to say! This is a rich field, as your father witnessed. It is, what we say, a sea of knowledge, aa, bahr ul-uloom.'

Arabic in a German accent. To Sami, glaring at the frozen floor, it sounded like Hebrew. And why did Schimmer keep bringing Mustafa into it? By what right did this German talk about his father?

Schimmer noted his student's displeasure like a naturalist spotting a rare insect, and warmth flickered over his thin northern features, sparkling at the sharp nose.

'Ach, Mr Traifi. You torture yourself too much, I fear. It has been a long time for you, this thesis, so many years and without, aa, progress. Now perhaps you should reconsider.'

Sami could tell what was coming next.

'Perhaps you go out into the world. Perhaps do something new. It may be that suits you best. You can always, aa, come back. We can arrange it, for the son of your father.'

Sami leapt to his feet.

'My advice, Mr Traifi, is only to look in front of your nose. Don't, aa, fret yourself with big ideas. The details, Mr Traifi. Truth and beauty are in the details.'

Sami walked to the plastic door.

'Have a break from these big ideas, Mr Traifi. See the little things clearly. Enjoy your life.'

'You're right, Dr Schimmer,' said Sami. 'You are right.'

So events were moving at last. At least that. The logjam was breached.

From there down to here, he'd had several warming drinks. Desire sloshed inside him like meltwater over rapids and he reached for a next step. He had no idea what it could be, but it had to be something sizeable, something as big as a Schwarzenegger bicep, as unwieldy as a capsized ocean liner. A great leap. Something towering and infernal.

Suited men were filling the pub. Suits expensive and sombre, in dark, unshowy tones. Every wearer meeting a common standard: upper middle class, middle-aged, of medium Anglo size or slightly larger, with steamed unreadable faces, conversing at medium volume. And all men. As if a detail of conformity doormen had arrived to police the entrance. Sami linked this obscurely with the Nazi Schimmer, who he sensed following him, sending in Aryan goons. (But how unfair he was to Schimmer in his bitter, wounded mood. Schimmer who was, in fact, an eccentric and sensitive scholar, a convert to Islam, a defender of diversity.)

Suits trooping in. Sami the only dark tone in an assembly line of pastels. The only extreme. The only willing drunkard. The only atheist Muslim. The only one with no future or past. He found himself – searching drunkenly for an analogy – surrounded by an alien army in the realm of Middle Earth.

In this case the old racist refrain held good: it really was difficult to tell them apart. Still more came, darkening the door, increasing the heat. Half had hair and half did not. Those with hair shared the same hair colour, midway between blond and brown. And the same haircut, sideparted, lank. They sat in rows on either side of rectangular tables. They clustered around circular tables. Gin and tonics on the surfaces, hands flat on knees. They queued against the bar, and their sound rose in a gnawing and humming.

Then Sami understood where he was. Each man held the same model of briefcase. So not in Middle Earth but somewhere just as cultish, among beings as incestuous and secret as elves or dwarves.

These were Freemasons. Rolled-up-trouserleg people. Bared breast people. In-house handshake people. Not people: a fraternity, a band of brothers. Its own species.

Lost, bereft, impotent, Sami had stumbled into the halls of power. Freemasonry was the organization of ruling dynasties, chief policemen, top civil servants. An international network hustling behind the scenes since Solomon's temple. The eye in the pyramid on the American dollar. This was significant. That he, a mess of feeling, pissed up, was in the middle of it. And placed here randomly? By coincidence only? Today of all days? He was at the centre of power, like antimatter. Like a black hole.

Black holes sucked in light, so were unseen. And sure enough nobody saw him, not even the barman. The barman's suit jacket was hung up on the wine rack. He made subtle signs of recognition to his customers. Sami rapped at the bar and called, 'Oi! Oi, barman!' to bring him over. He had mid-brown eyes, a say-nothing smirk. With Muntaha-like imperturbability he failed to notice Sami's rudeness, listened mildly to his order: triple whiskey.

All around the Freemasons were preparing, planning, taking control. Arranging for the last days. What to do? It couldn't be long now, thought Sami with sudden chirpiness, until there would be essentials to be busy with. He caught a glimpse of his future. Black holes sucked in surrounding light, and pulling faster than light confounded all the laws of physics. Theories suggested new universes blossoming on the other side of black holes. Through wormholes, something like that. Negative universes.

He sank the whiskey, banged the bar, held up a finger for more. If the master class here had organized itself, why, he could do his own organizing. Form his own group. He wasn't quite deranged enough yet, he admitted that, not yet confident enough in his lunacy to give it shape and force.

Sami felt hot. To slow down he decided to check the messages on his mobile.

From Muntaha: 'Where R U?' Something from Ammar too. He saw it. But he didn't want to read it. Now was not the time.

Where was he? That's right, he had an aim. Which brought with it a surge of energy. He would make an immediate start, to derange himself. To purify himself. A few minutes back he'd been considering a meal, even returning home. Mentally, he slapped his forehead. Stupid! That way lay sameness, and desperation. How easy it would be to fall back into that. No, something entirely different was called for. Something diverting. Here in the shape of the whiskey glass, for a start. Down in one, down deep, to close the gates on normality.

His throat anaesthetized, it slipped into him. Ice inside melted with it. To the furnace of his stomach.

The stool flounced away from his buttocks and he was staggering to the toilet, Freemasons bouncing gently off his shoulders. He seized on the cistern for stability, and made a tight little bundle there of the remaining grass. So much more important than just a spliff, this spliff. It was the plan. The answer.

Invisible even to himself, he reappeared at the bar. A fresh drink awaited. Down it went, whiskey and meltwater. He clawed money from his pocket and dropped it, and then he was out on the street, crowded night colliding with his cheeks, feeding himself spliff and flame, injecting smoke into the organism, sensing it pull him forward.

Time was rushing on. This is what he needed. Not thought, but action. He'd had a decade of thinking. What had it done for him? What did it threaten now to do? He clanked his eyelids shut and, hearing them open, was half a kilometre further on. Leaping across ten minutes in one bound. A superhero.

Consciousness located him at intervals. The city red and brown. The oil economy rumbling on. Scorched red buses, black cabs, police vehicles. Laughter and music and food steam in envelopes (smouldering cheese, kebabs, Chinese). Scalding darkness and reflected light. Through the riotocracy at fantastic speed, crowds parting like the sea before him.

He stopped with a click. Oh it was blissful how decisions were made, how the body functioned. That thumb undergoing evolutionary adaptation to the techno-environment. It switched on a mobile phone, summoned a name (Greek Chris), and dialled.

'Emergency situation, Chris. I need one gram of coke and two bags of weed. Three bags of weed. Yes, I'll pay. I'll pay the transport fee.'

He named a delivery point. Turned the mobile definitively off. Took his bearings. His mind, his body, was a bullet launching itself. It swivelled, locked on its northern target. It ran.

He made the connection in a sultry King's Cross pub. He'd extended his overdraft by way of a cashpoint on the way, and here between a fruit machine and a pensioner couple with nothing left to discuss he unpeeled blue notes and counted them thrice before yielding them triumphantly. As if they were proof of a wager won. Greek Chris stuffed the cash inside his shirt and winked. By magic there appeared on the polished plastic table a brimming, layered grey package. Sami snaffled it, cellophane damp on his palm, into a tight pocket.

'I'll have another one of these, squire.' Greek Chris shook his curls at an empty glass beneath him. 'Gin and tonic and lemon. Gentleman's drink.'

Sami at the bar. Two gins and two lagers. And another gin because he drank his while the barman oh so slowly, turning the glass like a key on a grinder, drew the lager.

'I don't drink that piss,' said Greek Chris.

'What's that?'

'That piss. I don't drink it.'

'What do you ask for it, then?' asked Sami.

'I don't ask anything for it. I just don't drink it.'

'What?'

Greek Chris scratched at incipient moustache.

'Having a mad one are we?'

'A mad one. Yeah. I am. Purifying myself.' Sami's nose twitched. A nerve jerked at his temple.

'Right you are,' said Greek Chris, and then he laid a stubby finger on the rim of the nearest pint glass. 'This piss,' he said. 'What is called lager by the commonality. I don't drink it.'

'Oh I see!' said Sami loud enough to rouse the sad-eyed old woman at the next table. She blinked in his direction. Her husband gazed dejectedly into his drink. The woman's hair the colour of cigarette stains. Her face puffy but sunken, like bread out of the oven.

'What a lovely fucking colour to dye your hair,' said Sami in a kind of wonder. Then, quick as sparrows, he took Greek Chris's lager and drank a third. 'I'll have it, then,' he said. He stood up, patted his pocket, sat down again.

'I think,' said Greek Chris, leaning in, 'you want to inspect the merchandise.'

Sami said, 'The merchandise. I do. I do.'

'Off you go, then.' Greek Chris, tonguing oily lips.

Sami in the toilet. Again by magic, a newly rolled spliff tucked behind his ear, and a line of cocaine arranged on a cistern clean enough to lick. It was that kind of pub. King's Cross certainly, but no sawdust on the floor. No TV football. No crowds. No whores permitted. In a Bengali neighbourhood. Staid and clean.

He snorted and bolted back up. It was sultry, though. A well-nigh tropical night, sleaze leaking in from outside, through the aspirator: flesh, coconuts, wet perfume, brine. A ramshackle bar on the docks. He banged the saloon door behind him.

No it wasn't. It was north of King's Cross.

Across from his dealer, on a low upholstered stool, bouncing a leg on the ball of his foot.

Greek Chris rubbed a curling eyebrow. 'The ear,' he said.

'Yeah, man,' said Sami. He had no idea what Chris meant.

Greek Chris. Old sea salt. On shore leave after a long, long time. Searching for fights and rum and easy girls.

'Good not to be cooped up, yeah?' Sami said. 'Get your feet on solid land at last.'

Greek Chris frowned. 'The ear,' he said, tapping at his own. 'The fucking doobie. This is not the place.'

Sami's hand hovered and fumbled about his head. It found the spliff. He examined it, a bit cross-eyed.

'Yeah,' he said. 'I see what you mean.'

Greek Chris hissed, 'Keep it under the table.'

Sami did as he was told. 'It's hot in here,' he said.

Greek Chris made a concessionary shrug. His shirt was V-necked, skin-coloured. His curls were fierce and spiky.

'Warm summer for these climes,' he said. 'That's the global warming.'

Sami nodded, and slurped at lager.

'Kicking off again, your lot,' said Chris.

'Football?'

'Arabs. On the news tonight. Settlers shooting up children and that. Tanks and planes against blocks of flats. It doesn't seem fair to me.'

'No, that's the Israelis,' said Sami. 'Anyway, I have a plan.'

And he jabbered on. It was about internationalizing the conflict, cosmopolitanizing it, by means of a secret organization, and hijacking the ships in the docks right now, and burning universities and de-religiousizing everything and getting rid of names so no one could tell who was who.

'I must tell you,' he said. 'It's been getting rather too slow in here. I've been talking you see. Which doesn't help. Slows things down. Last time I looked I was talking and now I'm still talking. You know what I mean?'

'What's keeping you?' said Greek Chris, with a curl flick to the door.

'I'll finish my drink first,' said Sami, but found he already had. All of them.

Next, a warehouse, thoroughly overheated. Jumping amid short girls in bras. In the toilets a lot, and queuing for Lucozade. Reverse-coughing coke from the back of a strobe-lit hand. Racing himself, mainly victorious, around the Bacchanal's perimeter.

Then the leaping began again, Sami the Time Lord vanishing

into empty space, into spectral cloud landscapes. In just one flash of the strobe. Maybe time stood still and he was everywhere at once. Alternative realities – that was what he wanted. Maybe he was going backwards, back so he could start again. Maybe the universe was shrinking to something more manageable.

He chunked and blipped. The blanks were soft and silent, and each re-arrival came with a boom as the sound-system invaded his ears anew, and he arrived each time in a clearing, flailing his arms and floppy fingers to force outward the storm-tossed trees which were dancers, fortunately too chemical-happy and endorphin-rushed to mind.

When he came out there was a crowd in the street and neon lights shining in the club's entrance. False-tolerant bouncers consulting their watches. Sami was everybody's friendly loon, pushing his way into freshets of people as they spilled out. The stars were ferocious above. He kept his eyes on the Earth.

Then eastwards in somebody's car, a tangle of limbs in there, Sami poorly balanced across knees, his head lower than his feet. The people he was with thought he was telling jokes. Everybody screeched.

They entered a terraced house of small rooms, open plan because the doors had been removed, brimful of stuttering junglistic sound. A house which represented, in the absence of crisis politics, what the city took to be its underground. Conspirators without a conspiracy, nodding to the drum plot, shaking to the bass.

Something pulsed in his shoulder and neck. He bent his head into it cat-like, purring, and touched flesh with his ear. Somebody's hand. He looked into a familiar face. A slow-rippled pelagic fringe, hazed-up blood-logged eyes, perfect teeth twinkling.

Matt had been a pretend student at the LSE while Sami was an altogether more dedicated poseur at London University. Where Sami considered himself full of meaning, Matt was entirely empty of it. Everything about him was ironic. He'd tried on ideas as teasingly as a stripper tries on garments – only to shrug them off again. He'd been through a mock-Maoist period. He'd spent a week of imitation Buddhist silence, with Valium, in his room. For the sake of anti-fashion he'd been a paid-up member of the Communist Party. His trademark speech was in happy-nihilist mode: 'It's over, man. It's finished. Oho! Fucked! It's all fucked.' Meaning the government, civilization, all history, the destiny of man. He was a non-believer. A high priest of meaninglessness. Exactly the right person for Sami's organization, whatever it was to be.

It looked like Matt. It wore a shirt which read: FUCK ME. But Sami wouldn't believe the evidence. Suspicious how this seeming Matt hadn't aged. As if the years hadn't happened to him. Not an ounce of fat added, or a wrinkle, or a hair removed from the fringe. Not a filling, not a stain on the enamel. No insect had trod here its withering trail. No toll taken by adrenalin, bile or smothered tears.

Sami narrowed his eyes at the apparition. 'What year is it?' he asked.

'It's all relative. But, 2001, mate. A space odyssey.'

The voice made of Sami a believer. He exploded volcanic joy.

'It's Matt!'

Not hallucination but a coincidental twist of reality. Why, then, were there no signs of age? In the absence of signs, perhaps there was a greater sign, a message. How had his old friend sidestepped time? By investing in neither feeling nor belief. By being chaste of all commitment. To paraphrase Dr Schimmer, by having no big ideas. Matt surely hadn't befuddled his nerves with romance. (That thought brought a dagger's turn of guilt. *Muntaha may be worrying, poor Moony*.) All this passed with some flares of resentment through Sami's brain as he hugged his friend, bubbling also lava of fiery love.

'Matt.'

'Sami.'

'Matt, would you care to have a tootle? Do a line?'

Matt turned on his heel. On the back his shirt read: FUCKWIT.

And off they danced to the bathroom. A proper green bathroom, with tub, basin, toilet, tiles, this being a proper house. Sami unpocketed the wrap; Matt removed his from a humid boot. He ejected an unbroken rectangle of speech.

'You make two lines I'll make two that's one of each for both of us times two is four.'

Then it was up in a burning chunk at the bridge of the nose and the flanges of the nose flaring and saliva white-water rafting down his throat, and Matt was attached to the mouth of a suddenly materialized bikini girl. Who brought her in?

Matt roared, 'You can kiss her too!'

Sami, to be sociable, did so immediately, slurping on tight lip-sticky lips, intent and towering, nipping and biting; but then the dagger in his ribs made a thrust. *What am I doing?* So instead he fixed a hand on each breast, smaller and harder than the ones he was used to. The girl giggle-crumpled to the tiles. Matt slipped into the bathtub, laughing hugely, and rattled about, limbs scattered spiderish. Sami's peeled head high above them.

When the blank came it lasted into a sinking darkness. A blackness deep and cold. Longer than the night so far. Longer than half his life.

Matt's elbows proprietorially hinged on both walls of the bathtub, damp face composed, pale against pastel green.

'What you need,' he said, 'is a spoon.'

That hot light was an interruption. No more than a flicker. And then again Sami engulfed.

His knees hurt. He could smell metal. An empty spoon pushing at nostril cartilage. The bones where his cheeks met his ears might crack. Bikini Girl's pink hands fluttering about his arse. His knees hurt because he was kneeling on them, watching Matt regal in the bathtub.

'So,' Sami said, scrabbling for a grip. 'What are you doing these days?'

The dark was galloping, closing in. Its preceding dusk had netted him already. Hoof beats thudding louder. He stood to fend it off, embracing the green-shaded bulb. A blow swung at him: broadsword, ball and chain. He dodged, breathing fiercely.

'Advertising,' said Matt.

He jumped again, but there was no darkness. On the contrary, there was light. From freezer to furnace. In the largest room (the living room) fifteen or twenty men circled an omphalos of sound, leaping, fingers pointing and waving.

This generation . . .

Overbrimming with energy. Becoming one soul.

Shall witness the day . . .

Horns blew and whistles screeched.

That Babylon shall fall.

Someone in the centre had a microphone. Names being big-upped. The massive saluted. Light streamed in flailing arcs and curves and arrows.

Following one of these brought Sami back to Matt, apart from the crowd, shoulders forward, arms loose. The fringe limp over his eyebrows and his jaw raised like the jaw of a ruminating sheep.

Sami approached.

'I have to tell you. You are Matt, still as ever. But I, I am no longer Sami Traifi.'

'What are you, then?'

'I'm nothing.'

'No you're not.'

'I am. I am attaining nothing.'

Matt peered sideways, head cocked. 'What are you in the meantime?'

'Sami's body perhaps.'

Matt put a sticky arm around his neck, gummy fingers at his teeth. 'Eat this.'

Sami did so. Something sour and yellowish. An E or an X or an A or a K.

A brief jump. A voice or the system slowed, or Sami's ears, to a chant distorted: *Ba-by-laan shaall faaaall.*

A bound through time. They were in the bathroom again, organizing spoons, lines, cash cards, notes. Sami knew the girl had been with them although she was decorously hidden now. He was slobbering sentences at Matt.

'I want to recruit you. That's why I came to find you. You're my first recruit. I can't yet say what for. Restricted information as of the present moment. Even to me, Matt, even to me. My first recruit.'

'I'm number fucking one,' said Matt.

'It's kicking off,' Sami continued. 'It's a cull like the Jurassic or something. Signs of the Hour. Like Freemasons. Getting ourselves in a group. Preparing for it. That was just the start. Not a lot of these, let me tell you, are going to survive.'

'The Black Survivors!' shouted Matt, clammy white, in his Birmingham accent.

A low-howling wind over flat lichenous moorland. The flapping of angry trees. Whispers susurrating through dark leaf-swamp, and too much fog to see – fathom deep, oily dark. A forest. Reddening.

Sami recognized himself in this scene by his fear. His heart stalled. His tongue swollen. He was somewhere he'd been before. A familiar presence with him, keening in the wind.

Back to glimmering light. The wind was his hasty breath. The light was hot and he was sweating. He was weeping. He had the Bikini Girl against a wall, grinding against her, hands pressing her bones. He licked her. She shivered and shook, bit his chin. Light flickering like a guttering candle.

Do such stories have happy endings? Down back steps behind a sturdy grey terrace in the latter part of dawn, in among old-fashioned clatter bins and fag ends and bits of yellow grass and scratchy soil and probably, from the smell of it, dogshit, and the London odour of grease and used petrol and spilt beer, Sami's elbows scraped and raw and his teeth bared in a snarl and his knees and groin aching, and his eye a microscope squashed against Bikini Girl's purple eye and tangled yellow hair. Up close. The gargan-tuan sour grain of her skin. An ash-flecked twitching earlobe. Her wheezing breath. Yes, the beast with two backs. Sami inarticulate, at a loss, fucking a girl whose name he hasn't asked.

But can he be blamed for that? Sami would argue not. Not when at his back, above him, there is the heavy thud of hooves, an equine slobber, a flurry of dust (thick, red Syrian dust), and the beast rearing on its hind legs, flanks shivering and scattering blood. He doesn't want to see the rider but Bikini Girl squirms underneath him, turning him so he has to look, and there is no rider, but something worse. The apocalypse horse is its own rider. It has a human face: the leering, fish-eyed face of Mustafa Traifi.

'Baba,' it says. 'Sami, my boy. Look at me. Look at me.'

Sami now on his feet, zipping and buttoning as he runs, too scared to scream. Up the steps through the house into the street and then down vortex pavements leading either into or out of the black hole's centre. Outwards, he hoped. Into the viscous morning.

17

Death Number One

What's time to a corpse? From the moment of its death, time becomes a foreign territory, a land stranger and more distant with every minute, every decade, until soon there's nobody left to put a face to the corpse's name, to the name of the dust, and soon the letters of its name have sunk into the graveslab's grain, and the stone itself is broken or buried or dug up. And the land which was once a graveyard is overgrown, or shifted, or levelled. And the planet itself is dead, by fire or ice, and nobody at all anywhere to know. No consciousness. As if nothing had ever been.

Unless there is Grace watching and waiting for our helplessness.

There is no permanence for a corpse, not even for corpse dust. Or corpse mud, in this country. All this graveyard sentiment. You may as well shoot a corpse into outer space. Into the stars.

The Royal Free Hospital, February 1985. Mustafa Traifi is dreaming intermittent dreams of war. He sees the city of Hama from above and within. Sees the black basalt and white marble stripes. The mosque and the cathedral. The thin red earth. The tell of human remains, bones upon bones. The Orontes River rushing red with the blood of Tammuz, the blood of Dumuzi, the dying and rising shepherd god. The maidens weeping on the riverbanks.

Life is precarious. This place is thirty kilometres from the desert. The river, raised by waterwheels, feeds a capillary network of irrigation and sewage channels, and agricultural land in the city's heart. Traffic is organized by the nuclei of marketplaces where there are householders and merchants and peasant women in red-embroidered dresses and tall men of the hinterland wearing cloaks and kuffiyehs, and mounds of wheat and corn, and olives and oranges from the hill orchards, and complaining oxen and fat-tailed sheep. Dust in the endless process of becoming mud and then again dust.

It is not a bucolic scene. Mustafa is dreaming of February 1982, the time of the Muslim Brothers' uprising and of the government's response which he so passionately supported. His disembodied eye discerns barricades across the main streets and graffitied edicts on crumbling walls. Directives are called from minaret to minaret, drowning the alleyways. He can smell delight and horror: the smell of recently spilled blood. The city's inhabitants withdraw into their cells, locking heavy wooden doors. Those still moving outside have the wild glint of certainty in their eyes.

Tanks and trucks ring the city. Tented barracks where soldiers splash about in boredom, nerves and cheap tobacco. Buzz-fly warplanes fill the sky.

It's no longer possible to distinguish insurgents from loyal cells. They've penetrated everywhere. They hide in families, among women.

Radical treatment. Excision. Then chemotherapy. There are side effects.

The flicker of twenty-seven days and nights. It's a huge noise, thundering, relentless, mechanical yet animal. The crazed purring of an astral cat. Its pulverizing effect on internal organs makes ears irrelevant. The first night's run disables roads in and out, isolating the illness. Flowers of fire bloom upwards. Artillery remakes the environment, opening it up to the tanks and bulldozers. Rhythmic and persistent work. There go the mosque and the cathedral. There go the twisting covered alleyways. There go human bodies, bad and good cells, men and women, old and young. Bodies broken down, sewers cracked open, the bitter crackle of hair and skin.

Is it worth it? That's what the professors in London asked him, in 1982, when the stories were coming out. Twenty or thirty thousand dead, to save a government which is, after all, a dictatorship. Is it really worth it, Mustafa?

Yes, it's worth it. Look, if Hama goes so does Damascus, and then it's war without end, the cities against the army, the cities against the countryside. Of course it's worth it. These people would take us back to the Stone Age. They would destroy us. The rot must be stopped. For the sake of the future, of progress. At any cost. At any cost.

Mustafa Traifi is dying. They'd sent him a bearded, turbaned Egyptian to offer stale words and verses. (Nur had written Muslim on his admission form.) The visit had been a confirmation of the death sentence, although confirmation wasn't necessary. Mustafa felt his power draining. With some of his last reserves he sent the sad cleric away, down the long unwalkable corridors, away to the mosques and to the past that would outlive him. Pasts should die before you, but this past, this religion, cast itself as child rather than parent. It stood at the foot of his bed and watched him disappear.

This humiliating thing. The thing that wasn't supposed to happen, not yet, not yet at all. Belief in an afterwards would make it easier, but there wasn't time now to cultivate a belief. Belief is a habit which takes years to establish.

He has a button he can press to release more morphine into his drip solution. Another drop. He has a moment of emptiness before his thoughts return. The same thoughts generated by the same feelings: anger and fear. Anger is better than fear. There are illusions in anger. There is the momentary sensation of power. 'I should have had longer,' he roars to himself. 'I will do such things.' But anger is tiring, and more temporary than fear.

Another drop. He concentrates on breathing and becomes calmer. If the brain could die first it would be easier. It's the superstition of the soul that terrifies him. The nonsense that he is a soul. If he understood himself to be an organism, a flesh machine, he would not presume to fear.

Decomposition fertilizes. Massacres provide food for archaeologists. Chaos is ultimately creative. That's what he told the English professors. Of course it's worth it. Whatever has to be done, even at personal cost, even if it involves sacrifice, even in your own family, it's worth it.

Each winter the shepherd god dies, and the earth with him, but each spring he rises again. Women scream on the riverbanks where the Orontes curdles. Blood flows with petrol and molten plastic. Each spring he rises again. If not him, then what he represents. The nation or the future or progress or whatever it is he represents, Mustafa can't remember now, he hurts so much, feels so much fear.

Blood has to be sacrificed. It's not an easy thing to make the decision. To follow your convictions. Was it easy for Ibrahim?

A drop of morphine. How many more drops are there? His breath fails to replenish his lungs. He hears its sound, like himself running. Like himself as a boy scared and crying into his mother's chest. That thought weakens him. He pants with rising panic. How much more breath? How many more exhalations?

His reputation will never be greater than it is today. He can accept it if he is stoical. Any achievement is small put next to the size of nothing. And all men find themselves here, in this kind of bed, facing this. All men are subject to the grip of time. All men have to labour through the business of dying. Alone.

It would be easy if he could do it now, this moment. If he could brace himself with a cynical smirk and rush at it, demonstrate to himself that his dignity could survive it. It's the waiting that weakens, and the useless thoughts.

Now Um Kulsoom is playing in his head like it isn't a head but a Syrian taxi cab, hung with shiny invocations, breasty pin-ups, tassels and slogans, othersuch jangling things. The voice of Arab nationalism. The voice of oriental romance. She's singing about the days that are gone. The weak spot: the pathos of past time. When Mustafa remembers himself as an intense ambitious child, in the early days when he overswelled with feeling and released himself into a bounteous future, it brings him back to his painful failure to breathe. Meaning and self-love hurt. Soon there will be no meaning, and soon the loved one will die. The little innocent beloved. Little Mustafa among the olive trees. Mustafa dreaming secret games in fields of tobacco and aubergines. Mustafa by the kerosene stove in the old stone house. Mustafa going to buy fish with his father.

The years have weight. It seems a long time ago, yes, but his consciousness of it is as new as this moment. He sees his memory of the boy Mustafa. The boy is already dead, died long ago. Does he care so much about him? Is he still so attached?

He can do without the boy. He would willingly sacrifice ten years of Mustafa the boy's life in return for a further ten of his, Mustafa the adult's. What he would become. What he is now can die, all right then, if the becoming Mustafa can live.

If there were someone to do the deal with.

He would sacrifice every moment until this moment. He'd miss a few memories. Times with his son. Having his book praised. Some others. But the memories are part of this moment. He doesn't own the past, can't return there, only remembers. For a little while longer.

That the processing of reality would not stop. That consciousness would continue. Continuity of self isn't necessary. Just consciousness.

If there were anyone to reason with.

How quickly a body becomes a corpse. It chills, hardens, becomes soapy to the touch. It smells sweetly of corruption. Back to the shit it came from, the angelic illusion over for good. Nur will have him buried straight away, in the way of hot lands, before the next sunset. As if he never was. As dead as the earth that covers him. Equal to the elements. What had been tripping airily above cancelled and brought down.

Two more drops. Mustafa sinks. He sees the mass graves of Hama. He sees the superstitious dead, the believers in eternity, sees them open their eyes and stare.

Sacrifice will not save him now. There is no redemption from death.

Mustafa opens his eyes after a time and sees his boy and his wife at the bedside. Nur leans greyly over him, the reproach of her. But Sami's uncertain face shines with the light of innocent love.

'Baba,' says Sami, the unshepherded boy. 'Baba, it's snowing outside. It's lying in the road.'

And when with two more drops he wills his hand to move and Sami to bow his head, he finds the boy's dark hair moist with melted flakes or the dew of dawn or sea foam.

Mustafa sinks with increasing velocity. When he sees again, Nur has gone. Sami's face glistens. Mustafa feels himself pulled away. He should speak now.

'When I close my eyes I'm in a hole. When I open them I'm here. There are two worlds. I can't reconcile them.'

This isn't what he means to say. But he holds on to the continuity of his voice. While it speaks, he still exists.

'Everybody dies. Not so bad if we all do it. You know, the problem is there's no solidarity. Better if we all did it together, at the same time, holding hands. But alone is unbearable. It's unbearable. It brings out the worst superstitions.'

Words form in the dark liquids of his lungs. Not sure if he can hear them any more. What do words mean?

'They hanged men ten at a time in Tadmor prison. They killed men and women and their babies all together in Hama. Tens of thousands. Don't be sad about it. It was worth it. And those people were lucky. They died in solidarity. Don't blame me. It's a question of principle, Sami. You have to be loyal to your principles. Sacrifices have to be made.'

Has he stopped now? Which language is he using? It isn't what he meant to say. He should find some wisdom for the boy, some comfort. But there is none. None of this is what he meant. None of it at all.

A Sufi proverb says: *The approach of the angel of death is horrific; its arrival is bliss.* For Sami, who was there at his father's end, the angel's approach was surprisingly chilly.

He'd been cooling for weeks as the process unfolded, as the waves of Mustafa's grief broke in cold spray over him. In resentful imitation too of his mother's frigidity.

A nurse tiptoed to the bed and nodded meaningfully at Sami, keeping her cool eyes on him long enough to ensure he understood. She pulled his father's eyelids closed with a smooth, practised movement, then turned to Sami again and asked, 'Where is your mother, dear?'

A tree of ice was flowering inside him. He felt crystals cramp around his heart. It was an exciting feeling, and also terrible. Concentrating on the sensation, he pointed to the corridor, then shuffled backwards towards it. He watched nurse and corpse while he retreated, in the same way that a pilgrim leaves a shrine, slowly probing with blind toes behind, always facing the sacred point.

At the foot of the Royal Free Hospital a layer of snow negated the ground. Flakes numbed his ears and nose and penetrated jumper and jeans. He'd left his jacket in the ward. He sped up across South End Green until breath forced high, inhuman sounds from his throat. Snow drizzled into his tearless eyes and glassy mouth. He burst on to the dead blank of Parliament Hill Fields.

Through exposure to stock narratives he had expected to be overwhelmed by a surge of pain, by screaming hysteria. But this didn't happen. On the contrary, life revealed itself to be simpler, cleaner, than he had realized before. So was his heart. There was no tension, no desire, no yearning. Just the purity of ice.

He stepped forward slowly. He experienced the crush of snow beneath his trainers more as vibration than sound. The swirl in the white air was indistinct from the earth, and his breath indistinct from the inaudible wind. The surrounding city's responses were silenced. There was no one else on the hillside with him, and then he too was absent, and instead of him there was emptiness. Timeless emptiness which didn't stop.

Nur was grateful when her frozen son returned after four hours' wandering, although she hadn't really been worrying. Wanting to be alone was a normal reaction to death. She was grateful because he gave her something to be busy with. And, once returned, Sami joined the game, separating himself from the cold so that he felt it and began to tremble, so that he blushed in the hospital's artificial heat. Allowed himself to be wrapped in blankets, and driven home, and fed, and put to bed. Attended his father's funeral, and as time passed, school, and then university, and grew heated with sex, ambition and argument, keeping his eyes on the concrete earth. He lived amid hectic human heat. But he always knew that beneath the warm appearances of things lay a solid foundation of ice. He kept this knowledge with cold certainty inside him. Until this summer. Until now.

18

A Great Leap

In seventeenth-century England the verb 'to leap' was slang for to fuck. Hence the tendency of Shakespeare's livelier characters to visit 'leaping houses'. Following the death of Thomas Hobbes, whose last words were: 'I'm about to take my last voyage; a great leap in the dark,' a new copulatory phrase entered the language: 'To go on Hobbes' voyage.' As in, 'I think my luck holds. I should be going on Hobbes' voyage ere sunrise.'

Sami had been leaping about in time. He'd evaded news of one death and, as usual, frozen out the reality of another. Drugged and stupid, he'd embarked on Hobbes' voyage, but had been brusquely hauled back to land by a hallucinated leaping horse. By his father.

We find him stumbling in a world which had also given in to its desires. A chain-smoking, junk-guzzling, substance-abusing world. A sweating world, whose temperature control was hopelessly disabled.

The weather this morning had turned. It drizzled in wavelets and upward eddies. Sami wasn't wearing his jacket any more and his shirt was grimed with the previous night's pain. When he came to an eastern section of the canal he slunk down on to the towpath. As he tramped along – modest tower blocks rising grimly above the canal banks – there were worm shapes forming from the mist, and overgrown flies, and sullen reptiles making the black water turbulent. But his other-worldly intimations had reached their climax. He could shrug them off. 'This isn't real,' he said, 'none of it is real.' All he had to do now was endure.

He rubbed more coke into his gums, and then he was so crazed by thirst and a desire for clarity that he kneeled, and bowed, and dipped his head into the canal. In among the who-knows-what, the mutant weeds and industrial acids, the human waste, the water not fit to drink when boiled, not fit even for twenty-first-century, hormone-boggled hermaphrodite fish. And here he was with his head in it. He sat against a lichenous wall and shivered, letting canal drops piss into his shirt and on to his belly.

Unfaithfulness hadn't been a feature of his marriage. He was sure of Muntaha, and on his side, he'd never before wavered. Certainly he'd been tempted, particularly during his sojourn in Paris, because they were apart, because of the city's reputation, because of the undoubted elegance of certain French women. Also because of Parisian North Africans – not just a street or two of Arabs like London before sanctions pushed the Iraqis out, but whole markets and high-rise suburbs of alienated noble-browed women. Rich hunting grounds. But he'd never wavered. He had pride then in what he thought he was doing, the research and all, an anthropologist high-mindedly not touching the natives. Muntaha would come over for weekends, or he would spend an occasional week back in London, for non-contemptuous carnal days stripped of familiarity, burnished by absence. And if he hadn't seen her for months and years he'd still have remained faithful. They loved each other. He'd loved himself through her eyes. And what had also kept him pure was a proper sense of standards, the belief that cheating was just that: cheating. Something humiliating. A betrayal of himself as well as of her.

But his sense of standards, and so much else, seemed to have melted. Nothing was solid any more.

Now had he really, this morning, an hour or two ago? Could he have? True, he couldn't rightly remember (and if he didn't own the pleasure of memory he didn't bear the weight of sin, surely? And surely it hadn't been him who'd done it; he'd done it while he was – what? – attaining nothing) and true, there was a chance he hadn't; he'd seen a centaur, after all, as clearly as he'd seen the girl under him. Were there centaurs in London? But looking the matter straight in the eye, no excuses, facing facts, well, yes, he had. He most probably had. He'd rutted lovelessly, not because it was in his destiny to do so, not because he'd encountered a beauty not to be denied, but just because he had.

Poor Sami felt very sick. Such guilt couldn't be swallowed immediately, not in his nauseated state. So mistaking Muntaha for himself, he tried to blame her, reasoning that it must have been her fault, at least in part. Oh they'd had love all right, and no major crisis until latterly, until the religion thing. Her failing. Changing on him after all these years, wrapping herself up in a scarf, saying prayers, mumbling mumbo-jumbo. She was supposed to be a support. What he wanted was for her to see things as he saw them. A natural enough desire. Not much to ask. Only that his wife would continue in their secularist consensus, and not disrupt their life plan. But she was all set on disruption.

He stood up and scratched in his pockets and snuffled more powder from the bag. Then he was off again at speed, his nostrils propellers carrying him through murky skies, up from the canal and over blighted, rainy streets. When he came across a shop he entered, addressing the frightened woman behind the counter.

'Do you have any ice?'

'You what?'

'Ice.'

'Ice cream?'

He thought about it. His stomach told him no.

'Just ice.'

She stared at him in horror. Sami Traifi, bloodshot, semi-dressed, canal-stained.

'No,' she said.

He bought a bottle of water and drained it on the pavement outside. And continued, zigzagging deeper into the city's sad orient. At a coin phone he paused to speak to his answermachine. 'I need to be alone.' Left his Greta Garbo message as Marwan's corpse was being driven to the mosque for noon prayers. And stumbled on, a hallucinated astronaut charting a succession of dead planets.

He landed, spasmodic with cold and hunger, in a deserted car park. He was experiencing blank patches again, but these were only the predictable consequence of exhaustion. Sheltered in a brick right angle, he made a spliff with jerky hands. Smoking it calmed him into a hypnagogic state in which, as he would in bleak moments, he spoke to his dead father.

'Despite whatever you've done,' he muttered, 'I don't hold anything against you. Despite it all. Just leave me alone, then. I'm doing this for you. Steering clear of the Muslims. No need to worry. So leave me alone.'

And here, for a while, he slept. Pleasant dreams of a rational world. Clean laboratories. Neat-shaven scientists in white coats.

Until he was rocked awake by a brown hand. A concerned, skullcapped face peering into his.

'Brother,' it said. 'Brother, wake up. Do you hear me? Are you ill, brother?'

Sami wept, 'Oh. Oh fuck.'

The old man wore a bristly white beard.

'Never mind, brother. Get up, please. Insha'allah you'll be very well soon.'

Sami said, 'I'm not your fucking brother.'

He climbed the wall until he was standing. And then for all the world as if he were a pure-blooded son of the islands, upstandingly English and true, he said, 'Piss off. Piss off you old Paki fucker.'

Leaving his spurned saviour in the background (undoubtedly in consternation, rubbing a bald patch under the skullcap), Sami loped out under the rain. Through brown brick and concrete parkland. Then high-sided, denser streets, colour bulging from video outlets and sari stores. Curry houses turning his already turned, shrivelled stomach. Hooded men and hijabbed women. Sami heading for the river. He had a half-formed urge to submerge himself, to clean himself up. Searching for an end point, or a beginning, for some kind of baptism. Perhaps he'd make for the Millwall bend, where they drag most of the bodies out, and pull himself together there.

He got as far as Tower Bridge. The tower itself drizzle-stained ochre behind him, something built of stone, modestly, in the contemporary glass and metal riverscape. The dead and regenerated docks in front. Outstretched mud expanse rushing underneath.

Suited men and women hurried stiffly past, chins to collars, grunting against the weather. At a distance, a tourist couple chirped under a red umbrella. Sami keened in turpitude, sodden, guilt-racked, filthy, his elbows on the railing, cradling his head. Nothing remained of last night's sense of mission. Like his Big Idea deconstructed: nothing. Under the veils he'd penetrated: nothing.

What to do now? Go home and sleep, eat cornflakes, drink tea. But Muntaha would arrive from work, and then he'd have to lie, he'd have to avoid her eyes. And probably she wouldn't have gone to work today, but somewhere else. Sami stopped the thought.

He took the last note from his wallet and tubed it into a nostril. (The male tourist quickly snapped his picture. Some authentic London colour, better than those dated punk postcards.) Sami snorted, and gave the packet to the wind. At the same moment English earth was being sprinkled on Marwan. The angels of the grave commencing their interrogation.

Sami absorbed the cocaine. It didn't make much difference. Still nothing to do but go home. Face things.

For the last time, he bolted. And, straight away colliding at the neck with a solid object, fell. And sitting on the pavement on the props of his arms, looked up into a policeman's face. For it was a policeman's arm into which he had collided.

'You appear, sir,' said the policeman, 'to have a fiver stuck in your nose. Now why would that be?'

Sami tried to shrug as the policeman plucked the note from his nostril.

'There's powder here.' Unravelling it with distaste.

Sami would have said, 'What of it?' if he'd been in a speaking mood. Eighty per cent of notes in circulation in the metropolitan area bear verifiable traces of cocaine. And Sami had finished his. Thus, arrest aborted.

Alas, not so. Sami, walked off the bridge to an expectant squad car (photographed again by zoom lens and crowning the tourists' day), was forced to remember, with his pocket contents laid out on the bonnet, that he hadn't finished the weed. Which meant he didn't have to face Muntaha just yet, but the inside of a cell.

He was packed into the car, a protective hand shielding his head as it went under. Then seatbelted. With official process setting in and the officers' formal, ironic language, Sami felt his safety was taken care of. Lurching on the back seat, bubbles rising from his feet and popping at the top of his skull, he was really quite pleased about it all, about the drama, the not being in control.

At the station he gave Tom Field's university address. Couldn't remember his own, he said, couldn't remember his next of kin. Muntaha was the wrong person to call after last night's adventuring, a woman in a hijab. Who else was there? No one.

'Take me where you must,' he said, offering wrists for cuffing.

The policeman he'd been handed to, a bland-faced, weary slab, looked heavenward for patience but found only neon and styrofoam tiles.

'Joker,' said the policeman. 'Fucking joker.'

Leaving Sami's hands free, he pushed and pointed him down a grey corridor, around a corner.

Here they met a smell. It hit Sami like something solid. He gasped. Clutched his solar plexus. Behind bars in front of him was the source of it: a huddle of clothed flesh – a tramp, a drunk – something perhaps dangerous, or perhaps not alive. Something, in any case, which stank.

Sami's sense of safety dissolved.

'You're not putting me in there with that?'

The slab smirked. 'To be honest, sir, I can't see much difference between him and you.'

The door opened electronically and Sami sidled in, keeping what distance he could from the stink. It was thick and heavy and full of horror. It prised open dark areas of his brain. Everything was coated in the smell, walls, bars, benches. Sami sat. He shivered. He looked at the heaving pile opposite. A coat, more cloth, and a body.

Even with nose and lips squashed together against dirty knuckles, the drunk had a semi-familiar face. It was round and red. Inflamed skin and bloated cartilage. Greyish hair curling to the shoulders.

The smell had become a taste. Sami had a mouthful. Yellow and harsh. Alcohol in it as well as stale sweat and urine.

Man at a loss.

> Verily, man is bound to lose himself
> Unless he be of those who . . .

He stopped the verse, stood up, and began to pace. Up and down, back and forth, through the medium of the smell. Dim light sheathed inside the ceiling. Up and down, back and forth, breath as shallow as he could make it. Then the drunk whimpered and growled, and Sami immediately sat back down. He tried not to breathe at all. Waited there for five minutes, ten, a quarter of an hour.

For the first time in this summer's story, Sami had come to rest. No more rolling, snorting, seeking or rushing. No more diversionary activity. No more awareness of the pains that shot through his back and neck and constricted his head. No more of those sensations that he usually employed as a hijab to drape around things-as-they-are.

He'd stopped running. Easier just to sit, in this silence, in this stillness. He slipped behind his breath, but not into oblivion. His silence was warm, not icy. Warm with a warmth that didn't disrupt the silence. A body temperature warmth, no more nor less. He felt he was on the verge of something. The lifting of a veil. The Greek word for it is apocalypse.

But then the drunk awoke.

'Ah! Me nephew!'

And as quickly as he'd been recognized Sami recognized the roaring man from the strippers' pub.

'Hello,' he said. 'I'm not your nephew, though.'

'Not me nephew?' The accent almost Irish, but then not, so

confused in the storm of urban accents that it contained features of all. 'Well, perhaps not. Perhaps I am mistaken. But still a brother. We're all relatives, you know. We all come from Adam.'

Sami nodded assent. The roaring man continued.

'Have you been living clean, lad? There's the question. Too much dirt in the world, you see. Oh dear me, yes. Too much dirt, and you know what else? Too much Satan.'

He sucked at air, made a 'hoo hoo' noise, wiggled his ears. With the clapping of his hands he was signalling either triumph or certain knowledge.

'No one believes in Satan now, not till they see him. I've seen him. In the bottom of a glass. Reflected in a whore's eyes. It isn't all fun and games, you know. You'll notice that when you see him.'

Remarkably straight-backed, he moved on to commandments.

'Stick to one woman. Reject liquor. Live clean. Stand in the way of Satan. Also beware of false prophets. Distinguish false from true visions. Stand in Satan's way.'

'What are you doing here, then?' Sami asked, not unkindly.

'Aha!' raising a finger and an eyebrow as if Sami had delivered the crucial point. 'Aha now! I'll tell you! Satan! Listening to Satan! Should have listened to the priests.' Shaking his head and grinning as if it was, after all, fun and games. 'But no one will listen to the priests. Not in these days. Nor should they, those fucking hypocritical bastards. Dirty bastards. Would you listen to them? A bright boy like you? Of course you wouldn't. Dirty bastards. Dirty fucking religion, the whole thing. Oh no, no, no . . .'

For some moments he indulged in negation.

'Oh no, I'd prefer Satan to that, to tell you God's honest truth. None of that. We'd do better to start again. Time for a new religion. New everything. A new heaven and a new earth. Ha!'

And he laughed hugely.

'Uncle,' said Sami. 'You need to have a shower.'

'You're right there,' uncle quietly said. 'And I'll do it directly, just as soon as this . . .' – gesturing at the walls – '. . . hospitality comes to an end.'

Sami stretched out on the bench. He looked up into grey light and the smell and uncle's subdued whispering. He was more tired than uncomfortable. The air swam above him, and for an instant seemed to solidify. Sami heard the briefest clack of hooves. Mustafa Traifi's face began to form.

'Oh fuck off,' said Sami. Mustafa disappeared.

There were tears in his eyes, but he didn't brush them away. What he did this time was face facts. Heard the echo of his own 'fuck off' in his ears. Words with no audience, for his father was really gone.

Really gone. He brooded on that, the injustice of it. That he too was bones and meat and vibrating pulp within a peel. That the body was coming to its end, if not tomorrow then after a finite number of tomorrows that passed faster and faster, losing illusory substance as they passed.

More than unjust. Terrifying. In any case, superstition wouldn't help. Nothing was left of Mustafa Traifi, it was time to admit that. Time to stop behaving as if his father was still here. And time, therefore, to examine all the superstitions he'd built around his father's ghost.

The God fiction, for instance. He'd believed as passionately as he could that it was fiction because he'd thought it was manly and worthy of his father's pride to believe so. And what did he believe now, now that his manliness no longer seemed a tangible aim, now that his father was gone? He searched for his belief, looking mutely into his own silence, and found none. Nothing solid there. He believed nothing either way.

What if he were to believe, positively, in a God, in the unseen? To believe that death was not death but another kind of life? Would that be wrong? Would it be wrong to at least aspire to such a belief, to hope? Was hoping wrong? Faced with the injustice, the absurdity, the unthinkability, of death. For it is unthinkable, once you've noticed yourself living, to stop.

No, not wrong. Perhaps not right either. But not wrong.

You could even say that the weight of blindness falls on those who don't stir to hope, so blind they are to the absurdity of death. The careless atheists, like him. The materialists who sneer at religious emotion. You could even say that it is they who are in denial.

For Sami this was a great leap, across, out, into the abyss. Towards what? Would something be there to meet him? To stop him falling through the void?

19
Enlightenment

Gabor could be defined in ethnic terms as Jewish or Hungarian – Hungarian is his largest genetic portion – but he thinks of himself as Russian, like his grandfather. Why? Because he considers Russia to be furthest away. Because Russia is the most distant from his mundane environment. Because Russia is most other to himself.

Otherness. The realm of the spirit which art gestures towards.

Gabor knows the spirit from certain numinous experiences of his childhood – certain signs and visions. He knows the world, if read properly, is a canvas of signs, hinting beyond itself. He knows the world when unread and meaning only itself, the material world, is as grey and damp as the Essex village he grew up in.

His parents were that world. Therefore, he'd always liked what that world doesn't. When he was at school he had Indian friends, because his parents didn't want him playing with Indians. Why not? Because Indians were 'superstitious people'. Now he goes out of his way to meet Indians, Africans, Arabs.

His parents were hygiene freaks. He suspected they worried about the Indians' dirty brown skin, although this was never articulated. Straightforward racism would be too low class and passionate for them. But they cleaned him extra hard when he returned from school, swabbed his fingers with medical alcohol before he was allowed to eat.

His mother was anxious to scrub away the central European grime of her own name. Angyalka introduced herself as Angie until she decided it was too cockney. She was Angela after that. Gabor wondered why they'd named him as they had. Was he meant as some kind of totemic propitiation of the primitive gods? Was that the deal – if he was named for the past his parents could comfortably deny it, and get on with their present ambitions?

Angela claimed to have forgotten both Hungarian and Hungary, although she'd lived there until she was ten. Her physique let her down – she was bonier and sharper featured than her neighbours – but in dress, accent and posture she was a typically nervy Anglo nouveau riche. She suffered something like the self-hatred of the working class, except her background wasn't proletarian. Her parents had been educated people, he a journalist, she a musician. When they fled, in 1956, after he'd unwisely authored anti-Soviet editorials, they became proletarian in the strict Marxist sense of owning nothing but their labour. Being dispossessed immigrants in London made them scum. Angela saw scum everywhere. Gabor remembers her scouring the bath and sink and kitchen floor even when they were clean.

His father was calmer and less ambitious. Richard was just scared of difference. Not of being different, because somehow he never was, despite growing up in a different home. He had not a word of Russian, not a smidgeon of Yiddish. Being the son of a Jewish mother makes him technically Jewish. You'd never guess. He looks English. Acts English. Has the stereotypical prejudices and ignorances of a sheltered Englishman. Put him in a bus with people of foreign origin and he flinches. Ask him his history and he screws up his pale cheeks in bewilderment. Jews? Russian exiles? Do such things exist?

As resistance, Gabor loved the strange and exotic. In the village there was a fourteenth-century church, with an eighteenth-century tower attached. It didn't quite do it for him, too close to home and to their foam-haired old lady neighbours. But out of the village, on a flat plain of tall white oxeye daisies and purple common mallow, was the seventh-century chapel of St Peter's-on-the-Wall. In the shape of a normal house, but taller. Built by Saxons, by an extinct people. Gothic mists and salty North Sea gales outside. Inside, bare stone, bare benches. As minimalist as a desert mosque. There were inlets of light too high to see out of. The outside sees in. Light sees in.

A monk named Cedd, called from Lindisfarne by King Sigbert, prayed, fasted and blessed the land before he built on it. The chapel was constructed from the ruins of a Roman fort, in the style of Syrian churches. Cedd died in Yorkshire of plague, a disease from the east.

Gabor squeezed his eyes half shut, imagined Cedd and the East Saxons through his lashes. Ghosts bubbling past him. Then one afternoon in his early teens, shortly after his grandfather's death, he dreamt of Vronsky while asleep on the church floor. Vronsky handing him the powers of art and lust. The vision lasted for half a minute after he awoke and rubbed his brow. Vronsky handing him light.

Beyond the chapel was the power station where Richard and Angela worked. A brutal rectangle against the green sky. A fact. A denial of transcendence. Their world.

When his parents knew he'd been at the chapel they sniggered and smirked. 'Been talking to God again have we?' They nudged each other and rolled their eyes. It was a moment of closeness for them, until Angela thought of the Saxon dust on the chapel flagstones and snapped Gabor towards the bath.

Everything about them was hyper-logical and counter-intuitive. Post-enlightenment people, they refused to believe in the soul because they couldn't see or measure it. Their hearts were neither seats of passion nor mirrors of divinity, but mere complex muscles pumping blood. They represented science in opposition to Vronsky's art, stability in place of his migration, surface instead of depth. Of course, it was inevitable that they would be like that. Human beings must rebel against their parents. It's a mechanism that moves the world on. Gabor too rebelled.

Despite himself, he was a gifted science student. The shame of it dissipated once he was able to dissociate the subject from his father and mother. Anyway, it was no longer their subject. In the brief space of a generation a sense of wonder had returned to science. The rigid boundaries between it and art had begun to dissolve. Science could be experienced as mystery. Outside school he read quantum physics, which was like reading Sufism. Appearances are illusions. Is the photon a wave or a particle? Our traditional categories break down when you look closely.

Reading science, and being an adolescent, taught Gabor that his parents' professions were evil. He leafleted the bemused villagers with anti-nuclear propaganda, and confronted his father.

'That power station should be closed down. How can you work there? You're poisoning your descendants.'

Richard said, 'Nuclear power's a lot cleaner than fossil fuels.'

'You don't care, do you? Your grandchildren will be mutants and you don't have the heart to care.'

Perhaps it was an urge to rub his father's nose in difference which made Gabor leap to this image. Mutants would be good. Dirty mutants best of all.

'Nonsense.' Richard chuckling complacently.

'I reject this. I reject your crimes, both of you. You two and British Nuclear Fuels. At Sellafield the child cancer rate is way up. It's probably happening here as well. You're probably helping them to cover up the evidence. You're monsters, both of you. No emotions. I don't have anything to do with you. You're not my kind of people.'

'We're your parents. You can't escape your past, any more than a fossil can crawl out of its rock.'

But fossils can be dug up and burnt. They can be liberated in the form of carbon dioxide. From rock to air, to the sky.

'My ancestor is my grandfather. Why couldn't you have been like him? He was a humanist and a spiritual man. He wouldn't have poisoned the earth.'

'You're very romantic about your grandfather. You forget I knew him better than you. He wasn't as you think. Not nearly so exciting. You've made up a fiction. You're not looking at the real thing.'

What did they know of reality? They saw only the absence of

Vronsky's body, while Gabor saw the man's spirit. Felt it in the breeze, in the borderless sky. The sky transcending and ignoring facts. If it notices facts, it mocks their pretension.

Gabor's father said he wouldn't escape his past. He had escaped, though. He had nothing to do with them now. Not with inflexible facts, and not with his parents. On one occasion they'd come down to sneer at his studio, at the ethnic mess of the streets outside. Only once.

Gabor taught physics and art to Bengali children. He ate in restaurants his mother would consider dirty. He walked the streets Vronsky had walked. He prayed for light before he created pictures.

And now, like Cedd the builder, he'd contracted a disease from the east. A disease called Muntaha. Swerve-bodied Muntaha, her nose broad at the bridge, eyes as tall as they were wide. Gabor returned tense from Marwan's ta'ziya and went straight to his painting.

A large canvas was already strapped up to his workboard. In its centre he marked out an empty square with a ruler. This represented the empty cube of the Ka'aba in Mecca.

Then he took off his shoes and placed them neatly behind the door, as the Muslims do. He'd have a shoe rack put there, to remind him. He removed shirt and trousers, folded them slowly, carried them like an offering on flat arms towards the cupboard that was his bedroom. The room he was painting in was a long bare-walled rectangle that had first been built, in the days of the city's tangible wares, to store textiles. Cotton brought from India and Egypt, milled in the north, exported back to the colonies. Now it was stacked with wooden boxes and computer monitors. Canvases completed or in progress. Potted plants on rough shelves. Jars and tubes of paint.

There was a rack of books near the entrance to the bedroom: Kandinsky's *Concerning the Spiritual in Art*, Paul Klee's journals, novels by Tolstoy and Dostoyevsky, stories by Gogol and Chekhov, the scientific and philosophical studies of Einstein and Max Planck. Also the heavy dark Qur'an Muntaha had given him, and a collection of ahadeeth, the traditions of the Prophet, which he'd bought in a

Finsbury Park bookshop. Between the books and his canvases there was a salvaged coarse-grain desk, and on it the framed black and white photograph of his grandfather.

Gabor pulled the four low windows open to their fullest extent, to ventilate the paint fumes, perhaps for a breeze. The night, to his ears, was silent.

He surrounded his ka'aba with a swirl of pilgrims moving anti-clockwise, like all the orbits in nature. He felt this was significant – one of the correspondences or artful patterns to be found at all levels – electrons around a nucleus, planets around suns, galaxies on their axes, all anticlockwise, like Muslims circumambulating the empty House. On holiday in Istanbul he'd seen the Mevlevi dervishes doing it in their sema, spinning, arms outstretched, one palm facing the heavens and another to the earth.

Gabor had faith in his art, real holy faith. For him, art was something primeval, something shamanic. He was engaged in the same sacralization of matter that had made men decorate cave walls, mummify corpses, fashion icons, and replenish the land's significance with earthworks.

He used thick strokes, and then a knife to highlight the colours with borders. Greens, reds and blues. He was trying for a rainbow effect, but a splintered rainbow, with leakages and leaps to defy tonal classification – a London residential mishmash instead of New York ghettoes. The viewer could read that in if they wished – racial mixing, miscegenation.

With a thin hard brush he stubbed dots of darkness, for heads or souls, on to the swirl. He wiped his fingers on his underwear. Next, he superimposed Bohr's famous atom symbol on to the pilgrims, brushing three broad oval orbits around the ka'aba nucleus. As he worked he repeated the first four ayat of the Qur'anic Surat al-Fajr, which he was learning for Muntaha.

> Consider the daybreak, and the ten nights!
> Consider the multiple and the One!
> Consider the night as it runs its course!

The 'ten nights' referring to the final third of Ramadan, the month in which the Prophet, before he became a prophet, withdrew to caves in the Meccan mountains for fasting, meditation and prayer, the time when he first met the angel, when the revelation descended. He recited in Arabic, again and again, with rhythm and rhyme.

> wal-fajr
> wa layaalin 'ashr
> wash-shaf'i wal-watr
> wal-layli idhaa yasr . . .

She would be impressed. He'd recite it to her when he showed her this painting.

He put down the brush. What now? He thought of Mr al-Haj in the grave. He thought of Mr al-Haj's daughter. He named the picture 'For Muntaha', and as he did so he felt a pat on his shoulder, and also a stirring in his groin. Grandfather Vronsky exhaled lustily behind his back. Light shone briefly on to the white centre of his painted ka'aba.

Is something going to happen here? Gabor wondered. I mean, where was her husband today? Why the embarrassment when I asked for him?

He ate a slobber of pickled fish from the fridge, brushed his teeth, and slept a deep, unbroken sleep.

20

Evolutionary Loss

Sami blinked at the ghost of himself until he could name his surroundings. Then he solidified fast: a hungry, numbed and dirty organism, bruised where his ribs had pressed the bench. He sat up and found he was alone in the cell. Knowledge leaked slowly from body into mind. For instance, he'd been asleep a long time. He'd been taking drugs, which were now flushed on to his surface. He needed to wash before he did anything else.

He was in the same neon eternity of trapped air he'd fallen asleep in, but the smell of the man he'd called uncle had almost completely dispersed. Whether it was night or day he didn't know.

He made a mental gesture of searching for his jacket, but before his arm or eyes moved he remembered its loss in the party house. Then he remembered other losses too, like the academic life, abandoned after his meeting with Dr Schimmer, and the marital moral high ground, which he may on previous occasions have occupied rhetorically, irretrievably tangled up back there in Bikini Girl's knickers and teeth. He'd lost too his childish ability to speak to his dead father, this most intimate of his comforts. His innocence was gone. The angry fidgeting state he'd been in up to then seemed to him like innocence.

Surprisingly, after all that loss, he felt bright and free. He'd have liked to sit a while and enjoy the sensation, but his body had its own priority. His bladder was excruciatingly swollen. As soon as he noticed it he began to sweat.

He called through the bars, embarrassed by his voice.

'Erm, officer, excuse me, I need . . .'

When he heard steps approach he wondered how to apologize. Wondered at last how much trouble he was in. At the same time he clenched his buttocks and counted to the time he'd be pissing. One to seven and back down to one.

As four reached three a policeman beeped his bars open. A new policeman, short and square.

'Had a good sleep, then? Your friend's here for you.'

'Yes, I need, officer, to go to the toilet.'

Which friend? So he could leave?

Dribbles of light reached through an airvent in the toilet. Daytime, then. He must have slept all night and half of the day before. He pissed a river, and then, slack-bladdered, set about washing head, face, neck and arms in the miniature sink, until the policeman struck the door with worried urgency.

'Out now, or I take you out.'

He emerged shrugging and apologizing. The policeman walked him through to the front office, which in the cold illumination of sobriety was drab and angular. It smelled of chipboard, paint and boredom. Sami saw his friend. Tom Field, professor of survivalism, Sami's source of wisdom, the man who'd nearly reconciled him to Muntaha's hijab. Looking very natural in contrast to his background, wearing organic fibres and exuding human passions, Tom stood among the seats of the waiting area. His face was leathery, burnt in the sun, and expressionless save his eyes, which glared at Sami. Pseudonymous, anonymous Tom: the last person he should have brought to a police station.

There was some bureaucracy to get through, and a tired warning not to do it again. Then a statement of the obvious to accompany a nod towards Tom: 'Here's your mate come to take you home.'

Tom hadn't spoken yet. He pointed to the front entrance. Sami thanked the police for their trouble in the same way he'd once thanked a teacher for slapping him, and followed the survivalist. He'd put himself in the role of naughty child. Well then, bear it. Take the admonishment.

Tom led the way to an anonymous car and let himself in the passenger side. A woman sat in the driving seat. Sami got into the back, behind Tom. The woman twisted to grin at Sami.

'I'm GR,' she said.

'Sami,' said Sami, then turned to his mentor. 'Tom, I'm sorry to get you down here. They wanted someone's name.'

Tom, glaring through the windscreen, replied staccato.

'Yeah, but not mine. I'll help you out in all kinds of ways, but not like this. My name written down in a police station. On someone's computer. That is what I do not want. Do you understand me?'

'Yes, Tom.'

'That is what I do not want. I do everything I can to cover my tracks, to keep anonymous, and you give the Tom Field name to the state machinery. You've set me back, Sami. You've got in the way.'

The tendons writhed in the back of Tom's neck. The sound of car engine. Torsos through the windows. They moved through light and shade into the densest section of the city.

In the cheeriest of voices, Sami spoke again.

'So, GR, that's an unusual name.'

'Yep,' said the driver. 'Signifying Global Resister.'

She wore a one-piece camouflage suit. Brown and green jungle camouflage. Not much use for the urban environment.

'And what are you resisting?'

'The whole thing. Capitalism. Imperialism. Globalization. The way we're being driven to Armageddon.'

She had nine-tenths of her attention on the road. This reassured Sami.

'I see,' he said.

Light brown hair was pulled up and tied on top of her head. Her neck smooth and unblemished. The hairs glistened sunlight blonde where they left the skin. Sami judged her to be in her late twenties, at least a decade younger than Tom. He knew nothing of Tom's private life.

'So you think Armageddon's coming. A war. The end of the world.'

It sounded silly when he said it, so he laughed once.

'Things'll get a lot worse . . .'

They lurched around a skip cooped off from the traffic by mesh, like the holy of holies screened from the mob in an orthodox church. The skip was radioactive green. A worker perched on its edge eating from a Pret A Manger bag, listening to a walkman.

GR had stopped talking to concentrate. Now she picked up again: '. . . then there'll be a revolution.'

The shadows of office buildings blotted them out.

'A revolution,' said Sami politely, glancing again at Tom's rigid neck, his tight-packed scalp. 'I thought revolutions were old-fashioned.'

'Marx is a lot more relevant now than he was in 1917. You know when Marx said the conditions would be right for revolution?'

'No. When?'

'Only when the entire world is connected up to the same economic system. That's when. One global system. Sound familiar?'

'I suppose it does.'

'Know what Marx said capitalism would inevitably lead to?'

'Revolution?'

'Apart from that.'

'No. What?'

'He said it would inevitably lead to the commodification of two things. Of nature and the human soul.' She pronounced each carefully. 'Nature, and the human soul.'

'Yes,' said Sami.

'See any signs of that around you?'

He saw her nodding in the mirror, smilingly serious. There was a madman on the pavement. Sami couldn't see his face, but could tell the madness from the ardour of his arms. A pigeon lit choking on the bonnet of the black cab to Sami's right, then swam into the air again. The city was coughing at him.

'Could we stop somewhere to get water? When it's convenient.'

GR reached under her seat without losing grip on the wheel. She handed back a leather bottle. A muscular arm where it emerged from the camouflage. Was she Tom's lover?

'It's filtered,' she said.

Not a bottle but a water sack. Sami liked that. He felt like a Phoenician swigging at it, or some other kind of ancient Semite. But then he understood the thought to be Mustafa-inspired, and allowed it to die.

'Filtered at a home base. That one's not a commodity.'

Sami drank and drank, wondering what a home base was.

'So, yeah, the revolution will come,' GR continued. 'It's inevitable. There are ups and downs, sure. Things'll get worse before they get better. But they will get better. Radically better.'

In the mirror Sami watched her eyes, flecked with orange, shining with quiet rapture. Somewhat less than nine-tenths of her attention on the road.

'Evolution is a proven scientific mechanism. Life develops to higher stages. In the present situation, revolution is the only way to break through upwards. Evolution is progress, and progress must happen.'

Sami took the water sack from his lips, held it on his lap, panting.

'Do you believe in progress?' he managed.

'Progress is inevitable. Otherwise there's no meaning to the human experience. But Tom Field and I disagree about this.'

She called him Tom Field. Both first name and last, like a code.

Sami watched Tom's unyielding ears and the stubborn stalks of hair. Save the internal agitations hinted at on the surface, it could have been sculpture. A backward bust. A work entitled: Anger Enwrapped.

'Tom,' Sami pleaded, 'I'm sorry, all right? I've learnt a lesson. It's been a learning experience.'

The Tom Field face whipped round like a sheet of metal in a storm.

'I hope it was worth it,' he said, with energy.

'Yes,' reflected Sami. 'Yes, it was.' He paused for longer than was relevant. 'I learnt that I am flesh and blood. We, I mean, are flesh and blood. We're made of matter, no more nor less.'

GR raised her forehead in satisfaction. These were necessary evolutionary stages: from woolly spirit to materialism, thence to dialectics and revolutionary action. Tom, however, squirmed impatiently.

'Actually, no,' he said. 'We aren't matter. We channel matter. Matter irrigates us.'

Sami, blissful because Tom was talking to him now, asked, 'What do you mean?'

'I mean we consume and excrete matter, we take it in and break it down. But matter isn't us. Matter seems to become us for a while, but it's always in flux. No cell in your body is the same cell as when you were a boy. On a smaller level, the particles that make you are always flashing in and out of existence. You aren't matter, you organize it. You're an organizing principle. The flesh and blood is produced by you, a temporary pattern you've made. It isn't you.'

Sami understood Tom's words a little differently, through his own filter. I am the by-product of a body, he thought. I am a changing breath, a transient unity of synapse flow. He heard a ringing in his head, caused by estrangement. Such knowledge resists comprehension. Does an ant also fail to understand that it is an ant?

He returned to simpler matters.

'Anyway, Tom, I'm sorry. I was in a bad way. I'd been up all night. I was coked up, drunk, stoned. I was going through a crisis. I'm sorry. I didn't think.'

'I know that,' said Tom. 'I know it. I'm making allowances for your circumstances. Wouldn't have come for you otherwise.'

'What circumstances? Did Schimmer tell you?'

'Yes, Dr Schimmer called. Your wife was looking for you.'

'My wife? Why? I didn't think Schimmer would call around to announce it. Didn't think it was that important.'

Tom wrinkled his eyes.

'He wasn't announcing. He was trying to find you, on your wife's behalf.'

'So he called her? Because I've given up the doctorate? She wants me to anyway.'

'You've given up your doctorate?'

'What else are we talking about?'

Now Tom's eyes opened wide.

'We're talking, Sami, about your father-in-law's death.'

GR steered towards the inevitable. Two cycle couriers sped past meanwhile, metallic and aerodynamically sculpted, adapted to their medium by wave-shaped helmets and snarling teeth. A woman in a suit waved across the road, shouting something silent through the traffic. Pollutants rose into the cooking sky. A shaft of light pierced the window next to Sami. He bowed his head into it.

'I'm sorry, Sami,' said Tom. 'I presumed you knew.'

'No, I didn't.' But there had been that message from Ammar on his mobile, in the pub among the Freemasons, the message he'd ignored. He flattened his palms on his groin and found that his mobile too was gone. Another loss.

'Yes, yes, I knew. I did really.'

Tom with forearm on the ledge of the seat, breath surging through his nostrils, watched Sami. In contemporary English there are no formulas for this kind of thing.

Sami raised his head.

'You'd better take me home.'

'That's where we're taking you. Remind me of the address.'

Sami gave it. After that there was no conversation, except for enquiries concerning the least clogged route. Sami, eyes down, touched his thumbs together, experiencing not so much butterflies in the stomach as a raging holy dread as to what he would find at home.

Marwan was dead, that was another father lost. But worse, Sami by his absence and betrayal had abdicated all pretence to husbandhood. So how did that feel? Not too unpleasant. As ever, the sense of drama lightened things for him. Bad news is always good news so long as it's dramatically bad. So long as there's otherness, newness, difference. Then everything can be borne.

That was the attraction of intoxicants for him, the pulse-stopping drama of difference they thrust him into. To be different from himself. For this second to be different to the last. For nothing to be settled or normal or real. He was aware of the possibility that his need for difference arose from misunderstanding what was real, or from a partial understanding, from a blindness. Perhaps reality seen properly would not be so dull.

Relying, for now in any case, on old habits, familiar drugs, he found solace in change. He didn't bother preparing a defence with which to meet Muntaha, but sat quiet in the back seat as the car prowled West London, sat and felt a new leaf being turned over, enjoyed the cooling breeze as it flopped heavily, greenly down.

His street. Their home. Sami exited the car. His legs shook. How long since he'd eaten? He approached his own unwelcoming front door as wobbly as a space traveller unaccustomed to local gravity. Took big careful steps across the pavement.

Tom wished him luck. Sami thanked him, and apologized again.

'Nice to meet you, Sami.' GR seen in patches, winking through the window behind Tom. 'I'll be in touch, when I've found some revolutionary action for you.'

He let himself in.

She was in the kitchen, wearing a nightdress. He heard her stand up and walk towards him. There was a kind of awful peace about her and, at first, a forgiving warmth. Her face was shrunken, making her eyes seem even bigger than usual, and blacker. An impressive vortex of rings surrounded them, which made Sami think of a near-death experience – darkness tunnelling in towards pricks of redeeming light – light enlivened, as she studied him, by developing horror.

'You're bitten,' she said. 'You've been having sex with someone.'

Sami mumbled, 'No, no,' fingering his throat. He hadn't yet had the luxury of a mirror view of himself. 'No,' he mumbled, 'no, no . . .' Not denying the accusation, just winning time. He spread his fingers, felt cool air between them. We have webbing there, remnants of webbing between each digit, because we have evolved from fish. We've gained nails, thumbs and fur, in return for gills, fins and scales.

'Either you've been fighting or having sex. And you only fight with me. Look at me. Have you betrayed me?'

He looked at her.

'Have you been out fucking someone?' The bowstring of her voice taut, the volume rising with each word.

Sami stood before her conscious of his size. Just irrigating liquid in flux, perhaps, but it felt solid to him, felt like bulk.

'Yes,' he said. 'Yes.'

'On the day of my father's death.' Her olive-oil voice distorted by an act of terrible vandalism, and still rising. The string of a lute pulled so far back from the body of the instrument that it has to break.

'Yes. I didn't know about that. I mean, I only knew partially.'

Muntaha watched him as if waiting for an answer, her eyes roaming about his face, which he knew to be just the same unresponsive face as usual, a face which doesn't give answers. He wanted to tell her so: 'It's only my face, the same one as before, there isn't any reason to it.' It took a long time for her to realize this. Then she cast her eyes down, and relaxed. The air whistled out of her. She returned to the kitchen.

He watched her move away. With her nightdress crumpled to her, her white arms sombre as moonlight, he glimpsed Muntaha as an old woman. There's a future he was excluded from, a loss not yet lived but already determined. But he didn't mourn. Newness was still exciting him. The stripping away of what he'd had whet his appetite for more denudation. A sense of anticipation, as if he was about to step into the steam of an old city hammam. About to get clean.

He climbed the stairs. Collected his toothbrush, laid out some clothes on the bed. Smelled the tranquillity of her there but resisted the urge to push his nose into the sheets. By his side of the bed were the wooden prayer beads he'd brought back from Syria for Marwan but had forgotten to give to him. He glanced from the window on to mud and wall, and glimpsed then the unvarnished truth: that he had betrayed everybody, in various ways. Mustafa. Marwan. His mother, of course. Now Muntaha. Not just now, but for a decade. He'd let down Mustafa by failing as an academic, even as an atheist. For Marwan, the betrayal was not being a Muslim, or a father. For his mother, he was not a son. For his wife, not a man. The pattern of his relations with the world was to betray its trust. Everybody's trust. Here the vision of the betrayed expanded to include Tom, whose name he'd given to the authorities, and Schimmer, whose efforts had been wasted, and Ammar, who he hadn't guided rightly, and Bikini Girl, for something obscure, and deeper into obscurity, his broken uncle Faris, in Damascus. Why was Sami responsible for that? The question posed itself in bright clarity, and Sami at once forgot it. Forgetful Sami. Leaving everything unpacked, he descended.

She was standing in the kitchen entrance, arms folded above her breasts. It looked to him that she needed somebody to give her a hug. He, of course, was not that somebody.

'Would you say you've been a good husband to me?' she asked, pouting slightly, brow knitted. Trying to work things out.

'Well, no,' Sami admitted. 'No, I wouldn't.'

There was a motionless interlude during which he absorbed his wife's appearance. Her dry dark lips reminding him of more intimate lips, if intimacy is in any way gradable once you've arrived at lips. No lips he'd wish to moisten more than these ones decorating her feeling face. Her tired skin taking the blows of death and loss. The night-time waterfall of her hair. Her sharp, intellectual angles. This was territory that he had denied himself. Pleasures he was exiled from. He took a last deep inhalation to keep with him. The sound of his breath stirred her.

'You'd better leave,' she said in a reasonable tone. 'I can't look at you now. You'd better go and sort yourself out. And me too, I'd better sort myself out.'

Lost land dwindling behind barbed wire. Sami, carried away by cattle truck, saw his home shrink to nothing. The Palestinians took housekeys. Sami's souvenir – her air, her odour – escaped slowly from his lungs.

'I'm sorry, Muntaha.'

'Don't bother with that,' she said. 'There's no point.'

He turned into his study. What did he need to take? What was essential? He regarded his shelves. The prefixed and affixed academic warblings, the expensive isms which he'd previously taken as sacred text – impossible to apply, impossible to fully understand, but of higher-order value and thus to be grappled with – these were now abruptly irrelevant. A necrotic crust expanded rapidly from books to pictures to the Mustafa relics in the desk drawer. Unworthiness colonizing each cranny of the room, inch by inch. What an evil, secularizing spirit his eye contained. As he cast his gaze about, divinity vacated his holy objects. Spreading, corrupting atheism was in his eye, the real thing, not the rhetoric of it. The real, deadly, God-killing certainty of atheism. Even the furniture had the dust of the grave on it. His upholstered Moroccan chair. The camel stool. He didn't need any of it.

He was going to walk away, but sat down instead on his old red sofa. From its fibres and springs rose memories of the strategic retreats he'd made here, the staged absences in mid-fight, usually to smoke spliffs and count time on the clock rather than to fume. All quite calculated. But it hadn't worked. He'd never won. She had scared him, not the other way round. How much like his mother she'd seemed during those arguments – wallfaced and heartless – he could die for all she cared. But in retrospect he questioned this version of her, the unlistening stubbornness. Was that the way she really was? Unbelief galloped backwards to infect his previous concepts. Strangely now, the hijab didn't bother him. He flashed a picture of her wearing it on to his inner screen. No, that was fine. Now that he'd renounced ownership, she could do what she liked. He even admired her for it.

Sami surveyed his domain once more as he stood up. It occurred to him that they'd never had a sitting room. Well, it would be good for her that he was going. She'd be able to use the space.

He closed the brown door behind him. Upstairs he had a very brief shower, covering his penis as guiltily as a thief in case he was disturbed. Then he dressed, and packed his clothes in a bag. The same overnight bag he'd arrived with and lied about.

As he stepped down the stairs, as they creaked against his weight, a miasmic updraught of novelty rose through his nostrils and earholes and into his sugar-parched brain, sparking momentary departure-related hallucinations. Of heroic Sami Traifi clicked into a rocket's cockpit. His mission: to slip into the emptiness between the stars. With toes folding from the ball of one foot, the next foot swinging forward and down, he chuckled at himself. Layers of transparent plastic fixed between him and his loved ones (blonde American wife flutters a handkerchief, freckled sons nod bravely goodbye). Hitting the foot of the stairs, not turning his head left to see her in the kitchen, nor right to the study – and fires roaring beneath him. Yellow ash clouds blooming, a countdown, and then with a whoosh and distant applause he is propelled through blue into green and black, up into the bleak insubstantiality of space, up up up through it, sinking backwards, drowning upwards, nothing holding him, nothing to get a grip on, losing the past and his natural habitat, losing context, losing any stable definition of himself.

'Bye,' he called.

There was no response.

21

It Soon Come

Have you forgotten that once we were brought here we were robbed of
our names, robbed of our language. We lost our religion, our culture,
our God. And many of us, by the way we act, we even lost our minds.

Khalid Abdul Muhammad sampled, and then with a 'Here it is:
Bammm!' Chuck D in black, the serious, unstoppable, pile-driving
voice, slamming the words home with a wheeling and battling arm.
Pure anger. Skipping and hopping past him, the funny man Flavor
Flav, in white, floppy at the waist, pulling faces to show off his gold
incisors. Pointing to the swinging clock hung from his neck, big
and round enough to hide his chest. Calling once again, 'Gotta let
dem know what time it is, boyyeeee.' Nothing but entertainment.
The backdrop to both: the Security of the First World patrolling
the stage in light camouflage and red berets, doing a tiny-step
shuffle and a military scowl. And at the sides of the stage, a big, big
sound system. The speakers Carnival sized, but this was inside, the
noise walled in and echoing upon itself.

Sami was remembering this as he found his way to his
(still, officially) brother-in-law's underground mosque. He'd called
Ammar the day before on his new bottom-of-the-range mobile
phone to do the necessary condoling and apologizing. Ammar had
been understanding. Don't worry about it, brother, he'd said, and
then he'd invited Sami to visit the mosque. Sami had guilt to
appease, and nothing else to occupy his time, and even mosques
didn't frighten him since he'd stopped believing in Mustafa's ghost.
So here he was, feeling unwrapped and chilly, descending a blustery
western hill.

But back to the remembered concert hall. It was hot in there and wild, the screams and the whistles, the raised fists. The crowd swell moved you, mainly male, mainly black. Just standing still you were moving. Your body one cell of a bigger body. A London Leviathan stretching itself out to touch beyond London, and being touched right now by New York.

By Public Enemy. PE in full effect, at the Electric Ballroom, Camden, late 1991. A younger, still innocently arrogant Sami bounced and whooped, and beside him, occasionally glancing at him with eyes of love and admiration, the boy Ammar. Both lives were looking up: Sami at the start of his Muntaha years, just beginning his doctorate, and Ammar on the cusp of purposeful (hip hop-oriented) adulthood, stepping forward into the big-beat urban night with his newfound big brother. Both felt the tickle of roots going down, of futures flowering, and in this heaving, sweating place that tickling was indistinguishable from the abdominal tickles the music made: the muscular scratching at the turntables, the sirens, the demented saxophones. The political frisson of the sound.

It was sounds for the barricades, but in its layers and contradictions more complex than the Trotskyist or Green agitprop you could hear beyond the Ballroom, out there in the vegetable market or outside the tube of this fairly white, fairly straightforward inner suburb. PE's brain-busting militancy was wrapped around a warm funkiness – something very sexy and very soft. It suited Ammar down to the ground (as Flav put it, it rocked his boots to da roots). It gave him access to his inner sweetness, his sensuality, and then led him to cut it off again with masochistic violence. Sweetness and violence. Violence and sweetness, spinning together, arm in arm. Their mutual embrace looked like home to Ammar. Because London at the end of the millennium was neither a time nor a place for just dancing, not only, not with slavery only half ended, and corporate empires ruling half the world, and your lost country half forgotten, and the people there half starving, and pictures of them on the TV that you only half recognize. Maybe half of you could dance, touch girls, smoke weed, but the other half must do something more darkly energetic.

He turned to Sami with an eager-beaver snout and hands funnelled around his mouth, shouting. Sami couldn't hear until the hands bumped into his ear, the lips squashed against his earlobe and jaw. Then he picked up the enthusiasm.

'It's good being here, innit. I mean in London. We get to see all this, yeah?'

There was that in Ammar too, Muntaha's capacity for unalloyed happiness.

'It's good. It's good,' Sami gestured in reply.

Spotlight on Chuck D. He was telling the crowd about a game slavemasters used to play with pregnant black women. The thud and crash of the bass behind his baritone. The woman, he said, would be tied up naked, and the whites would place bets on the sex of the fetus. To settle it, the white men cut the baby out of her. Cutting her from breast to vagina, settling their bet in her black blood.

The happily furious crowd booed and wailed.

'Four hundred years!' Chuck declaimed.

The anger and the heat intensified.

'Four hundred years of Jack's bullshit!'

Screaming. Coordinated grunting.

'What we gonna do about it?' asked Chuck, very rhetorically indeed.

And as an answer, the spotlight on him faded, replaced by two beams shone on to the speakers at the extremes of the stage, and a member of the Security of the First World standing on each speaker, and in their upraised arms, Uzi sub-machine guns. Fake Uzis, but the point was made. The crowd leapt and roared approval. Ammar leapt and roared approval, almost weeping with excitement. Sami, however, raised his shoulders and looked towards his feet, which he couldn't see for movement and shadows. Ammar grabbed at his arms, but Sami held them to his sides.

'Join in!' screeched Ammar. 'Fight the power!'

No, signalled Sami. And Ammar asked with his face, why not? And Sami, trying to shrink from the public noise, trying to detach from the common body, attached his lips to Ammar's ear.

'It's a black thing,' he said. 'It's a race thing.'

They moved heads so Ammar could reply.

'Don't worry about it. It's our people. We're black.'

Ammar held up a rigid finger as if he was about to offer some proof. He turned to a neighbouring Negro. Sami changed position to lipread.

'Yo, brother,' asked Ammar, waving a hand back at Sami. 'Are we black?'

Sami remembering, coming to the foot of the hill. On his way to Ammar's mosque. Feeling naked.

A gym fanatic of a sun flexed rays towards the city. Tom's speech on the changeability of matter had lingered with Sami. He was all flux. And the sun was all flux – all explosive transience – hot, and bright. Infecting the atmosphere. In climatic terms this was the calm before the storm. It promised flood, fire, and plagues of insects. But for now the city seemed healthier than he'd seen it in a long while, as if its illnesses had been burnt away – healthy in comparison, he supposed, to himself. It would be wrong to describe Sami as less healthy than before (he hadn't been drunk or spliffed since his arrest on Tower Bridge), but he had become more aware of his health, or lack of it. So we can say that his picture of himself was less healthy than before. In present circumstances, he trusted neither the seeming health of the city nor his own strength.

These streets he walked through, strung out around different varieties of chickenshack, undertakers and keycutters, were embalmed by wind and neutered pollen, and by glancing light, producing the healthful sheen in which he had minimal confidence.

He remembered for a flowing moment the plumber, vaguely a family friend, who'd lived down the road of his childhood home, the plumber who'd kept him and his mother up to date with the progress of a brain tumour. He remembered the decay of this man into something less than plumber, and then his deceptive recovery. They'd visited him at home twice. On the second visit the plumber could speak again, drink without dribbling, and smile. He looked forward to returning to work. For the half-hour of the visit it seemed that the cancer was decaying and the plumber gaining health. But a week later the plumber was dead. Mustafa had used the episode to teach an anti-superstition lesson, which Sami remembered grimly. And then the memory was gone, blastomaed into the afternoon, leaving Sami with the glassy heat, the numbing haze.

He was living in student accommodation near Euston. In a concrete and plastic block, with undergraduates above and below him and on either side. Dr Schimmer, pulling strings like an Arab, had found the room. Sami could stay there until late September. He paid a student's token rent.

He'd arranged further credit with his bank: the bank believed in him even if he didn't. And he'd taken a tour of a Kilburn job centre. (He'd been walking in Kilburn when resolution swayed him.) Yes, the economy was booming, and there was a range of work available. Like labouring (but he didn't own hard-top boots, and didn't trust his strength); machine operating (he didn't have the necessary qualifications); secretarial work (he couldn't see it). There was one job advertised he thought he'd be able to do right away: public convenience cleaner's assistant. He'd called to arrange an interview, but they said he was overqualified. What was his niche? he wondered. What lay between holding a bucket and driving forklift trucks? These were questions he'd never had to ask himself before. Anyway, he was trying. His new life had just begun. He was doing his best.

This morning he'd gone home. He knew Muntaha was at work, but he didn't let himself in. He just looked at the front for a few minutes, and the neighbouring fronts, and the black street surface. Then he'd walked to the barber's.

Harry the Barber was reading the sports pages when Sami arrived. Too early in the day for rum or company. Some dub reggae playing on a cassette deck. Trumpets, drums, blues guitar.

'Sami! What can I do you for?' asked Harry, rising.

'Haircut, please, Harry.'

'Yes indeed.' Harry ushered him into the blue chair and cracked a barber's bib. 'You looking like the seventies.' Tying it motherly around Sami's neck. 'Like a disco king. You building up to an afro there.'

Harry fitted a pair of scissors to his hand and limbered up, making 'chop chop' sounds to the rhythm of the dub.

'Why don't you just use the machine this time,' said Sami.

'You want it short?'

'Short and simple.'

'What about your bald bit?' Harry pointed to his own shiny top and chuckled indulgently. He knew his customers' issues.

'I suppose it's time to come to terms with that.'

'You're the boss.'

Harry was a short man. He stood and worked, his head not far above Sami's, wielding the relentless machine. Sami's curls came sprinkling downwards. The twists and turns of his previous vanity.

It was the dub poet Linton Kwesi Johnson playing. An extended version of 'Time Come'.

> read di vialence inna wi eye;
> we goin smash di sky wid wi bad bad blood

'And a shave, I think,' said Harry.

Sami considered the hours and days he must have spent scraping at his face to make it smooth and secular. Sculpting concepts, carving modernity on to his cheeks and chin. As if facial hair signified evils beyond itself.

Shaving had been one of his obsessions. He didn't see the point of worrying any more.

'No thanks.'

'Well then.'

> look out! look out! look out!
> but it too late now: I did warn yu

'And you'll be wanting some green?' asked Harry.

'No thanks.'

'No thanks?'

'Not this time.'

'That's a change.'

Seeing his face in the mirror made him uncomfortable. He closed his eyes and willed himself towards a pampered slumber.

> now yu si fire burning in mi eye,
> feel vialence, vialence
> burstin outta mi

'New leaf turning?'

'I suppose so.'

Barbers were one of the good things in Syria. Most men visited every week, for more than a mere haircut. The barber would do a lot. By tapping a flaming wax taper against your ears he'd burn the hair, more plant than human, that grew inside. He'd shape the left and the right of your beard, if you had a beard, in perfect parallel. (Sami, of course, hadn't had a beard. He hadn't been that sort of person. But he'd observed it done.) The barber would pull the skin taut to shave around your lips, he'd snip your wiry nostril hair, he'd clip your Arab eyebrows. He'd massage perfume into forehead and neck, and pause while you sipped the tea he provided. Throughout the process he'd complain about business and tell you coded political jokes. Your only job was to luxuriate in such excessive service, to trust the luxury. To stretch your throat towards his open razor. It was like giving yourself to the sea in the dark. Like putting yourself in God's safekeeping.

But not just yet. Sami wasn't ready.

Impatient to continue about its business, Sami's head rejected the chair's specialized support. Harry pushed it gently back, and worked the machine to the music. 'Time Come' was recorded on a loop. It came round again with steady inevitability, coming with its deep base shuffle.

> It soon come
> It soon come
> Look out! look out! look out!

'More tribulation in the Middle East, I see,' remarked Harry, still working.

Tribulation indeed. Sami checked it each morning in the residence's internet café. Yesterday morning: helicopters rocketing police stations in Gaza, six Fatah activists killed in the West Bank, fighting in the Aqsa mosque compound. Today: Jamal Mansour from Hamas killed, with seven others, in a helicopter raid in Nablus. Dead children stiff in the rubble. Pictures of living children bearing stones, fighting for Palestine with chunks of Palestine. Untrained and ragged gunmen. Pictures of the hi-tech enemy: their metal insects spitting fire. Their tanks tearing up the olive groves. And every day photos of funerals. Processions of flag-wrapped corpses, with their faces uncovered – the tradition for martyrs – tossed by waves of angry mourners.

> Look out! look out! look out!

It made him think of the brother-in-law whose mosque he had to find this afternoon. The anger of the Intifada youths, and their frailty – it made him think of Ammar. In 1991, when Ammar was a proper youth.

The second time Sami met Muntaha was the first time he saw her brother. She'd called him for long enough to suggest a meeting at a café in Queensway, and Sami got there early to prepare for her. He found a section of wall with his back. He pressed against the alternative culture advertising, and swivelled slowly on the balls of his feet, trying to scan the crowd. The busy and the exiled swaying past. He was above the level of bobbing heads, dreadlocks, hats, hijabs. He tried to remember the swing of her hair. He couldn't make her out.

Then she was beside him, smiling as if at a joke. Sami opened his mouth to say what he'd planned to say, but next to her was a scrawny teenager, thin to the point of emaciation inside his leather jacket. A Public Enemy target was printed on his T-shirt.

'Hello, Sami,' Muntaha said. 'This is my brother, Ammar.'

'All right,' nodded Ammar.

'Yeah, how you doing?' Sami tuned his delivery to streetspeak, and extended a hand to be shaken. It was met by a clenched fist. Sami realized too late, and they ended up somewhere between a slap and a fumble, embarrassed.

'Ea-sy,' breathed Ammar, the first syllable like he'd been slapped on the back, the second radically unstressed. He rolled his thin head on the thinner pivot of his neck, making a great show of sizing Sami up, bunching his lips tight closed, narrowing his eyelids.

Has she tasked him with taking my measure? Sami asked himself. A teenager whose head looks like it's been squeezed in a vice, to take my measure? He looked straight at the boy and spoke in Arabic: 'Is everything all right?'

Ammar's attitude broke. 'Yeah, yeah, all right,' he replied in English. 'Do you want to go in?' He smiled weakly at Muntaha and Sami. They smiled back, like a couple.

Inside they huddled on stools, three points to a triangle, knees touching.

'I see you like Public Enemy.' Sami pointing at Ammar's chest.

'Yeah man,' said Ammar through falafel. Oil crawling along his sharp chin. 'I give them maximum respect.'

'Public Enemy,' began Sami. He was conscious of Muntaha's lips. Red and full and turned up at the edges, as lips are drawn in comic books. He was conscious of her silence too, and couldn't tell what it meant. As inscrutable as a Sumerian statue, he thought. Upright, wide-eyed, but for what? Intent on the conversation? Judging him? In awe?

'Public Enemy,' said Sami, 'have taken music to a new level. It isn't even music any more, which I mean as a compliment. It's the news, it's politics, it's preaching. And also the roar of the crowd, and the noise of the metropolis.'

Ammar was leaning so far forward their noses nearly touched. But the sister? Sami worked on not looking at her.

'What they do is layer different sounds. TV adverts, traffic, the police. Allusions to Farrakhan and Malcolm X. Old soul music spliced up and given new meaning. It's very postmodern.'

'Wicked!' ejaculated Ammar. Muntaha, meanwhile, had finished her shawarma sandwich. She folded the grease paper into a tight, neat square.

'A PE track,' Sami went on, 'is not a song. Not only that. It's a cacophony of voices in competition. It's the media attacking the media. It's a history lesson. It's both tribute to and parody of the black music tradition.'

'Yeah man,' said Ammar. And after a pause, 'Word!' Sami wondered if he was reaching the sister through the brother. Did she see his future as he saw it, as lecturer, speechmaker, as a man who is listened to? He saw the blackness of her hair, and worked on avoiding her face. Just chatting casually, to the brother, that's all he was doing.

'What they do is take the language of the street and make it allegory, symbolism. It's the most apt sound for the end of the millennium. It's end of the world stuff, global revolution stuff. It's nothing less than apocalyptic.'

'Wicked, man, wicked!' squeaked Ammar, jigging with great frequency on his stool like a praying Jew or a Third World child learning the Qur'an, like a convulsive from any culture.

'Sami's going to do a PhD,' Muntaha explained.

What had she meant by that? What had he looked like to her? He looked to himself, in retrospect, like a hollow character. If you rapped your knuckles on him he'd feel like tin, and make a hollow metal clang. What had he meant by speechmaking? He was a face painted on a balloon, his brain a bubble of roiling air. He was too lively, too self-staged, to be true. If that was how he'd really been. Was his picture of himself accurate at all? He wondered how the film played in Muntaha's head.

It was a month or two after that meeting that he took Ammar to the PE concert. They were firm friends. At home Ammar had to listen to his music on headphones, to avoid his father's frown, so he used to come round to Sami's flat to blast it. Flicking the Miles Davis or Mingus or Coltrane cassettes with disdainful thumb from the deck, or discs from the turntable (this is back in the day), using *A Love Supreme* as a frisbee: 'Now get this bollocks away from me! Listen to this one mash yu head!'

He also picked Sami up in a variety of cars, driving licenceless at first, to circle the city with windows unwound. Showcasing the vehicle's booming system by playing PE's sonic collage, and eery Schoolly D decadence, and NWA ('Fuck da Police'), and BDP's more positive rhymes. There was also Naughty by Nature, Big Daddy Kane, Stetsasonic. As time went by (by which time driving had become his profession) Ammar expanded to Brand Nubian, Snoop, the Wu-Tang.

It all felt like dangerous fun with your arm hanging loose against the car's exterior, nodding your brow to the beat but keeping your expression disengaged. The thrill of being driven. In those days Sami still wore a kuffiyeh. Ammar wore wraparound shades, especially at night. You'd expect difficult moments, what with Ammar half standing at certain climaxes, one hand on the wheel and the other raised out the window in fist salute or flagging at spectators, mouthing lines like:

> if yo fucks wit us
> we gots to fuck yo up
> nigga . . .

But there never was any difficulty, because they were moving, and because it was a private city, one of the most spread-out and low-rise in the world, with enough space for all manner of private madness.

Ammar stabbed his speech with 'jew na wat ameen' and 'jew na wat am sayin'. His accent slid from Jamaican (Shabba Ranks, Cutty Ranks, the general badboy dancehall phenomenon), through New York (PE, Schoolly D), to LA street drawl (Ice T, Snoop). He could reference them all in a sentence. His preferred exclamation was 'cha!' He expressed comprehension with a long deep 'seen!' He called his sister 'man' and sometimes 'brother'. Sami, being male, he addressed as 'bro', as in, 'Yo, bro! Whassup?' His multicoloured associates were 'G' or 'Negro' to their faces, and in the third person, his 'associates', his 'crew', or his 'brothers in arms'. For Panther-stylee speechmaking he got articulate, clipped and resonant in a contemporary Black London tone. When asked for commentary on a film or a piece of music he said things like, 'I question its blackness.' He quoted PE a lot in general conversation. If Sami laughed at his Farrakhan references, he rapped: 'Don't tell me that you understand / Until you hear the man.' Or: 'Sami treat me like Col-trane / In-sane!'

A couple of years on, and Sami stopped paying so much attention. He was fruitlessly busy in academia, and then travelling. But bumping into Ammar after weeks or months of library-bound absence he noted the stages of his transformation. The adolescent became a sort of man, which was advertised through his clothing. He matched his sunglasses with unmixed plain colours (mostly black), and shiny shoes, and a straight-line mouth. He had his hair cut close and disciplined. He no longer gestured provocatively from car windows, emanating now a harsh sobriety which wouldn't allow it. For those in the know, he was mimicking the Nation of Islam lifestyle, except when it came to spliffs. Then he was much more Five Percenter: 'Given that the black man's God, we all divine. We make our own commandments. So chill, bro. Skin up and pass the dutchie.'

Only the tip of Ammar's tongue was in his cheek. He was reading pamphlets about how the mad scientist Yaqoob invented the white devil race by genetic experiment. There were bits of Islam and bits of Christianity cut up and sampled and redefined in the mix – very hip hop.

'See, it's written in the Qur'an, yeah? When Yaqoob creates the whites, yeah, the other divine black elders, they saying, wat yu doin man? That one gonna spread corruption and shed blood. And he say, "I know what you know not." That's Qur'an, second sura.'

'That's the angels asking God what He's doing creating man. It's got nothing to do with whites and blacks.'

'Yeah, in your forged version.'

Sami chuckled at him. If Ammar wanted to mangle Islamic text into chunks of absurdist rap, he could be Sami's guest.

Ammar took to breaking down everyday language into esoteric particles to reveal hidden political significance. This was a technique learnt from the Five Percenters, so prominent in the rap milieu. Otherwise known as the Nation of Gods and Earths, they'd split with the Nation of Islam on the logical grounds that the returned God of the blacks, Master Fard Muhammad, who taught that the time had come for the black man to regain his divine place in this world, time come therefore for the final race war and defeat of the devil – this Master Fard could not be God because he was in fact white. Most probably a Syrian Druze.

'They call it library,' Ammar would say when Sami told him where he'd been hiding. 'But lies buried is what it is for the open-eyed.' Or, 'Television? That's tell a lie vision. Don't believe a word of it!'

Sami laughed. 'Shit, a dictionary of etymology would sort that out for you.'

'Don't complicate things, bro. Keep it simple. Ya cyaan run no revolution if yu na keep it simple.'

Ammar seemed to Sami very much like the immigrant that he was. If he understood the social codes of the place better he wouldn't make himself so ridiculous. And that was also why Sami went easy on Ammar's accent issues. He'd seen other cases of the same syndrome. A Pakistani friend at the university, for instance, who'd arrived with an Oxbridge accent, and then met a girl with a Mancunian twang and switched overnight, apparently without being aware of it, to her flat vowels and clogged-up consonants. That's the adaptive strength of the stranger. A strength in most of its manifestations. If you're not stuck hard in your habits you easily pick up new ones.

But the lunacy went a little too far. Sami feared that Ammar would be hurt. He tried to explain.

'We can call ourselves black politically speaking, in that we're not white, and for solidarity, yeah, agreed. But ethnically, racially, I don't think so. I mean look at my skin. It's a lot more white than black. The Five Percenters is an ethnic movement. They're blacks, meaning of African origin. They don't much like whites. Believe me, you wouldn't fit.'

'It's a movement for the original black Asiatic man.' Ammar waved the argument off. 'I'm an Arab, guy. You don't get no more Afro-Asiatic than me.'

There was truth in this, but useless truth, because the black nationalist definition of Asiatic was a religious mythical definition. It was like the Rastafarians talking about Zion and the tribe of Judah. It didn't mean they had common cause with the denizens of Golders Green.

'Keep it simple,' Ammar said, in speechmaking mode. 'We're black. We need to know who we are, and then we need to stand tall.'

Simplicity. A dangerous refuge.

'It's about power, bro. It's about making knowledge the servant of power.' He illustrated this with a rare reference to Marwan: 'I mean, look at my father. Why he so hunched up, man? Why he so, like, fuckin' defeated and shit? Reads his books and goes to the mosque, but how's that ever going to give him any more power? He needs to know who the devil is, and who his allies are.'

To Sami, black nationalism smelled too much of blood and semen. And not his. It felt too much like rigid Black manhood. In its American context it was attached to claiming some land on which to establish a black state. Like Zionism, it was a perverse response to oppression. But he wasn't going to get angry about it. The Five Percenters had no power to realize their ideas, which decontextualized in England meant very little anyway. In practice, it was no more than sexy identity-assertion, and Sami of the kuffiyeh and Intifada T-shirt could understand that well enough. Strange that Ammar wanted to be a black rather than Arab nationalist, but not that strange. Ammar's Arab nationalist option had been shut down in his distant boyhood when people calling themselves Arabists shattered the al-Haj family. History had squashed the possibility of Arabism. Moreover, there was no hardcore Arabist rap.

So Sami, usually so intolerant of any shabby mysticism but his own, allowed Ammar's rants. They didn't trigger any of his taboos. They weren't religion, at least not the religion he'd been trained to despise.

He also empathized with Ammar's view of Marwan. It reminded Sami of his own childhood perspective on the Muslims. What the Muslims lacked was the power aphrodisiac. They lacked the superficial values of the street. There was nothing new or exciting about them. They didn't look good. He could only be ashamed of them.

Then there was envy. Sami envied his brother-in-law's capacity for self-definition. Another immigrant strength. When you're up-rooted you get to plant yourself in a new location. You have a kind of choice. And yes, you might choose shallow soil, if only it looks like the sun shines on it. How can you know how deep the soil is, anyway, until you grow roots?

Back to the future. Sami in 2001 was a fragile flower. Heavier, balder, and altogether less stable. He searched for Ammar's mosque with a warm breeze playing cold around his temples, his sense of nakedness heightened by the fact that curls no longer kissed his ears. He was like a man accustomed to a hat suddenly unhatted, like a muhajjiba woman stripped of her scarf. Feeling old but new, weary but nervily awake. 'Look out! Look out!' jumbled up in his brain with old-school hip hop, and flash memories of mildewed prayer halls.

He was in the right sunlit-grey street. The paper in his hand said number 7a. Number seven was a house with its curtains drawn. There was an unsigned peel-paint door beside it. This? Sami knocked.

Following a pause, it opened a suspicious crack's worth. Then it swung wide, and Ammar opened his arms, and his voice sang out. 'Na'eeman!' – referring to the haircut – the formula literally means comfort, tranquillity, softness. Sami was grateful for that old-country courtesy. Instead of returning the correct response, however, he started into what he'd come to say.

'Your father, ammu Marwan. I'm sorry . . . you know . . . allah yerhamu . . .' The religious phrases always stuck in his throat.

Ammar repeated it. Allah yerhamu. God have mercy on him. Then he turned and led Sami down a dark stairwell. Down into a long flat room hazed in artificial light. The neon echoed between bare plaster walls. There were curls of plaster and cracks on the ceiling. A smell of paint but no visible sign of it. Plastic mats imitating straw on the floor. A concrete floor. Hidden, windowless and unaesthetic, the room was an ideal location for Ammar's pared-down protestant faith. Six other men occupied the space, separated: two at prayer, three intensely whispering, and one cross-legged, bobbing over a text.

Ammar took Sami's hand again, intent on his eyes.

'Tell me. Something going on with you and Muntaha?'

'You know,' Sami mumbled. 'Some thinking time. I've stopped the doctorate. We'll see what happens. I need time to think at the moment. Get a job and so on.'

Ammar nodded. 'Learn to drive and there's a job waiting for you.'

'Well, thanks,' Sami said. 'But I don't know if I approve.'

'What?'

'Messing up the environment. Exhaust fumes. Global warming. Driving a car, you're contributing to that.'

Ammar's cheeks rose by force of habit to exclaim 'cha!' – but he transformed it to an emphatic 'masha'allah!' He was clearly as amused by Sami as Sami was by him. He tugged on Sami's hand.

'Come meet my brother Mujahid.'

Mujahid sat directly under one of the neon strips. Seeing them coming he closed his book quickly, stood up and smoothed down his clothes. He said, 'As-salaamu alaikum, brother.' An Irishman, by his accent. Greenish skin. A blood-red beard. A shalwar kameez.

Sami, in concert with Ammar, replied, 'Wa-alaikum as-salaam.'

They shook hands. Mujahid had fingers like spider's legs.

It seemed that the house upstairs was inhabited. They heard the scrape of shifting furniture, something being dropped. Ammar and Mujahid exchanged glances.

'We have trouble with the neighbours,' Ammar told Sami.

'Oh yeah?'

'They don't want us here.'

'They call us Pakis,' said Mujahid. 'They even call me Paki.'

'There've been incidents,' said Ammar.

Mujahid explained, 'Brothers have been punched. They spit on us from upstairs when we're coming in. They throw beer cans at us sometimes.'

'We haven't responded to it,' said Ammar.

Sami couldn't think of a useful comment. He searched for something. The book enclosed in Mujahid's hand was not the Qur'an.

'What are you reading, Mujahid?'

'*Teach yourself Arabic.*' Rolling a thin eyebrow between fingertips. 'Brother Ammar is giving me conversation lessons also. It is my knee-yeh, you see, to perform heej-rah to a pure land.'

I beg your pardon. Sami stared in bewilderment at this strange foreign gentleman.

'His "niyah", his intention,' Ammar translated, 'is to migrate to a Muslim country.'

Back before the millennium turned Ammar had actually gone to a Five Percenter meeting, and he had come back subdued. They are misguided, yes, he admitted, and said nothing more. But it was obvious that he'd reached a turning point. His accent calmed down immediately. His hip hop fixation waned. Farrakhan and Mr Yaqoob departed his conversation, and Malcolm X entered. Malcolm had worked out that the Nation of Islam's leadership was fraudulent. Disillusioned, he'd travelled to Mecca for Haj, where he performed the same rituals and ate from the same plate as white Muslims. 'The "white" attitude was removed from their minds by the religion of Islam,' Malcolm wrote. The story of Malcolm's conversion to orthodox Sunni Islam was a story that Ammar told again and again.

Now Ammar and Mujahid were describing the benefits of Muslim lands, tossing the ball of idealism between them. A sustained volley: hospitality, sexual morality, social responsibility, racial equality, honesty, piety, peace.

'Well, I don't know about that,' said Sami. 'You might be disappointed when you get there. I'm not an expert. I'm not . . . a conventional believer.' He was floundering. He knew that the converts (Ammar was surely a convert too, an ideologically displaced person, a changeling) were projecting their dreams on to countries they were ignorant of, but wasn't it his own habit to do the same? He was cramped by self-doubt. 'I mean, I don't suppose I'm the man to comment, but I expect Islam is something you find inside yourself rather than in any specific country.'

It sounded like a metal ball bounced on the upstairs floor. Mujahid's head flicked up nervously.

'But you don't get those people in Muslim countries,' he said. 'That's something.'

'But Sami's right,' said Ammar. 'It's all "dunya". The world is godless matter. It's all the realm of annihilation. Without Islam there's no meaning in it, not in the east and not in the west.'

The world means nothing. It was easy for Sami, in his new father-free state, to agree. The stars are merely rock and fire. Nations are dreams, or perhaps nightmares. None of it has any importance.

'That's right,' he said. 'I agree with you.'

'Brother, I tell you.' Ammar spoke with glinting eyes. 'It does me good to hear you speak like this.'

Then Ammar checked his watch and pointed at Mujahid. 'It's time,' he said. Mujahid turned his head and walked forward to where an arch had been pencilled on the wall. He cupped his palms around his ears and tunelessly called the believers to the Asr prayer.

They came at a frantic pace, springing athletically to their feet and into place. To quote Public Enemy, the posse got velocity. Ammar moved into imam position. The others lined behind. The white convert in Pakistani gear. The two subcontinentals dressed like Arabs, in white gellabiyas. The Arabs and the Somali (Sami guessed) in tracksuits, like Ammar. What they had in common was that their garments were all hoisted above the ankle. Only Ammar bucked the trend. In his case, a vestigial natty dress sense overruled prophetic tradition.

After a pause, Sami found himself going along. He joined the right end of the line. He had no opinions to prevent him from doing so. He'd renounced them.

He touched thumbs to ears and folded his hands on his chest. Each body was in the same position. He anticipated the coming movements, and his self subsided. But the prayer's calming discipline was offset by Ammar's military delivery: a long sura barked fast.

In any case, Sami hardly heard it. He had entered Ibrahim's world – the world of sacrifice. On his inner screen he saw glimmering images of himself with the knife at his throat. No, to be clear about it, with a razor slashing at his ears, and feet kicking at his testicles. Being whipped, tied by his feet to the ceiling. He kept his eyes resolutely open and focused on the earth-coloured plastic mat. And he kept on with the prayer despite his confusion, as if to do so was to win some sort of victory. Over Ibrahim. Practising Ibrahim's religion in order to defeat Ibrahim: what misty and knotted logic was this?

There was vibration like dub sound between his ears. Like the 'look out! look out! look out!' of the barber's, or was it the absent-hair sensation he'd brought away from there? A headache announc-ing itself, wordless but full of sound. He could hear or feel the grinding and gnawing of Ammar's metabolism in front of him and to the left. And the noise of the others on occult frequencies. He heard or felt their amplified whispering to God, and also amplified anger, desire and anguish. He was in the crossfire, in the centre point of their reverberating unanswered passions. Volume rising.

He tried to tell himself he was observing only what he was observing, only the concrete floor beneath plastic, and the back of Ammar's legs, only some unsettled young men gathered in a shallow basement to try to concretize things, but he couldn't prevent the process of fusion whereby memories and dreams adhered to the moment like flies to fly paper. The mosques of his childhood stretched out beyond this one like a hall of mirrors diminishing into the infinite. And the screams of Syrian detention chambers, for reasons he couldn't quite pin down, not yet, echoed around the basement walls. The histories of these others too weighed down the present. The Arabs, the Indo-Pakistanis, the Irishman, the African. From what tortures had their fathers fled? Over which jagged topographies of pain? Arrived like far-flung stumps of desert trees following explosions and a long stretch of failed rains. Most of each structure dead, the trunk dead, root and branch dead, only one green shoot twisting from the dead wood sideways and up.

The prayer finished, heads turning right and left to salute the recording angels. While the men counted praise on their fingers and then prayed further raka'as individually, Sami rubbed his scalp, trying to breathe the phantoms away.

'I should go,' he said when Ammar faced him. 'I'm getting a headache.'

'No, stay. We'll talk a little bit.'

The men had adjusted themselves into a seated circle. Ammar introduced them and Sami leaned forward to shake. Shafeeq and Abdullah (gellabiyas). Sulaiman, Tariq and Abd ur-Rahman (tracksuits). Brother, they called him. They were willing to make him their brother.

'Brothers,' said Ammar. 'One of the reasons we are here is to gain knowledge. To gain and share knowledge.'

Some of the brothers said yes. Others gestured their agreement.

'Knowledge is what we need to solve our problems. But knowledge isn't going to solve problems unless it's practical. Unless it gives you power.'

And more agreement.

'Perhaps some of us,' Ammar looked significantly at Sami, 'don't see the importance of gaining power. Or of knowledge. But this is the time for power, and soon it will be too late.'

A chorus of 'yes' and 'that's right' in English and Arabic. There was plenty of affirmation among these brothers.

'The signs of the Hour related to us by the Prophet give warning as to when the end shall come. And the signs are being fulfilled. The minor signs, at least, we can be sure of those. The earth has become smaller, like the Prophet said it would. Vast distances are crossed in short spans of time. People jump between the land and the clouds. These things are happening now.'

'That's planes and the internet,' Mujahid confirmed.

'And the space shuttle,' said Shafeeq.

'Before the Hour comes,' Ammar said, 'rain will be burning.'

'Acid rain, man,' said Tariq.

'And fog will appear over cities because of their evil.'

'Read the news and you see it,' said Abd ur-Rahman.

'The Hour will not come before the Beduin compete with each other in building high buildings.'

'Look at Dubai and Abu Dhabi,' said Abdullah. 'Look at the skyscrapers in the Gulf.'

'As a result of European persecution, the people of Iraq will have no food and no money.'

'The sanctions,' said Sulaiman.

'Men will look like women and women will look like men.'

'This city full of that weirdness.'

'Family ties will be cut.'

Sami directed his eyes at the mat.

'The signs are being fulfilled. These are some of the minor signs. There are others. You know them, brothers. It can't be long till the major signs come, and then they come fast. It's almost too late. But most so-called Muslims don't even know what time it is.'

Everybody nodded. Sami may have nodded too, in physical sympathy. An unstable plant in a forest of nodding trees.

'The worst of a people,' Ammar continued, 'will be its leader. There will be an increase in killing to the extent that people won't know why they are killed. Not even the killer will know why.'

Examples given from the Muslim and Western worlds.

'The Dajjal will rule, the False Messiah, the one-eyed beast.'

'Seen the eye on the dollar? Masonic sign. One eye, not two.'

'Or the TV, brothers! One eye in every sitting room!'

'The Dajjal,' said Ammar, 'will have a mountain of bread, and the people will face hardship except those who follow him.'

A sudden hammering from upstairs silenced the gathering. Loud, metallic and intent. The brothers switched their gaze from face to face. How to interpret that? Home repairs or a warning of imminent violence? Or something else entirely?

Sami sat still. Waiting.

22
Brother and Sister

Ammar launches from the Nissan into an angry floundering on the pavement beside her. Arabic radio news wafts behind him. He's had it on at full volume, dense as car-trapped cigarette smoke. There's no greeting.

'Something needs to be done about it. You see how our brothers are living in Palestine. You see how your sisters are living. And in Iraq. You see how our people have been starved and broken by the West and by that tyrant they put there. I tell you, something needs to be done.'

'So what are you doing?' Unperturbed, she poses her challenge into the storm. It may snag him enough to say hello. She can hardly see his eyes for the jerking of limbs. He wears long white sleeves. His shirt buttons are done up to the top. He is thin and overworked and handsome in an impoverished way. Is it only coincidence he's found her on the street? What has he come to tell her?

'Yeah. I'm making a start. I'm strengthening my Islam. Islam's coming. I don't know how yet. But we're going to do things. The time's getting nearer. I tell you, I've got two burning towers of anger – Iraq and Palestine – and I've got the rule of Allah coming up BOOM! between them. We'll get rid of the traitor governments for a start. And then we'll sort out the Jews.'

Muntaha had been on her way home. Normal people would arrange to go for coffee somewhere instead of such car-crash rendezvous. She's happy to see him, anyway.

'Not all Jews are interested.' She talks back, amused and concerned. Ammar is on the cusp, as usual, of comedy and desperation. He's her attractive energetic brother, and he's also a complete loon.

'What do you mean?'

'I mean some of them don't care about Israel. And some of them oppose Israel.'

Ammar releases tongue from palate with the kind of explosive violence he'd like to detonate under the complacent world.

'Jews is Jews, Muntaha.' He shakes his weary head.

'No. That's too simple. There's different kinds of Jews like there's different kinds of Muslims. Some of the Jews help us.'

'That's wrong thinking.' His right hand chops into his left palm. 'You've been tricked by their game, man. Jews is Jews and kuffar is kuffar. Unbelievers. You got to know the boundaries.'

Muntaha smiles at being called man. Littler versions of Ammar poke through.

'Which brings me to something else.' He scowls, sensing her sympathy and resisting it. 'Something we must have words about.'

His face is cocked obliquely, his nose quivers. He's trying to be big-brotherish, and the strain tells, his vulnerability. Muntaha is open with curiosity.

'Speaking of the kuffar, I mean. You got to watch out, sister. Don't trust their motives. Do you follow me?'

'No, habibi, I don't.' But she's starting to sniff his purpose.

'I'm talking about one particular kafir. That Gabor. Round you like a fly round honey. Talking his philosophical shit to try to manoeuvre in.'

She'd wanted to respect his authority, so as to not hurt him. She watches the stream of her breath. There's a stream too of kuffar around them, married women and single men with Freezerland bags which steam in the afternoon heat, boys with beer cans, more boys on mountain bikes, rapids jostling around this obstruction in streetflow. But the al-Haj children don't respond to it.

'It's my duty here to set you straight.' He isn't meeting her eyes, but frowning skywards. 'You're innocent in this. Naïve. I know that. So I'm giving you advice, from brother to sister. Stick with your husband, with your Muslim man. He's your fortress.'

Her breath is fast and scorching. He can't see her.

'Keep away from the kuffar. They're waiting for you to make one wrong step, that's all, and then they pounce.'

This illustrated by his knuckly hand, a leaping spider.

'What,' she asks, 'are you suggesting?'

Clipped vowels and plosives. He knows he's overstepped a boundary. Backtracks.

'Nothing. I'm suggesting nothing. Just advice. Just warning you.'

'Warning?'

'Warning you. You're innocent, I know it. I meant him, not you.'

'What about him?'

'Forget about him. Stick with Sami. He's a brother. You're safe with him.'

'I wouldn't be talking to anybody I wasn't safe with. I respect myself. I don't need to be warned, little brother.'

Two teenage girls have stopped to spectate. They chew gum in synchrony, chins bucked upward, insolently close.

'Yeah . . . yeah.' Ammar dissolving into small hard pieces. Pebble-dash. Shingle. 'Just, you know, Sami's, you know, a brother.'

'A Muslim brother?'

'Yeah.' He brightens. 'A brother.'

'What makes you think so?'

'Oh, don't be like that, Muntaha. He's never said he isn't a Muslim.'

'I'll tell you what he's said.'

But Ammar snarls and windmills his arms as if she's going to describe her orgasms. Nasty dirty incestuous stuff. Her bras and knickers abandoned on her bed. Opening the bathroom door on her. Her female smell. He doesn't want to know.

'No, but if you think you can judge people so easy . . .'

'It's between a man and Allah.'

'Let me speak.'

'I don't want to hear.'

'And I don't want to hear you. You're still a boy. A little brother is all you are.'

Ammar flinches.

'And what's this "they"?' She continues the onslaught. Words born through the hot vibration of her lips, blood ringing around her eye sockets, eyeballs burning. 'All this kuffar stuff? What's that about? People are individuals, not shapes to fit your categories. Not shapes you slot through holes in some fucking baby game.'

Muntaha swearing. He's misstepped badly.

He attempts to firm up. Makes the gesture, at least. There isn't much more in his repertoire.

'Watch what they do, not what they say. Watch what they do in the world. They have this nice cop nasty cop thing, but it's all bollocks. The result is the same. They started it. I'm just responding. Believe the propaganda and you end up defenceless.'

'You were talking about Gabor. He's one of my colleagues. He's a teacher.'

'Yeah, whatever. But they all stand together at the end of the day.'

The spectating girls lose interest. They shuffle towards the news-agent's for better distraction. Brother and sister remain, enwombed in private drama.

'Ammar, you're insane. You need to have your head checked.'

'And we need to stand together too, is what I'm saying. Muslim with Muslim, that's all.'

'Slow down.' Speaking into his face, she exaggerates the shapes of the words. 'This isn't politics. You were talking about one of my colleagues.'

'They divided us, you see.' He continues blindly, for the sake of his pride, down this doomed leaden road of contradiction. 'They invented sects and parties among us. Divide and rule, you see.'

'Who did?'

With softened nose fallen towards the ground and a voice sunk into monotone, he continues. 'The English, the Jews, the Christians, America.'

'What's that got to do with . . .'

'You know, created these traitors among us, the Shia, Communists.'

Abruptly, she pities him. At the moment when he merits her anger most. She speaks quietly, sorrowfully.

'Your mother was Shii. You should be ashamed of yourself.'

At last he is quiet. His eyelids flutter. He is overcome by a glottis-tangled cough. Is he starting to cry?

'You can't talk to me like that,' he says.

She waits.

'I'm the head of the household,' he says.

A strangled hiccup in his throat.

'Then behave like a grown-up.'

The drying up of his speech reveals barren cracked silence beneath. It's awkward. Muntaha wants to move things on before she sees insects crawling out. Millipedes from their sand dens. Clicking exoskeletons. Shiny black pulsing things.

'I don't know what you put into each other's heads in that mosque. You were better off into Public Enemy. It made a lot more sense.'

His head hangs below gaunt shoulders, unresponding.

'I mean, the Jews invented the Shia? It's ridiculous. You should read some history books.'

Which does the trick. 'So you believe what they write in their books?' he says. 'Sister, they're taking you for a ride.'

'For God's sake.' Relief breezes through her. 'You read more than one book and make your own mind up. If you don't want to read their books, improve your Arabic and read ours. For God's sake.'

'A sister,' he says, 'requires proper guidance.' And he's speechifying again. About sisters ideological, not actual.

She disconnects, like leaving a meditation. There's the street around her: its stark lack of sisterhood. Everyone by themselves, doing the Anglo thing of avoiding contact, whatever their religion. And departing again, she remembers Baghdad. Was that her there? If time hasn't cheated her, and she knows it has, the city of her childhood was like a storybook village, traffic and dust and heat notwithstanding. The neighbours there were sisters to her mother, at least she called them sister when they met. Muntaha used to be sent around to the neighbouring flats with pots of rice when her mother made a big meal. The women were aunties to her. The market men were brothers and uncles.

Ammar has realized that he has no audience. He glances at the Nissan.

'So what did you want?' Muntaha asks him.

'Oh fuck, nothing.'

'You just came to say your piece about Gabor.'

Wordlessly, he concedes it.

'I know what I'm doing,' Muntaha says. 'And I'm not doing anything anyway.'

He nods. There's a condom smeared on the pavement between them.

'You were listening to the news, and you had a little emotional rush from the news, so you decided to drive by and give me a speech about kuffar.'

He nods again. Glances at the Nissan, which is playing Egyptian dance music.

'Well don't let it all drive you mad, all right? There's enough madness.'

He bunches his lower lip forward and scratches at wispy beard. His voice is level. 'You want to go somewhere to pray Asr?'

'No, habibi, I don't. You don't make me calm.'

'All right then.' He affects a nonchalant gait as he steps around the car. Swings the door open.

'Be calm,' she says. 'I'll see you.'

'Insha'allah.' He scallops into the cockpit, fires the engine, pulls away fast.

She's left all alone in the busy city. Orphaned, but connected by fate to her genetic simile. Whether she likes it or not.

23
Muntaha's Prayers

Muntaha's prayers are much more peaceful than those of the men in her life.

When she prays, her heart is a shining mirror reflecting the light of God. She can almost say that only God is present. She is aware of Him only. Her consciousness continues, but Muntaha, the daughter of Marwan and Mouna, is nearly absent. Aiming at absence. She is the flame of love blown out by the Beloved. She is the reed and He the breath, He the music too. He the cause and the consequence and she obliterated in between.

God is closer to her than her jugular vein. I am inside God, she thinks. God is inside me.

When she prays, she enacts a drama of scale. She is worshipping the absolute Light, in the centre of it, conscious of herself at the midpoint of extension into inner and outer space. Out there the larger volumes, the stars and galaxies, and out there in reverse the smaller sizes, atoms, electrons, and particles yet more abstract.

When she prays, she looks at the prayer mat and what is implied in it like ripples reaching its surface: first the wooden floor, then brick and plaster, and the local history of the room below (Sami's), and pipes and sewers at ground level, next ratlands, archaeologists' London, and soil and rock, and then through layers to the inner earth, the molten core. She looks at the physical world and considers how it balances on a needle of time. How it is swallowed and folded into packets of nothing, zapped, as soon as God closes His eye. It is real but unreal in the face of God. It emanates from God but God is beyond it. She says 'allahu akbar' as she bends, kneels, and prostrates. Allahu akbar. God is greater.

Each moment God creates anew. The Sufi Suhrawardi called God 'the Maker Who transfers existences from non-existence to existence'. Muntaha notices existence forming every time she puts her foot forward. This is why she is soft-footed and open-mouthed. She feels the sacred. Her actions, therefore, aren't only her own.

In the days following Sami's departure she performed the tasks that presented themselves. She met a solicitor to execute her father's will: a straightforward business. Marwan had arranged everything according to the letter of Sunni inheritance law. That is, Hasna took an eighth of his wealth, and the rest was split two to one between Ammar and Muntaha. In the event of Muntaha divorcing, Ammar would become financially responsible for her. Sons inherit twice the share of daughters because sons must provide for their families, while a woman's money remains her own. Islam works when men are noble. In other cases, however, the regulations seem questionable. Once he'd finished his dead father's money, Sami lived off his wife. And off the state.

Marwan's wealth was the house where Hasna and Ammar continued to live, its future undecided. There was also a modest sum of money deposited in an Islamic bank, and a box of gold which Marwan, with his Arab mistrust of institutions and paper money, had kept locked in a bedroom cupboard. Muntaha's share came to a few thousand, enough to buy a small car if she'd wanted such a thing, or to go on a couple of exotic holidays.

She disposed of Marwan's stuff in one busy afternoon. She brought one suit jacket to live in her wardrobe along with her dresses and Sami's unclaimed garments. The jacket smelled deeply of her father, though less so every day. His clothes didn't fit anybody they knew, so the other things, trousers, shirts and vests, she packaged in black bin liners and delivered via Ammar's taxi cab to the same charity shops in Kilburn they'd originally come from.

There were also, dusty on a shelf behind Hasna's Iraqi memorabilia, photographs of life in Baghdad, including portraits of Marwan when he used to smile and stand straight; of Muntaha's beautiful mother; Ammar as black and white child from a foreign land,

Sunday supplement-type studies of him amid palm trees or against flat scrub backdrops; and uncles and aunts whose faces Muntaha had forgotten, who stirred emotions she couldn't properly recognize.

There was an album of drawings done by her and Ammar before they could write, happy dinosaurs and multicoloured goats depicted with the expressive primitivism of the very young. She took the photographs and the drawings and stashed them in the heart zone of her bedroom. Her own private bedroom now. She considered Ammar too clumsy to care for them. He'd already taken the Islamic pamphlets, and Marwan's prayer rug.

She took a few pieces of cutlery that gleamed something of the past, and one or two plates and cups. Ammar kept his father's out-of-date and in-other-ways invalid Iraqi passport, symbolic of the only journey done with it. And then there was nothing else of Marwan. Having distributed his remains thus, Muntaha experienced a satisfying sense of completion. She felt as she did when she finished a long novel, or as an artist feels when he's put the final detail to a canvas – paradoxically, because instead of achieving and synthesizing she had divided and disintegrated something that had previously been one.

A condolence letter came from her uncle Nidal. He invited her to visit Iraq, and she thought perhaps she would. Perhaps she'd request a year off work and try to do something useful, teaching English to Iraqi children, for example, or collecting schoolbooks to donate. They needed them. They even had a pencil shortage. Pencils were on the sanctions list because graphite was classed as 'dual use'. Meaning it could just as easily be used to manufacture a weapon of mass destruction as to copy notes from a blackboard. And meanwhile, because of the American depleted uranium, cancer rates and birth deformities had increased by hundreds of per cent. Just to imagine the country she had come from was to weep. It made her private grief irrelevant, and so it was comforting to imagine it as often as she could. She should do her bit, she thought. She should spend her inheritance on this.

At school between meetings she contemplated some sort of a

memorial for her father. Writing something maybe. For the local paper, perhaps, or the school bulletin. At a staff-room desk she noted sentences and scrubbed them out again, trying to find a way of making him representative of all the city's migrant lives. She went so far as to plan a project for her history class called 'History Starts At Home', intending to use Marwan as model text. Photos, maps and narrative. 'Marwan al-Haj was born in Iraq and died in England.' 'Marwan al-Haj came to England to build a better life.' 'Marwan al-Haj knew the libraries of both Baghdad and London.' But it didn't capture anything of her father. Written down like that, Marwan was nothing special. Everybody migrates. Everybody changes and disperses. And life is too complex, too large, to encapsulate. Nothing can be summed up, least of all a human spirit.

So Marwan slowly became defined as a personal memory, or more precisely as a collection of images and sensations which summoned something of him for a candle-flickering instant, and this memory joined the mental objects of her world as one of a series of signs in a glorious book, signs which were resonant if not symbolic of an inexpressible, ungraspable realm.

Ammar kept his inexpert eye on her. Her college friends came round, and she saw friends at the mosque. At school she confided in Gabor a little, between meetings, and he pieced things together. He understood that Sami had gone, and imagined what he didn't understand. He saw himself as a support for her. They ate at the same table in the canteen, and sometimes went for coffee after school. Things were looking up for him. He had an exhibition planned in a fashionable gallery, and at the same time, Muntaha became available. When he asked her to come to eat at his flat she said she'd be more comfortable if he came to her. On Saturday afternoon, she said.

Gabor brought flowers, arriving early.

Just as he put his hand up to the bell, Ammar burst from the door. His hand collided with Ammar's nose. Or Ammar's nose smacked into Gabor's palm. It happened very fast. Ammar was already angry when he came out, before the collision.

'God. Are you all right?' Gabor asked. He'd stepped back, but now went towards Muntaha's half-felled brother, put his hand to the hand with which Ammar was cradling his nose.

'Fucking Jews,' said Ammar.

He pushed Gabor away.

'And you expect us to lie down and let you do whatever you please.'

Ammar clenched his fists. His eyes watered. He spat, fiercely, at the pavement. A puff of summer detritus rose from the place of impact. A tail of spittle hanging to his lower lip.

'You've misunderstood.' Gabor was working out that the Jew comment specified him. That Ammar had him implicated in a collective drama, larger than this doorstep coincidence. 'No, you've got it wrong. I didn't mean to hit you. I was going to ring the bell. I was looking for . . .'

Ammar hit him, hard, in the head. So fast Gabor didn't see his arm move. Just the ghost of something to his left.

Yes, it hurt. Gabor wobbled. A flash of general pain and greater surprise made his body want to fall, to stop. Then he steadied himself and touched the side of his face. It was roaring red. Still numb, but heat came through his fingertips. He watched Ammar.

'Now turn the other cheek,' he taunted. 'That's right, turn the other cheek.'

'What do you mean?'

Gabor felt blood swelling at his temple. Is there a weak point in the skull there? He pictured a skull, with its fragile curve down to the eye socket. Was his brain all right?

'You're a Christian, aren't you? That's what they pretend to do. Turn the cheek, boy.'

'Didn't you just call me a Jew?'

'Whatever the fuck you are.'

'I'm not a Christian.'

Gabor found himself flushed with fighting hormone. Throat dry and mouth unresponsive, it wasn't easy to speak. He negotiated an agreement with himself not to do anything regrettable. Here was Muntaha's little brother, at Muntaha's front door, in the grip of a crisis which had little to do with Gabor. He was much smaller than Gabor. If Gabor hit him he'd do him real damage. All the same, butterflies were zooming about his intestines. Imam Ali said the strongest man is he who can fight against himself. Hard to be so strong. Gabor forgot his aching head. His body wanted to strike.

'I'm not a Christian,' he said again, through bloodless lips.

'Whatever the fuck, then. Whatever the fuck you are.'

Gabor thought of saying he was a Muslim, in the true linguistic sense of 'one who submits'. He'd been preparing to tell Muntaha that anyway. 'One who accepts' is better, one who accepts reality, because in Islam God is the Real, the True. But Ammar was there frothing at him, dribbling saliva, reddening as shame replaced anger, trying to make himself angry again. A dangerous spinning man on a dangerous spinning earth. He wouldn't want to hear it.

'I'm an agnostic,' Gabor said.

And that was also true. Gabor was a not-knower whose prejudice was to wonder how anyone could be otherwise. When you consider that our sense of reality depends on the structure of our brains, that the matter we assume to be real and solid around us is ultimately points of light in empty space, when you consider big bang theory and superstrings and chaos, and the varieties of religious experience, the people who see ghosts and the people who don't, when you consider these things, then certainty doesn't seem to be a logical response.

'I'm an agnostic,' he said. 'Not a Christian or a Jew.'

He was pleased to see Ammar, who hadn't expected theology, bewildered by this. His brows descended, his nose flattened. Meanwhile, blood flow was returning to Gabor's face.

The door opened, first slowly, then fast. Muntaha lurched out, still tying her hijab.

'What's going on?'

It was a shriek. She shrieked next in Arabic. She stopped and looked at Gabor, pointed at him, and demanded something of her brother. He answered in Arabic, shrugging and shaking his hands. Then she hit him, slapping him with open palms on the crown of his head. Most rewarding for Gabor, who stepped back and decorously turned towards the street. Three sniggering boys on bicycles across the tarmac who'd stopped to watch. When their eyes followed Ammar down the pavement Gabor turned again.

'My God,' she said, in a passion. 'Are you all right?' That had been Gabor's response when he saw that Ammar was hurt. Gabor, now very grateful for his injury.

She steered him into the hallway and raised her large hand to his cheek. She touched him, which both stung and didn't. He thought her fingers stroked his hairline as she removed them. The hint of a caress. He felt something of the adrenalin flush he felt before, so he loosened, weakened. Saw her in his imagination as a spirit woman, a Sufi Sophia, eastern like his grandfather. The opposite of his materialist parents.

She led him to a ground-floor bathroom. The hallway made of wood and roses, a tempting smell of onions and clean red meat from the kitchen. But when she closed the door behind him he was in Sami's territory, dark and claustrophobic, the walls tightly packed with cartoons cut from Arabic newspapers, a lot of maps and guns, men with globes for heads. Gabor washed his own head in cold water before inspecting it in the mirror. Nothing serious. The skin raw but unbroken. A bruise already gathering colour. He padded his hair dry with a perfumed towel.

When he came out he found her silhouetted against the kitchen window's blue. He remembered the flowers which he must have dropped when Ammar hit him, so he creaked over the floorboards and let himself on to the pavement where they still lay, blue like the sky against stained grey. They'd been trodden on once, but not maliciously. He picked them up, rustled them into shape somewhat, and returned to the house.

With the door open the hallway was a suspension of sun motes, and they played over Muntaha, her skin, the fabric of her clothes.

Her lips were parted and moist, her lubricated eyeballs shining unalloyed white, and their blacks glistening. A third of her face retreating coyly into shadow. A few strands of satin hair escaping the hijab. For Gabor, time was suspended, a gateway to the ancient world ajar. The past present. No time, so no weight, no obligation. No husbands or rules or social codes. They could kiss.

'I'm so embarrassed,' she said, studying his bruise. 'I'm ashamed of him. He's going to get himself into real trouble soon. He's off the rails, really off the rails. I don't know what to do about him. I've thought about getting him to live here with me where I can keep my eye on him. His problem is, he isn't really old enough to have no parents.'

She interrupted herself when he lifted the flowers for her to see.

'Flowers,' she said. 'That's nice of you. They'll look good on the table.'

Gabor watched her step into the kitchen and crouch at a floor-level cupboard to find a vase. She blasted some tap water into it, added a spoon of sugar, then scissored off the flowers' lower stems and put them into place one by one. She moved past him with the vase and through a brown door. He followed.

'This is Sami's study,' she said, 'but I've made a few changes. This table, for instance, I've brought in here for when I have guests. What you have to remember about Ammar . . .' – she continued as if the table and Ammar were two facets of one conversation – '. . . is that he's a motherless child. He was only six when he lost his mother. And his motherland too. Six is old enough to be very socially aware, so to be pulled out of your country suddenly like that is very disturbing, even for a child who has a mother to comfort him. I don't think he's got over it yet. I mean, part of him is still six years old waiting for his mother to come back. He was smoking cigarettes and worse when he was fourteen, and he could drive when he was fifteen, but that's not the same as being a grown-up. In fact, those are compensations for being a little boy still. It's a shame. He'd make a lovely grown-up, he really would.'

Gabor wondered if we must always be making excuses, if we

can't judge just a little more. But it would have looked insensitive to argue against sisterly sentiment. He let her get it off her chest.

'He has all this undirected anger. I wish he'd, you know, channel it. Do something positive with it. He gets angry about Iraq and Palestine. I mean, all right, we all do. But what can we do about it? We must be able to do our little thing, whatever it is. That way the world might improve. Getting aimlessly angry isn't going to help.'

She talked herself back to the kitchen, leaving him alone in Sami's former study. He took the opportunity to nose into its contents. In the desk drawer there was star stuff, curl-edged photographs, a miniature whiskey bottle, a book.

Muntaha came back bearing loaves of flat bread and a dish of paste the same colour as her. 'Matabal,' she said, laying it on the table. 'Aubergine and olive oil and tahina and yoghurt.'

He'd pushed the drawer shut and turned to the bookshelves.

'Looking at the books? Most of those are Sami's. But you see those ones, those are mine. I've been clearing his notes from the shelves. He agreed. We spoke on the phone. He says he doesn't want them any more.'

On her half-shelf there were Sufi texts, books about Iraq, some magical realism, a few Arabic titles. Also the copy of *Anna Karenina* Gabor had given her a week before, still in its pristine, untouched state. And in Sami's larger section, texts about Sufi texts, theories about theory.

Eventually they sat on straight-backed chairs on either side of the table, with the cramming of Sami's uncollected furniture not allowing much room for manoeuvre, his rank old sofa and obsolete camel stool pressing at their sides. Between them steamed a leg of lamb which had been marinated overnight in sour yoghurt and garlic. Succulent meat which Gabor carved and then forked on to the plates, and which disintegrated creamily in his mouth. They were discussing sharia law, starting with her father's will and moving on to sexual misconduct. She was arguing that sharia is inherently flexible, much more tolerant than either Muslims or non-Muslims assume. Gabor half taking it in, being greatly disturbed, greatly exercised, by the leg of flesh in front of him and on his tongue, by an extending metonymy of legs, of shanks and thighs, and of the area where they meet. He understood why cartoon Victorians, fearing for a gentleman's moral equilibrium, covered up female-suggestive piano and table legs. Except that covering draws your attention to what is covered. The imagination comes into play, and an imagined uncovering becomes the first stage of foreplay. Those covered nipples. The fabric of the bra meeting them, hard against soft. Then in the gap of the thighs, in the centre point, the wonder of the intermediate zone, part skin and part internal organ, that boundary of known and occult, both dry and moist, the texture of it. And what is its texture? Gabor wanted to know. Is it true that Arab women shave there, not shave but – so much more feminine – wax? Does she?

His desire was a very practical sort of lust. A lust requiring fulfilment. The opposite sort of lust from Sami's in the strip pub, although both men's imagery of Muntaha have much in common. Gabor's orientalism maps reasonably closely on to Sami's more self-complicated version. Symbolic thinkers both, left behind in abstraction. While their perceptions freeze like brittle glass, and fall, and crash gently to the ground, Muntaha is one step ahead, poking a toe into the pre-perceived, into the primal raw mush of it.

'It's a hadeeth qudsi,' she was saying, meanwhile. 'Not from the Qur'an, but still the word of God reported by the Prophet. "My mercy is greater than my wrath." And that's the balance in sharia: mercy and wrath, severity and lenience, to the extent that the penalty can almost never be applied. So the punishment for zina, for adultery, is whipping for an unmarried person and death for a married person.'

Gabor's fork was stuck in the leg between them. Strands of leg between his teeth.

'Pretty severe, yeah? But now look at the conditions that have to be met before the punishment can be applied. There have to be four witnesses to the adultery, which means witnesses to the actual act. You know, to the intercourse itself. And the four witnesses have to be reliable people, known for their honesty. Now who would commit adultery in front of four prayerful, honest witnesses? No one. And if an accuser can't prove his charge, then he gets punished for slander. So the message is, if you suspect your neighbour of adultery, keep quiet about it because you can't prove it, and speaking about it will damage the public peace. And Islam as a social system aims at social peace. How you get from that to the kind of laws they have in Pakistan is a different story.'

She paused to chew some leg.

'But the severity of the punishment remains. If you're guilty of adultery you know the severity of the crime. It's a sin, a serious sin. And God sees it all, every detail.'

24
Following the Heart

Sami awoke from a dream of a rotting corpse, and the sweat in his nostrils was at first indistinguishable from that imagined stench. Against the surface of the regulation university wardrobe his eyes still saw maggots thriving in the corpse's slurry eyes, the jaw cracking open to reveal a turd tongue, pus leaking from the ears.

He shook himself and rose. Drank water from a shiny alloy tap, and instead of braving company on the route to the communal shower he splashed himself there in his armpits and groin, noting with distaste his beltline roll of fat. Then he stood at the in-slanting window, over a street recovering in the sun from student-blighted Friday night, and smoked a bitter cigarette. As he did so he produced a freshly toxic sheen of sweat to be blotted by the day's T-shirt.

In the internet café he learnt of further Israeli revenge attacks for a suicide bombing in a Jerusalem pizzeria. He downloaded a TV report for the third time. Through fuzzy BBC blood decorum you could still see defunct bodies scattered on the floor and against furniture. The correspondent was moping about it. You could see religious Jew volunteers picking up hunks of flesh and putting them in bags. Sami watched it through until the headshaking of Israeli spokesmen sent a spurt of venom into his stomach, on the strength of which he ventured forth, towards violence of more random genesis.

He walked from weekend-quiet Euston to the wide markets of Camden. Up there a crescendo of car noise expanded within a larger crescendo of simulated excitement – music channelled through the glass doorways of leather shops and poster shops and body-piercing parlours, and also voices, of criers of wares and slogans, of different brands of youth yo-ing or oi-ing to each other on the pavements. Groups of young natives half-heartedly looking for war, and innocent blinking boys in football shirts, tourists from the outer suburbs disconcerted by the richer varieties of uniform here. People purchasing all manner of sophisticated identities, making all manner of consumer choices, and all believing they deserved them. Sami, who had just decided to shed his addictions, including shopping, hadn't brought his card with him. He moved left on to the lock, and westwards on the towpath.

Plenty of people, the summer permitting their privatized enjoyments, individuals and couples and groups preserving the ritual boundaries around themselves. Everyone on his own altar. Everyone in his own fantasy. Just enough cooperation to pretend the others weren't there. Just enough suspension of disbelief.

Sami cooperated, ignoring people. The backyard vegetation and the canal steamed deeply. Long low houseboats rocked easily on the green, self-contained with plant pots, mugs, curtained windows. He indulged sketchy fantasies of houseboat life and furniture, of peaceful isolation.

'As-salaamu alaikum!' A grinning skullcapped black man of Sami's age had spied him for a brother, and passed on. An instant of fraternity, an exclusion boundary split open to absorb him. Sami wriggled out again.

He considered how different to his illusions the world actually was. He'd thought he was holding the fort of secular humanism, but the fort had already fallen. In its rubble a marketplace of religion had set up, where people thrashed and struggled to attain uniqueness of belief. True, tradition had decayed so long it had crumbled into itself, its crumbs had been thoroughly mulched in the jaws of various modernisms. But like an imploding star, tradition hadn't simply disappeared. Instead, the old material was sucked in and spat out into a new dimension, transformed into what would have looked like parodies to previous generations: the bump 'n' grind pop stars tangled in Kabbala string, the London Sufi groups made up entirely of ageing white hippies, the smack-addicted trans-

vestites chanting mantras, the counterculturalists battling the ego
with LSD. The New Age spiritualities – a bit of this and a bit of
that, to fit advertising: the world is as you want it to be, because
you deserve it. And so on, everywhere you might care to look.

Secularism had collapsed under the weight of the new beliefs.
Instead of catching up with the empirical West, Third World
religion became more strident, more nihilist. And the religion of
the comfortable metropolitan natives was ever more Hellenized:
physical, sexually liberal, requiring spectacle and heroism, requiring
feats of strength and human drama, with the divine focus dispersed
to allow for a variety of household gods. There were consumer
cults, body cults, the Greek perfections of Schwarzkopf or Schwarzenegger, the kick-ass warrior aristocracy worshipped on exploding
screens in arcades and living rooms. Empirical cults.

It wasn't as he'd thought as a boy, that all these religions
would cancel each other out. Instead they existed in bubbles. As
bubble hit bubble more bubbles were formed. It was clear to him
now that secular humanism was a late nineteenth-century hiccup,
an antiquated European gentleman's daydream. And Mustafa's
daydream too, of course.

Across hot canal vapours he saw the zoo's nocturnal mammal
house, and then, nosing through the fencing, oryx displaced from
the Arabian Gulf. Next, on his right and above the towpath, an
aviary dense with the chirps and squawks of competing species.

Surrounded by these twittering potentialities Sami again confronted Mustafa's death. How someone could fall off the edge of
the world like that. It seemed like a joke, like some kind of trick
played on him. Until recently he'd half believed his father was going
to burst through a door one day with his cynical laugh – *Ha! got
you! you believed in death like these fools believe in God!* And why
shouldn't he? Mustafa had never said goodbye.

Another fact: Marwan's death. Marwan dispersed. The corpse in
the soggy ground and the spirit, the character, in the sky, in the air.

Two facts. Two absences. Two sets of guilt and pain arriving
from a void.

Sami thought: the past is a nightmare determining the present, and the present is empty. And then: death is the constant and life an aberrant moment. Being here, being present, is an aberration.

To his left, glistening sombrely in the sunlight, the false gold dome of the Regent's Park mosque. Where prayers had been said over Marwan's body, and over Mustafa's body too, once he was unable to resist. Would Sami go in? He remembered the peculiar Englishness of it from his previous visit. Coats and scarves hung up on hooks, the smell of damp wool, wooden panelling on the walls. Snow through the windows against a red and yellow sky. He'd never seen a mosque with windows in an Arab country, where light is something to be escaped from.

His foot waggled at the point of decision: right and up and across the bridge and into the community of believers, or left and onwards to the west, along the canal bank, towards his formative haunts. West, then.

He continued to philosophize. Ascertaining physical facts. The matter that irrigated him, the incidental, time-bound stuff. But he, Sami the personality, the consciousness, Sami the intangible which couldn't be measured, he was a mere possibility. Like God.

And here stretched out a sorry, partial pathway to belief. A via negativa. Sami the soul doesn't exist, nor does God. If he's going to believe in himself, he may as well believe in God. It seems only fair. Sami and God appear to be, in some sense, brothers.

Sami addressed God: You don't exist. And I don't exist. You don't exist and neither do I. We belong together, therefore.

This bemused him pleasantly, for a short moment. A smile played to extinction on his dry lips.

He left the canal and threaded through mid-rise towers until he was on the Edgware Road and heading south. Following the heart.

And who said that first? Follow the heart. Some poet who failed the biology test. I mean, Sami murmured, what heart? Where to? The dumb organ, the notoriously convoluted chunk of gristle, all twists and turns, pointing in ten thousand directions or none at all. Uncle Marwan's heart hadn't led him anywhere special unless you count the mud. Follow the heart? If only we could do otherwise.

In Sumer they followed the messages they read in the entrails of sacrificed animals. They read the liver, the liver being the seat of the soul.

When Gilgamesh rejected her, fierce fateful Ishtar asked Anu for the means of vengeance. Her father Anu of the air. Anu of the sky. She raised her voice in insistence until Anu granted her the Bull of Heaven, although he knew the Bull would muddy the waters and parch the earth with drought. Ishtar sent the Bull to ravage the lands of men. But Gilgamesh with his friend the wild man, Enkidu, killed the Bull on Cedar Mountain. They scorned the gods. And so Ishtar sent disease to kill Enkidu. It ended in the killer's death.

Father killer, Sami murmured at himself. Denier of dying men's wishes. *My own little Enkidu, my wild man.* What Mustafa had called him in the nightmare past.

He strode past (striding now) a flyer for an evangelical meeting in Earl's Court. More evidence, if more were needed, of the spirit rushing to adapt to new realities. Instead of churches and modest little English chapels it was conference centres, stadiums, concert halls: these the helipads on which the spirit today descends.

He moved south practising detachment – from evangelism, from his thirst and the stickiness of his T-shirt, from the meanings of argileh bars, Lebanese restaurants, Islamic banks, from Arab property dealers and from the quiet doorways down to noisy whoring spots. At the point where he felt fully liberated from particular responses the city agreed with him, losing its Arab specificity to enter a stretch of nondescript, post-human concrete and tunnels under the marble arch. His heart was as cold as the suddenly clammy absence of sun.

So when he re-emerged into superficial heat at Speakers' Corner he was hermetically insulated in his equanimity, so he thought, even from salaaming brothers. His eyes were set high and far, on to the trees and the scrubby lawns of the park.

Seven or eight soapbox heads harangued their respective audiences. The same theme rehearsed in different accents: repent, convert, step on to the straight path. Repent before God or Gaia or the black race seeks revenge. Sami strode through with rigid gaze and intention, their words breaking weakly on his impassive ears.

It was this phrase, spoken in an American accent, that stopped him short: 'The destruction of Damascus.'

He turned towards it.

'The destruction of Damascus is a sign and a wonder soon to be witnessed.'

A figure on a box bearing carefully intertwined Israeli and American flags, a thin figure, pale and loosely put together. Lost like an infant posed in its father's clothing, in an overlarge Star of David T-shirt. A slight breeze flapped the flags against his face and obscured the volume of his sub-biblical, self-announcing diction.

'. . . for I am here to tell you that evil can be defeated and eradicated. Not only that, but that the time is nigh. Isaiah seventeen verse one: "The burden of Damascus. Behold, Damascus is taken away from being a city, and it shall be a ruinous heap." Damascus, the capital of the rogue Arab Muhammadan state of Syria, the enemy of Christ and Israel, is the oldest . . .'

Sami's brain completed the formula. The oldest continuously inhabited city on earth.

'Damascus has never yet been a ruin, so this prophecy is still to come. And verily, it shall be us of this generation who shall witness this wonder.'

He wasn't loud or muscular enough to draw significant numbers. His ten or fifteen spectators made a limp and listless audience, committing themselves to only a few paragraphs before moving on to sample another loon.

'For I am here, people of England, to tell you. I am here to announce the tribulation.'

He picked the tail of a flag out of his eye.

'Yeah,' he said. 'Yay, for the Jews have returned unto Zion. Ezekiel thirty-six verse twenty-four: "For I will take you from among the heathen, and gather you out of all countries, and will bring you into your own land." So sayeth the Lord, and so it has come to pass. And, yay, the endtimes are nigh.'

He took breath.

'So I'm telling you all, this is the time to wake up and change your life around. I'm here to say, repent ye and join the faithful. Turn ye to Christ. For the time of the rapture approaches, when the true faithful shall be transported unto heaven. And for those remaining there shall be a tribulation and a purifying fire and a pestilence and a . . .'

The apocalypse ended in a spluttering as the flags once more intervened. The preacher had raised an arm skyward at the mention of the rapture.

'Then one hundred and forty-four thousand Jews, as it is prophesied, shall repent their error and accept the risen Christ. And the Antichrist shall rule from Babylon, and he shall make a covenant with Israel. Until such time as the final battle on the field at Armageddon. The remnant of the Christians with the converted Jews shall defeat Satan, and Christ in his glory shall return. For the unbelieving Jews and Muhammadans there shall be hellfire unending.'

He added an afterthought.

'And hellfire also for the United Nations world government and for Communists and the Chinese hordes.'

The audience had changed half its composition, which made Sami one of the old guard. The preacher tried to catch his eye.

'Now, brethren, I am here to rouse you with my wake-up call. People of England, it is decision time. Are you with Christ, brethren, or do you stand against him? Are you girded for Christ's work? For at this time we must prepare Christ's way by supporting Israel against the Muhammadans. The in-gathering of the Jews is our priority. Muhammadans and Communists shall stand against us, as it is prophesied. But Damascus, yay, shall be a ruinous heap. And the Lord God shall smite those who oppose him.'

Sami extricated himself and walked off quickly, stabbing the ground with his feet. He was hot and thirsty and sunblind. His thoughts chained through clasps of anger – plenty of anger as he associated the preacher with the morning's news – and fear, which displaced hunger as his dominant intestinal mood, and self-pity. His head steamed up with it as he stepped on to the grass, and on his inner screen he directed an angry fantasy, in which he identified himself with a Palestinian of the camps. A man grown up surrounded by death, shaped by death. Who has seen death take his father, his brother, his neighbours. Death operating out in the open, not veiled like here. Faces of the dead pasted on the walls. The streets named after those who have died in them. Neighbourhoods named after dead villages. Militias named in honour of the dead. Death everywhere in the ruinous heap of the camp, imprinting itself on everything.

His gaze was down, stuttering over cracked turf and cans and crisp packets. Dehydration stopped him sweating but his face was burning. On the inner screen he was a man who defeats death by choosing it. Who conquers humiliation. Conquers the fear of death by walking towards it, cold-hearted. Cold in the heart like crushed snow on a blank hill.

He remembered Muhammad ad-Dura, the boy who was first wounded then killed as his father screamed for the Israeli troops to cease their fire. Huddled under a useless wall. The humiliated father humiliated with the ultimate humiliation. Once the boy was dead, finally, after twenty minutes of it, the father dropped his head into the blood, his blood and his son's drying blood, his dark eyes dulled, no longer registering pain or terror or anything at all once he'd failed to save his son. Killed in the crossfire, the English news said.

So Sami saw himself in this early Intifada scene. He would give himself up to save the father, whose head would now be raised in a new kind of awe as he hears the triumphant cry of the leaping crowd as Sami rushes through, forgetful of himself, with only Palestinian stones in his fists, into the line of fire, a bullet meant for the child's corpse thudding into him in a spatter and a gouging but he only coming faster because they haven't yet hit his heart, the Israeli boy soldiers in awe also, aiming and firing but unable to deflect the perfect fury of this dying body, gaining velocity, raising its arms, expanding to the size of a nation, an earth. Mr ad-Dura brought to his feet, the cringing soldiers in defeat. And Sami in another realm embracing the boy while the earthly Sami, the corpse, sinks into its inescapable blood and bone.

He jerks on over the baked grass. It's not enough. So he blows up the Israeli soldiers and their Western weaponry in a fountain of metal and gore, and blows up the fucking American supporters of Zionism too, the preachers and moneymen who don't have the excuse of the Holocaust for their derangement, with their humane God hypocrisy and their freedom and civilization hypocrisy and their double-standard racism hypocrisy and their weak Disney-Torah rhetoric and all their power.

A bracing, crushing halt. A real hand closed around his throat.

'Cunt,' spat the owner of the hand. 'Cunt. What you looking at.'

A skinhead had caught him. Pub odours spurting from lipless mouth, shaven head glistening, a cross the blue of tears tattooed on the forehead, round eyes unblinking, puckered pink nipples sitting fatly on hairless chest. Two pierced women on the ground behind kneeling upright and aroused.

The hand tightened, raising Sami's chin, bruising glands and tonsils.

'Cunt,' it said again.

'Nothing,' Sami tried to say, but his throat instead made a wet gurgle. Some sweat was squeezed out of him, as out of a stone. His eyes watered. Eventually he made a twisted, high-shouldered shrug.

The crusher, the bearer of the cross, relinquished Sami, the cunt, with post-coital disdain, and turned to his flushed consorts with his palms flattened, bouncing a nodding grin to beckon applause.

Sami heard it in their sniggering. Prayers for their Hellenic hero, their man of action. He staggered away towards the Serpentine, there not being anything else to do, swallowing painfully on the shame. He ignored whoever may have seen him, wished he could ignore himself. At a time like this you think you need a hug from your loved ones, but thank God, thought Sami, that his loved ones were dead, or rejected, or sick of him. Even himself is sick of him. And thank God for it. Sympathy would destroy him. Much better to swallow the pain alone. Humiliation is a worse enemy than loneliness.

In the high sky, above trees and the lake, a carbonate-tinted cloud found shape like spreading blood, forming shoulders, breasts, hips, triangulated elbows: an Ishtar of the approaching evening.

Sami in the burnt desolation of Hyde Park, in a wilderness of disconnection, trying to see inside his head a winter scene, a coolness and emptiness, but it's far too late for that. He can't recapture the purity of snow. What flickering visions he manages are of half-thawed city slush, browned by exhaust fumes, spattered by phlegm, yellowed where it's been pissed on by dogs and drunks.

25
Fast

Sami could take no pride in himself. This statement needs no further explanation, except to say that his body by itself was a humiliation. An empirically verifiable humiliation.

According to the principle that an indulged and flabby body bespeaks an indulged and flabby spirit, Sami began to renounce his pleasures.

Lager and whiskey had been the first to go. He fancied this left him unbloated, less bitter. And there was the added advantage of keeping him out of pubs, away from people.

And he'd discontinued smoking spliffs. After that he was clearer-headed, but still felt he had weight – literal and metaphorical – to shed. Clarity needled and prickled him. There was a lot of time. A lot of distance to his vision. He went for hasty, pointless, broken walks. He fidgeted in the room. He pushed the plastic campus furniture about.

Chewing on his cheeks, dust-chested, dirty-mouthed from the extra (compensatory) cigarettes, he frowned upon the plastic ash-trays. He kicked tobacco.

It wasn't enough. Noticing that the desire to smoke was almost the same voidish sensation as hunger, he set out to eliminate the most immediately gratifying foodstuffs. Cafés and restaurants, with their trapped crowds and trapped air, were now out of the question, and so, therefore, was Balti sauce, battery flesh, glutinous fast food of all varieties. He abjured the white substances – the processed breads, pastas and rices – only one remove (in a fast absorptive blam! of lazy intestine) from glucose.

He worried about preservatives, flavourings and other

E-numbers, about genetically modified foods. He worried about the smeary fingers of packing workers. He sought out produce that was organic, though the word reminded him of what he'd rather forget. He repudiated sugar and salt, which effort made him less sweet, less sour, and more neutral, closer to the middle path. He worried about origins too. He'd always made a point of avoiding Israeli avocados, but now it was environmentalism rather than nationalist politics that dictated his buying. The further a foodstuff was made to travel the more carbonate was belched into the air, and the more filth rained or wheezed back on to Sami. Through such filth he walked to markets for lettuce, carrots, tomatoes, radishes, marrows – the muddier the better. On his return he spent half an hour at the basin scouring them skinless. And English apples and pears. Occasionally, for luxury, some Mediterranean citrus, which made him guilty, polluted and ill – the thought of heavy vehicles swinging like blistered whales along grey motorways, through choking tunnels.

He contemplated the eating of meat. The shovelling of chunks of one rotting body inside another. Meat which defiles the intestines for forty-eight hours after ingestion. Who has sniffed meat left standing for two days at body temperature? Who has then wondered why shit smells like shit? Anyway, the packaged shit on supermarket shelves is swollen with those chemicals which made Sami want to go organic. Even the halal shit sold by Sami's mother, Nur, is machine-hacked from pilled-up steroid-sick neon-lit creatures. It's called halal because there's a voice on a cassette player coughing 'In the Name of God' between pulls on a fag, between machine swipes at the animal's false-fatted neck. So Sami gave up meat. Which meant he needed less sleep.

He cut down on sleep, from eight hours to seven, to six, to five. He felt less comfortable, less cushioned, but more awake. He understood how deceived he'd been in his presumed requirements. This inspired him to omit his evening meal. For two days he was hungry, or looking for a smoke. Then he adjusted to his new habit. He perceived a glimmer of power here: that he could organize the beast by setting its habits, that he could programme himself. He realized too how easy it was to deny himself things, now that he lived alone. So many of his previous needs had been demonstrations for Muntaha's notice, muffled invitations to her to fill his gaps.

Sami aimed for self-control. The body, he reasoned – and the self is what he meant – was a monster that could be weakened through lack of sustenance. A bit of self-applied Sufism. The less food, he reasoned, the less metabolism. The less farting and burping, the less inner churning. Not that it worked out like that. There was a particularly nasty gut exhalation that became impossible to ignore after six hours of non-ingestion. The Prophet said: *By Him in whose Hands my soul is, the smell coming out from the mouth of a fasting person is better in the sight of God than the smell of musk.* But Sami's olfactory perceptions were less than divine.

He fasted Muslim-style, dawn to dusk, no liquids or solids. He also tried a week-long juice fast, though he grew squeamish at the sibilance of the word itself. Juice. The wormy lip-puckering sound of it, as if he was squeezing juice as he spoke it. The thought of it, the carrot and parsley and marrow mulch spurting through intestinal tunnels – a kind of reverse colonic irrigation – made him wriggle. All those associated slow-vomit words did: 'spill' and 'spew', 'purge' and 'purify'. Somehow they brought him to Syrian detention chambers. Hanging parties. The detergent of bombs. Liquidation: there was a word suitable for a juice fast, and for an eradicating regime. For anyone in a hurry to build a new, secular consciousness.

Around the clock he heard a child screaming, wishing it to shut the fuck up but then stopping himself because he knew the child's universe of suffering was more vast than his would ever be again. It being a child. Him being an adult, conscious of the changing nature of emotional states. Conscious of flux. He didn't know where the screams came from, what with the stale modernist architecture ricocheting sound waves in all directions. The child was a mystery, wailing at unknown injustices. Sami thought the area had been purged of families.

Sami, increasingly aware of basic facts. Of his body palpitating, processing, without his consent or control, twenty-four hours a day for all the days of his life, entirely indifferent to his ideological pursuits. Atheist, agnostic or Muslim, the body paid not the least attention, so busy it was producing aromas.

He smelled pinkish at the tip of his penis, a little closer to the core there, not quite skin. Where most Englishmen were protected, or where their attendant English penile biomatter was protected, by a flap. It was the best smell his body managed, but its curdling, pointless sweetness nauseated him nevertheless.

His fungal groin gradated through the tugs and tangles of wiry hair from balls to arse – his arse was undoubtedly the hairiest part of him – arse which was citrus-sour but more darkly tanged, something of a Balti in it, or something still more southern, still more tropical, a South East Asia of a smell, containing all the regional diseases. Yellow fever, typhoid, Japanese encephalitis. All these were latent at his lower entrance. Which made him wonder about inside proper. What equatorial vapours did he contain? What toxic inner worlds? (He'd got on closer terms with his arse since he'd started post-defecatory washing in the Muslim style, rather than just smearing it around with paper. Rather than rubbing the waste against his skin and curls, pushing atoms of it back into him, through the pores – how had he done that for all his life?)

He was a weary explorer through the body's olfactory moss, wanting only to hack out of it, to slash and burn, to get home, to get to civilization and a warm bath. But a real warm bath, a literal shower, provided no exit. For we're talking here about Sami in a clean state, as inoffensive odour-wise as it is possible for him to be. Unwashed, it's a different story.

Sami unwashed. His unclean underarm aroma was brownish, greyish, ashland air, the wind of the grave, of the crematorium. There was the grey stuff secreted in his nostrils, London stuff to remind the citizens of their city's sooty past and car-carbonate present. (He took to another Islamic habit, snuffing water into his nose up to the sinuses and then blowing, snorting it out.) There was his goaty piss and his shit rising to him like evacuated organs.

On these days of scrubbed leaves and local fruit it came like abrupt moist bullets. Dirt attacking on two fronts, from inside as well as out. How could he cleanse the inside?

He showered morning and evening and whenever he returned from outside. He did head, hands and feet more frequently at the basin. He brushed his teeth five times a day. He brushed his heart-like cow-stubborn tongue. Towelled orange wax from his earholes. Washing was a race against time, and given the starting blocks of basic stink he was always at a disadvantage. His smell at zero point was a block of concrete tied to one foot, a rope tied tight around his knees.

He read a newspaper article about the two hundred toxins found in human breast milk. Over-concentrations of fluoride and chlorine, the poisons of a benevolent state, and corporate pesticides, carbonates, lead. There was no escaping. Shampoo and soap contributed their own artificialities. The degenerate metal of the shower pipe, the water itself, was filth.

Muslims wash before the five daily prayers, to be clean before God, to not offend their fellows, and also to consider their moral taints. Old-time desert logic. Logic reliant on water filtered and salted through the rocks of an unraped earth. How do you get clean now? How do you eat clean? For halal meat you wash and pray and calm the animal with recitation and tender strokes before 'In the Name of God' slicing the throat. You bleed the animal to drain out hormones. Assuming a world which doesn't inject the hormones into muscle from the creature's supervised birth. No such thing as clean slaughter in an industrial age. Too many consumers to fuel. Not enough profit to bloody your margin if you take your time passing out the commodity. Which makes the hygiene laws about as relevant to the internet generation as a Qur'anic education. To make hygiene relevant, Sami was in need of that desert which didn't exist any more. The Arab desert before depleted uranium and plastic bags, before metal shafts thrust like fingers into the throat of the waste to bring up its black oil. He needed ancient, parched, sterile atmospheres, too dry even for ghosts.

The child's screaming worked at his thoughts, shaking his memories out of place and into sight – obscured screaming the rattling background theme to his mental life.

Under scalding water one showertime Sami remembered a Faris. An uncle. This Faris had visited at least once in Sami's boyhood, once among the more readily recalled visits of his mother's family. Fadya, Shihab, old Haj Ahmad Kallas. And Faris. Handsome, neatly bearded, swaggering slightly. Sami remembered him sitting at the kitchen table drinking tea, telling jokes. Nothing like the loon in Fadya's back room. But he'd come to London, he'd existed. So Nur hadn't exactly kept the knowledge from him. It was Sami who'd forgotten, until now.

Back in the room, towelling himself, he heard the high inhuman wailing of the mystery child, keening like seagulls. Let it wail, he told himself. Don't be angry. He remembered his aunt's anger as she told the story of Faris. He remembered the question his cousin had asked. *I wonder who informed on Uncle Faris? I wonder who told the mukhabarat?* They'd stared at him, waiting for him to respond. As if it had something to do with him.

The child had ceased wailing. Its forgetfulness of suffering was vaster too.

And what of sex? Our culture's first advice to a man in Sami's position (not much of a man, but perhaps becoming more manly), to a man alone, is: get over it. Get out on the pull. There's a few more fish in the overfished sea, a few more birds staggering in the sick air. Liberated from the marriage bonds, Sami owned the gift of the new century. Namely, the freedom to choose, to unwrap, to possess. But promotion of yourself as a suitable partner, from what he could work out from a glance at the zeitgeist, requires a promise of service. And after his decade of marital commitment – all right, sexual commitment; all right, a decade of failure or fear to stray – he wasn't too sure of his ability there. Sex beyond habit – how was it done? He wasn't about to trust the body's instincts, any more than he could trust the heart.

Back home, lying on his crumpled couch, legs buckled up, not fitting, he had masturbated half-heartedly, sometimes finishing, sometimes not. A sign of his passed youth that these days it took something exciting to excite him. But now in the student room he never started. Another discontinued pleasure. Another horror, the pulsing of the ducts, the alien production of clotted liquid.

These were some of the reasons he lived autonomously of women. But the main reason was, he harboured hopes of returning to the much more hopefully liberated Muntaha. Muntaha with the doors of opportunity open. He wasn't going to find better. That was obvious. For him, it was either a recognition of his place with her, if she closed her doors and let him, or some form or other of suicide.

He spoke to her about twice a week. He'd made three full apologies, for his general selfishness and lack of direction as well as for his specific unfaithfulness. She'd neither forgiven him nor rubbed it in. She just paused to hear it and then raced on, in her own direction. Telling him her plans for a year in Iraq and charity work. Plans which didn't seem to include him. She wasn't in need of any of his education. Entirely self-sufficient.

Many pre-dawn mornings Ammar banged the door, jerking Sami up against his sheets, in the subdued orange illumination that insinuated through the curtainless window, the glow of London's night sky reflecting the student surveillance lights of the compound.

Ammar strode in salaaming, Mujahid shuffling behind. They waited for Sami to shower, and while he dressed Ammar would make Islamo-affirmative commentary.

'Sami depressed again. Subhanallah, this gifted brother here, with all the blessings Allah gives him, miserable and depressed. Look at yourself, brother. You're a Muslim, you're worth something.'

Look at yourself. Something Brother Sami didn't wish to do. Not at the physical surface anyway. He had considered smashing the mirror, but it was institutional property and fixed to the wall. He'd covered it instead with a shimmering green cloth Blu-tacked to its corners.

The believers waited while Sami brushed teeth and tongue,

Mujahid as silent as Sami, embarrassed. Sami flossed, wrinkling a long nose at the presumed chemicals on the thread. He washed them off his fingers. Then Ammar nudged Mujahid.

'Time for Fajr prayer, brothers.'

Mujahid wheezed the call, and Sami huddled up next to him, toe to toe, black beard to red, and followed the motions behind his brother-in-law. He did it because it was too early for debating. And he did it for brotherhood. As prayer, he told himself, it didn't count.

Some mornings Ammar drove them to sleeping suburbs in the north west (less state militia up here, he said), where he stopped to move Sami on to the driving seat. In Sami's control the car shuddered around the crescents and cul-de-sacs, an oaf in the presence of more monied vehicles. There were detached brick houses overcrept with ivy, occasional shops and pubs imitating village architecture, with whitewash and gables and pretend Tudor beams. Arched windows and rose-trellised passageways. Professionally tended gardens. Bird baths. Churches moated by graveslabs and deep grass. Paperboys. Milk rounds. Things that were extinct further in.

The car triggered burglar lights when it stalled. An early-riser frowning at them from the even pavement, dressed in expensive tracksuit and paunch. Ammar leaned from the window: 'Yo, faithless, your time's coming.' Mujahid nodded, ready to be the enforcer. Sami felt like nodding too. Out here in the comfort zone he felt put upon, deprived. His vulnerability in the driving seat increased the anxiety. As a driver, Sami was not a gifted brother, his foot cramping with tension on the pedals, his lungs making shallow inhalations to avoid exhaust fumes – breath as juddery as the fuel fed into the engine – his fingers fluttering on the electricity of gear stick, indicator, wheel.

Sami remembered how it was to feel good, talented, a creature of potential, writing clever essays at school, holding his own in precocious conversation with Mustafa's colleagues. Talented through other eyes, usually his father's. Others' definitions had sufficed him. He remembered sharing whiskey in the hospital room.

Jameson's. His father liked Irish whiskey, said it was less complicit in empire. The kind of comment Sami took with religious seriousness then. The whiskey warmth in his gut made him tearful. Never liked whiskey really. But the compensation was being admitted to the warmth of manly intimacy, credited with the keys of adulthood. He was a prince, an inheritor. The president's son.

'Don't worry, brother.' (Ammar reassuring a shaking Sami, who'd accelerated through a red light nearly into the side of a truck.) 'You're safe with your brothers. Say bismillah, nothing can hurt you.'

'If Allah had wanted to,' Mujahid joined in from the back, 'he'd have mashed us then.'

'That's right. We're in His hands. Nothing happens but what's meant to happen. Put your trust in Allah, feel no fear.'

None of this seemed appropriate to Sami, stalled in the car somewhere beyond Finchley in the grey morning, but he couldn't respond. There was an engine jam in his brain.

'If Allah wanted to . . .' said Mujahid, doing something very Irish with the last syllable of Allah. This was his favourite line. If Allah wanted to. This Islamo-hippy. Bush of a beard, flowing robes, jumping the ethno-barrier. Three decades previously he'd have been into flower power, not the power of the umma. If Allah had wanted. Like Allah was a giant fairy ready to swoop down and interfere with every little nugget of human history. For instance, during one of their in-chassis educational talks on the Sunni–Shia divide: 'If Allah had wanted to, He'd have made Ali the successor to the Prophet. Peace be upon him. But He didn't want to, so He didn't.'

'That's right,' said Ammar. 'So they should shut up about it.'

'I don't know.' Sami broke his usual silence. 'I don't know anything about it. But it was politics, wasn't it, after the Prophet? I suppose it's justified to have a political opinion.'

'If Allah had wanted . . .'

Ammar cut his student off.

'These Shia, they're kuffar really. They split us up when we need unity. They do the devil's work whether they know it or not. We have to purge these impurities, brother. Become one.'

There it was again. Purge, purify, imprison, torture. *I wonder who informed on Uncle Faris?*

Some mornings Ammar drove them west, for training. 'While the Crusaders sleep,' he said. The early roads still loose as flushed bowels, Ammar would indicate left before swiftly lurching right, or manoeuvre screeching U-turns.

'This is how not to do it, yeah? Not when you're driving the cab. This is how you lose a tracker.'

'Someone tracking you?'

'You never know, brother.' Then, noting Sami's swallowed-lips grin: 'Nah, not now. But this is training.'

In slow dawn on Wormwood Scrubs, with Ammar barking whispered orders, they stretched, did sit-ups, press-ups. Military crawls through morning-moist weeds.

'We could do this nearer you.' Ammar giving the impression of measuring words by the millimetre. 'Regent's Park. Hampstead Heath. But we're safer on the Scrubs.' And more cryptically: 'We've got it . . . erm . . . pegged.'

Pegged? Reference to tents? The pavilions of the first holy warriors? Sami let it go. There was dogshit everywhere, at this hour like icebergs hidden in a dark sea. They jogged a long circuit. Planes in the cloud above, traffic rumble occult on the horizons. Training finished with a race, which Ammar, spider legs clicking, always won. Mujahid second, with the tighter movements of a crustacean. Sami last, being early middle-aged. Blood tubes in his brain constricted above the ears, chest sputtering like the combustion engine, stealing oxygen, puking carbonate. Now his more urgent race began, to have them deliver him to the student room, and the shower. He had only minutes before the sweat sheen staled on him.

He jogged to the car when they wanted to stroll. 'Training's never over,' he said, successfully, to enthuse them. He wanted to get back fast, but they wanted to educate him.

They quoted Qur'anic prophecies concerning cars: *And (it is He who creates) horses and mules and asses for you to ride, as well as for (their) beauty: and He will yet create things of which (today) you have no knowledge* (Qur'an 16.8).

Between Westbourne Park and Marylebone they explained how light travels in a day the distance the moon travels in a thousand years, how the Qur'an contains this information. Statistics, equations he didn't understand. By Marylebone, and the shops opening for business, he had a millennium's worth of self-stink in his nostrils. New wax in his ears. The Qur'an says the earth is egg-shaped, that the mountains move like clouds, that stars and planets swim in their orbits. Sami swam in encrusting sweat, in brewing shit. The shower, please God, fast. The Qur'an gave hints to brain science, describing the cerebrum – *the lying, rebellious forehead!* – as the site of lies and aggression. Sami's forehead yellowed, full of heat.

But strangely enough, Sami felt at ease with these boys talking science. There was little otherworldly in it. It was his own dirt that made him panic. So to forget it, to keep it at bay, he steered the talk to more local issues.

'How's everything at home?'

'Fine. Aunt Hasna's upset. You heard about Salim.'

Salim. Her good, obedient, Iraqi son. Doctor Salim.

'No.'

'He's engaged to a Nigerian nurse.'

'Fuck.'

'That's right. Without his mother's permission, of course. Which is not good, if you ask me. The ties of the womb and so on. Otherwise, good for him. She's a sister. Hausa girl. Muhajjiba.'

'What else?'

'My sister's missing you.'

'Did she say so?'

'Not so much say so. But I see it, man. I know.'

Mujahid sank in silence on the back seat. Silence all round. The lack of words seemed to stretch the minutes out. So Sami brought them back to their favourite topics.

'What exactly are you training for?'

'The last battle, brother.'

'So it's coming up, is it?'

'Coming fast.' Ammar bowing his forehead in satisfied assent at his own comment, as if he'd found a bonus in his pay packet.

'Well, you know better than me on the Islamic thing. But at the time of the Mongols there were Muslims who thought the endtimes were around the corner.'

'Irrelevant. Read the traditions of the Prophet and his companions. The signs are falling into place.'

Their interest, like Mustafa's, was ancient and modern, cutting out the centre of Islamic history.

'Palestine, brother. Iraq. Crusader bases all over the Gulf, on holy soil. Vodka-addicted atheists raping our sisters in Chechnya. Brothers in Bosnia blockaded so they can't defend themselves from kuffar. Hindus desecrating mosques in Kashmir. Oppression all over the umma. But we waking up now. Palestine's the start of it. Soon there'll be a world Intifada, and then this training will have a purpose. You too, Sami. There'll be purpose for you.'

'Is God not purpose enough? Not my place to ask, I suppose, but . . .'

'God's not here, is He? I mean His nation's here, and His rulebook. His constitution. It's our job to implement His law. To change this state of oppression.'

Ammar, in the absence of God, must find the absolute elsewhere.

'But if Allah had wanted . . .' put in Sami, sly.

'Shit, Sami.' Ammar slipping. 'Don't play games. It's a different issue. Action is what we need. Allah doesn't change the state of a people until they change what's in themselves. You not learning that yet? We need to be ready.'

26
Pyramid Power

'Action is what we need.' Ammar's sentence reverberated in Sami's idleness. His pride had already been swallowed, pushed fibrously through his cleaned-up system, and shat out into the bowl of past time. There was therefore no reason why he shouldn't take the first job he could find. He was even learning to drive, which meant accepting his status as damned and helpless contributor to the Earth's death – as carbonate merchant. Who was he to resist? The system was greater than him, and he was ready for any indignity, economically speaking. Anything to earn his daily bread. In one evening's *Standard*, he read:

Pyramid Power
Marketing Professionals Urgently Required
The Future Starts Here
No Experience Necessary.

He pitched his voice to self-sale and called the number. A machine answered, telling him success was waiting riverside at eight every morning. He rubbed his shoes with a cloth and scissored the edges of his beard. Ammar provided him with suit and pressed shirt. He set his alarm for five, making time to shower and to progress across the city gently enough not to bring forth sweat.

The address in his pocket named a two-storey building crammed beneath a railway arch. He arrived early and paced the pavement, practising smiles. Some booming vibration swam from upstairs to meet the traffic in fishy embrace. Young, brightly dressed people skipped E-happy through the door. It looked like a morning-after party. Sami even wondered if he'd misunderstood the advert. Had it been cryptic warehouse-rave code? 'Future Starts Here' sounded junglistic enough, and of course 'Pyramid Power'. Rave, or New Age, or Masonic. But Marketing Professionals? How out of touch was he?

At five minutes to the appointment he pushed the steel door open. A wooden door to his immediate right was handleless and marked with a no-entry X. Otherwise, a stairwell. He had to step through a triangular polystyrene frame to start climbing. An A4 printout reading 'The Ascension' was stapled to the apex. He ascended, approaching trance tones, a clickety beat, big booms. At the top, two more doors of unadorned, gouged wood, labelled 'Initiated' (to his right) and 'Uninitiated'. Sami supposed he was uninitiated, and knocked. The door was opened.

A blonde in business skirt and blouse said 'welcome' into his eyes. The South London accent didn't match the greeting. She ushered him inward and pointed to an imitation-leather couch. A black girl perched there nervous as a deer, hands clasped around slim stockinged knees. The corners of her wide mouth twitched upwards. Sami smiled hello.

'Welcome,' repeated the blonde. 'Be seated if you will. A few minutes only.'

She swished into a back office.

Sami sat, subsiding further than he'd expected into the couch's numb reception. The rave sound was quietened, as if the room were soundproofed. His couch companion rolled involuntarily towards him, touched her hand on his thigh to steady herself, and grinned 'oops!' to make it friendly.

'I'm Aisha,' she said, lifting her hand from his thigh to shake.

He took it. 'I'm Sami.'

'Pleased to meet you, Sami.'

She sustained her smiling, unbroken as a river's flow. Liquid black eyes unblemished. The whiteness of her teeth. The pinkness of her tongue. It was revelatory to Sami to remember that a human could be pure. He couldn't name her smell but it was inside him like spring-cleaning. Molecules of her floating inside his brain, sparking receptors.

She asked him, 'Any experience of this kind of work?'

'No. Well, I don't know what it's going to be really, but no anyway. I was trying to be an academic until recently.'

'Academic? That's interesting. I think it's sales. I've done a little. It's all right if you keep thinking positive. I need this one, though. No money in the bank. I need this one.' She flicked crossed fingers between their noses. 'I need it, God,' she prayed.

The blonde returned, bearing papers. 'Welcome,' she said, to Sami's eyes, then Aisha's. She dropped her gaze to give instructions, and kept it dropped as she turned and sashayed away. An efficiency of skirt-bound buttocks.

They each had a form to fill. Name, Age, Birth Sign. Then an open question: How Much Do You Want To Win?

Sami Traifi, Sami wrote. Virgo. He put twenty-seven for age. How Much Do You Want To Win? He answered in genre: One Hell Of A Lot.

He waited for Aisha to finish. She wrote a paragraph about winning in tiny letters, the pen pushed hard into the resistance of her folded leg.

'Aisha. That's a Muslim name.'

'Don't know. It's Aisha Smith. My Mum says it's African, Aisha. You Muslim?'

'Well, in a way. By birth, yeah.'

'Fair enough.' A sporting smile.

'Aisha was the name of the Prophet Muhammad's favourite wife.'

The blonde returned, face to carpet. 'I'll gather these,' she said, 'if I may.' And next into Aisha's eyes, Sami recognizing this contact to be scripted: 'Welcome, Ee-sha. It'll be your turn first.'

Aisha rose, smoothing herself down. As he watched her legs recede, heels striking the tiled floor, Sami felt a twinge of fear on her behalf. Deer hooves clacking on concrete.

Someone came forward to meet her, tall and padded, suited like a mukhabarat man. Neck erupting from a tight, white collar, and a fleshy chin, a roast-tomato tan on tumescent nose and cheeks. Sunken green eyes, pools bordered by red anemones. His moist forehead bulging. Creamed brown hair. He slapped at Aisha's palm like she was a male. Like a rugby player in the bar. 'Antony,' he said.

Left alone, Sami sat forward, thinking American artifice to put him in the mood for the new economy. Cartoons in technicolour, novelty, fast food, gadgets, gloss. Muffled rave through the wall. Aisha's neat shape engraved next to him.

No more than two minutes passed and she was back, over-shadowed by Antony's bulk.

'Thanks a lot now.' He dismissed her. 'That'll be all for today.' His smile slapped on like sunscreen.

Sami stood. Again she presented her hand. A fact, unarguable.

'I know you'll be selected,' she told him. 'You have personality.'

Her face was curved and full like the stages of the moon stitched together, but seamless. Her skin didn't mask any of her emotion, which made her vulnerable in this environment. She was upset, and she also wished Sami well. Genuine on both counts. No script. Old-fashioned, really.

Sami took his turn, swinging into the mid-Atlantic shake-slap presented him.

'I'm Antony. In charge of this operation. On the peak of the pyramid.'

'Pleased to meet you, Antony.' First names are important. The mask of intimacy.

'Firm shake. I like it.' Antony smiled into Sami's eyes to indicate the liking. 'Please step this way.'

He sat in an imitation-leather armchair on one side of an empty desk, Sami on the other side, on a plastic chair. On the wall behind there was a portrait of Antony framed in imitation gold leaf. Lines like rays or roots were drawn downwards from the photograph into a descending base of more photos, fifty or sixty, passport sized. In the portrait Antony beamed as he was beaming now.

'Sami, my brother.' Raising his head from Sami's form. 'I call you brother because we're a family here at Pyramid Power. You can think of Pyramid Power as your home. Now. You say you want to win one hell of a lot. Can you expand?'

'Not so much want,' Sami said, 'as need.'

Antony cocked his head with worry. Sami noted it, and inspiration flowed.

'Not so much need,' he said, 'as desire. Desire strong enough to be need. I'm already a winner. Let me out there, I'll bring home the trophies.'

'I like it!' Antony congratulated him. 'Sami, Sam. You know what the S stands for?'

'Success?' Sami offered.

'That's another possibility. Not what I was looking for, though.'

'Er . . . sales?'

'Sex, Sam, sex. That desire you mentioned, very aptly. You're a . . . think of yourself as a penis, yeah?'

'OK.' Sami grinned.

'Seriously. A throbbing member, Sam.' Thin lips curled. 'I'm going to set you free. You're going to penetrate the world out there, find the sale, and – boom!' A handclap. 'Orgasm, Sam. Sex, Sam.'

'I'm ready for that.'

'I know you are. I know more than you think.'

'All right.'

'This is S for safe sex. You don't lose, Sam. I'm going to give you twenty quid just for returning home this evening, sale or no sale.'

'OK, then. Thanks.'

'You're on board.' Antony springing erect, hand groping in his pocket. 'I'm gifting you something special now. Something – I jest not, Sam – something sacred.' Extending a silver key across the desk. 'The key to the manor. The key to the future.'

Sami took it. Smeared his fingerprints on it.

'Thanks a lot.'

'One more thing, Sam.' A low, confidential tone. 'The beard will have to go. You know what they say about beards?'

'No, not really.'

'Beards bedevil business.' Antony sympathizing. 'Off with it by tomorrow, OK?'

'Sure. It's only recent.'

'Good. Jules will guide you.'

With a flapping of palms markedly less feel-good than the interview, the blonde directed Sami from the office and through the Uninitiated room. Through the door and to the next. Initiated.

'Your key,' she said, pointing at his pockets.

Sami unlocked the door.

The sound dipped into a hollow.

'Sam!' announced Jules.

'Welcome!' A crowd of perhaps thirty in integrated greeting. Not much space between them. A high frequency of blacks. And Bengalis. The whites breaking off into accents of recent arrival – Spanish, Slavic – as the music rose again, and Jules steered Sami to a square-headed black.

'Scoop. He's yours.'

They did the knuckle thing.

'Right, Sam. Let me give you lesson one.'

'Your name's Scoop?' Sami shouted.

'Skittle. Pyramid name's Scoop.'

'I'm Sami, with an "ee".'

Jules stood diagonally to him, glaring. Skittle followed Sami's incomprehension to its source, and whipped back, furious.

'Keep to the fucking pyramid name!' Skittle, Scoop, mouthed, then recovered himself. 'All right. Lesson one,' he said. Probably said. Too much clickety bump in the background – into which Jules had dwindled – for aural clarity. 'The Three Ps. Means Package, Present, Promote. That's a philosophy, Sam. You know anything about philosophy?'

The lesson lasted until Antony bounced in, red and wet. With a body twist and an upper cut he shouted, triumphant, 'Pyramid Power!' And the initiated shouted it back, with spittle and breath.

'The pyramid.' Antony quietened them, broodily scanning their half of the room. 'A sacred structure. A power structure. A way,' he whispered, uptilting his fat chin, 'a way up.'

There was awe in the air, but it hadn't reached Sami. What was wrong with him that he couldn't share people's enthusiasms? The awe hung viscous, until Antony snapped it down.

'All right. Sisters and brothers. It's another morning. It's time again for me to tell you a tale. The tale of me, your leader.'

He spoke with a weariness.

'You've heard it before. You hear it every morning. And to tell you the truth it's a tale I get more than a little bored of telling. Until I reach the end. Why bored? Because it could be anyone's story, the first bit. It's probably the story of most of you, change a few details. So I'll be brief. The details not being in the least bit interesting, or in the least bit important. Just background. You'll have noticed, by the way, that I didn't ask any of you about your backgrounds when you first ascended these stairs. Because I know. It's happened to me. I've been there. And it isn't in the least bit important.'

A pause which indicated both humility and hard experience. Then a sigh.

'Right then. Let's get on. Me, in my case, I was in Australia. And I thought, to put it bluntly, I thought I was fucking God. Oh yeah. Fucking marvellous. And there'll be no more cursing because it doesn't fit the package that we are, so I won't be having it, but just to let you know my mindset at the time. I was a fucking king. On top of the fucking world. Right. That's what I thought.'

He allowed a pop-eyed chuckle.

'Right. I thought I had the world sussed. Lying on the beach. Drinking beer. Smoking the wacky backy. Girlfriends. Books. Oh yeah, books. Tell you what, thought I was Jean-Paul Sartre, a philosopher.'

And on that word he became more toxic.

'A philosopher, for God's sake. A beach-arse philosopher. Until one day, a simple thing, my tooth started hurting me. Really hurting. And I didn't have the cash to go to the dentist. So I ask my so-called friends to help me out, and it's all, sorry Antony, man, like be cool, yeah, but there's no moolah for you. But I'm in agony, I'm crying with it, and they've disappeared, so I've learnt something. I've learnt, there's no friendship, there's only respect. And I commanded none. Which depressed me. I wanted to come home. But I had no cash for the ticket. What I was, was helpless. What I was, was nothing. I was shit, that's what I was. No cursing, but making allowances for the mindset, for my new awareness of my basic situation. I was shit. Worth nothing.'

At last Sami felt a mild splashing of emotion. He cupped it protectively inside himself, to keep it safe, to be one with the others.

'So I was shit slopping around on the beach, when I met someone. Jeff.'

A collective lightening, and some gasps of relief. Jeff was a known deity.

'Jeff. You've seen his picture. That man was my saviour. At the present moment – and I jest not – one of the wealthiest people in the world. He gave me the cash to have a haircut, and sent me to work. In three days I'd made enough to have my tooth fixed. That was three days of smiling through the agony, good training, three days of packaging the pain. Then it was steady ascension. Learning what value meant. Getting on the second tier, the third, respecting myself, being respected, the fourth tier, the fifth.'

It became a mass-participation exercise, the counting. 'Sixth!' called Antony and the initiated in chorus. 'Seventh! Eighth! Ninth!'

'And where am I now?' Antony at top volume, straight-backed and glistening.

The response came: 'At the apex!'

'What car do I drive?'

'You drive a Porsche!'

'What star hotel do I sleep in?'

'Five!'

'Where's my third home?'

'Paris!'

'That is correct.' Antony wound it up. 'Don't be shy to imitate.

This is your future too, if you really want it. This, and more than this. You see, I'm at the apex of our family here. But there's a bigger pyramid.' He made a modest shrug. 'There are people above me. Internationally. Globally. There are more things in heaven and earth than are dreamt of in your philosophy. Horatio.'

Jules flicked a wall switch. Music exploded, high notes and a woman's voice rolling in sugary orgasm.

'Now. If you want it. Come forward! Cross the line!'

They crossed in pairs and threes, disappearing fast through the door. Skittle pulled Sami's forearm and they moved forward together.

Antony laid a heavy hand on Sami's shoulder as he passed. 'Remember, Sam. A penis. Out you go. The lady's opening her legs.'

Out into the surprising sobriety of the London morning. To the frenetic stepping of a train station, echoes and glass and lights beneath a high Victorian roof. Skittle paid for two tickets. They found seats, and their train shunted out and over a bridge. Elevated, Sami looked on the surrounding city, glimpses of Thames like silver foil, the knobbly mould of towers on hilly horizons, concrete vistas of cruel mechanism. It struck him, he didn't know why, as magnificent. He admired it as you admire a boxer dealing his opponent brain death.

Sami told Skittle, 'Antony said I was a penis.'

'Wow.'

Sami laughed.

'No, man. That's profound. That's a teaching. Think on it. Look for its significance.'

'I think it's sales talk, Skittle.'

'Scoop. Call me Scoop. He knows more than you think.'

'Where do you live, Scoop?'

'Lewisham. But my first aim is a beach house in Jamaica.'

They gloomed into the suburbs. Red roofs and melancholy green parting occasionally to reveal kids on bicycles, delivery vans, minicabs. Intermittent cloud above, shadows and light strobing over the streets like the hands of a clock. A sky tasting of rain but not quite releasing it, sighing up its tears.

Square-headed Skittle, eyes pouched in suspicion: 'How old are you, Sam?'

'Thirty-one. Getting older every day.'

'Not twenty-seven, then.'

'You've read my form. I wanted the job. It looks like a young people's place.'

'You lied. That's bad.'

He settled back, arms folded, not tall enough for the seat.

'Skittle . . .'

'Scoop. Shouldn't have told you that. You're a slow learner.'

'Scoop, then.'

'Scoop the moolah, you see? Scoop the deal.'

'How much money you make in a day?'

'Not much, yeah? But I'm still learning. You're my first subordinate. Which means I'm on the second tier of the pyramid. Which is more important at this stage. Which means I won't even be doorstepping that much longer. You do well, I'll get more. Then *you* get subordinates. And I'll be in the office, watching the cash grow.'

'Well, perhaps. What music you into?'

He was into hardcore gangsta rap. The conversation lasted them to an outer suburb, in the green belt, almost a town in its own right. The squat pink public buildings of the centre were shaped like slices of pie. Beyond these the streets were winding, leafy, and white.

Their products were a never-experienced-before range of phonecards and membership of a super-exclusive sports and leisure club. Skittle spent two hours showing Sami how it was done, although he never made a sale. The housewives flinched as they opened the door. From Skittle's black skin, the piss of stained Lewisham walkways tainting him, and needle-strewn playgrounds, rain and desperation. The city they thought they'd escaped, that magnificence in Sami's eyes, still chasing them out here.

Sami would have preferred to be accompanied by Aisha. He initiated a fantasy to help him smile behind Skittle. Unstocking her hard legs. White garters and knickers rustling on ebony. Purplish up close. Tingle of returning sex against the groin of his borrowed suit trousers. Aisha, fading to dark wheat, morphing into Muntaha. Heavy breasts. The wind wept a burst of drizzle. Sami stopped himself.

Skittle had brought a boiled potato for lunch. 'Don't really have enough to go round,' he said. Sami struck off on his own, to a minimarket near the station where he bought a bag of carrots, and a public toilet where he washed them. In the afternoon he knocked on doors, peering past chain locks, talking above the barking of dogs. When the sky finally let itself go, in thick waves of hysteria, he sheltered in the station waiting room. Skittle turned up at five, soaked, having made six sales. Commission of thirty quid.

'It was your beard stopping us this morning. Wrong image. And your attitude, Sam. Yeah, but I've still got faith in you. Antony wouldn't have chosen you otherwise.'

Antony was flaccid at the end of the day, cheeks deflated and skin greyed. On his empty desk surface there was a wrap. Most probably coke. He caught Sami's gaze on it.

'That'll keep me up, Sam, my brother. Want some? So make some sales. Earn your tootle tomorrow. The beard. The beard's in the way.'

Past seven thirty and the sales rave continued in the Initiated room. Commitment. Faith. But not for Sami. He wasn't quite that badly off. Today had been an indignity too far. With his compensatory twenty in his pocket he descended the ascension stairs, for the last fucking time.

But for immediate cash, and a sense of action, he had another option. A one-off. Dr Schimmer had told him about it.

'One of my, aa, scientific friends. A table companion, Professor Fencestoat. He requires, aa, guinea pigs, for which he pays very well. It is what you might call, aa, weird science, more neurotheology than neuropsychology. Interesting study for one of your background.'

Sami made the call.

Two mornings later he was looking into Fencestoat's inverse triangle of a face, a slight face atop a slight body, sloping from a comparatively wide forehead to a pointed chin. The temples hollow enough to house shadows, and a perfectly bald dome, with bad patches of scalp and complicated bumps – a phrenologist's paradise.

Fencestoat was introducing the topic.

'A tendency towards or against religious belief can be inherited, just as blue eyes or bad temper can be. In other words, as far as ideology is concerned, it's nature as well as nurture. We've known that for a long time.'

Car beeps skipped up and away beyond the office walls, reminders of carbonate.

'But what we are studying here is the religious experience itself. The experience of meeting the numinous. Traditional mystics would tell you that they meet something outside of themselves, but it turns out . . .'

'Some of them found God within.' Sami, apprehensive, felt he should stake some authority. 'The Sufis said the pure heart is a mirror for God.'

'Certainly,' continued Fencestoat. 'Arts and sciences. Different ways of saying the same thing. God, anyway, with a capital G. But it turns out that religious feeling is all in the brain.' He chuckled at his joke, which Sami had missed. 'Not all in the mind. In the brain. We can locate it. You see,' he squared his shoulders for the hard facts, 'research has shown the frontal lobes to be particularly active during prayer or meditation. Brain imaging shows this clearly. And the same activities seem to deactivate the parietal lobe, or perhaps just starve it of input.'

'I see,' said Sami, not seeing at all.

'The parietal lobe,' Fencestoat, making allowances, spoke more slowly, 'is responsible for orienting the body in space. It therefore provides the brain with its concept of the boundary between the body – the self, if you will – and the external world. Subjects who meditate often find they have a clumsiness after their meditation. And for the same reason they feel at one with the universe, or God, or whatever their culture has told them to feel at one with. Because of the deactivation or deafferentation of the parietal lobe.'

'But,' Sami struggled to contribute, 'I thought you said belief can be inherited.'

'Indeed. The tendency towards belief.'

'But just now you said people's culture shapes what they believe.'

'What they believe, yes. But the tendency to believe, and the spiritual experience, which is what we've moved on to now, these are hardwired.'

'I see.'

'The question that arises is, why? Why do our brains produce these illusions? There's a good case that our psychosexual development is involved. The experience of orgasm, in which we seem to overspill the boundary of ourselves for a moment, to become one with the other, this experience so useful to building close familial bonds and loyalties . . .'

Sami butting in, 'In the Renaissance they called it dying.'

'Dying?' Fencestoat cocked his head. 'Yes, very apt. Dying. Good. The end of the self. Well, that's more evidence of a kind, I suppose. That we travel the same neural pathways to reach either sexual or spiritual bliss.'

'It seems too simplistic to me.'

'Nothing simple about it, Mr Traifi. I simplify, of course, when I talk to a layman. Many parts of the brain are involved. Millions of neurones. Millions of synaptic connections. The brain is a very complex machine.'

Grey matter. Sami had eaten sheep's brains in Syria, boiled, with a squeeze of lemon.

'Evolution has developed this very complex, very useful machine, the brain, and has incidentally fitted it out for spiritual experience. The irony is that the brains of the future may well be more spiritual than ours, even as we discover the physical causes of spirituality. Evolution will ensure it. Spiritual people live longer, happier lives. They tend to have more success at work, and better interpersonal relationships. Even if it's illogical, spirituality appears to be good for us.'

'I see.' Sami blankly observing Fencestoat's slight, busy face.

'It probably started as an accident,' Fencestoat went on. 'Like wings. In fact, like everything gained through evolutionary mechanism. A religious person would say it's God's plan.' He snorted softly. 'That's probably what we'd like it to be. Wishful thinking.'

Sami sensed himself reddening, and an obstruction in his throat, became aware of the downturn of his mouth.

'Arts and sciences,' Fencestoat conceded. 'It's a matter of interpretation. The body, after all, is the temple of the soul. Or of God, I can't recall my divinity lessons.'

Sami sniffed. 'Anyway,' he said.

'Yes,' said Fencestoat. 'Moving on. What we'll be examining today are temporal lobe experiences. Temporal lobe epileptics frequently report supernatural visions, of the demonic or of the divine. Even between seizures they can be religious to the point of fanaticism. Fyodor Dostoyevsky was a temporal lobe epileptic. Have you read *The Idiot?*'

'No,' said Sami. 'I'm a specialist in Arabic literature.'

'Very well. The Prophet of Islam, then, who used to shiver when his trances approached, and to fall from his camel under their weight. There is a theory that he was an epileptic.'

'I'm a specialist in mysticism too. Not only Islamic.'

'Very good.'

'And English Renaissance poetry. John Donne.'

'Good. Good.'

'I've stopped now. I'm not an academic any more.'

'So Dr Schimmer tells me. Yes.'

'Go on,' said Sami.

'So. Our research stimulates the temporal lobes of our subjects with weak electromagnetic fields. We provoke microseizures, and observe the results. That's what we'll be doing this morning.'

'You're going to give me an epileptic fit?'

'Oh, nothing so dramatic.' Fencestoat waved a hand too quickly, as if it was something he'd practised in front of a mirror. 'Tiny doses of electromagnetism. If it wasn't safe it wouldn't be legal.'

Sami, more Englishman than Arab, trusted legality. And there was money coming.

'All right, then,' he said.

There was a form to fill in, boxes to tick. The thrust of it was, to what extent are you a loon?

I am personally important to the course of history.

Strongly Agree, Agree, No Opinion, Disagree, Strongly Disagree.

Important interests want me silenced.

I attend church/mosque/temple on a regular basis.

I am angry with the world.

I am never clean.

It is possible to communicate with the dead.

And so on.

When he'd finished, Fencestoat handed him a cheque for two hundred pounds. 'We are unusually lucky with our funding,' he said.

Fencestoat led him into a dim inner chamber. A snappy blonde assistant smeared conducting cream on his temples. 'And Persinger's helmet,' said Fencestoat, producing a green motorcycle helmet and squeezing it with a damp pop over Sami's head. 'Fitted with solenoids,' said Fencestoat, 'for the transcranial stimulation.' The blonde, in a white coat, hair cruelly tied back from pinched but foxy features, pressed goggles around his eyes. They closed on his skin in an airtight gasp. She lowered him, blind, on to an imitation-leather recliner. It was Fencestoat's talk about sexual bliss, orgasms, that made Sami feel he was involved in something perverse. Some new form of unfaithfulness.

He pictured himself on the institutional couch, used by so many before him, under the pyramid of suspended brain tools he'd seen before they removed his senses.

'Now relax.' Fencestoat's voice muffled. 'We'll be next door, measuring and observing. It'll take about thirty minutes, a little more maybe. You don't need to do anything at all.'

And Sami told himself, *enjoy it*, like a man with scruples who's taken the leap and paid a prostitute, handed the cash over and his pride with it. Half an hour ahead of him. Enjoy it. Money in his pocket, independently earned. A neutral temperature. No car noise here.

Packaged up, his head is large and the world small, becoming smaller. Unseen, unreal. He thinks he might sleep. His ears lost in the helmet, his bones puffed up against the goggles, their aerated spongy interior inflating until his head isn't there at all nor his body, just relaxed cloud buffeted in a roofless sky. On a silent breeze. If anything is thick it's time, widening, expanding, absolutely still. He floats. Not him. Cloud floats.

A black and sickly thundercloud angry at the sky's edge.

Nur finger-combing his curls. Little boy Sami. She hums an ancient tune. He ends not at his scalp but at the top of her hand, which the cold air kisses.

A boy's voice singing Qur'an on the stereo:

He deprived them of their garment (of God-consciousness) in order to make them aware of their nakedness . . .

Each Arabic word ending on a long 'maa' sound, like mama, *mama*, says Sami, *maama*, but he isn't naked, he's wrapped up in towels, in the couch of her body, her fingers in his curls, he ends where she does, against the wind:

yanzi'u 'anhumaa libaasahumaa liyuriyahumaa saw'aatihimaa . . .

The wind over the recitation takes a desolate turn.

Slamming a door. His father's voice wanting to know, 'What's that bloody noise?' A constriction. The force of Sami's adult body bearing down on him. Black and bloody walls. Detention chamber. Screams. Animal breath: *ullahullahullahullahu*. The looming secret, Mustafa looming.

Part of him saying, not again, I thought I'd done enough of this. I thought I'd finished this.

And really it's so old, so déjà vu, that it holds no more novelty and no more fear. Freed of fear he is free to hate. Or to love properly. He turns around, finding a sword's handle in his grasp, and the centaur snorting and galloping at him. He stabs it upwards through the throat, through flank and gristle, pushing hard.

'You did it?' he asks.

'Yes, I did it. You know I did.'

'Why?'

'I thought it was worth it. Now, you know what to do.'

More stabbing, more gore. The son sacrifices the father, whose horse body quickly dissolves. Mustafa raises a palm in farewell. Leaves lightly, in human form. Cloud dissipates into light rain.

The blonde removing the goggles from his eyes. Harsh light. Unsticking the helmet from his head. Helping him to his feet.

Sami stumbled from the chamber, past a sage Fencestoat, to a narrow bathroom. He washed the gel from his hair, but didn't bother doing a thorough job of it. Walked over to Fencestoat's paper-strewn desk, more steadily now.

'So,' Fencestoat tapping on a keyboard, 'tell me what happened.'

'Difficult to put into words,' said Sami. Water trickled into his beard.

'So first you felt . . .' Dry voice scratching at scabs of meaning.

'Relaxed,' said Sami.

'Right.' Fencestoat entering data. 'Caused by what we call Burst X. A very pleasant frequency. And then?'

'I don't know. A childhood memory perhaps.'

'A sensed presence?'

'Something like that.'

'Please, Mr Traifi, don't be embarrassed. Subjects have seen . . .' – swiftly fanning the practised hand – '. . . Buddhas of compassion, little green men, deceased family members, tunnels of light. The lot. All from a little brain crackle.'

'Nothing so dramatic, professor. No visions of God. I saw my parents.'

'Right. The Thomas Pulse causes the sensed presence. Because of mismatched left and right hemispheric activity your normal sense of yourself is misinterpreted. You feel some "other" is with you. The amygdala and the hippocampus make the experience more emotional.' Peering at Sami, 'Perhaps, more personal?'

'Certainly it was personal. They were my parents.'

'Can you expand?'

'Not really. I saw my parents. I was a child again. I hope your funds haven't been wasted on me.'

'Not at all. We have some excellent readings. Thank you, Mr Traifi.'

Sami stepped out into the noise. Above the Earth's steady magnetism there was the ongoing crackle of millions of human nervous systems, and power lines, car electrics, radio receivers, fixed phone lines and mobile radiation, TV reception, stereos, refrigerators, air conditioners. The net. Gossamer strings of the web intersecting through his cerebrum. Sami standing inside an overarching dome of electromagnetism, a stone thrown into a pool, his feet at the centre of the ripple, throbbing outwards for ever.

27
To Be Touched

If there are aliens out there they'll hear us soon. We're getting louder. Our radio waves spin out on concentric ripples: polite broadcasts first, received pronunciation boldly going into the void, then wars, speeches, pop music, disaster reports, to shock jocks and jungle pirates. Accumulating until our current cacophony. Relentlessly to the stars. Screaming to be heard.

The human urge for contact has brought us a century of noise. We want to go beyond the body, beyond the planet. It's a desire which we all share: the desire to touch another. To be touched.

It was the opening night of Gabor's exhibition, the night his fingers would reach through canvas to probe the public mind. He intended, also, a more carnal probing: to achieve the climax he believed the summer had been leading to. And here she was: Muntaha arriving, slipping gracefully through glass doors, dipping her profile with mixed pride and modesty away from the art crowd in attendance. A hasty breeze blew through her nostrils and over her silken upper lip, wind from her exertions on East London's thin pavements and narrow, sometimes cobbled streets. These hyper-urban, post-imperial streets walled by four-storey converted warehouses, towers at their horizons brown and yellow like Liquorice Allsorts – streets Gabor felt proprietorial about, since he'd chosen to live in them, since his grandfather had trodden them before him. And Muntaha's feet treading them now.

She was dressed up, in long black skirt, patterned blouse, swirling hijab, smarter still than usual. For him. And she entered this place at his invitation. Into an atmosphere cohering around him, for tonight at least. Emanating from him and his success.

Her dark, intelligent eyes thudded from face to face as she smoothed her skirt, finding her bearings. She picked out his mother's jutting chin and brows, the pinched Hungarian merchant expression melted to approval for once, bathing in his reflected glory. Muntaha's eyes rested on the journalists with notebook and dictaphone. She noticed the beautiful women in her shadow, and Gabor noticed her noticing, and hoped she understood his history with them. History he'd renounce for her. She registered the easily assimilated crowd of all styles, colours and influences, nearly as much brown as white, overwhelmingly mobile and optimistic.

There were bulbs of champagne being handed around, cocaine if you watched carefully. What has been called space reggae bubbling in the corners. And Gabor the sun, the nucleus. She his chosen one. He let everyone see this was the case, by his gaze and his open palms. Music and people parting like the Red Sea to let her through. Her nose broad and strong between her eyes, a masculine force in her, but still archetypally female in his vision. A woman caught sparkling in the summer evening sunlight which washed the gallery's white rectangle in gold, atoms dancing around her, light and shade, nesting in her swells and depressions. Her skin had a recent surface darkness like the ghost of reddish brown on Assyrian wall paintings, museum faces ready to flake but kept timeless with sealant. She was darkened beyond her usual tone just from walking down the street. Good to have skin like that, he thought. Good to rub your fingerprints against it, to push it on to the bone.

She took both his hands, and from the discomfort of her smile he judged his offering of both to have been overly theatrical. But it was a special occasion, and she was the guest work of art. He didn't tell her that yet. He saved it for later.

She looked away from him at the postcards on a nearby table. Like the banner over the gallery entrance, they read: *The Paradox of the Particle/Wave Duality: Connected Work by Gabor Vronk.*

'The theme of it all is connection. Unity.' He tried to make his voice warmer. 'Connection, Muntaha. Let me show you around.'

He was thinking, tonight's the night. He'd made his preparations for the long-hoped-for connection. Scissored pubic beard and razored armpits, as Muslim men do. So he'd heard. Made of his studio bedroom an advertisement for himself and an elaborate trap. Clean but artfully cluttered, with paintings and sketches and notebooks, enough to suggest an inexhaustible well of creative energy, strewn with rhythmed intensity towards the bed. Islamic books within eyeshot, the paths to sexual and spiritual bliss neatly enfolded. Gulf frankincense burning in the kitchen to cloak the Slavic odours of pickled fish. Windows open to the balmy East London night. Clean sheets on the mattress. The climax, he was thinking, perhaps a couple of hours away, and so much ahead of him to learn and experience in those two hours. A woman like that, when she chooses to unlace herself, fireworks are expected.

Fireworks from the east. There's nothing prudish in Islam. Gabor had thoroughly researched it. The original faith doesn't ask anyone to lie back and think of Mecca. It holds sex in high regard, despite the puritanism of some contemporary clerics who, out of touch with their own tradition, imitate Victorian Christianity. Ali said: 'God created sexual desire in ten parts. Nine parts he gave to women and one part to men.' Foreplay is recommended. So much so that the Prophet gave as an example of cruelty a man having intercourse with his wife without arousing her with foreplay first. Sexual pleasure is a marital right. The failure of a husband to pleasure his wife is legitimate grounds for divorce. And divorce in Islam is quick and easy. If she'd married Sami according to Islamic regulations she'd be free of him by now. So Gabor saw no cultural or legal obstruction to their first night of knowledge. It's the tribal background that turns women's bodies into suitcases of honour, and she'd liberated herself from that.

He showed her the first canvas to the left of the entrance. It was called 'Standing Wave'.

'A bull's eye?' she asked.

It did look something like a target. Rejecting a proffered champagne glass and turning his back on the room, he said, 'Read the caption.'

The caption said: *What we observe as material bodies and forces are nothing but shapes and variations in the structure of space. Particles are just appearances (Erwin Schrödinger).*

'So it's something to do with quantum physics.' Muntaha chewing on her puffed-out lower lip. In the morning, thought Gabor, they would wake up and everything would be different. Fresher and simpler, having tasted the fruit. They'd understand directly, not in code.

'Matter exists as spherical wave motions of space. The wave centre creates the illusion of a particle. Or, if you like, the illusion of separateness.' He moved closer until he was breathing her. An Arab perfume. 'In reality, everything is one. Matter and space and time are one. It's Islamic, isn't it? I could rename this one "tawheed".'

Tawheed, or unity. The foundation of Islamic thought. The concept that had made them friends.

'Well, it's very nice.' It sounded like a concession. Then she added wistfully, 'Sami would talk about the Bull of Heaven.'

'Bull of Heaven?'

'From the Gilgamesh epic. It was one of his and his father's favourite stories.'

'Sami's obsessions!' He chuckled too richly.

'But it's art. You can interpret art as you like, can't you?'

'I suppose so. Let's move to the next one.'

He took her arm, and met some resistance. She didn't want contact in public, perhaps. Or perhaps not yet. Her elbow squirmed until he let it drop.

Arabs, Gabor theorized, are either sensuous or violent, or both at once. You can see that from the news. Look at her brother, Ammar, who had called to apologize, two days after smacking him, when his bruise was still visible. Ammar described himself as having been 'well out of order'. Gabor was magnanimous, assuming Muntaha had ordered the apology and would receive a report of the conversation. Ammar had surely got Gabor's number from her. But as he talked on it sounded like his own idea. Very genuinely, very eagerly, he suggested Gabor hit him back, as a proportional punishment, an eye for an eye. When Gabor had thrice refused Ammar offered him fifty quid, a kind of blood money, he said. 'Punishment should be proportional. Proportional punishment keeps the peace. I oppressed you, and oppression is worse than violence. So either you smack me back, or I pay. We're Muslims. This is what we believe.' Weird.

The next picture was called 'Tsunami'. It was huge, from the floor to the ceiling, a wave made of faces which disintegrated into unreadable letters or symbols which could be cuneiform or hieroglyphs. And plants and planets, masks and machines, fire, mountains and streams, all morphing into each other. Colours collapsing into white foam.

'This is the same idea. Same theme. Tawheed again, very Islamic. Endless multiplicity arising from basic unity.'

Waves are symbols of passion, of course. Gabor's surged with phallic force. It should have taken her breath away.

But she said, 'Why don't you let me think about them first?'

So he remained silent. Silence can be powerful. He steered her to the next, called 'Vision'. An eye with a galaxy in the pupil. The eye in fact modelled on her eyes, black in a black sea, but he didn't tell her that, not yet. Gently does it, he thought.

She cleared her throat, or it could have been a grunt of appreciation, or comprehension. Hard to tell.

They moved to 'Kitchen Table', which depicts points of light in empty space – what any mundane object actually consists of at the subatomic level.

'Now this one,' he explained, 'is about illusion. Solidity is unreal. Even the particle is unreal, as a solid particle. It's something we want to see but which isn't really there.'

'It looks like another galaxy,' she started. Gabor should have paused and listened to her, but he had too much momentum built up to stop.

'What we see is illusion or, better put, interpretation, and we ourselves are illusions or interpretations, just blips of consciousness looking at themselves. Mirrors hung on the curtains of the real. That's what we are.'

'I don't know,' she said. 'But it reminds me of a hadeeth qudsi. You know, not from the Qur'an but still considered to be the word of God, not of the Prophet.'

This was the point he'd wanted to arrive at. She was making connections, him to her.

'"I was a hidden treasure that desired to be known, so I created the creation."'

He waited a respectful moment. 'So we are God's self-consciousness, is that what it's saying?'

'No.' She seemed resentful of his formulizing. 'Or not only that. He is greater than our imaginings.'

On this her jaw closed and she clicked a heel on the tiles as if declaring her withdrawal from a team game. She was putting herself at a distance, and Gabor needed proximity. Proximity enough to measure her nipples between his fingers and thumbs, to weigh breasts and flanks, to annotate her curves and chart her, to claim her for science. To gather empirical proof of her.

Would it happen, or would it not? He'd been sure of it, and now was radically unsure. Didn't know where he stood or what the future would be. Like Grandfather Vronsky with his feet sinking into the heaving sea of Europe. But all was not lost. Uncertainty added intensity to the situation, an upgrade in excitement, as from West London to the grittier East. His groin tingled. He concentrated.

Quiet and predatorial, he followed her to 'Twins'. The picture showed two faces, one male one female, one black one white, spinning to opposite sides of the canvas from a central point of origin. He'd have said something about electrons paired with positrons, protons with anti-protons, about the work of scientist Paul Dirac. He'd already said that to a journalist, who took a lot of photos of 'Twins'. But now he didn't say a thing, only pointed to the caption: *Limitless in His glory is He who has created opposites in whatever the earth produces, and in men's own selves, and in that of which (as yet) they have no knowledge (Qur'an 36:36).*

Paired opposites, you see. Spiritual-scientific awe, you see. Gabor choosing the Qur'an as a source reference for his art, while Sami scorned it. Was this working on her?

He followed her to 'Atom'. Another vast canvas, with a grain in the centre, in a void, and specks orbiting at a distance.

'It looks like a galaxy again,' she said, as if to herself, 'or a solar system. And it looks like Jackson Pollock, but more minimalist, less expressionist.'

So she knew more about art than Gabor had presumed.

They cornered with the wall and walked at her pace through the section labelled 'Scale Studies'. The first exhibit, 'Traffic', involved three screens. One showed haemoglobin, slowed down, pulsing through capillaries. The next, commuters fed through the channels of the tube, speeded up, clotting like platelets at the turnstiles. And the third, headlamps flowing through a road system, on slow exposure so you see rivers of red and blue light.

No comment from either of them, although she seemed interested. She watched each film twice, in order, as a traffic of guests wove around her. Gabor allowed the distance between them.

'Microchip City' was on three blocks: two repainted photographs of a magnified microchip, and between them an aerial shot of city blocks. The point being, they look the same. He nearly said so, but it seemed evident.

'Mountain: Triptych' contained a close-up photograph of piled earth at a roadside, a shot of a mountain face, and a satellite image of the rising Himalaya.

He didn't speak until they arrived at 'Bubble Chamber Tracks'.

'Bubble chambers are particle accelerators that physicists use to make protons collide. When that happens you get new particles, really tiny, just for a millionth of a second before they collapse. But it's enough time to catch their tracks. They make beautiful patterns.' He flapped his fingers at the images he'd made. 'Only a little tweaking makes them roses and roots. Don't you think they're beautiful? They remind me of mosque art, arabesques, spiritual abstracts.'

She didn't answer the question. Fair enough, it had probably been rhetorical. At least she was looking hard. He waited for her to find the last of the series, a track which he'd developed into a calligraphic Allah, in Arabic. There, she saw it. No clear sign of recognition. No lingering over it. The calligraphy was obvious, but she didn't comment. So neither did he. Didn't want to patronize, or to say the wrong thing. She was an unknown particle herself. Gabor could understand her in the zone of middle dimensions, which is what physicists call our human scale of perception, the size at which traditional physics predicts accurate results, where things make sense. But what was happening in her mind, at the quantum level, at the cosmic level? This he couldn't map.

Nearing the end, at 'Dostoyevsky's Brain', Gabor was flipping like a hooked fish to regain the initiative. To make her talk before the final picture.

'You know Dostoyevsky?' he said.

She nodded once.

'Of course you do. He was an epileptic, and perhaps for that reason a visionary. Here . . .' He touched the cross-section of brain on the canvas. (It was his picture. He had a right to touch it.) 'Here are his temporal lobes glowing. He's having a seizure, you see.'

Muntaha briefly laughed.

And so they reached the picture called 'For Muntaha', the ka'aba inside Bohr's atom. Dedicated to her by name, a privilege granted to no one else, not to these buzzing media people or to any of his previous women, not to a relative, not even to the memory of dead Vronsky.

'I painted this when I got back from your father's ta'ziya. You remember the conversation we had that day?'

'Yes,' she said. Yes, and a full stop. She wouldn't look at him.

'You know what I recited while I was painting it?'

'Recited?'

'Recited.'

'What?'

He pulled himself up to his height, way above her, viewing the slope of her hijab to her spine, and the hair and cool hats of all his visitors, the sparkle of glasses, cameras flashing, people curling their heads to their phones like cats to caressing fingers, and he tried out what he'd practised so much:

> wal-fajr
> wa layaalin 'ashr
> wash-shaf'i wal-watr
> wal-layli idhaa yasr . . .

The multiple and the One. The night as it runs its course. Meaning, tonight. Meaning, now, at last. Out of many, one. One body. The beast with two backs. But her eyes faced the floor tiles. Gabor had a view of the hijab on the nape of her neck. Wasn't she getting this? Hadn't they been leading up to it all summer? The lake of meaning in his eyes, the glowering brow, the power and the presence: she wasn't seeing this at all.

Her strangeness struck him with a slicing shiver, in his groin and belly and also at the roots of his teeth. Her strangeness was erotic, and it was terrible.

Gabor spoke honestly to himself. The thing about Arabs – they're freakish. More like us than Africans are, or Chinese, so like us sometimes they're almost interchangeable – but the thing an Arab face must have to distinguish it from a European is at least one element of freakishness, of disproportion. They're like aliens wearing human masks. He feels affection for this: it's what was Arab about his grandfather, Vronsky. And Muntaha – she's rich in freakishness, her nose, mouth, in particular her eyes, big like baby eyes, and bigger top to bottom than side to side. A Disney dream of eyes. And her eyebrows like fur, like things borrowed from a black cat's back. And the shape of her face not what we normally call heart-like but like an exaggerated sketch of a heart, cartoon again. If Gabor has exaggerated, it's her Arab face that has made him do so.

She still hadn't raised her head. Action, then.

'I've been here long enough,' he said, louder. 'Why don't we walk over to my place?'

'No. You talk to the others. I'll look at the pictures a bit longer.'

'It's walking distance. You'll see some pieces I've been working on recently.'

'No. I should get home anyway.'

'All right. Let's walk. You'll love the area. The restaurants we have round here.' He was like an athlete who wouldn't reach the finish line. 'There's Bengali, loads of Bengali. There's Vietnamese, Mexican.' Like a stand-up comedian running out of air. 'Greek, Brazilian, and fusion of course . . .'

'No, Gabor.' She lifted her chin, confronted him with her nose. Her eyes directly on his.

He picked at her upper arm. He held on to the flesh, harder than expected, which threatened to slip his grasp. Out of pity she didn't dodge him.

'No?'

'You've been a good friend. You're a lovely man. A good artist, a good teacher.'

He let her arm alone. 'These are compliments I don't want to hear.'

'But I think you misunderstand our relationship. I'm married.'

He said, 'Sami isn't living at home.'

Irritation flashed like windscreen wipers across her misshapen eyes. 'What do you know about it?' Then more kindly: 'I'm married. Marriages have ups and downs. And . . .'

'I could help,' he said stupidly, dry-mouthed.

What did he mean? Help with what? Help her put her marriage back together? Anyway, she hadn't heard. He'd croaked, and she hadn't paused to hear.

He was speaking into her words, she continuing: '. . . even if I wasn't married, I'm not interested in you like that, as a husband or boyfriend. I like you as a colleague. I thought you were interested in Islam. That's all.'

She blinked, and she turned to go.

'I am,' he said weakly.

She said no. She was through the glass doors. Tens of trendy, chirpy profiles were directed at Gabor, scenting scandal.

She said no, and so prevented the story from moving into the universal territory we can all relate to. She said no, choosing to remain in her particularity. In her own ethnic group, in her religio-cultural space, in what they call a 'community'. She said no, and made the story a local one. Limited the story's scope. Her choice, not Gabor's.

Gabor slipped out too quickly to attract attention. Walked home, checking his shoulder for the deracinated Muslims who might spill up from Brick Lane. Climbed stairs, and unlocked triple locks. Instead of leaving his shoes in the shoe rack he kicked them off next to the bed. The pointlessly clean sheets. He washed his mouth with tap water and lay down fully clothed.

It was just him. Gabor and his imaginings.

28
Devils

Sami stepped out. Just walking distance, to a London University venue where the famed Rashid Iqbal would be delivering a speech against religion. Rashid Iqbal: of Indian birth and British nationality, postmodernist, controversialist, author of *Taboo Buster*, *Haris of the Harem*, and *I-Slam-Slim: Representing Islam, Aggression and the Human Image*. Sami's kind of thing, previously. In fact, Iqbal's books were on Sami's shelves, in the house where Muntaha lived.

It was nostalgia for his previous certainties that brought Sami out, plus the opportunity to disrupt his routine of window-gazing, tight-knuckle driving lessons, and pseudo-subversive dawntime training. And perhaps even sociability. Tom Field would be in attendance, and Dr Schimmer.

It was the holidays, but the most committed student groupuscules were there in the conference hall's forecourt and corridors. Such activity was, for the militants, either a prelude to disillusion and drugs, or training too, for more serious, more right-wing lobbying later on. Blacksoc, Leftsoc, Beersoc, Gaysoc, Greensoc, and unformed youth picking among the stalls like it was an early freshers week. Asking, which soc is coolest, and which can I fix a CV for? Which does the best T-shirt? Which will most suitably define me?

Miniature demonstrations had been organized in specific reaction to the visiting speaker, and they hectored the audience as it washed into the hall.

There was a huddle of Hizb al-Hurriya girls flapping in jilbabs and niqabs on one side of a plastic, leaflet-strewn table, and skullcapped bearded boys on the other. The boys held banners whose meanings were obscure if you couldn't supply the context:

'Palestine, Chechnya, Iraq . . . And Now Our Faith Itself!'

'Truth Is Distinct From Falsehood!'

'War in the North!' This a reference to ethnic disturbances in the old mill towns, white versus brown, and police versus brown, and Bengali versus Mirpuri, but understood here as Ignorance versus Islam, the original battle.

On the other side of the queue, activists of the Radical Humanist Society, dressed as logically and badly as scientists, chewing on limp roll-ups, represented the pro-Iqbal perspective, bearing a banner of their own. 'Outlaw Faith!' it declared.

There were also delegations of politicos whose positions were more obscure, such as Revolutionary Solidarity with Third World Peoples, and Class Fight, who were undecided – despite tens of emergency policy meetings – if the struggle against pipe-dream false consciousness should be prioritized, or alternatively, the necessity of winning over proletarian Asian energies, and who therefore changed their accents according to the colour of the nearest listener, and handed out safe pamphlets on the strike weapon or black rights.

Middle-class whites of the Socialist Workers Party and Revolutionary Communist Party had come simply to show their relevance, entirely avoiding the Rashid Iqbal question in favour of spitting insider insults at each other. Like 'Tankies!' Or 'Trots!' Or 'Big moustache boys!' Or 'Infantile Leftists!'

Then, arranged in a secondary ripple of offence taken, at mocking distance from the primary stalls, were the reactions to the reactions. An Out-Rage! posse chanted 'Mullahs Kill Queers!' towards the Hurriya crew. The Jewish Students Against Muslim Nazis were also engaged in low-level taunting.

Tom Field had hooked Sami's elbow in a pincer grasp, hurrying him through the noise. With the other gnarled hand he flicked at the activists.

'This, in their totality, from religious to secular, right to left, is what we call opposition. What we call, at this late stage, the hope for a brighter future.' He made one cracked cackle. 'Feeling optimistic?'

One of the Hurriya brothers clocked Sami's beard.

'As-salaamu alaikum,' he shot at him in level tone.

'Wa-alaikum assalaam,' Sami shot back. He was thinking of a cynical enough response to make to Tom, and realized too late he'd fallen into a trap.

'You're one of us, boy. Why you going in there?'

'To hear the ... to see what ... doesn't mean I agree or disagree ...' Sami, feeling an answer was required, watched guilty-browed over his shoulder the expectant, hurt face of his bearded brother.

Tom pulled him on through institutional doors. The crowd behind them chanted their public slogans with personal urgency, as if this was the last chance for them to make a point. The sound became wordless crackling and crows' screeches as they made distance into the hall.

It was a full audience which Sami surveyed. In the front row, university VIPs and athletic cameramen in leather and straps. In the rows behind, excited students pretending not to be, and tweedy academic and writerly types including Dr Schimmer, and then a mix of colours and styles and snarls, some very natty, some very grungy. Some niqab girls had infiltrated. There were Africans wearing all their wealth, and brown and yellow intellectuals with thin spectacles and folded legs, and Indo-Pakistanis from rich to poor. At the very back a white but dreadlocked pair sat together, or at least side by side, with each a pair of big headphones muffling their already muffled skulls. Sami and Tom bustled into place at the front of the mixed-up rows, behind Dr Schimmer.

Just in time. A reedy, jaundiced fellow stood and pushed air at the audience to win a partial hush.

'Our guest today requires no introduction. Nevertheless ...'

Polite laughter tinkled from the rows in front of Sami.

'Nevertheless, a very brief introduction must be made. Rashid

Iqbal is one of this country's leading cosmopolitan intellectuals. Rashid's groundbreaking novel, *Taboo Buster*, was described as "a continent finding its voice". This voice, at once powerful and subtle, demands to be heard. No stranger to controversy, Rashid has recently called for the hijab, or Muslim headscarf, to be banned from British educational establishments. A similar debate is, of course, taking place in France. It is on his more general theme, against religion, that we will hear him talk today. So, before my brevity becomes long-winded, I give you Rashid Iqbal.'

The same section of audience heartily applauded the round, brown man in brown corduroy who rose the short distance to his feet, supporting himself with arms braced on the table beneath him. He had a bulging square face like too much dough risen out of the mould, its creases of experience ironed out by self-satisfaction, and low-hooded crab eyes on stalks, and worm hairs sprouting not only from ears and nostrils but from the mushroomy grey nose itself, from the temples, from the highest contours of his cheeks.

Jaundice waited for the clapping to subside, then continued.

'Responding to Rashid will be our own Daoud Jenkinson, a historian at the university, a convert to the Islamic religion, and a founder member of the British Muslim Committee. Daoud's latest book, *Secular Fundamentalism: A Panic Discourse*, has been described as "a timely riposte to contemporary fanaticism". So, therefore, thank you, Daoud.'

The speaker took to his seat amid dimmer clapping from the front and, behind Sami, a fast crop of whooping. Daoud, a beak-nosed man in a faded, wide-lapelled three-piece suit, squinted his acknowledgement past a sparse and pointy beard.

Rashid Iqbal, still precariously on his feet, inflated above the table.

'To begin with,' he began, 'two images.'

Pause One.

'The suicide bomber.'

Pause Two.

'The book burner.'

A pause more pregnant than the previous.

'I present to you, ladies and gentlemen, Homo Religiens. Willing to kill for no other reason than his belief.'

Pause.

'His belief in a world that does not exist.'

Pause.

'A belief not based on evidence.'

Pause.

'This vengeful father in the sky.'

He stretched out his arms in welcome or entreaty and smiled benevolently.

'Have we not, by this point, had enough of him?'

Into his swing now, Rashid Iqbal dropped the dramatic timing.

'Where does it come from, such blind, destructive belief? From misery, of course. As Freud and Marx taught, religion is illusion and opiate. Opium. It is painkiller for sick, for hurting people. A man or woman who has no problems is a man or woman who has no god.'

His voice reached Sami's ear as a stick tapping on hollow wood. There were echoes from the lobby, a rising hysteria, words as intense and thickly matted as branches and twigs in dark forest, too layered to be distinct.

'It looks grim.' Rashid Iqbal, man of letters, unperturbed. 'But, friends, it isn't. What can't be stopped is progress. As surely as our ape ancestors developed large brains and delicate voice boxes, so Homo Religiens will become Homo Secularens.

'The religious tell us that above us there is a divine law, a divine master to be obeyed. The master who, in his various guises, has commanded the Inquisition and the religious policemen of Saudi Arabia. Why should we obey such a cruel master, with so much blood on his heavenly hands? What have we done so wrong that we cannot trust ourselves?

'Fear of freedom, my friends. The human being observes his own capacity for destruction and fears himself. To be precise, he fears the responsibility for the pain he creates. Better, he decides, to blame something superhuman for his pain. Us causing the pain? he asks. No, we are only following orders. And so he reconciles himself to his misery, and stays in its depths for centuries and millennia.

'So where is the hope? The answer to misery is technology. Technology and wealth. Technology and wealth are enemies such as religion has never met before.'

A piercing, speechifying voice called out from the back rows: 'The white man developed tricknology when he got free of his debased tyrannical religion! But the Muslim got undeveloped when he let go of his true faith!'

The audience, entertainment on its face, twisted towards the voice.

'Our friend mentions the Muslims.' Iqbal grew an inch in response to the challenge. 'Islam once offered a theory of unity. And now it has been superseded by practical unity. A world linked like one body by the arteries of flight paths and the nerves of the internet, a world rushing inevitably to embrace itself, in one economy, one legal system, one entertainment industry. This is not a world destined to remain attached to dusty dreams.'

Shouting blew and swirled in the corridor. And angry whispering inside the hall, repeated by Dr Schimmer, who was worrying at the narrow bridge of his nose, grunting, 'Too, aa, simple!'

'But won't the Third World need its dreams? No, it's false to think so. It could even be racism to think so. Those of us who think the dark-skinned and hairy have to remain in their delusion, for reasons of authenticity, they should look clearly at the world. The youth of Iran and India and Nigeria aspires to Hollywood and hip hop as much as our youth here does.'

Iqbal raised a chubby finger.

'Pause a moment here. Hollywood and hip hop. The providers of stories. These are the alternatives, and this is where I come in. The storyteller liberated from Islam. Islam, you see, is not a civilization of narrative. It's rules, that's all. Rules and hygiene. It's washing. A religion of the bathroom.

'So I present literature in opposition to religion. With the little wealth needed to teach people to read, and the little technology needed to connect to the internet, literature can become available to all. What if the mosque is across the street? The screen is in the bedroom. Doesn't have to be the written word even. It can be films, or songs. This is my wide definition of literature. Instead of the dominant narrative, I offer a competition of narratives, a hubbub of voices, a Babel. Instead of the one Word, I offer infinite words. Histories, novels, characters, fantasies. I do not say we do not have spiritual needs. I say that we can fulfil these needs more profitably with literature. The imagination.'

Having arrived at the nub, Iqbal leaned back to watch its reception. Mixed results. Ha-hums of comprehension from the front. A bubbling drizzle of complaint at the periphery. Squalls of dissent rushing in the corridors.

'Literature,' he continued, 'isn't clean. Literature is impure, as blended and mixed and polluted, as transgressively tainted, as a curry, a spiced Bombay curry, into which all the influences of a continent have been poured.'

Applause for this simile. The Daoud brother, meanwhile, was furiously scribbling, forehead red and crinkled, pointy nose and beard rising from the point of his pad like the tail of an exclamation. Scribbling about the spicy mix that was Islamic Spain. About the Greco-Judaic-Indo-Persian masala of medieval Baghdad. About Qur'anic allusions to Alexander the Great. About syncretism and Sufi visions and Muslim travelogues.

Now Iqbal addressed the front rows, the swishing academic eyelashes, the flashing jaws of cameras, at an intimately low volume.

'Let us isolate some enemies from the darkness of belief, and shine our enlightening torch upon them. Let us start with what we have here in this city. To start with, African exorcism. Here in this metropolis, in this new millennium, witch doctors whipping and burning their victims in order to expel evil spirits. Here in London, today. Do you not feel the need to expel some of these evil spirits yourselves?'

'Indian!' A proud African bellowed. 'Don't stereotype our traditions now!'

'And further witcheries,' Iqbal skipped on, louder, enjoying the temperature. 'For instance, female circumcision, barbaric mutilation to give it its less polite name. A barbarism which must be stamped out! I call for compulsory hospital examination of African Muslim girls as a means of ensuring their genital rights!'

'Get your hands off!' someone male blasted from mid-hall.

And another: 'Hands off our women's vaginas!'

The audience swerved from side to side hunting for drama.

'*Your* women?' Iqbal rejoined. 'They own themselves, my primitive friend. And the vagina, being hidden, is not your target. It is the vulvas you want! It is the visible vulvas that offend!' Forgetting in the heat of combat to touch lower lip to teeth, Iqbal pronounced it 'wulvas'. Wisible wulwas.

'Oi! Leave our vulvas alone!' One of the flappers there.

And another, clearly also British-born, mocked, 'You take our wul-was, Iqbal, but leave our vulvas alone!'

Someone barked, 'Female circumcision got nothing to do with Islam anyway!'

Booing and hissing to that.

'That's not his business! That's our business! That's our discussion!'

'But he's pretending it's part of Islam!'

To which, a clamour of agreement.

Two voices in concert urged, 'Propaganda!' It was unclear whether they opposed propaganda or wanted some, and who they thought the propagandist in question was.

'He called us suicide bombers!'

'Terrorists!'

'Don't insult our martyrs!'

'Fucking murderer!'

'Shut your faces!'

'Fundamentalists!'

The audience tossed like wind-pulled waves. Even the front rows lost their unity. Faces couldn't agree which direction to turn. Unruly eyes and fingers splashed all ways like foam. People were standing up, which made others strain and stretch to better view the action. Shouts spattered like bursts of rain on foliage.

'Ladies and gentlemen,' Iqbal made a preacher's sweeping gesture over the mob, 'I present my characters.'

Iqbal had always liked rough and tumble. It was a long while since he'd written notes for his speeches; the confidence conferred by fame had made them unnecessary. He preferred to speak on his toes, feeding on nervous energy and on the responses of the crowd. Hecklers aided his improvisation, summoning sparks from him and electrifying the audience. Hecklers were welcome. Violence was welcome, so long as it was at a reasonable distance. He got a buzz out of it. Whenever he wanted a bolt of inspirational lightning he remembered the communal fighting of his youth. Mainly Sunni Shia in Lucknow, but Hindu Muslim in other cities. Or the street battles between language communities. The primitivism of it, the wild men roaring, the keening women beating their breasts. His headmaster called it 'the human comedy', those mornings when the dayboys from the inner neighbourhoods couldn't come to school. 'Smaller classes today, boys. The human comedy is in performance once again.' Seen on television as arms and legs and teeth and police sticks, or with the rolling naked eye as purple smoke rising above the old town, it was enjoyable, it was colourful. Rough and tumble. Slap and tickle. Colour and trees and birds on the largest scale. Mother India. Monsoon leaves slapping against the windows. Illuminated dreams.

'Mosques are taking over abandoned churches,' he shouted. 'Are we happy with this? Is this what we call progress?'

The tempest met his voice. Sonic Iqbal and the hecklers struggled like clashing pressure fronts.

He shouted, 'Some of our young, excitable friends are taking offence. Well let them! Let obscurantism and demagoguery take offence! Let us fight if fighting is necessary! Proactively. Pre-emptively. Let us fight in defence of the right to offend!'

With a transposition of atmospheric volumes, Iqbal was drowned out.

From mid-hall: 'Fuck your progress!'

From the stage, behind Iqbal: 'Please! Please!'

General pleading from all around. Whimpers of distress. Chorused cursing not at anyone specific, but just because the world was bad. Combative chuckles and howling. Disruption, as a longbeard pushed through from the centre, jostling chairs: 'Come down and fight, then!' Photographers prowled between seats and stage, shooting at random.

Daoud Jenkinson, wearing a magisterial frown, reached his feet and opened his mouth. At this rate, he would miss his chance to answer Iqbal.

'Uncle fucking Tom!' someone called, presumably at Iqbal.

'House Nigga!'

'Fuck your mother! Am I offending?'

The gridmarked doors from the corridor wheezed open and shut and trickles of protesters forced their way through into the already brimming hall.

'The headscarf,' Iqbal persisted. 'Why should a secular and modern society have to put up with it? It oppresses women and it oppresses those men who might wish to see women's hair without being accused of perversity. Why should we allow this?'

'If I may respond,' mouthed Daoud. 'If I may calm tempers by responding to this assault.'

Too late to calm a cloudburst. Eschewing the guerrilla tactic of striking and ducking, people now stood on chairs and sloganized, attracting punters from the no-longer seated, milling crowd.

'They weaken our culture so they can steal our land!'

'There's your multiculturalism! Chaos! It's a Paki invasion!'

'Imperialist!'

'Imagine,' screamed Iqbal. 'Imagine the future. Freed from mind tyranny, free to design the heavens for ourselves. Freed of religious war, liberated by control of the material world, the only world we have. And then there will be no grieving. Freed to explore the imaginary realms. No grief will touch us.'

A crumpled ball of paper bounced off his forehead. More followed, like Himalayan hailstones.

'Traitor!' was screamed at him.

Sami, meanwhile, vague and amused, had risen from his seat into a quarter crouch. Debate had crossed a line and was becoming riot. As the first chairs were thrown he sensed the supernatural presence of ruptured normality, of danger. Unable to believe it, an ambiguous grin spread from one side of his heavy beard to the other.

A knot of brothers occupying a section at the front were haranguing Daoud: 'What colour are you? Sitting with the kuffar! He's one of the kuffar!'

Daoud responded with splutters, enraged: 'What colour am I? Islam is above race!'

A chant started: 'Al-Jihad! Al-Jihad!'

And another, more weakly: 'Black and white / Unite and fight!'

'Time's coming to get you!' threatened a voice with time on its side.

A pained, tormented voice: 'Consultation, brothers! Seeking to come to terms!'

Someone ordered, 'Restore order!'

And this was the last widely registered word. A dam burst followed. When Sami saw brawny white males in cheap suits and T-shirts and football colours pouring through the open doors he clutched his throat protectively. BNP, it looked like, restoring order with urgency and dedication. They hadn't been represented at the stalls outside, but here they were. Here they were. Fists into ears, boots and neatly toed office shoes into balls and vulvas. Chairs not thrown but beaten against the floor until they could be recycled as batons and clubs. A screaming, and a thickening rain of blood drops.

Mujahid unexpectedly wheeled into sight. 'Brother Sami!' he yelped, pulling at him in his panic.

In the same moment the drunken man Sami had called his uncle ran unevenly past Sami's right eye. 'Devils!' he proclaimed. 'Possessed by demons!' He'd either had a good wash since his police-cell sojourn, or fear had removed Sami's sense of smell.

Sami found himself gripping a metal bar, formerly chair leg, protecting Dr Schimmer's eggshell skull. His hands stung. The ballhead facing him grappled back his weapon and swung at a frozen Mujahid. Sami's hands connected again, stinging more. Sami and ballhead both expressionless. It was all too quick to be personal. Mujahid ball-eyed, quivering, understanding once more what he'd let himself in for with the floppy clothes and the beard.

Now police flooded in to establish another brand of order, and added to the crowd. It was as packed as Carnival, as Haj. A lot of earnest, busy, unselfconscious noise. Sami looked round for Tom Field but didn't find him. (Tom had slipped out when Iqbal made the headscarf comment.) Sami had decided to get out of the way himself when he realized the police were heavy truncheoning only the Muslims. The black beards and hijabs and dark skin and skullcaps taking the brunt. Ballheads dropping their chair legs and strolling to the sides, and out. Sami gathered his beard in his fist.

He heard a thundercrack. Not heard; felt. It was heart-shaking. He'd done a strobe dance of defensive contortions and turns before he told himself what the sound was. Gunshot.

The hall was stilled. Everybody stationary. The dreadlocked headphone couple stood up slowly and pressed their backs to the back wall.

29

Reclaim the Streets

The Westway above Shepherd's Bush was thunderous not with traffic but rebellion. Or with the techno sound which signalled one self-conscious sort of rebellion. A high-stacked sound system set up against the base of the central reservation was blasting a trance version of Public Enemy's 'Party For Your Right to Fight', which is what several thousand young and older were doing, shaking, swigging, smoking, smooching. Drumming and juggling. And agitating: a long Reclaim the Streets banner was hung from the flyover railings. Because this wasn't Carnival. Carnival had been a fortnight before. Here on the Westway, which Carnival never touched, anarchist flags flew. A Jamaican flag. A Palestinian flag. A ganga-leaf flag. Children of the radicals kicked castles over in a sandpit hastily constructed on the east-bound carriageway. There was free food of the bean and brown rice variety being ladled out. Stalls selling natural highs, on both carriageways, and thin men moving through the crowd advertising 'Bush, Bush'. A lot of shabby-as-normal people, some surprised in formal working clothes, alongside others dressed especially for the bacchanal and masquerade, like the clowns and the silly top hats. Like the women on stilts under whose absurdly hooped skirts hidden eco-guerrillas drilled holes in the tarmac, holes to be filled with peaty soil and small trees smuggled from black bin liners, and before that liberated out of commercial forests in the Home Counties. The structure heaved and vibrated under all this weight. It heaves under the weight of cars and lorries too, but on ordinary days there are no feet to feel the heaving. The smoke of spliffs and sparklers rose, but no petrol carbonate, not from this half-mile of concrete, not at the moment. The Trellick Tower glistened from the east. Wormwood Scrubs prison visible to the north, and towers and inter-arterial no-man's-land to the south.

Sami was there, reading a leaflet. *The whole of our enculturation,* it said, *consists of being told to stay inside. Remember Don't Talk To Strangers, Keep Off The Grass and No Ball Games? We're told that outside doesn't belong to us. It belongs to private vehicles, to business! Reclaim The Streets says Bollocks to that! Dis-enculturate yourself! Clean your brain out! Go Outside! Go into the streets!*

He'd come because GR had invited him. She'd promised revolutionary action the day she'd driven him from police cell to Muntaha. The day Muntaha told him to leave. GR made good her promise: stopping cars was her revolution, at least her first step. It looked like a little bit of fun, but not so much fun that Sami would feel guilty or overcome by it. Still avoiding hedonism, he'd only skirted the edge of Carnival (all his life was there in the noise and the throng: old Moroccan ladies swaying on the pavement, liberal Arabs on the al-Muhajir float, spliff and lager, reggae and hip hop, the steel pans you hear practising when you walk canalside in the summer, booming systems, *The Final Call* sold by Nation blacks, and Muntaha in it somewhere munching a corn on the cob, watching the procession). But this Reclaim the Streets thing was new for him, and new was good. It had nothing to do with Muslim or Arab controversies. Enough of that with Rashid Iqbal and bullets in the ceiling. Enough of that with Marwan and Mustafa.

Global Resister in karate kit handed him a clay mugful of carrot juice.

'Shutting the city to cars, Sami, is opening it to us. Opening our lungs too. The combustion engine is the single worst invention of capitalism, I tell you. Just filth. Smoke for the lungs, heat for the planet, cash for the bosses.'

He remembered his driving lessons, a dirty secret.

'Where's the public space,' GR cheerily continued, 'except when we steal it back? You know, we used to have town centres, common land, public squares where we could meet and talk and sing and protest. Now a square is something for cars. Something for privatized transport. We're only allowed to walk across it at designated points, when the lights tell us we can. Town centres are corporate owned. Instead of markets we have malls. All policed and mood-controlled and surveyed by closed-circuit TV.'

The space was increasingly rammed. 'Street Now Open', signalled a sign. And: 'Car Culture: No Future'. And: 'Road Rave', the 'v' busting a 'g' out of its way.

'Where's Tom?'

'He thinks it's too late for this kind of resistance. He's a pessimist. And he doesn't want to be seen by the cameras.'

Police vans at the protest perimeter banked against the human flow, and policemen wielding shock-absorbent cameras standing on the bonnets. Lenses also extended from helicopters which Sami hadn't remarked. You stop noticing helicopters in London just as you stop noticing flies in Syria. Some of the Reclaim the Streets hardcore, the people working the drills, wore balaclavas and kuffiyehs.

'But he should have come,' said GR. 'Don't you feel optimistic, being here?'

Sami searched and found an abdominal effect not unlike belief. 'I do,' he said.

'That's the power of direct action. It gives you a sense of your own strength. It shows you what you can achieve. You're interested in the Arabs. It's a good time for the Arabs too, isn't it? At last.'

So here we go. Arab controversies. But from a new, non-Arab perspective.

'Why do you say so?'

'The Intifada, for a start. I know it's sad they're being shot. But it's good to see them in open rebellion. It's an inspiration. It's terrifying the ruling class.'

She wore only karate trousers and a karate jacket. And sandals. Hair tied up and flowering from the crown of her head. Bird's feet of enthusiasm radiating from the sides of her eyes and mouth.

'It looks unstoppable,' she said. 'It looks like nothing can be done to quieten them. Wouldn't the Israelis like them to get out of the streets! And the Americans, and the Arab rulers. But the streets are being reclaimed. In Egypt, Morocco, Indonesia. You know, even the Gulf Arabs are in the streets demonstrating for Palestine. Gulf Arabs out in the streets for the first time ever!'

'It's true,' said Sami. 'It's something to be proud of.'

'And Hizbullah kicking the Israelis out of Lebanon. There's a turn-up for the books. Farmers defeating a First World army. People liberating themselves.'

'It was impressive.' Sami shouted over ballooning music.

'And so well managed, media-wise. They were doing what we're doing today. Making their own spectacle. Remember when they liberated that prison?'

'Khiyam prison. You saw that?'

'Oh yeah. It was so emotional. When they broke down the doors and let the prisoners out, these prisoners who'd been tortured. There was a BBC report. And someone sent me translated footage from Al-Jazeera. And the Hizbullah channel.'

'Al-Manar.'

'That's it. Very inspiring.'

Sami handed back his mug.

'It's all hopeful,' GR said. 'This breed of Islamist, like Hizbullah. They're very interesting. You know, it reminds me of liberation theology. South American leftist priests. You know about that?'

'Vaguely.'

'I've read Hizbullah speeches. It's not knee-jerk reaction. It's not just anti-Jewish stuff. What's he called, the boss?'

'Nasrallah.'

'That's him. Hassan Nasrallah. One of his big influences, apparently, is Che Guevara.'

'Really?'

'Really. You know, that kind of religion, politicized, can shake things up. One place Marx went wrong is religion. He didn't understand how much people need it. Opium maybe, but what's so wrong with opium? People need a painkiller sometimes. They need a drug to give them visions. Capitalism's been winning because it says that drugs are all right. It doles out drugs.'

'Capitalism doles out drugs?' Sami bemused.

'See what I'm saying. Not literally. Consumerism's a drug. Advertising's a drug. The idea that you can spend your way to fulfilment, that's a drug.' GR gasped with a fresh idea. 'But literally too. All the corporate-administered drugs. Nicotine, alcohol, Prozac.'

'All right. I see what you mean.'

'So the Islamic movement seems to have captured the imagination of the masses. It's given them a revolutionary vision. Tom thinks there'll be some kind of massive escalation now to counter it, but like I said, Tom's pessimistic. I can't see the Intifada being countered. What I see is it spreading to all the Arabs, and then to here too.'

Sami left GR to another of her friends and bumbled grinning through the crowd a while, sugared-up on the candyfloss of her predictions. Amid the general drunkenness and staggering there were groups involved in similarly rosy educational sessions, pointing at text in leaflets, tracing historical inevitability through the air with wide-arcing fingers. Some talking about the fighting at Rashid Iqbal's speech, testing out who-shot-the-shot conspiracies. The fact that the fired bullet had been found in the ceiling laid events wide open to interpretation. The sort of people who shut down motorways blamed neo-Nazis or the police, or a combination of the two. The newspapers and the police (although the police hadn't explicitly said so) had their money on vengeful but clumsy Islamic fundamentalists, aiming for Iqbal. Iqbal had made no comment. Ammar and Mujahid blamed Zionists in the British government preparing the atmosphere for an anti-Muslim crackdown. Sami suspended judgment.

The wind was whipping up. It was a clear sky but with a late-lunchtime haze gathering. A tint of autumn in it. A touch of cold. Panning down again, Sami noted several others gazing upwards, more than seemed natural. Man is the only creature that looks into the sky, so he'd heard. It can't be true. Sky-gazing must be a survival mechanism for plenty of small mammals, guarding for air-borne predators. Maybe it was star-gazing we do. Or maybe we're the only thing that looks up just for the sake of it. He also noted more than a few people wearing expressions of shock. Strange. It gave him an adrenalin spurt. But no police charge, no collapsed bodies. No gunshots today. The shock must be something to do with their stage of drunkenness, or trip, or whatever.

It was three o'clock, and Sami was hungry. He passed an eye over the food stalls. Then registered a surface-familiar face heading his way. Head-down. In attack mode, but hampered by the crowd.

'Skittle!' he called in recognition, and to defuse Skittle's obvious anger. But the anger made Sami scornful, so he added, 'Still scooping shit?'

'You let me down,' Skittle declared as he arrived. 'I'm still fucking doorstepping thanks to you. Still on the streets.'

Sami raised both hands. 'What's the problem? The job wasn't for me, that's all.'

'The key's the problem. We need it back, or I have to pay for new locks. And also the personal thing. You were my subordinate, yeah? And you fucked it up.'

'The key,' said Sami, remembering. 'Well, I don't have it with me. I don't carry it around.'

'Not good enough, Sam.'

For all his shortness, or because of it, Skittle seemed to be considering violence. But Sami felt Ammar's training in his fists, and all those summer days of disillusion.

'I'll post it to you,' he said. 'I'll post it tomorrow.'

Skittle thrust a card at him. The Pyramid Power address. He chewed his lower lip, snorted, porcine.

'People like you make the society break down. Fucking Arabs and shit.'

'Calm yourself,' said Sami, and turned away.

He checked his optimism level and found it much diminished. His shoulders were cramping. He felt distaste for the revellers. Not very representative, the revellers. Not what you could call the masses. Just a sect, a minority trying to feel like a majority. Didn't think much of the music either, or of their dancing, which was shambling and crashing and fists shaking from stiff elbows. As they did at televised party rallies in Syria. *With our soul . . . with our blood . . . we sacrifice . . .* Opportunists shaking their fists and looking bored. These London counterculturalists weren't bored, but the politics was just as false. They were here for the fun of it. Not ready to be shot at. Not ready to be crushed by tanks. So not much of a revolution. They knew they were going home when it got dark, earlier if the beer ran out.

Sami saw people on their phones, blocking their free ears with palms. More people than was natural. Obedient to the herd, he unpocketed and checked his own mobile. Seven missed calls. And very few knew his new number. Strange. Plus two messages.

The first from Ammar:

Subhanallah! Victory! Brother Come West! Urgent!

The second from Muntaha:

Habibi were at Babas house come watch.

The first time since he'd left that she'd initiated communication. And the 'habibi' was encouraging.

He blocked an ear to call her. Network busy. Meanwhile, the crowd around him was rapidly diminishing. Like tired children suddenly giving up their naughtiness, Street Reclaimers were dropping their banners and sloping sheepish through police lines. Sound system faltered. Something was afoot.

Tried calling again. Network busy.

30
Historical Events

He walked for ten minutes, very conscious of car carbonate. Toxic syrup sliding down his windpipe. He kept on calling, but either the network was busy or Muntaha's phone was engaged. Something important was happening in the world. Who could have died now? His mother? Aunt Hasna? But this was a public event. Everyone was reacting.

He waved down a cab. He wanted to ask the Somali driver what he'd heard, but the driver was screened off, gabbling into his mobile, driving one-handed. Sami saw him thin and toothy in the rear-view mirror. They drove past a betting shop where people huddled around a screen. Too much sky on the screen for it to be sport. Past an open-door pub and again a screen gathering. Something urgent or celebratory about the angles of the heads, the grip of hands on arms. Every driver they jostled with was talking on the phone, or dialling. Perhaps that was normal. The only phoneless traveller was a cycle courier darting around cars and vans, grinning as he succeeded in each manoeuvre, each dart an inoculation against despair.

Muntaha stood in the door of her dead father's house. He had the shock of familiarity when he saw her, like looking in a mirror but seeing something more solid and knowable than himself. He wanted to hold on to her face.

'You've lost so much weight!' she said, with that Arab concern which thinks a thin man is an ill man.

'You look more or less the same.' He kept his eyes on hers to show this was a compliment. In truth she was a little thicker, a little more written upon.

She thought he looked too calm for the situation. She checked, 'You know what's going on?'

'No.'

'Why not? The whole world's talking about it.'

'Not to me. The world's talking on the phone.'

What was going on was this: first one tower of New York's World Trade Center had been hit by a passenger plane, then another. Technology crashing into technology. Then both towers fell. But it was bigger than that. It was a collapsing tower of Babel to start the millennium.

Sami laughing. 'Nah! Be serious!'

The Pentagon had been hit by a third plane. A fourth smashed from on high, a fallen techno-angel, into a field.

Sami chuckled, 'What you on about? Talk sense!' Conscious that he hadn't wanted to patronize her any more, that he'd planned to respect what she said, even if it didn't make sense to him – but the circumstances weren't on his side. 'Stop, you know, babbling, Moony. Tell me what's going on.'

He entered the sitting room. No Marwan there. Obviously. Aunt Hasna paid him no attention. She was attached to the TV as to the Egyptian soap-opera episode of the decade.

TV. What we take for proof. The first plane ramming purposefully into the building, and the second. Again and again, for emphasis. To drive it home. The smoke bloom pink in the clear New York morning. Seeing is believing. But still.

Sami took Marwan's seat as Ammar burst in, saluting.

'I'm back for a while only. The brothers are calling a meeting.' He had returned from the mosque: 'What's happening now? I need an update.'

He was activating his laptop as he spoke, and pacing between the slack-jawed beady-eyed others and the TV screen, and unshrugging his jacket to reveal a tight black buttonless shirt. On its front it said: ISLAM. On its back: THE ONLY SOLUTION.

What was happening? Sami couldn't tell. He had no scale to measure the event. Nothing inherited from Mustafa. No nationalist way of judging. No Qabbani verse to help him. Here was life imitating disaster movies, more or less. But where was the hero?

The screen showed the second plane hitting the tower. The plane appearing from icy blue, out of normality, and exploding, again, melting the frame of everything, making history collapse. The voice-over reported a claim of responsibility from the Popular Front for the Liberation of Palestine.

'Yo!' said Ammar. And: 'Booyakka!' But remembering himself, 'Masha'allah! It's the Jabha! PFLP boys! It's the brothers doing it. Now we'll see what goes down. It's us against them now, you know what I mean.' He bounced from foot to foot, stabbing a witnessing finger in the air. 'It's the Muslims, blood. It's us. Get on the train before it leaves the station.'

There was a buzz and a click as the internet connected.

'There were people in that plane,' said Muntaha without breaking her gaze.

'No there wasn't.'

'There were. Pay a bit more attention.'

'No, man, there wasn't.'

He pranced balletic to the corner of the room, to the laptop, texting on his phone as he went.

The screen showed the second plane hitting the tower. Boom! A moment of history. It made you feel special to be seeing it. The voice-over reported a claim of responsibility from the Japanese Red Army. Revenge for Hiroshima.

'Yo!' Ammar turned urgently from the laptop. His lips were pushed forward as if he was sucking a bullet. 'Japanese brethren! Respect!'

The screen showed the second plane hitting the tower. An expansion of fire. A mass catching of breath. New Yorkers screaming for God.

'But they're not Muslims, are they, the Japanese,' said Muntaha, in an academic tone.

'Shit, religion isn't the only thing, man. Point is . . .'

The screen showed streets of rubble. The black and white tribes of New York uniformly ashen grey. Briefcase refugees streaked with dust-caked liquids – with blood or tears.

'Point is, this the heart of America. This the belly of the beast. And it looks like Gaza, man. It looks like Baghdad. And that is something to restore a man's pride.'

Sami heard him. It was true, he noted an intestinal rush of excitement, something like worthiness and justification. He also felt the guilt Freud says a boy feels when his father dies, because the boy's been beaming death wishes for so long.

The screen showed a flabby, wobble-voiced American. 'I don't know what's going on here,' he was saying. His hands circling. Gathering and pointing his intention into the camera. 'All I know for sure is, we gotta nuke the entire goddamn Middle East for this. We gotta reply to this.'

Ammar was up at the screen with a fist and plenty of saliva.

'Fuck you,' he snarled. 'Fuck you.'

Hasna, stunned since her son Salim's engagement to the Nigerian girl but coming to life now with the events, inhaled sharply.

'Language please,' she said. 'There are standards, whatever the occasion.'

The occasion. Was it justified? Sami fulminated a while. America attacks Iraq. Puts military bases in almost every Arab country. Military bases in more than a hundred countries of the world. They attack Vietnam, Panama, Nicaragua, Sudan, Libya. Undermine popular governments and prop up hated dictatorships. Put the bullets in the guns which kill Palestinians. Export their films to everywhere, in every one of which they're the heroes. As aid to poor farmers they give seeds which impoverish the soil, so it'll only produce crops if treated by expensive American fertilizer. Which is a metaphor for their whole economic system. They control trade. They seed the earth with depleted uranium. They are the empire.

The screen showed workers dropping from windows. Insects falling, some in spasms of terror, some unmoving. Paralysed or submitting? Protesting or ecstatic? Falling, in any case. As Muntaha will fall. As Ammar is falling – ageing – if he could see it speeded up. As Sami himself is falling. Marwan gone. Mouna gone. Mustafa gone.

Death was happening inside the building too. Invisibly. Before the towers fell. Repetition of footage made it all one moment – planes hitting, people jumping, towers falling. Sami watched the walls being carbonized. Smoke going up. How this makes the time run out a little quicker. Although all planes are grounded, meaning less carbonate overall. But the wars there'll be if Muslims did it. This chokes us quicker. A lot quicker.

Ammar texting and speaking. 'It serves them right. It's payback time.'

Muntaha said, 'What about "My mercy is greater than My wrath"?'

Ammar said, 'What about fight them wherever you find them?'

The screen showed the collapse of the towers. First one, then the other. The half hour between abbreviated, and the ten seconds of each crumpling extended beyond time. Such a beautiful demolition. To die all at once, Mustafa said on his deathbed, to die with solidarity, takes the sting from it. So maybe they're lucky, like the dead of Hama.

'It's probably nothing to do with Muslims,' said Muntaha. 'Remember when Timothy McVeigh blew up the building in Oklahoma. They were convinced it was Muslims. Men of Middle Eastern appearance, they said. Remember that? He was blonde, McVeigh. Nothing like an Arab. Looked like a soldier.'

Sami helped her. 'He *was* a soldier. In the Gulf War. It was being a soldier that pissed him off with the American government.'

'Language,' said Hasna.

'You see,' said Ammar, in the act of discovery. 'One of the signs of the Hour is there'll be a fire from the Hijaz visible in Basra, and we thought it was the Kuwait oil wells in '91. But it's this. It equals this. Everyone in Basra will be watching this on TV.'

Muntaha tutted. 'The fire's in New York, Ammar.'

'Yeah, but, think about it. A TV station transmitting from the Hijaz, from Mecca or Madina, and watched in Basra. Yeah?'

The towers collapsed and dust storms rose. The desert, vertical, claiming its place. Would America be destroyed in just one day? The temples of its power were burning, financial and military. The political still to come. Some reports said a fifth plane was unaccounted for. Sami decided it was heading for the White House.

Muntaha rolled her eyes. 'It'll be a relief for you when the Hour comes, won't it?'

'Can't stand in the way of reality, sister.' A strong strain of Jamaica in Ammar's voice. 'Ya cyaan stand in the way of jihad.'

'Jihad?' Muntaha rose, half straight, twisting her body towards him, not giving up her chair. 'Islamic rules say you can't kill women or children. You can't kill civilians. You have to fight on the battlefield, not in the middle of the city.'

Ammar made his hands into scales, explanatory. 'They attack our cities. We attack theirs.'

'So call it politics, then. Or straightforward war. Don't call it jihad.' She sat down, addressed the screen again.

Varieties of heat roiled and smouldered under Sami's skin. He agreed with Muntaha and Ammar both. And the studio experts. And the Japanese Red Army. A hot prickle of fear, mainly beneath his scalp. What if it was Arabs? What kind of excuse would this give America? A studio expert was talking about Pearl Harbor.

Muntaha held her face as Sami would have liked to, between her hands, and whispered, 'God, I hope it wasn't Arabs.'

Ammar prayed, 'Let it be the Muslims!'

Hasna announced, in loud English, 'It serves them right. But still, those people.'

Sami rolled his head to inspect her. Her eyes dry and desperate, her skin pale as ceilings. Her body worn out by exile frustrations, the deaths of husbands, and shaken now by Salim's bad marriage. A body receiving blows, slowly disintegrating. And all we are is body, as far as nature is concerned. Nature being all there is, here at least, in this empirical dimension. Our condition being that we rot when we're not burning or falling from windows.

'Celebrations in China!' Ammar reported from the laptop. 'Celebrations all over Latin America!'

So will Sami defend it to his non-Arab acquaintance? If it was Arabs who did it, it's all anyone is going to talk to him about. Ever again.

Ammar speaking into his mobile: 'That's right! As many kuffar killed as brothers and sisters martyred in the Intifada!'

Muntaha, from her chair. 'What's this kuffar? Kuffar means the ungrateful and arrogant. How do you know who they are?'

'The unbelievers, sister.'

'Christians and Jews aren't kuffar. They're People of the Book. Maybe even Hindus aren't kuffar. There weren't any in Arabia, so the Prophet didn't talk about them. You can't call just anyone you want a kafir. The kuffar are the pagan Arabs who rejected the Prophet.'

'Shit, keep it simple. Kuffar is kuffar is kuffar. Just . . .' – he waved at the TV – '. . . cheer up. Look at it. Cheer up.'

She made a sound with her lips like a pressure cooker.

'What you're saying,' said Ammar, 'is we should just let them kill us and never strike back. Turn the other fucking cheek.'

'Them?' Muntaha pointing at the screen. 'They aren't the people killing us.'

Her voice was high like the day she'd told Sami to leave. But this wasn't nearly so serious. It wasn't a real day. It was Eid or Christmas, a deathday or a birthday. Nothing had weight. More precisely, nothing that they did had weight, not in comparison with the historical events on the screen.

'Language,' said Hasna.

'Collateral damage,' said Ammar conclusively.

'That's what they say when they kill Arabs.'

'And why should we be better behaved than them?'

Unexpectedly, Hasna asked, 'What would your father have said?'

A silence while everybody contemplated this, a question Hasna hadn't really intended. Marwan, thought Sami. Marwan would have cursed a lot. He'd have called the Americans and the Arabs and the Jews pimps and dogs and sons of donkeys. He'd have wondered what the response would be. For a brief moment Sami found Hasna and Muntaha and Ammar's eyes on him. Not on him, on his chair. Marwan's chair.

'Shit,' said Ammar. 'I was on the phone. He's gone now.'

He dialled, glowering down at the little keyboard. Muntaha, meanwhile, shuffled her chair towards Sami's. She ignored the TV screen.

'I'll tell you what's jihad,' she whispered.

'What, then?'

And they were immediately conspirators. Or bomb-shelter acquaintances, marking off territory around themselves. Us in here. Ammar and Hasna out there, a little nearer the exit.

'Marriage is jihad.'

They smiled into each other. She touched his hand.

'I heard you were at the Rashid Iqbal talk. Didn't see you on the news.'

'That was an experience.'

'So what did he say? Or was it fighting from the start?'

Rashid Iqbal was one of the topics they used to argue about, Sami at least. Sami praising Iqbal as a post-Muslim genius, sacrilegiously placing Iqbal books on top of the Qur'an, bringing Iqbal into discussions of sport, weather, TV, irrelevantly, just for a wound to worry. Muntaha's tactic had been to wear her tolerant expression.

Sami told her, 'He made a distinction between literature and religion, and preferred literature. As you'd expect.'

'But why make a distinction? Whatever raises the spirit.'

'He meant religion only allows one truth.'

'One kind of religion. Depends how you read, doesn't it? Same with novels. How does he expect people to read novels properly if they can't read religious text? Also, fiction is fictional. Religion isn't.' Her words spun wistfully heavenward, and she twirled her hair. 'I suppose religion's somewhere between fiction and non-fiction.'

'He seemed confused,' conceded Sami.

'Everybody is. Then what happened?'

'Then everybody started shouting about everything at once. Nobody knew what was happening. Then people mashed the place up. BNP mostly, and the police. But I can't judge properly. It was so much chaos. Then someone fired a shot. No idea who. Could have been anybody.'

'Could have been anybody,' she repeated. 'So was it exciting to see him in the flesh? You've been reading him for years.'

'Not really. Feet of clay, I suppose.'

Their eyes trailed to the screen, which showed the second plane hitting the tower, and back to each other.

'And did anybody hurt you?' she asked.

She touched his face. Tugged his beard gently. He couldn't reply.

'What's this? Sami with a beard! Wonders never cease.'

From now on the beard would be a magic charm for them, and a souvenir of this world-turning summer.

He asked, 'Will you have me if I have a beard?'

'I'll have you if you're you.' She paused. 'But good you. Loyal, sorted out, not depressed. Not taking it out on me. Not so scared, if I may say so, Sami. Habibi.'

She fixed him in such warm, unblinking focus that he sensed the abyss of himself – his ancestors falling infinitely away inside him – and his shallowness, just a skin's thickness of conscious time between the deeps of past and future. But he kept his bearings. Muntaha was only as deep and shallow as he was. No more nor less than him. Very like him, yet not identical. Not a mirror. She was a woman. A human being. Obviously.

While he was failing to respond to her conditions she reached over the chair arm for his hip. She extended a chaste hand into his pocket, and withdrew his mobile.

'You need to talk to your mother,' she said, typing and saving Nur's number. 'You need to be more responsible. Think about others.'

He nodded obediently. 'I was thinking about that anyway.'

'Good. She'll die one day.'

'I know,' he said.

The screen showed the second tower collapsing.

Sami said, 'I understand what it means that you lost your mother in Iraq. But sometimes I feel you've lost her less than I've lost mine.'

'Well there's a paradox,' she said, quizzically.

'Something to do with you being a woman, I think.'

The phone interrupted them. The land line. Muntaha rose to answer it. From her side of the conversation Sami worked out the caller was her mother's brother in Baghdad, Nidal. He was asking what would happen now, expecting her to have inside knowledge because she was there, in the West, hearing what the Westerners say.

Sami noticed the extra junk accumulated in the room since Marwan's departure. A framed 'To Battle!' calligraphed on Celtic (and Islamic) green, purchased from Sinn Féin sympathizers on the Kilburn Road, was propped on the sideboard. A shiny stick-on 'Allah', in Arabic, placed over the tricolour. That would be Ammar's contribution, juxtaposed incongruously with plastic flower and fruit arrangements, strawberry red and apple green, and burgeoning Iraqi memorabilia – vague terracotta reproductions of Sumerian statuary, black and red woven saddlebags, a naïve portrait of a Beduin with a falcon. That would be Hasna. Strange housemates, these two.

Both sat staring at the screen, which showed New Yorkers trekking over a long bridge. Hasna's jaw hung low, her mouth slightly open. Ammar, who'd taken his sister's seat, finally silenced in contemplation of the event. For someone whose world-vision is predicated on humiliation, on personal powerlessness extended to an imagined community, the planes were redemptive, miraculous. They didn't fit the mundane narrative. They were mysteries. For Ammar, a real sign, at last. Something concrete. Something you didn't have to try hard to make significant. At last, God in the world.

Sami watched his wife talking. Connected. Using her mother

tongue. Her 'lughat-al-umm'. In Arabic, 'umm' means mother, and also origin and basis. 'Amma', meaning to lead a prayer, derives from the same root, as does 'umma', meaning the nation or the Islamic community. For Muntaha, her people, her ancestors, didn't mean trouble. She was as she was, accepting her past, hopeful for the future. Sami watched her and considered.

Chilly dusk on the doorstep, Sami startled by his own laughter. Their hands rising like sparks to each other's faces. Too fast. They stopped, caressing the breeze at shoulder level. The unfamiliar familiar.

You can't take anything for granted. Not a woman, nor an idea. Not a political situation. Not life or death. Nothing is simple. Everything is always changing, and always – if you pay enough attention – surprising.

31
Escape

'What?' asked Sami, gulping and blinking. 'What are you doing?'

'I'm getting out.'

What Tom Field was doing was pulling books from his office shelves, twirling them before his knife-like nose, his furrowed brow, and allotting them to piles on the wooden floor. In front of each pile was an A4 sheet labelled with marker pen: Pile 1, Pile 2, up to Pile 7. Number codes for the recipients.

He'd already signed a pre-prepared letter of resignation and announced to his doctoral students that university was a distraction they could no longer afford. Pulled out of a lecture programme ('Surviving Collapse: Remnant Societies Post-Rome to Post-Industrial') at the start of the new term, too late for rearrangement. He'd left no number or forwarding address. Burnt his bridges.

'Why?'

'Why?' Tom, incredulous. 'Why? Well, what do you think? Because it's starting now, if you haven't noticed. Stage whatever-it-is. The next stage. A much more pivotal and violent stage. Haven't you noticed how hectic things have been, even before this . . . event?'

The event didn't yet have an agreed-upon name.

'I said something big was planned. And there you have it, a couple of days ago. The catalyst. The trigger. Well then, watch it unfold. Enjoy the . . .' – his flow broke and resumed as he stripped and stacked – '. . . the oil wars. Or not. As the case may be.'

'You mean,' started Sami, but couldn't find an apt conspiracy to continue with. 'What do you mean? Who planned it?'

'Oh, I'm not being simplistic. Could have been who they say it is. The Saudis they used in Afghanistan. Could be. Or maybe not. Too soon to say. Not really important, in any case. Not really relevant. It's how they'll exploit it that's the point. And that isn't difficult to predict.'

His hands, busy as bees, denuded the walls of books. Sandbags removed from a shelter.

'My favourites are here,' he said, tapping Piles 2 and 3. 'Survival narratives. Not particularly the academic analyses. Just the raw stories, told by the survivors themselves. War stories. Camp massacres. Sabra and Shatila. Rwanda. People lost in the desert, or shipwrecked, or fallen down crevasses.'

His eyes shone. His Adam's apple worked.

'I suppose there'll be some good ones from New York soon. The stories Hollywood doesn't get its hands on first.'

Tom took himself back to the labour, swiping heavy volumes, swinging them to their fate. His unbuttoned cuffs fluttered. His forearms flexed. His elbows sharp.

'Reading those,' he said, 'pumps the adrenalin. Operates the glands. I think that's why I got waylaid writing books and researching. I've had an addiction to the excitement. To the feeling real. Visiting the militiamen in the American forests, interviewing a fighter from Grozny, a man who started thinking rubble was the way home should be. That's been my buzz: just thinking about the challenges a human being might have to face. It wakes you up. It's like being in the mountains, with your senses all working. Feeling like an animal, on your instincts. Feeling healthy. Feeling properly alive.'

Out of the window and below was the year's new intake, trusting, fizzy-optimistic, sparkling with the sense of new beginnings. Pitifully vulnerable. And inside again, to Sami's slowed and pensive eyes Tom was a blur. The man most aware of what was approaching was moving too fast for the rest, for all the slow beasts. Sami felt like a member of the herd. A bison when Europeans cropped America. An Aborigine when smallpox cropped Australia. Waiting for doom. His closeness to Tom meant at least he knew the doom was coming.

'But I don't need to read them any more. From now on it's the genuine article. Not metasurvival, but survival. You want a pile?'

'What?'

'One of these piles is for you.'

He indicated Pile 7. Something rag-eared on top concerning Sufi responses to Mongol massacres in the medieval Middle East. Pile 7 a leaning tower of Pisa in comparison with the Petronas Towers of Piles 4 and 5, the Chicago-scape of 1, 2 and 3. (Pile 6, to be fair, was as Old World low-rise as 7). Seven or eight lurching books. Was that reasonable compensation? Sami considering himself tragically abandoned once again. His shaikh rejecting him before he'd advanced through the stations of the spirit, so now he would be a mere beggar, not a knower. Merely a shabby, failed faqir. But he got on top of his sentiment quickly. His personal dramas, the paternal-familial if not the philosophical, had burnt themselves out. And his resentment dimmed further with another glance through the porthole, another reminder of the innocents out there, laughing, posing, like him a decade ago, unbruised by the world. Thin shells of bone sheltering inner matter from whatever was coming first, bus-bombs or missiles or tidal waves or plagues. Those with something to lose to the outside, at least, those that didn't have an enemy already growing inside, some new millennium brain fungus or alien spore ready to burst. Their shouting poked its way in, sound bent by the window angles, the calls of boys and girls wanting to mate, to demonstrate strength and fitness in the time allowed.

'A question, Tom, before you go.'

Tom dropped discs into a brown cloth sack and pulled its string mouth shut before grunting his readiness.

Sami asked, 'Are you a believer?'

Tom Field squinting, disapproving. Tugging the string of the sack over his head.

'Everyone's a believer. Don't believe anyone who says he

isn't. You can't breathe without belief. In gravity, for instance. How can you step off the floor without believing you'll come back again? You can't.'

'Ah,' said Sami. 'No. I meant . . .'

'You mean God, whatever that means.'

Sami nodded, wrinkling his chin in embarrassment. These aren't questions to ask in society. Tom was crumpling papers and mounting them in pyramid formation on to a tray.

'Let's simplify. You want to know what I think to help you know what you should think. Am I right? Well, that won't work. Either you're a born believer, meaning you subscribe to a cultural belief like you subscribe to gravity, or you decide for yourself. The latter, in your case. Decide for yourself. It's a matter of choice.'

'Choice?'

'Yep. And whatever you choose to believe, there's a good chance you'll be wrong.'

He fished a match from the hidden pool of his pelvis, struck it on his palm it seemed like, and in the last act of his tactical retreat lit the papers. They caught angrily. With solemn caveman instinct they watched together the pyre flare and die. Carbonate rising. Carbonate. Tick. Tick.

'Like I said, we all believe in something. It helps to know what it is. Know yourself, in the famous formulation. Meaning, know what it is you believe.'

Sami sighed audibly.

'More help? All right. Belief is good when it increases knowledge. It's bad when it doesn't. If it develops what we can call spirit, or awareness, it's good. If it smothers it, it's bad. If it helps you to survive, it's good. The ex-professor of survivalism tells you this. Asks you. Will it help you to survive, or will it make you an easier target? That's the way to judge these days. Self-preservation. And now, my friend, I have no more time.'

Tom made a farewell reconnaissance of the smoky room, ready now to abandon position.

'One more thing,' he said. 'A lesson from the concentration camps. Those who survive are not necessarily the physically strongest, but those who see purpose in their suffering.'

'Purpose?' asked Sami. 'Things are too confusing to work out purpose. Everyone interprets, and it seems arrogant to imagine one interpretation's more correct than another.'

'There's your answer, then. Yet you could be mixing up your categories. What a believer does is to find the world significant. You don't have to know what the significance is. A believer says God is the Knower. Isn't that right? Your field, not mine.'

'That's right.'

'Well then.' Tom turned to the bare desk and withdrew from its innards a surviving pencil and piece of paper. 'But wait,' he warned, although Sami wasn't going anywhere. He scribbled, and presented the paper. 'Here. Read it.'

Sami read it.

'Have you learnt it by heart?'

'By heart? No.'

'Well, do so.'

Sami did so. The name of a mountain and the nearest village.

'All right,' he said.

'So give it here.'

Tom crumpled it, placed it above the sparse ashes of the tray. Struck a match and lit it. It floated and danced, free of gravity.

'You never know,' Tom said in response to Sami's doubting smirk.

Once they'd watched the information burn, Tom said, 'And one more thing.'

'Another?'

'A brief thing.' He paused for effect before delivery. 'Relax.'

'You're telling me to relax? You?'

'Why not?'

'Look at you. You're getting out. You're running. Panicking.'

'Panicking? That's what I'm not doing. I'm acting. I know exactly why. Beyond that, I'm perfectly relaxed.'

In the door frame he made his parting speech, a set of recommendations.

'Be as intelligent as you can when dealing with human beings. Take evasive action when you need to, like I'm doing now. But after that, relax. There's still big nature out there. It's big and you can't understand it. So what? War and politics is all part of it. Just relax. Do what you can. Then surrender to it.'

Sami took the first bus that passed. East through the thickness of the city. He paid no attention to outside. As the vehicle thrummed and rocked he saw concentration camps, refugee camps, torture cells. Insect people leaping from collapsing towers. He considered annihilation. Then his own aching uniqueness. His unbearably lonely sense of being special. The man who put this in him is dead. Dead and buried organic matter. Carbon on its way to being fossil fuel.

But none of this knowledge hurt him. He descended and walked, without too much heat, balancing terror with lightness. He opened his eyes to outside. Smartly dressed Bengalis hustling and bustling, making money, unembarrassed. A community on the up. Also businessmen from the City checking restaurant windows. Women in suits or jilbabs or tracksuits. The grind and the warmth of human activity. Just relax, thought Sami. He'd turned into Brick Lane, land of blood and beer. The tall brick chimney, a red reminder of imperial pride, behind him. To his right the mosque. Formerly synagogue. Formerly Methodist chapel. Formerly Huguenot church.

Just relax. If he could suspend disbelief. Just for a moment. Then he can review the experience. He won't lose himself. He promises. Here we are.

Splashes cold water on his feet, forearms, head. Then there's a corridor before a narrow doorway into the prayer hall. A very English building. Hooks for coats and scarves. Wood panelling. The hall wasn't built to look at Mecca. The direction for prayer diagonal, not fitting the rectangle of the room, so he stands facing a corner. Someone snoring on the carpet. Another man kneeling, clicking beads. Sami sidesteps the thought of his Uncle Faris. Sidesteps Mustafa and Marwan, and the female body, and the

Intifada, and the Arab nation. For only a glimmer he sidesteps the idea of himself. Sami Traifi, inhaling abstraction, inhaling void. He touches thumbs to earlobes. Folds hands on solar plexus.

'Bismillah ur-Rahman ur-Raheem,' he starts. Immediately he's crowded by idle memories, and by his voice, the proof of himself. Breathes a while longer, inhaling abstraction. Starts, 'All praise is due to God alone, the Sustainer of all the worlds.' Shudders and stops. When he isn't following a leader he remembers fragments only. Breathes some more. Just relax. Notices here that he's broken into two separate pieces: the piece that advises the other piece to relax. The two pieces in fact not two selves but two functions of the words. Speaker and speakee. The order to relax has made him briefly disappear. He speaks from below or above his reason. The Opening Prayer, and another verse.

> Consider the flight of time!
> Verily, man is bound to lose himself . . .

He hears himself saying the words internally and asks himself, what do I feel? The question is also words. He hears two sets of words, then. Two selves speaking and one listening. And now another, marvelling at this thought. He splinters. Mirrors looking into mirrors. Photons reflected.

As many bits of him as stars. And a sky containing the stars. He has only a hint of it. Something overarching and complete.

He bows, stands, prostrates, kneels. Stands. Folds hands. He concentrates on the words.

> Say: He is the One God
> God the Eternal, the Uncaused Cause of All That Exists.

Repeats this verse until there are only words. And afterwards kneels for five minutes, returning to himself. It has made him calm and peaceful. It has opened something spacious in him.

*

He stood outside, enjoying the tickle of moving air on his face. The mosque was a blending block of brown brick with white paint on the window sills. High on a wall was an optimistic sundial and engraved above it 'Umbra Sumus'. We Are Shadows. His eyes craned to street level. Despite its veneer this part of London recalled the imperial-industrial age. It grimly chugged and steamed. Within its narrowness, skulls, mouths and words. Clicking carbon heads. Hanging above them, an immense sentence, being arranged and rearranged. On the street, feet. Pedestrians. And between pedestrians, shades cast by absent Lascars, by Yemenis, Somalis, Malays. The very first Bengalis. If he could stand on the street like rock, like the sundial, he'd see the history of Muslim settlement, the shifting, accumulating sands of his praying, murmuring brothers and sisters. If he weren't trapped in time he'd sense a brotherhood even larger than that, with all the others offloaded at the docks, Russians, Chinese, Irish and Jews. And with the rural English arriving by land, coming to the slaughter. Brotherhood.

The miasmic sky opened above his head to reveal a spot of blue. The world was significant. He allowed significance to massage its way in. Then decided he might eat some curry. Until time gripped him more firmly than ever. Gripped him and jerked him by the beard.

He felt the touch of two hands from behind him, between his shoulders and the nape of his neck. He thought it must be an acquaintance playing that frequent but unfunny trick. Expected sweaty clumsy fingers to wrap his eyes next, and a voice to ask, 'Guess Who?' So he prepared himself to be graciously amused, and primed his ears to identify the coming voice, to get on top of the situation. But no voice came, except his own voice spluttering, 'What?' and a sudden whirl as of one of the scarier fairground machines and hard arms bending his arms behind his back and pressure on his scalp and the flinching glance of a grey-skinned passer-by and his own sense of guilt breaking in his mouth as he was bundled into the back of a car. Sticky seats. All too fast for him to know he was surprised. There were plastic cuffs on his wrists, and a face in front of his, close-up, wearing a gummy grin.

'Hi!' it said. 'I'm Jeff.'

Shortly afterwards he was in a police station, once again. But unaccountably, for this time he'd been behaving. Acting grown-up. No drugs or long sleeplessness. No Bikini Girl or centaur hallucinations. He gave his mother's name for next of kin, copied out her number from the list on his mobile. How things had changed.

He was taken to what he presumed from TV experience to be an interrogation room, and was sat on a chair across a table from two more. For twenty minutes on the wall clock he was left alone. He thought of Uncle Faris, picturing the TV flicker of light on his prematurely old, unresponding face, and in the intervals when the picture faded he snatched at Qur'anic half-lines as they danced, just out of reach, behind curtains of forgetfulness. He resolved to buy a good Qur'an, the heavy black bilingual Qur'an that Muntaha liked, when he got out. He formulated it to himself like that, when I get out, as if he would be inside for a significant time.

In came his interrogators and sat opposite. On one chair the man called Jeff, whose fat hand for most of the numbly silent car journey had patted Sami's knee, Jeff in jeans and blue rugby shirt, and glumly smiling. On the other chair, leaning at him, a slack-faced, brown-haired woman. It was their heavy-plotted seriousness which showed an interrogation was coming, and Sami thought, fair enough. All summer he'd been trying not to face interrogations, detention chambers, the rest of it, torture and terror, too Third World to fit this scene, but still. He was ready. The effort not to look at the truth could no longer be sustained.

'Country of origin,' the woman snapped.

'Britain.'

She repeated, 'Country of origin?'

'England. I was born here.'

She slapped the table. Jeff scratched an ear and wanly smiled. 'We mean originally,' he said.

'Syria. If you mean where my parents came from.'

'Syria.' The woman sneered at a notepad. 'Isn't that a Muslim country?'

'Yes,' said Sami. 'Yes, it is.'

Of course it is. He visibly flinched from himself when he remembered his childhood answers to the question. *It's a Mediterranean country. Would you call the Mediterranean Muslim?* What else? *It's a mixture of everything really.* He cringed now at his previous denial as much as he'd cringed then at the imputation that he had something to do with Muslims. Why deny what's in front of your nose?

'Muslim country,' the woman said, as if listing charges. 'False name. Suspicious appearance and behaviour.'

Sami frowned back at her.

She was called Kate. Jeff revealed this when she asked Sami how he'd celebrated the burning towers. 'Oh Kate,' Jeff said, with dramatized tolerance and hurt, playing good cop.

Why was Sami in this situation? The burden of the beard, he supposed. The burden of belonging. Just when he was sorting himself out the external world took a lurch for the worse. Yet another. Tom said those who survive are those who see purpose in their suffering. Not much suffering yet in this episode, granted, and no purpose in it that Sami could see. But significance, yes. It assuaged his guilt, the guilt that wasn't his but Mustafa's. He hadn't betrayed Britain or the American ally, he was paying for older treasons.

All relative. He paid not with his blood but by tolerating wilful stupidity. He even wore a tolerant expression (smiling inside to Muntaha) as they asked him, in staged off-the-cuff style, about routes to Kabul, or what he thought of the film *Braveheart*, didn't it fire him up, all that violent resistance to occupation? At one stage they went into a stock routine, rapid-fire and repetitive, demanding his name, address and date of birth, Jeff grinning through it all and Kate determinedly snarling, but tripping themselves up, tangling their tongues on the questions as if only in the twenty minutes before they came in they had skimmed freshly downloaded Israeli disorientation techniques.

Sami didn't know if he'd been arrested or not.

'Just having a little chat,' said Jeff.

'I think either I should get a lawyer, or I don't need to talk to you.'

Kate said, 'You still get your lawyer, but it isn't going to be nice. Thousands of people have been killed. Times have changed.'

'They have.' Jeff sighed.

'This is a matter of saving lives.'

Sami considered what was coming now, after the planes, after the towers. The New York events were big. Not as big as the media thought, not in comparison with Beirut or Baghdad, but big. Big for the First World. The events were historically big, and the response would be too. In Britain he expected a two-pronged attack of, on the one hand, co-optation and Working Together rhetoric – nice cop – and on the other, some heavy security work by the cerebrally challenged, like these two, clearly unable to distinguish Wahhabi nihilists from the plain dull religious, or even from the vaguely, perhaps, spiritual, like Sami. And there'd be a predictable political attempt to paint everything Muslim and oppositional in the same bloody colour. Would that work? Depended on to what extent Marwan's theory was true, the theory Muntaha had told him about: that the English are trusting and sheeplike, that they believe what they're told. Marwan had never articulated the idea in Sami's presence, although according to Muntaha it had been one of the old man's favourite themes, and Sami supposed this was because Marwan was being polite, that he considered Sami to be a sheep. And perhaps Sami had been. Certainly trusting. If not in the news, then in Mustafa's official version. Certainly deluded.

Kate said, 'We don't believe you're Sami Traifi. We've had him in, you see, Sami Traifi. The real one. He doesn't have a beard. He takes drugs, drinks alcohol. He's an innocent whose name you've adopted.'

'We have his parents next door.' Jeff apologetically spreading hands. 'They say you're not him.'

'Really?'

'I'm sorry,' said Jeff. 'I am. I'm sorry. It's a shame. And so's all this conflict between our peoples.'

'You've got his father too?'

This upset Kate, who waved a finger across the table. 'You leave him alone. Leave Traifi and his family alone, you hear me? He's the kind you kill, isn't he? You consider him a traitor. An apostate.'

It was lilting, oriental music to Sami's ears, Sami the apostate to atheism, traitor to his traitorous father.

The questioning resumed.

'What is your position on the Arab–Israeli conflict?'

So would the English, sheeplike, believe the official version? That Hizbullah is the same as al-Qa'ida? Hamas and the Taliban one? Sami would see. And he'd do what he could. Self-preservation, Tom had said. Evasive action.

There was a significant rapping on the door. Jeff went to it quickly. His fingers remained curled around the door frame while he conferred with a uniformed man in the corridor.

'Kate,' he called. His voice up a note.

She frowned as she got up, without the drama of her earlier frowns. Sami had a view of her back slumping a little as she received information. She wheeled away from the door, losing rigidity, compensating with a pinching of the mouth, a hard stare at the floor. Then swished her head sideways to her body, and smiled.

'Mr Traifi. I owe you an apology. It seems you are who you say you are. Not an extremist at all.'

'No hard feelings, mate.' Jeff, unsmiling now, made a jovial slap to Sami's shoulder. 'See it from our point of view. You were standing there, outside the mosque, in a suspicious manner. All perfectly innocent, of course, we know that now.'

'And you have grown a rather thick beard recently, haven't you?' Kate chiding gently.

'Imagine,' said Jeff. 'Imagine if under the questioning then you'd given us a lead. Something important. We could have saved lives.'

Sami stood up.

Jeff grasped his arm. 'Why don't you work for us?'

'With us,' corrected Kate.

'Work with us. We need the help, I don't mind admitting. We're not prepared for the new scenario. Lack of resources, lack of legislated powers. It'll take time to come through. We don't have many contacts in your community.'

His community. Society splitting up into sects for safety, into fraternities, everybody sticking with their own kind. The day of Tom Field had arrived.

'Whereas you, Mr Traifi, you could infiltrate. You look the part.'

'In the mosques. The beard and all.'

They were following Sami through the door, down the corridor.

'Think about it at least.'

'Give us a call.'

There was his mother. Nur Kallas. Her hijab tight. He'd seen her last perhaps a year earlier, briefly, in the street with Muntaha. He hadn't looked at her face then. Now he did, and it was creased and pale.

They shook hands.

'Thanks for rescuing me.'

She nodded. Jeff, smiling and stooping, ushered them to the exit.

'They thought you were an Islamist,' said Nur when they were on the street. A soft single chuckle died in her throat. 'It's true you look like one these days. Your beard's longer than your hair.'

It was the first time in a long while he'd heard his mother's voice.

Sami said, 'Do you know what they wanted at the end? They wanted me to be an informer. They wanted me to shop Islamists, to be mukhabarat.'

Nur raised her eyes to his. A hint of Faris to her, some family resemblance in the curve of the cheeks. They walked towards the tube.

Nur said, 'You're lucky, though. In Syria they'd have tortured you. We wouldn't have seen you for years.'

32
Late

Someone on the tube was reading an evangelical thriller called *The Late Great Planet Earth*. On the cover, the globe was cracked open. Sami and Nur sat opposite, in silence, rocked by the movement of the train.

She hadn't invited him home but they'd both known he was coming. They spoke about the circumstances of his arrest for a couple of minutes, Nur less outraged by it than he felt she should be, and then they submitted with awkward reserve to the journey, not saying anything, saving it up. A meditative nothing for fourteen stops.

They alighted, redundantly pointing the way to each other, and slowly walked a section of high street. Not too many people here owned cars so the corporations hadn't yet won total victory. True, there was a hyperstore within bus distance, but local specificity survived. As well as KFC there was the Harrow Hen House, etcetera, and to look on the bright side, Mr Patties Soul Food Kitchen, the Lebanese grocer's, the Sari Base. They turned right, past token front yards hemmed in by migratory traffic, but people out in them nonetheless, perched on brick walls, on bikes on the pavement, talking. Portuguese neighbouring Poles, Chinese neighbouring Algerians, and so on. Everyone mixed up. Flitting shadows.

The sight and sound of children made Nur speak, in English.

'No children yet? You're a man, Sami. You're here to have children.'

'You only had me.'

'I'd have had more if your father had agreed. He was father to his book.'

337

A child would mean Sami was a link in a chain, would make Mustafa a grandfather (deceased), and Sami a father, not the inheritor. A child would make Sami an attribute, a descriptor, not a subject. Not the chief subject. Sex is the defeat of individuality and the victory of the species. But sex, though. Sami thought of Muntaha undressed. He was ready for that.

There was no eye contact with his mother. They'd spoken with false gruffness, a manly kind of Anglo-Saxon distance. From the side he noted her deterioration. Her skin was old-woman fabric now, and it was too late for any reconciliation that would take him back to the boy in her lap, wrapped in towels. It provoked anger in him, or the memory of anger, and he was quite open to himself and calm about it, observing all his emotional habits: his traditional loyalty to his father, his old hatred for the hijab. The hijab that marked her as a female and a decaying thing. A woman, not a girl. The bearer of a body.

She turned the key in the old door. The old house. Even the old smell, though she'd changed perfumes and foodstuffs in the intervening years. Everything heavy with sad nostalgia.

Nur unpinned the hijab. Her hair was dyed chestnut brown, as he remembered it from early childhood, but otherwise she was rumpled, dressed less formally than before, quite un-Syrian. It was too late for her to be what she had been.

Yet in the house some ancient habitude had an influence, relaxing them both. They spoke Arabic.

'Those planes in New York,' she said. 'I dreamt it before it happened.'

Sami removed his shoes and followed her to the kitchen, where she was already preparing Turkish coffee.

'I was in my family's old home in Damascus, in Muhajireen. It was hot and it smelled like home. I was hanging washing on the terrace. I heard a crash and turned to the mountain. There were two towers burning. Exactly the same towers. I kept the image of them after I woke up.'

She arranged small cups and saucers on a tray.

'It was two weeks before it happened. Strange, isn't it? And what about this. I have a friend, a Lebanese, whose son's an accountant. He works in the City for a company which has a New York branch, in the Trade Center, in the towers, and he was offered a transfer over there. Of course he wanted to go, and his family wanted him to go, but he'd fallen in love with a girl here in London, an English girl. All the family complaining, why give up this opportunity for a girl, but he wouldn't listen. Two weeks later the girl left him and he cursed himself for not going. But look. The romance is over, but look how he was saved. It wasn't his fate to die, not yet.' She took a cigarette from a packet next to the sink. 'Smoke if you want to.'

'I've left it.'

She lit the cigarette, and peered through smoke to spoon powder into simmering water. She took two proper drags, then poured the coffee.

'So you stopped your university work.'

'Yeah.' He didn't want to talk about it. The fact was too much an admission of failure, of bad direction-taking and stubbornness. 'How did you know?'

'Muntaha told me. She always keeps in touch.'

Cardamom and coffee steam and smoke rose between them.

'I was going to call you.'

'It doesn't matter.'

Sami carried the tray to the front room. They sat down, and Nur leaned forward to add sugar, stirring. Her hands and his were the same, the flatness of the fingernails, the thick knuckles. His hands were his inheritance from her. Also the ridge of his nose. These were the visible things, coded from twists of DNA.

'We should talk,' he said, 'about Baba.'

'What about him?' Nur intently driving ash around an ashtray.

'About him and your family. My uncles.'

'Mustafa. God have mercy on him.'

'God have mercy on him,' repeated Sami.

'Mustafa with my family was like a bull in a china shop, as the

English say. He thought he had a duty to offend their values. He seemed to expect to be thanked for it. Respect is important in our society. Etiquette.'

'Does that explain it?'

'Explain what?'

'The problems between you.'

Nur sipped coffee, and stubbed out her cigarette.

'We didn't agree about things, as you know.'

'Tell me again. I want to hear it again. It's different now.'

Nur looked towards the window.

'Your father,' she said, 'had dreams concerning the Arabs. He thought it was only a matter of time until everyone would work in an office, productive eight-hour days, and go home in the evening to read novels, or go to the cinema to watch art films. He thought everyone would own a car and a house to fit a nuclear family, and that they'd all drink whiskey and smoke cigarettes. He thought that would make them better. He thought they wouldn't need anything more than that.' She snorted: 'Well, the cigarettes part came true, just when they were giving up here.' She pointed through single glazing to the street. 'A lot of us believed it, enough to forget what we'd believed before. Long enough for it to be too late to go back.'

She lit another cigarette, pulling deep. 'But his dreams were dreams. What he wanted, it's not possible. There aren't enough schools in the world. Not enough money. Too much history. Why should it happen, anyway? They wanted us to be powerful, like Europe. To an extent they had good intentions. But we aren't Europe. And maybe we were happier the way we were, even if we were underdeveloped, so-called, even if we were easy to colonize, even superstitious and weak. They wanted progress, whatever the cost. Progress, so-called. But maybe it wasn't a good idea, modernizing us. They made the country a prison to do it. A very modern prison.'

She veered from 'he' to 'they', from Mustafa to the Ba'ath Party. 'He thought there'd be one nation. One Arab nation from the Ocean to the Gulf. What we have now is everything but. We have everything smaller and everything bigger. Little sects and ethnicities, little nationalisms, and big Islamism. But no Arab nation. If they hadn't tried so hard to force us into it, maybe it would have happened. We're Arabs, after all.' She seemed to become stuck to her cigarette, her hand at her mouth, facing away from Sami, to the window. 'Anyway. You didn't see your father getting rich out of it. Most of the others were in it for money. Your father was an idealist.'

She stopped speaking and smoked noisily. Sami was embarrassed by her emotion, but he wanted to know.

He asked, 'And what happened between you? There was something specific, wasn't there? I remember when you two stopped talking. It happened suddenly.'

Nur was curling up, wrapping her arm around her waist as if there was pain inside which needed to be massaged. 'Deeply wounded' we say, talking about psychological trauma, and language speaking its wisdom through us. Because it's physical too, emotional events leave physical scars. Nur winced as she smoked, exhaling grey cloud into her lap.

She said, 'I think he thought, if his dream couldn't come true, then neither could anyone else's.'

Sami said, 'I visited Aunt Fadya in Syria.'

'I know. She told me.'

'I met someone called Faris. My uncle. I'd forgotten him completely, but recently I've remembered. He came here, didn't he, to London, when I was a boy?'

'Yes.'

'He wasn't well when I saw him in Damascus. He seemed much older than his age.'

'Yes.' She nodded, looking into the middle distance.

'They seemed as if they were blaming me. Fadya and her sons. I couldn't understand them.'

Nur said nothing.

'They said, "I wonder who informed on Uncle Faris? I wonder who told the mukhabarat?" Staring at me, as if it was me. But

I never knew anything about it. I was only a boy when he was arrested. I wasn't even there. "I wonder who informed on Uncle Faris?"'

Nur, softly: 'God knows what's true and what isn't.'

Sami said, 'It was Baba, wasn't it?'

Looking into the middle distance, she sighed.

'It was him, wasn't it? My father.'

'Nobody should tell anybody that their father was a traitor.'

'But I know. I worked it out. You just need to confirm it. Baba told the mukhabarat about Uncle Faris.'

She turned and faced him. Her eyes the colour of light honey.

'Yes.'

'Baba sent your brother to prison for twenty-two years. My father destroyed your brother.'

'He probably didn't want him there for twenty-two years. People get lost in those prisons. And your father died.'

'But he told the mukhabarat.'

'Yes. That's right.'

Sami dipped his head in acknowledgment, and paused, and continued. 'But he was living here in London.'

'He visited there. He had Party friends. Even here, he had Party friends.'

Sami neither cold nor hot. Sami, at room temperature, only wanting information: 'Why did he do it?'

'An excess of loyalty,' replied Nur. 'Not necessarily because he was a bad man, although I, of course, interpreted it like that. Perhaps because he was good, according to his own definitions. Betrayal of one thing is usually loyalty to something else.'

They had another cupful of coffee each, and Nur smoked two more cigarettes. Then she went into her bedroom (still the small one, that had first been a guest room) to pray alone. Sami didn't suggest he join her, but waited, tapping his teeth, asking himself how to communicate reconciliation. The right thing was probably to embrace her, but it felt too late, or perhaps too early, for that. He was still squeamish of bodies, except his untouched wife's. Plus, he was suspicious of his own tricks, and wanted to keep drama at arm's length.

When she returned from her prayer he caught, squeezed, and kissed her hand, taking refuge in culture, in this impersonal yet moving signal of filial respect and duty.

She said, 'Thank you,' wobble-voiced, nervously happy.

Sami was by the door, flushed, putting on shoes.

'You should come to eat with us sometimes,' he said.

'Are you living at home?'

'I will be. I'm moving back.'

'Yes, I'll come. If you want.'

'Yes, I want,' he said. 'I understand now.'

The moment for eye contact had passed, so he looked at the wooden door, saying, 'Muntaha likes you. She'll be happy to see you.'

Nur said, 'She's a good woman, a good wife for you. If you want my advice, Sami, stop making a fuss about her hijab. She tells me all about it, your hijab arguments. Maybe it isn't necessary, but it's her business. Don't make trouble over an abstraction. You should be loyal to people before ideas. Be flexible. Don't force people to be what they aren't.'

Sami parroted, 'Maybe it isn't necessary? The hijab?'

'Allahu 'aalim. God knows best.'

'So why do you wear it?'

'In protest, I suppose. And in hope. All you can do is hope. And try to be yourself, what you hope you may be. If belief isn't always possible, hope is.'

33
Awe

Sami, with Muntaha headscarfed beside him, was driving a West London Cabs Nissan north and west through a carbonate-beautiful late afternoon, into a rural, pre-apocalyptic zone of varied green. They'd had a long day's driving up the M6, talking pasts and futures, and listening to the radio: pirates on the FM dial on the way out of London, and while skirting Birmingham too. Otherwise classical music, and news.

George Bush, out of hiding and belatedly stepping into hero role, not saving but avenging, had told the New York firemen, 'The people who knocked these buildings down will hear all of us soon,' which reminded Sami and Muntaha of the Prophet talking to the dead, saying, 'Look, do you see now?' Given that the people who knocked the buildings down were dead too, of self-administered punishment, burnt with their victims. But Bush was talking of this world, of coming shock and awe, and commentators excitedly discussed imminent explosions, in Afghanistan, perhaps Iraq, the son Bush wishing to outdo his father there.

The village whose name Tom Field had written for Sami was easy to find on the map. Then they had to ask the staid, slow villagers who squinted quizzically at their foreignness – English foreignness – for directions to the mountain.

They stopped where the road did, clambered over a stone wall, and grinned at each other in their confusion. City people out of their depth. There were bushes and trees and reeds and no evident pathways. But Tom met them within five minutes, emerging from the wilderness even before they summoned the courage to shout his name. They climbed in the lingering northern indeterminacy between day and night up to Tom's house, which was in a hollow very close to the summit, on ground high enough to survive glacier-melt. It was also, Tom pointed out, fairly invisible from the air, sheltered by indigenous forest, by birch and ash, rowan and willow. Built of reclaimed wood and glass, as he explained, walking them around it. It had a bathtub, outside by the vegetable patch, on stilts, with space beneath for a woodfire to heat the water. Water had to be brought in buckets from a stream. Tom filtered it to drink.

'I'll need solar panels and so forth. More technology. I haven't spent a winter here yet. We'll see how it is.'

From a clearing he gestured downhill at the overgrown traces of an abandoned road, an illustration of the frailty of human endeavour from which he drew unbounded reassurance.

'Wilderness, you see, we should count as our friend. That's what I'm trying to do, partially. I admit I'm domesticated here. Ideally I'd be nomadic. But the world's not large enough any more. And it's too violent. More important to be hidden.'

He made them comfortable, served them filtered water and fed them palaeolithic food. As they ate he described the local barter system. Tom knew a glass blower, a weed grower, a cheese maker, a potter, a bowl lather, a knitter, a weaver, a candleshaper.

'The problem is getting to them without a car. I have a bike, but it takes time. These people are in a thirty-mile radius. It makes you ask yourself if a journey's really necessary.'

There was no sign of GR or any other companion – until Muntaha found a box of female grooming and hygiene items near the plate-washing area. She wasn't exactly snooping; there were none of the markers of private space that a house normally has.

Tom talking, in candlelight, against Sami's suggestion that he might feel disconnected: 'I'm at peace with disconnection. No ancestors up here, no past. Like the whole world soon. Give it fifty years. We're at the end of a loop.'

And Sami, smiling: 'There's signs of a companion here, Tom. Not my business, but . . .'

'There's no survival in this world without reproduction.'

'Children, then?'

'That's on the agenda, Sami. Serve the species, you know, serve the genes. We'll see. For now, I'm mostly alone. And that's good.'

But Tom talked on like a lonely man who's captured rare company, like an ex-lecturer who misses the lecture theatre.

'No clock here, you'll notice. So there's a rhythm of day and night, but no diary time, no squashing us into boxes, none of that kind of control. No phone either. But I think I knew you were coming. Didn't take me long to find you, did it? It's been suggested that hunter-gatherers had advanced telepathic powers. Perhaps that kind of thing is natural to us, and we've lost it as we developed technology. Perhaps we'll all find out, I mean those who survive, when the technology burns out.

'Bushmen can see four moons of Jupiter with the naked eye. Some tribes see Venus in the daytime. I have the feeling that all this is possible. I do sense exercises up here, alone. To enhance smell and touch. I blindfold myself and walk the mountain.'

'It's attractive,' said Sami. 'An attractive sort of life.'

Muntaha laughed, 'Have you got a mosque up here?'

'The mountain's my mosque.'

She regarded him playfully. 'The mountain's all right for you, Tom. But I'm an Arab. I need to keep warm in the wintertime. And there aren't so many of us in this country, better for us to stick together.'

'Where, in London? Under the bombs and the floods?'

'I'll worry about them when they happen. Right now I'm worried about finding Arab culinary ingredients. I need that Syrian shop on the Uxbridge Road, for a start.'

'True,' said Sami. 'Where's your olive tree? Also, not much jungle music up here.'

'No jungle music,' said Tom, 'but plenty of jungle. Plenty of reality. Art may only be an attempt to remember what we've lost. But the Arab culinary ingredients – I see what you mean.'

And with that fortuitous prompting Muntaha revealed from her bag an array of foodstuffs: stuffed vine leaves, kibbe, tubs of hummus and matabal.

Sami and Muntaha slept the night in the separate bedroom. So separate they had to walk for five minutes in the dark, across moss and leaves, to reach it, a square wooden structure between trees, containing only a wooden bed and a feather mattress, and without even candles – but with glass panels in the ceiling so their night was lit by the stars, so their eyes became accustomed to the dark and to the tones of each other's body in starlight. In the morning they lay on their backs and watched squirrels leap branch to branch.

They breakfasted on berries and some kind of tea. Then Tom went mushroom gathering, and Sami and Muntaha set out to walk all day. They prayed together at lunchtime and in the middle afternoon. Out in nature, prayer felt easy to Sami. Out in nature, marvelling in it, Muntaha quoted her favourite hadeeth:

> I was a Hidden Treasure which desired to be known
> So I created the creation.

And remembering her mother's lessons, she quoted Imam Ali:

Man is a wonderful creature; he sees through layers of fat, hears through bone, and speaks with a lump of flesh.

Sami nodded at the miracle of sight. He no longer experienced body-claustrophobia, but something like its opposite, a sense of openness and space. Now he claimed a doctrine of radical unknowing, and the beginnings of acceptance.

Our language is adequate for the detail of social relations, and for the objects made by us, or those for which there is an obvious human use. Language is primarily economic. However, for the economically useless, for the natural more-than-human, words are silly, shiny labels signifying only their own poverty. Words like star, sky, sea. Words like blue when applied to the sky, or to distant trees, or mountain rock (applied to the paintwork on a car it does fine). Silly labels tacked on mystery.

Imam Ali said: *There is enough light for one who wants to see.*

In another long dusk they washed with dust, prayed, nibbled sandwiches, held hands.

Stars became distinct in stages, as suggestions first, then as fixed ideas. Bright Venus, once called Ishtar. And the Pole star. The Plough. And Orion and Taurus, the constellations of Sami's childhood, oscillating in a stretch of time which has no economic meaning. Mustafa said he'd be up there, among the stars, but didn't specify which. Which constellation? Orion-Gilgamesh? Gilgamesh who'd rejected Ishtar's advances, Gilgamesh the king who didn't need gods. Or Taurus, the Bull of Heaven who ravaged the earth with drought? Bull in a china shop, Nur said.

Sami gazed on them. Fire and rock, the distance of time. Constellations to our eyes, telling the stories of culture. A little bit of science tells you how arbitrary the patterns are. Of course his father wasn't up there. His father was far too small, like any of us. Sami felt fear and trembling. Felt the emptiness of a burning heart.

Truth and beauty are in the details. The details on the mountain were bacteria, heather, a fox, some starlings, tribes of rabbits. The rumour of a golden eagle, and a cloud of late midges descending to gobble on the human couple. Everything gobbling everything else, relentlessly teaching a very simple lesson: of the power of change. Nature's plans don't include us.

Or perhaps they do. Sami had developed a trembling, contingent faith, not necessarily expansive enough to house an eternal heaven, certainly not for Sami as he is. For what is he, now? Not much any more. Not Mustafa's son, nor Marwan's son-in-law. Not the child of corpse dust. Not an academic. Not a member of the eternal Arab nation.

So what, then? He's Nur's son. Muntaha's husband. These are facts. But to define himself as other people's attributes – it isn't much. Even his name was given to him by other people. In the dead past. So what else?

He's a bit more of a man now. Meaning, a moment of conscious-ness. Awe and dread.

For now, that's all he can manage. Perhaps it's enough.

Acknowledgments

All praise is due to the Maker Who transfers books from non-existence to existence.

Thanks to my wife for putting up with a writer in the house. Apologies to Ibrahim and Ayaat for all the times I snarled when they opened the door. Thanks to Bashaar for answering questions and to Ḥadya for telling me her dream. Thanks to my friends Adrian Barnes, Giles Coren, John Liechty and Tariq Yusuf for patient reading and suggestions. Thanks to Simon Prosser, Juliette Mitchell, and especially my agent, Camilla Hornby, for their expert advice. Thanks to Francesca Main for helping with practicalities.

The Qur'anic 'We shall show them Our signs . . .' in chapter 6 was translated by the author. Otherwise, all Qur'an quotations come from Muhammad Asad's *The Message of the Qur'an*, which is in my opinion by far the best translation in English, and the only one I would recommend to English speakers. My thanks to The Book Foundation for permission to quote.

Thanks to Hadba, Zeinab and Omar Qabbani for permission to quote the poetry of their father, the great Nizar Qabbani.

The line 'wordlessly sensed by the mind' comes from the Nizar Qabbani poem 'I Declare: There Is No Woman Like You', translated by Lena Jayyusi and Naomi Shihab Nye, from *On Entering the Sea: The Erotic and Other Poetry of Nizar Qabbani*, published by Interlink Books.

Khalid Abdul Muhammad sampled by Public Enemy is quoted in chapter 21.

The great Palestinian poet Mahmoud Darwish is quoted in chapter 2.

Thanks to Linton Kwesi Johnson for permission to quote from his poem 'Time Come', from *Selected Poems*, published by Penguin.

He just wanted a decent book to read ...

Not too much to ask, is it? It was in 1935 when Allen Lane, Managing Director of Bodley Head Publishers, stood on a platform at Exeter railway station looking for something good to read on his journey back to London. His choice was limited to popular magazines and poor-quality paperbacks – the same choice faced every day by the vast majority of readers, few of whom could afford hardbacks. Lane's disappointment and subsequent anger at the range of books generally available led him to found a company – and change the world.

'We believed in the existence in this country of a vast reading public for intelligent books at a low price, and staked everything on it'
Sir Allen Lane, 1902–1970, founder of Penguin Books

The quality paperback had arrived – and not just in bookshops. Lane was adamant that his Penguins should appear in chain stores and tobacconists, and should cost no more than a packet of cigarettes.

Reading habits (and cigarette prices) have changed since 1935, but Penguin still believes in publishing the best books for everybody to enjoy. We still believe that good design costs no more than bad design, and we still believe that quality books published passionately and responsibly make the world a better place.

So wherever you see the little bird – whether it's on a piece of prize-winning literary fiction or a celebrity autobiography, political tour de force or historical masterpiece, a serial-killer thriller, reference book, world classic or a piece of pure escapism – you can bet that it represents the very best that the genre has to offer.

Whatever you like to read – trust Penguin.